THE MAILMAN

Bentley Little

AN ONYX BOOK

For Wendy

Special Thanks To:

My agent, Dominick Abel, again. Keith Neilson, for his advice, criticism, and his knowledge of all things dark and terrible, all horrors great and small. Don Cannon, book-seller supreme. Jeff Teets, photographer extraordinaire. And my family, for their problems with the post office.

ONYX
Published by the Penguin Group
Penguin Putnam Inc., 375 Hudson Street,
New York, New York 10014, U.S.A.
Penguin Books Ltd, 27 Wrights Lane,
London W8 5TZ, England
Penguin Books Australia Ltd, Ringwood,
Victoria, Australia
Penguin Books Canada Ltd, 10 Alcorn Avenue, Suite 300,
Toronto, Ontario M4V 3B2
Penguin Books (N.Z.) Ltd, 182-190 Wairau Road,
Auckland 10, New Zealand

Penguin Books Ltd, Registered Offices:
Harmondsworth, Middlesex, England

First published by Onyx, an imprint of Dutton Signet,
a member of Penguin Putnam Inc.

First Printing, February, 1991
10 9 8 7 6 5 4 3

PUBLISHER'S NOTE
This is a work of fiction. Names, characters, places, and incidents either are the product of the author's imagination or are used fictitiously, and any resemblance to actual persons, living or dead, events, or locales is entirely coincidental.

BOOKS ARE AVAILABLE AT QUANTITY DISCOUNTS WHEN USED TO PROMOTE PRODUCTS OR SERVICES. FOR INFORMATION PLEASE WRITE TO PREMIUM MARKETING DIVISION, PENGUIN PUTNAM INC., 375 HUDSON STREET, NEW YORK, NEW YORK 10014.

1

It was the first day of summer, his first day of freedom, and Doug Albin stood on the porch staring out at the pine-covered ridge above town. It wasn't technically the first day of summer—that was still three weeks away. It wasn't even his real first day of freedom—that had been Saturday. But it was the first Monday after school ended, and as he stood at the railing, enjoying the view, he felt great. He took a deep breath, smelling pine and bacon, pollen and pancakes, the mingled odors of woods and breakfast. Morning smells.

It was cool out and there was a slight breeze, but he knew that that would not last long. The sky was a deep navy blue, devoid of even a single cloud, and by noon the temperature would be well into the nineties. He scanned the horizon. A hawk circled lazily overhead, moving in ever-widening circles away from its point of departure. On the ridge, he could see the thin gray line of a single campfire rising into the air above the line of trees. Closer in, small animals flitted about, stirred into hyperactivity by the breeze: rabbits, squirrels, hummingbirds, quail.

Although he had arisen with the sun the way he did every Monday morning, he had done so out of choice not out of necessity, and the pressure of impending work that usually marred his mornings was absent. He didn't have to rush to get dressed, he didn't have to speed through his breakfast and read only the headlines of the newspaper. He didn't have to do anything. The whole day was before him and he could do with it as he pleased.

The front door opened behind him and he glanced around, hearing the sound of the latch clicking.

Trish stuck her head out from behind the screen. "What do you want for breakfast?"

He looked at her wild hair and her still-sleepy visage, and

he smiled. "Nothing. I'm not hungry. Come on out here with me."

She shook her head dully. "No. It's cold. Now, what do you want? You can't skip breakfast just because you're on vacation. It's—"

"—the most important meal of the day," he finished for her. "I know."

"Well, what do you want? French toast? Waffles?"

Doug breathed deeply, smelling other breakfasts from other homes. "Eggs," he said. "And bacon."

"Bran cereal," she told him. "And wheat toast. You've eaten enough cholesterol lately."

"Then why did you even ask me?"

"It was a test. You failed." She closed the screen door. "After you're through communing with nature, please come inside. And shut the door behind you. It's freezing this morning."

He laughed. "It's not that cold," he said.

But she had already closed the door, and he stood alone on the porch, looking out across the acres of ponderosa pine at the rocky crags of the ridge on the other side of town. The thin trail of campfire smoke had grown larger, dissipating, a gray stream in the blue ocean sky. He took another deep breath, hungry for summer, longing to breathe in that delicious freedom, but something had changed and the odors on the breeze brought with them something bittersweet, a vaguely familiar fragrance that awoke within him a subtle sense of loss he couldn't quite place.

The mood gone, he turned away from the railing. A hummingbird buzzed his head on its way to the feeder next to the kitchen window as he walked inside the house. Trish had already started breakfast and was busily cutting up slices of homemade bread for toast. She had relented a little on the bran cereal, but not much, and an open cardboard cylinder of oatmeal sat next to the pot on the stove. A pitcher of orange juice stood on the counter next to her. She looked up as he entered the room.

"Wake Billy up," she said.

"It's summer," Doug said. "Let the boy sleep if he wants. It's vacation time."

"I don't want him wasting his whole day sleeping."

"His whole day? It's six-thirty."

"Just get him up." She returned to her bread, carefully slicing the round loaf into thin equally small pieces.

Doug walked loudly up the stairs to the loft of the A-frame, hoping his exaggerated footsteps would awaken the boy. But Billy's still feet were sticking out from under the sheet at the head of his bed, and his head on the pillow at the wrong end of the mattress was covered and unmoving. Doug walked across the rug, stepping over the underwear, socks, shirts, and pants strewn over the floor. Sunlight was streaming through a crack in the green curtains, a wedge of brightness illuminating the posters of rock stars and sports figures on the slanting wood roofwalls. He pulled the covers off his son's head. "All right, bud spud. Time to get up."

Billy moaned incoherently and reached groggily for the sheet to pull over his head.

Doug kept the sheet out of reach. "Rise and shine."

"What time is it?"

"Almost nine."

One eye opened to squint at the watch hanging by a string from the sloping wall above his bed. "It's only six. Get out of here!" He reached again for the sheet, this time more aggressively.

"It's six-forty-five actually. Time to get up."

"Okay. I'm up. Leave!"

Doug smiled. The boy took after his mother. Trish was always a bear when she first woke up: silent, uncommunicative, nasty. He, on the other hand, was exactly the opposite. He was, as one of his old roommates had put it, "disgustingly cheerful" in the morning, and he and Trish had long learned to stay out of each other's way the first half-hour or so after waking.

He let Billy reclaim the sheet, and although the boy instantly hid his head, he knew he was awake and would soon be coming down.

Doug walked downstairs, offering a parting "Get up," which received no response. He sat down at the formica counter that separated the living room and the kitchen and that they used as a breakfast table.

Trish, stirring the oatmeal, turned around. "What are your plans for today?"

He grinned. "It's summer. I have no plans."

She laughed. "That's what I was afraid of." She turned off the burner on the stove and moved over to the cupboard from which she withdrew three bowls. "I thought you were supposed to get that boy up."

"He is up."

"He's not at the table, and I don't hear any noise upstairs."

"Want me to go up there and get him?"

She shook her head. "I'll do it." She moved into the living room and looked up at the railing of the loft. "Time to eat," she called out. Her loud voice had an edge of anger in it, whether real or not Doug was unable to tell. "Breakfast is ready."

A moment later, they heard the sound of feet hitting the floor and two minutes later Billy was coming down the stairs.

After breakfast, Trish went out to work on the garden. Billy finished watching the *Today* show, then took off on his bike to practice motocross moves in the forest. There was a bike tournament coming up at the end of July, and he wanted to be in it. "Be careful," Doug called from the porch as the boy pedaled furiously down the dirt path that wound through the trees toward the hill, but Billy either didn't hear him or didn't intend to be careful and didn't say anything back.

Trish looked up from her weeding. "I don't like him riding that bike the way he does."

"It's okay."

"It's not okay. It's dangerous. He's going to break an arm or leg someday. I wish you wouldn't encourage him."

"I don't encourage him."

She smiled teasingly. "Come on, don't tell me you don't feel a little macho thrill every time he goes careening off into the underbrush?"

" 'Careening off into the underbrush?' "

"All right, Mr. Teacher. It's summer. Quit lecturing."

He chuckled. "Those who can, teach."

She playfully stuck her tongue out at him, then returned to her weeding.

Doug went back inside and turned off the television. He stood for a moment in the middle of the living room, thinking. There were a few things he had to take care of this morning, some correspondence he'd let slide through these last two weeks of finals and graduation, and he figured he'd better get them out of the way before settling down to some serious non-work. He was going to give himself a week off before starting his big project for the summer: the storage shed. It had been three years now since he'd first promised Trish he'd build a storage shed in the back yard to house their tools and firewood and extraneous garbage, and though each June he'd sworn that he was going to build the shed, somehow he had never actually gotten around to it. This year, however, he had finally broken down and bought a prefab construction kit. This year, he was going to do it. He figured he'd spend this week reading, lounging about, and just relaxing. Knowing his ineptitude with tools and his incompatibility with manual labor, the storage shed, which theoretically should be a one- or two-week project, would probably take all summer, and he wanted to make sure he enjoyed at least part of his vacation.

He walked through the kitchen and down the short hall to the bedroom. His desk was on the other side of the brass bed, inconveniently close to the closet. A stack of books and papers sat next to the dusty uncovered typewriter, and he pushed everything aside as he sat down on the hard metal ice-cream chair he used in lieu of the wooden swivel seat he'd originally wanted. He quickly glanced through the pile. Bills. Bills. More bills. A letter from an ex-student who'd joined the army.

His application for the grant.

He dropped everything else on the desk and held up the yellow application form, staring dumbly at it. The application was for a federal program that offered teachers in specific fields year-long paid sabbaticals so they could conduct independent research. There was nothing he really wanted to, or needed to, research, but he desperately wanted the year off and had managed to put together a rather convincing application. He thought he'd sent it in last month, but apparently he hadn't. He looked at the deadline date on the form.

June seventh.

Five days away.

"Shit," he muttered. He placed the application in an envelope, addressed it, and affixed a stamp. He went back outside and walked down the porch steps.

"What is it?" Trish asked.

"My study grant. I forgot to send it."

She grinned up at him. "Those who can, teach."

"Very funny." He walked across the gravel driveway to the mailbox, opening the metal door, throwing in the envelope and pulling up the red flag. He walked back across the gravel, stepping carefully in his bare feet. Ronda would pick up the mail around lunch; it would get to the post office around four, get to Phoenix by the next morning, and probably arrive in Washington two or three days after that. It would be cutting it close, but he would probably make it.

He went back inside to make out bills.

Doug and Tritia ate lunch on the porch, sandwiches, while Billy ate inside and watched reruns of *Andy Griffith.* The weather was warm but nice, and they tilted the umbrella on the table to keep out the worst of the sun. Afterward, Doug did the dishes and they both retired to the butterfly chairs on the porch to read.

An hour passed, but Doug could not relax and enjoy himself. He kept looking up from his book, listening for the sputtery cough of Bob Ronda's engine, the metallic squeal of old brakes, thinking of his application wasting away in the mailbox, curiously annoyed that the mailman had not shown up on time. He looked over at Trish. "The mail hasn't come yet, has it?"

"Not that I know of."

"Shit," he muttered. He knew it was stupid to turn Ronda into a scapegoat when it was his own stupidity that had led him to wait this long before sending the grant application, but he could not help feeling a little angry at the mailman. Where the hell was he? He returned to his book, trying to read, but soon gave it up, unable to appreciate the words in front of him. His mind kept wandering and he found himself reading the same sentence over and over again, not comprehending. He placed his book on the plastic table next to him and settled into the chair, closing his eyes for a moment. He heard Trish get up, open the door, go inside. He heard the humming wash of water through pipes as she poured herself something to drink in the kitchen.

But he did not hear the mailman's car.

Trish came back out, her bare feet loud on the creaking wood, and he opened his eyes. Something was wrong. Bob Ronda inevitably came by about eleven or, at the very latest, twelve. He was a talker and he often stopped to chat with people, but he also knew his job and was extraordinarily efficient in his work. New people were added to the route each year, families arrived to vacation in their summer homes, but somehow Ronda found the time to talk, to deliver the mail, and to still finish his route by four. He had been delivering the mail for the past twenty years, as he would tell anyone who would listen, since Willis had been on a star route with so few people that being a mailman was a part-time job. He now wore a postal service cap, but he still favored Levi's and western wear, and he still drove his beat-up blue Dodge. A tall heavy man with a white beard and mustache, Ronda took his postal-service credo very seriously and had been known to deliver mail even when he was ill. Which was why he had never, to Doug's knowledge, been late with his delivery.

Until now.

He glanced at his watch. It was two-fifteen.

He stood up. "I'm going to go into town and drop off my application at the post office. I can't wait any longer. Mail leaves town at four. If that thing doesn't get in on time, I'm dead."

"You shouldn't have waited so long."

"I know. But I thought I already mailed it."

Trish stood up, pulling out her sweaty shorts where they stuck to her buttocks. "I'm going into town anyway, I'll drop it off."

"Why are you going to town?"

"Dinner," she said. "I forgot to pick up everything I needed yesterday."

"I'll go."

She shook her head. "You'll stay here and rest. Because tomorrow you are going to paint the porch."

"Oh, I am, am I?"

"Yes you are. Now go get your letter. I'll put on my shoes and sort through the coupons."

Chuckling, Doug walked down the driveway to the mailbox. He withdrew the envelope from the box and returned to the house, stepping inside. The front curtains were drawn to keep out the afternoon sun, and there was a fan perched on the small table next to the hat rack. The swiveling head turned at a ninety-degree angle, creating an indoor breeze that cooled everything from the Franklin stove and the bookcase along the left wall to the couch where Billy lay watching *The Flintstones*.

"Turn that off," Doug said. "Why are you wasting your day watching TV?"

"I'm not wasting it. It's *The Flintstones*. Besides, it's summer. What should I be doing? Reading?"

"That's right."

"You don't read for fun."

"Your mother and I do."

"I don't."

"Why not?"

"I read when I have to. That's good enough."

Doug shook his head. "After this show's over, the television goes off. You find something else to do."

"God," Billy said disgustedly.

Trish came out of the bedroom, putting on her sunglasses, her purse over her shoulder, keys in hand. She was wearing new white shorts and a thin white sailor shirt, her long brown hair tied back in a ponytail. "What do you think?" she asked, turning around, fashion-model-style. "Susan St. James?"

"Abe Vigoda," Doug said.

She punched his shoulder.

"That hurt."

"It was supposed to." She picked up her grocery list from the counter. "Anything else we need besides milk, bread, and dinner food?"

"Cokes," Billy said.

"We'll see," she said, putting the list into her purse.

Doug handed her the application envelope and followed her onto the porch as she walked outside to the Bronco.

"Cokes!" Billy called again from inside.

She smiled, getting into the car. "I'll be back in an hour or so."

Doug gave her a quick kiss through the open window. "Okay. Thanks."

"Tomorrow you paint, though."

"Tomorrow I paint," he agreed.

Tritia backed out of the drive and headed down the dirt road toward town. She rolled up the Bronco's windows to keep out the dust and turned on the air-conditioning. The first blast of air was stale and humid, but it quickly turned refreshingly cold and dry as she drove past the other houses scattered along this stretch of forest. The road curved around the side of a hill, then dipped down to the level of the creek.

She sped over the lowered crossing with the confidence of a native, the Bronco's tires spraying up water as they rolled through the stream.

She slowed down as the dirt became pavement and she passed the first cross street. She was glad that it was summer, that Doug was off work, but she could tell she was going to have to lay down a few ground rules—the way she did each summer. Yes, he was on vacation, and that was good, but she needed a vacation too and, unfortunately, there was no way to take time off from being a mother and housewife. They were full-time, year-round occupations. If left to his own devices, Doug would spend the entire summer veging out, reading on the porch, doing absolutely nothing. It was up to her to point out that the meals he ate had to be cooked, that the dishes afterward had to be washed, that the house required constant maintenance and did not just rejuvenate itself. He couldn't be expected to be a mother, but he could help out around the place: vacuum, do the dishes, rake the yard. She would still do the lion's share of the work, but it would help immensely if some of the duties were divided.

The road wound past the trailer park before hitting the highway. She signaled and turned left. The town was quieter than usual. There were some cars in the Bayless parking lot, and a few campers and station wagons were on the road, going to or coming from the lakes, but the usual Monday-afternoon work rush was nowhere to be seen. She drove past the Exxon station, past the Circle K, and turned down Pine Street toward the post office.

The post office was always crowded, and today was no exception. The small parking lot was filled with old cars and dusty pickups, and seemed to be more crowded than usual. Three cars were lined up in the street, waiting for the next available parking spaces.

Rather than wait, Tritia decided to pull into the parking lot of the chiropractor's office next door and hike it in. She parked under the shade of a ponderosa and walked across the lot and around the low brick fence that separated the chiropractor's and the post office. She noticed that both the American and Arizona flag on the pole in front of the tan brick building were at half-mast and tried to recall if someone important had died on this date. She didn't think so.

Maybe someone famous had died and she just hadn't heard about it yet.

She moved up the sidewalk steps and pushed open the door, walking inside. The swamp cooler on the roof of the post office had lowered the interior temperature but raised the humidity, so the trade-off was just about equal. The line inside was long, stretching from the counter, through the double doors, into the lobby next to the P.O. boxes. Howard Crowell, the postmaster, was at the counter, and Tritia saw immediately that he was wearing a black armband. She felt a sinking in the pit of her stomach, an instinctive intuitive reaction. She got into line behind Grady Daniels, who, for once in his life, was standing completely silent, completely still, unmoving.

He turned around to face her. "Shame," he said soberly. "It's a damn shame."

"What is?"

"Ronda," he said.

"What happened?"

"You didn't hear?"

She shook her head.

Grady lowered his voice. "Blew his brains out this morning. With a shotgun."

The postmaster looked dazedly up as the customer he had been helping turned to leave. "Next."

Tritia kept her eyes on Howard as she moved forward in line, feeling strangely cold. The postmaster's eyes were red and watery, his cheeks flushed, and it was clear that he had been both shocked and deeply hurt by the tragedy. His voice, ordinarily loud and boisterous, was a subdued whisper, and his hands shook as he handed out stamps and change. Bob Ronda had been not only his employee but his best friend, and it was a rare Saturday night that the two of them were not seen at The Corral, listening to the country swing of the Tonto Trailblazers, downing a few cool ones, and discussing the fate of the world. It was no secret that Howard's wife had left him two years ago, though he continued to insist that she was in Tucson attending to her invalid mother, and since that time, he and Ronda had been nearly inseparable. Ellen, Ronda's wife, had even complained that he spent more time with Howard than he did with her.

The line continued to move forward until she and Grady were at its head.

"Next," the postmaster said.

Grady moved forward. "I need to pick up my mail," he told the postmaster.

Tritia's eyes were caught by a sign taped to the front of the counter: "Mail will be delivered on Mondays, Wednesdays, and Fridays until a new postal carrier is appointed. The post office will temporarily be open on Tuesdays and Thursdays only. Sorry for any inconvenience."

Next to the sign was a funeral notice for Bob Ronda.

"How long's it going to be before you hire a new mailman?" Grady asked.

"I'm not going to be hiring one," the postmaster said. "The main office in Phoenix holds an open enrollment once a year and they do the hiring. They're going to appoint someone. I called in this morning and put in an application for a new carrier, but it'll probably be a few weeks before they send someone down."

"It's a damn shame what happened to Ronda," Grady said. "A damn shame."

Howard nodded silently.

Grady got his mail, waved good-bye, and Tritia moved to the front counter. "How are you, Howard?" she asked kindly, putting her hand on his.

He shrugged, his eyes blurry and unfocused. "As well as can be expected, I guess."

"I didn't hear until now. It's—it's hard to believe."

"Yeah."

"Bob just didn't seem . . . I mean, it didn't seem like he'd do something like that."

"That's what I been telling people all day. I can't believe he killed himself. People always say that when something like this happens, but usually there are reasons. A guy gets divorced, his wife dies, he loses his job. But there's nothing. I was just over at Bob's house last night, and me and him and Ellen sat down, had a good dinner, some good talk. Everything was normal. He wasn't depressed at all. He wasn't happier than usual or sadder than usual or more talkative or less talkative. There was nothing out of the ordinary. He hadn't been fighting with Ellen, 'cause when they fight me and him always go out and get something to eat instead of staying to home." He shook his head, looking down at the counter for a moment, then he looked up at her and tried to smile. The effect on his grief-stricken face was oddly gruesome. "Anyway, what can I do for you?"

"I just came to deliver a letter and to buy a book of stamps."

"A book of stamps it is," Howard said, reaching under the counter and placing the stamps before her.

She paid him the money, then gave his hand a small squeeze. "If you need anything just call," she said. "Anytime."

He nodded tiredly. "Will do."

She stepped away from the counter. Behind her, she heard the postmaster's dazed voice. "Next."

2

The funeral was well-attended. Almost everyone in town knew Bob Ronda on a first-name basis, and almost everyone liked him. The cemetery was packed and many of the latecomers were forced to stand outside the wrought-iron gates on the side of the small hill. Bob had never been a churchgoing man, and Ellen had decided to have the entire service conducted outside at the gravesite. She stood next to the preacher, dressed in a simple black dress, staring down at the ground. A wilted wet hanky was clutched in her right hand, and she twisted it absently between her fingers. Rumor had it that she had nearly gone crazy when she'd found her husband's body, screaming and yelling, tearing apart the house, even ripping off her own clothes, and that Dr. Roberts had had her heavily sedated ever since. Looking at her now, supported on both sides by her grown sons, Doug could believe it.

The newspaper account of the mailman's suicide had been sketchy and general, a polite glossing over of the facts in deference to the survivors, but in a town the size of Willis news sometimes traveled through quicker and more efficient channels than the press, and by noon the day after, nearly everyone had heard the full story. Apparently, Ronda had gotten out of bed before his wife had awakened, had walked into the garage for his sawed-off shotgun, and had gone into the bathroom. There he had taken off his clothes, stretched out in the tub, placed the tip of the shotgun in his mouth, and blown a hole through his brain. The blood and bone and tissue had splattered against the tile behind him and was dripping into the tub by the time Ellen had run in.

There had been no note.

There were other versions of the story. One version, one in which Doug put no credence, said that Ronda had sat on the shotgun, greasing it, placing it to his asshole and blow-

17

ing out his insides. Another said that he had shoved the barrel deep into his eye socket, putting out his eye before pulling the trigger. These false reports had died almost immediately, however, and by the day of the funeral there was only one story circulating.

Billy had been very shaken by the news of the mailman's suicide. He still had all four grandparents, had never lost a pet, and this was his first real experience with death. He had also liked Ronda a lot, as had most of the kids in town, and it had been a shock to learn that the mailman had killed himself. Billy had been quiet and subdued for the past two days, unusually pensive and well-behaved, and Doug and Trish had discussed at length whether the boy should go to the funeral. In the end, they decided against it, agreeing that the sight of the mourners and the coffin would probably be too traumatic for their son, and they had found a babysitter to watch him for the morning. When they returned, they would talk the funeral over with him, make sure he understood what had happened.

Standing at the head of the grave, in front of the closed casket, the minister read selected excerpts from the Bible. He tactfully refrained from mentioning the cause of the mailman's death and instead discussed the positive aspects of Ronda's life and the loss to his family and to the community his death had wrought.

Doug listened to the preacher's generic comments but found his mind wandering. Although he felt sad, he should have felt sadder. He should have been as moved by the words he was hearing as by the thoughts and memories in his head. What was missing from the minister's well-meaning words, he realized, was the spirit of the man himself, and he thought that there were many people who could have given a better, more heartfelt eulogy, people who had known and loved the mailman on a personal level. The bartender at The Corral, for instance. Or George Riley.

Or Howard Crowell.

His eyes scanned the crowd until he found the postmaster. Howard was standing next to Ronda's family, dressed in a new black suit bought especially for the occasion, sobbing openly. He was obviously listening to every word the preacher said, and his gaze appeared to be riveted on the casket.

Doug frowned. Standing next to the postmaster, wearing a light-blue postal uniform that contrasted sharply with the somber black conservative attire of the other mourners, was a man he had never seen before. Tall and thin, with a shock of red hair topping a long pale face, he was staring off into the distance, obviously bored with the funeral. Though Doug was not close enough to see clearly the expression on the man's face, he sensed an arrogance in the newcomer's stance, a disdain in the tilt of his head. The man turned lazily to look at the minister, sunlight glinting off a series of gaudy buttons on his jacket. On anyone else, the uniform might have looked dignified, even respectful, but on him it seemed mocking, clownish, and it served only to trivialize the proceedings. The man turned again, gazing outward across the crowd, and Doug had the sudden inexplicable feeling that he was looking directly at him. It was an unnerving experience, and he glanced quickly away, his eyes shifting back to Howard.

Tritia, too, was looking at the postmaster, but she did not notice the stranger next to him. Her gaze was focused on Howard's face, on his wet cheeks and shattered expression. He looked so lost, so hopeless, so helpless. They would have to invite him over for dinner sometime, she decided. Probably half the town had extended similar offers to him this week, but she knew that he liked her and Doug more than most, and she thought they might be able to cheer him up a bit.

She glanced over at Ellen Ronda, on the other side of the postmaster. She had never really liked the mailman's wife. Ellen had always seemed too hard, too driving, too status-conscious for Bob, who had always been an amiably laid-back man, but it was obvious from the pain, evident even through the drug-induced haze of her eyes, that Ellen had loved her husband deeply and that his loss would not easily be borne. Tritia's heart went out to the widow, and she felt welling in her eyes the tears that had eluded her until now.

Above them, the sky was a rich deep blue, the sun hot already at ten o'clock. From here could be seen most of the town: the dull-blue wall of the diner peeking out from behind the Valley National Building and the small Chamber of Commerce office; portions of the shopping center revealed through the trunks and branches of the trees; the brightly colored signs of the gas stations and fast-food restaurants in the newer section beyond. Closer in, across the meadow that separated the cemetery from the golf course,

was the original nucleus of the town: the newspaper, the
library, the bars and the police department—conveniently
located within a block of each other—and, of course, the
post office.

The post office.

Tritia found that she could not look at that empty building for any length of time. It seemed sad and forlorn, almost
abandoned, though it was only closed for the day. She
wiped her eyes and concentrated on the words of the minister, focusing her gaze on the dark rosewood of the casket.
Smooth and rounded, it looked almost like a large polished
stone. Tritia knew that Ronda's family couldn't afford such
an obviously expensive coffin, and she was pretty sure that
the insurance provided by the Postal Service would not
make up the difference. She would have Doug find out if
someone in town had started a memorial fund to help defray
the funeral expenses. If no one had, they would institute
one. The mailman's family would have a tough-enough time
just living with the pain and getting on with their lives
without having to worry about financial burdens as well.

"Ashes to ashes," the minister said, "dust to dust."

Tritia and Doug looked at each other, then grasped each
other's hands, holding tightly.

"Amen."

Ellen and the boys moved forward as the casket was
lowered into the grave. Between the sobs of mourners, the
quiet hum of machinery could be heard as the motorized
jack folded downward. The town was silent. Since most of
the residents had come to the funeral, there were not even
the occasional noises of car engines or power tools to mar
the stillness.

Ellen reached down to pick up a handful of earth. Before
dropping it into the open grave, she mouthed something
inaudible, pressing the dirt to her lips. Then she collapsed,
dropping to her knees and pounding her fists against the
ground. She began to scream and one of her sons lifted her
to her feet while the other spoke softly to her, trying to calm
her down. Dr. Roberts pushed his way through the crowd
toward them. Most of the people in attendance looked away
out of deference, out of politeness, but Doug saw that the
newcomer was staring boldly at the widow, bouncing a
little on the heels of his shoes as if enjoying the sight.

A moment later it was over. The doctor held Ellen's hand

and she stood stiffly erect next to the grave as her sons dropped symbolic handfuls of earth on top of the casket.

The minister said a final prayer.

They walked up to Ronda's family after the service, waiting in line to pay their condolences. After her emotional outburst, Ellen once again seemed dazed and drugged, and her teary-eyed sons found the strength to support her between them. The minister stood with the family, as did Dr. Roberts and Howard. Next to the postmaster, on the outer ring of this inner circle, was the newcomer. This close, Doug could clearly see the man's features: the small sharp nose, the piercing blue eyes, the hard knowing mouth.

Tritia grasped Ellen's outstretched hands firmly. "You're strong," she said. "You'll get through this. It may seem as though the pain will last forever right now, but it will pass. You'll survive. Just try to take things one day at a time. Just try to get on with your life. Bob would have wanted you to go on."

Ellen nodded silently.

Tritia looked from one son to the other. "Watch your mother. Take care of her."

"We will, Mrs. Albin," said Jay, the eldest.

Doug could think of nothing to say that wasn't trite and ineffectual. But then words from others at a time like this were bound to be meaninglessly superficial. "I'm sorry," he said simply, taking Ellen's arm for a moment, then shaking each of the boys' hands. "We liked Bob a lot. We're going to miss him."

"That's the truth," said Martha Kemp in back of him.

Tritia was already talking to Howard, echoing similar sentiments. She gave him a quick hug. Doug moved next to her and clapped a sympathetic hand on the older man's shoulder.

"He was the best friend I ever had," Howard said, wiping his eyes, looking from one to the other. "Usually your childhood friends are the best, the people you grow up with. It's not often you find someone who's as close as that."

Tritia nodded understandingly. Doug took her hand.

"I miss him already," Howard said.

"We know," Doug told him.

The postmaster smiled wanly. "Thank you. And thank you for the card and the call the other day. Thank you for listening to a crazy sentimental old man."

"You're not crazy, and you're not that old," Tritia told him. "And what's wrong with being sentimental?"

Howard looked at Doug. "Keep her," he said. "She's a good one."

Doug nodded, smiling. "I know."

"We want you to come over one night this week," Tritia told the postmaster. She looked him in the eye and there was something in her voice that forbade argument. "I'll make you a good home-cooked meal, okay?"

"Okay."

"Promise?"

"I promise."

"Okay, then. We'll see you later. And if you don't call us, we'll call you. Don't think you're going to get out of this."

Howard nodded good-bye as they began to move off. He had not introduced the man next to him, but Doug knew without being told that he was Ronda's replacement. The man held out a pale hand, which Doug reluctantly shook. The man's skin was warm, almost hot, and completely dry. He smiled, revealing white even teeth. "Nice day," he said. His voice was low and modulated, almost melodious, but there was an undercurrent of mockery in his tone, an attitude that only amplified the casual callousness of his words.

Doug said nothing but put his arm around Trish, ignoring the man and moving down the hill toward the parking lot with the other townspeople. As he turned around to unlock the car door, he happened to see the new mailman standing tall among the mourners. It was hard to tell from this distance, but it looked as though the man was watching them. And it looked as though he was still smiling.

Billy told Mrs. Harte he was going to go out and play, and she said that was all right as long as he stayed within calling distance of the house. His parents could come back anytime, and she didn't want them to think she had lost him.

Billy said he was just going to The Fort; it was right behind the house, and as soon as he heard his parents' car, he'd run immediately back.

Mrs. Harte said it was okay.

The Fort was located in the green belt behind the house but was not visible from any window. He and Lane Chapman had built it last summer out of leftover materials from the construction of a summer cabin down the road. Lane's father's company had built the cabin, and Lane's father had given them posts, two-by-fours, planks, and even some cement—enough material to build the basic structure of two rooms. It had taken them most of the summer to scrounge up the rest of the wood and the signs, decorations, and furniture for the inside, but after they'd finished, The Fort was perfect. Even better than they'd thought it would be. The front and sides were camouflaged with branches of sumac and manzanita; the rear wall was backed against a tree. You entered from the roof, climbing the tree until you were on top of The Fort, then pulling the string that unlatched the hinged trapdoor. There were no stairs and no ladder, but the jump was not far.

Inside, the Big Room was decorated with cast-off knicknacks salvaged from garbage cans around town: old album covers, bamboo beads, an empty picture frame, a bicycle wheel. Lane had added a stolen Stop sign given to him by another friend in order to lend the place a touch of class. The other room, the HQ, was smaller and carpeted with a stained throw rug they'd scavenged from the dump. It was here that they kept the *Playboys* they had found in a sack of newspapers destined for recycling.

Billy walked down the short path in back of the house. He could have called Lane and had him meet him at The Fort, but he wanted to be alone today. He felt sort of strange and sad and lonely, and though it wasn't exactly a pleasant feeling, it was not something he wanted to push away and force out of his system. Some emotions just had to run their course—you had to think about them, experience them, let them pass of their own accord—and this was one of those.

He also didn't feel much like talking, and with Lane around talking would have been unavoidable. The boy talked more than anyone he had ever met, and while sometimes that was fine, it was not always appropriate, and he just wasn't in the mood for conversation today.

Still, he felt slightly traitorous coming here alone. It was the first time he'd been to The Fort without Lane, and it seemed somehow wrong, as if he were breaking some type of pact, though there had been no such agreement either spoken or unspoken between them.

He reached The Fort and quickly clambered up the fork-ing branches of the tree, swinging himself onto the roof and opening the trapdoor. He dropped into the Big Room and stood there for a moment, looking at the old metal ice chest that they had turned upside down and made into a chair. The ice chest had been given to them by Mr. Ronda, who, when he had seen them sorting through a pile of garbage at the side of the road, had offered to give them the ice chest as well as a few pieces of plywood paneling he had at his house. He'd brought the materials by the next day, leaving them next to the mailbox.

Billy thought of Mr. Ronda's kind face now, of his blue laughing eyes, of his thick white beard. He had known the mailman all his life. He had seen him every day until he had had to go to school, and had seen him every Saturday, holiday, and summer after that. When he had needed rubber bands for a school project, Mr. Ronda had saved rubber bands for him, delivering them along with the mail each morning. When he had done a report on the post office, Mr. Ronda had taken him on a tour. Now the mailman would never help him again, would never drive by to drop off the mail, would never talk, would never smile, would never live.

He felt his eyes filling with tears, and he moved through the curtains into the HQ. He wanted to feel sad, but he didn't want to cry, and he forced his mind to think about something else for a minute. He would come back to Mr. Ronda in a while, when he was ready.

He sat down on the rug and picked up the top *Playboy*. He flipped through the thick magazine until he came to the first pictorial. "Women in Uniform," the headline read. His eyes scanned the page. There was a woman straddling a fire hose, wearing only a red fireman's hat and a red slick raincoat. Underneath that photo was a picture of a topless woman with large breasts wearing a police cap and licking the rounded tip of a nightstick. His eyes moved on to the next page. Here was a nude woman wearing nothing but a smile and the hat of a mailman. One hand clutched a group of sorted letters; the index finger of her other hand hung from the bottom lip of her pouting mouth.

Billy felt something stir within him. He pressed down on the rising lap of his jeans.

Was this the way the new mailman would look?

He stared for a moment at the woman's triangle of reddish pubic hair and the pink hard nipples of her breasts. He felt guilty for thinking such thoughts, and he quickly closed the magazine and put it on top of the pile. He tried thinking of Mr. Ronda again, of the things the mailman had done and would never do again, of the man he had been but was no more, but the moment had passed and, try as he might, he could not make himself cry.

3

They neither saw nor heard the new mailman come by the next morning, but when Tritia walked out to the mailbox around ten to drop off a letter, the mail had already arrived. "Damn," she said. Now she'd either have to go down to the post office and mail the letter herself or put it in the box and let the mailman pick it up tomorrow. She reached into the metal receptacle and took out the mail, sorting through the envelopes. There were only four pieces of mail today: three for Doug, one for her. There were no bills, she noticed, and no junk mail.

She closed the mailbox door. Doug would be going into town sometime today for groceries. She'd let him drop the letter off at the post office.

She studied the envelope addressed to her as she walked back up the driveway. There was no return address and the postmark was from Los Angeles. She opened the envelope and unfolded the letter itself, glancing first at the signature. She stopped walking. No. It couldn't be possible. Paula? She looked again at the signature. Paula. She ran quickly up the porch steps into the house. Doug was rummaging through the junk drawer in the kitchen, looking for something. "You'll never believe it," she said as she walked into the kitchen. "I just got a letter from Paula."

"Paula?" He looked up. "Paula Wayne?"

She nodded, scanning the letter.

"I thought you didn't know where she moved to."

"I didn't." Tritia shook her head. "I wonder how she found me?"

"Your parents, probably."

"But they've moved twice since the last time I saw her. And they have an unlisted number." She grinned happily. "I can't believe it. I don't know how in the world she found me, but I'm glad she did."

"Well, aren't you going to read the letter?"

"I am," she said, looking down at the paper, waving him away. "Wait." She read quickly, her eyes moving easily through the neatly scripted, almost calligraphic letters. "She divorced Jim and moved to L.A. and now she works as a paralegal."

"Divorced him?" Doug laughed. "I thought those two were a perfect match."

"Shut up," Tritia said, continuing to read. "She says that she's happy but misses Santa Fe. She hopes I haven't forgotten about her. She may be taking a trip to the Grand Canyon in August and wants to know if she can stop by and see us."

"I'll think about it," Doug said.

"Ha ha." She read in silence, turning the page.

"Well, what else?"

"It's personal. Girl talk." Tritia read the second and third pages, then folded the letter and put it back in the envelope. She shook her head. "Paula. I can't believe it."

Doug pulled a screwdriver from the drawer and closed it. "You miss her, don't you?"

"Of course I do. Oh, here, I almost forgot. Some mail for you." She handed him the other three envelopes.

He tore open the top letter. "You're not going to believe this," he said.

"What?"

"It's from Don Jennings."

"Jesus, you haven't seen him since—"

"—you saw Paula," he finished for her.

She laughed. "That's a weird coincidence." She moved forward to peek over his shoulder, but he pulled away, hiding the letter.

"It's personal," he explained.

She hit him lightly on the arm. "Very funny." She stood next to him and read along, catching up on the events in Don's life. Don had taught social studies at the high school and had been hired at about the same time as Doug. The two neophytes on the faculty had become friends out of necessity, but they had grown very close. A city boy, Don had never really been happy in Willis, and about ten years ago had taken a job in Denver. The two families had kept in touch for a while, writing letters, calling on the phone. Doug and Trish and a baby Billy had even visited the

Jennings in Denver one summer. But new friends had come along, responsibilities had grown and shifted, it was no longer as convenient to keep in touch, and gradually the families drifted apart. Doug had said to Tritia many times that he "should call Don" or "should write Don," but somehow he never did.

Now Don had written to say that he and Ruth were moving back to Arizona. He had gotten a job at Camelback High School in the Valley and suggested that when they moved and got settled in, the two families should get together.

"Are you going to write him back?" Tritia asked when she finished reading.

"Of course." Doug opened the other two letters. One was from the district, announcing that an agreement had been reached with the teachers' union for a cost-of-living raise next year. The other was from the Department of Education, announcing that the deadline date for the grant application was actually a week later than stated on the form and apologizing for any problems caused by the misprint.

Doug looked at Tritia incredulously. "Let me get this straight. You and I both hear from friends we haven't seen or contacted in years; we're going to get the raise we asked for; and my application will have no problem getting in because the deadline is a week later than I thought?"

"Hard to believe, isn't it?"

"I'm buying a lottery ticket today. If our luck holds out, we'll be millionaires by midnight."

She laughed.

"You think I'm kidding? This isn't just a happy coincidence. This is luck." He grabbed her around the waist, drawing her to him. "We're on a roll, babe."

" 'Babe?' "

Doug turned around. Billy was standing in the back doorway. He seemed tired, but he smiled as he walked into the kitchen. "Can I call you that too, Mom?"

Tritia pulled out of Doug's arms, turning toward Billy. "Very funny. Your father, as usual, is being a buffoon. I expect you to observe his mistakes and learn from them."

Doug tried to grab her, but she pulled away from him on her way to the bedroom and he managed only to slap her rear. Billy watched them mutely. Ordinarily he would have joined in, but now he stood passively, a blank expression on his face.

Tritia put away her letter, then went into the bathroom. Billy continued on into the living room, turned on the television, and sat silently down on the couch. Doug stood in the kitchen, carefully watching his son. They had talked to him last night, a long intense discussion of death and dying in which, he'd thought, a lot of fears were faced and confronted, but apparently little if anything had been laid to rest. Billy was obviously still quite disturbed over the mailman's suicide. And, Doug had to admit, so was he. Like Billy, he had never really had to face death; it had never hit close to home. Although he had known people who had died, they had all been, like Ronda, acquaintances rather than close friends, and he was not sure what he would do or how he would react if his parents died or Trish was taken from him or something happened to Billy. Despite his talk with his son, which was filled with the current psychologically accepted beliefs concerning the necessity of facing negative feelings and fears, he preferred not to dwell on such subjects. It was a shallow and easy way out, but rather than seriously confront his own feelings, he chose to joke, to laugh, to go on with his life as if nothing had happened.

He found himself thinking of the mailman now, though. Imagining how he must have looked with the top of his head blown off, blood and wet brains splattered on the tile behind him. Death, in any form, was a difficult subject to deal with, but violent suicide was messy and gruesome as well.

He looked down at the letters in his hand and thought of the new mailman. The coincidence of receiving so much good mail in a single day was wonderful, but it was also a little creepy. If Ronda had delivered these letters, Doug would have been ecstatic, although he would probably not even have noticed the coincidence. But knowing what the new mailman looked like, imagining those pale hot hands slipping the envelopes into the mailbox and then carefully closing the door, he could not help feeling that they had been tainted somehow, and though nothing had actually happened to affect his mood, he was not as happy as he had been a moment before. He looked over at Billy. "What time did the mailman come by?" he asked nonchalantly.

"Didn't notice," Billy said, not taking his eyes from the TV.

Doug recalled the mailman's mocking smile, his arrogant attitude. He found himself wondering what type of car the mailman drove. He found himself wondering the mailman's name.

Doug stopped first at the store for bread, charcoal, tomatoes, lettuce, and peanut butter, then dropped by the post office on his way home. He arrived between the noon and midafternoon rushes and had no trouble finding a parking spot. The tiny lot was virtually empty. There were two old-timers sitting on the bench outside the post office as he walked up the steps, but there were no customers inside. Howard, as usual, was at the counter, wrapping a package. He looked haggard, his face red and blotchy, eyes teary, and Doug guessed that he had probably spent the night before drinking. The sight of the postmaster filled him with an uncomfortable feeling, but he forced himself to smile as he approached the counter. "How goes it, Howard?"

The postmaster looked up distractedly. "Fine," he said, but there was no conviction in his voice. It was a stock answer, an automatic reply, and meant nothing. "Can I help you?"

"Actually, I just came by to drop off a letter, but I thought I'd see how you were doing while I was at it."

The shadow of a frown crossed the postmaster's face. "I'm fine. I just wish people'd stop treating me like I just got out of a mental hospital. I'm not that fragile. I'm not going to have a breakdown or nothing. Jesus, you'd think I was a little kid."

Doug smiled. "People around here care. You know that."

"Yeah, well, I wish they'd care a little less." He must have heard the annoyance in his voice, for he suddenly stopped wrapping the package before him and shook his head, smiling sheepishly. "I'm sorry, I guess I haven't been myself lately." He shot Doug a warning glance. "But I don't want any sympathy."

Doug laughed. "You won't get any from me."

"Good."

"So who's the new mailman?"

Howard placed the package on the scale, putting on his steel-framed glasses and squinting through the thick lenses to read the weight. "His name's John Smith."

John Smith?

"Got here pretty quick, didn't he?"

"Yeah, that surprised me, too. I'd never had to go through

this before, but I heard it took four or five weeks for them to transfer someone. I put in a request down to the main office on Monday, though, and he was here on Wednesday."

"He's from Phoenix?"

"I'm not sure. He don't talk much. But I'm sure I'll find out soon enough. I told him he could stay with me until he found a place of his own. Murial's room is vacant while she's gone, and I told him he could sleep there so long as he makes the bed and picks up after himself. It's cheaper than a hotel, and it'll give him some time to pick out a place. Usually, postmen end up taking the first place that comes along because they can't afford to stay in a hotel any longer. The Postal Service don't give you no moving allowance, and God knows they don't pay carriers enough to stay holed up in a hotel for weeks at a time." He wrote down a number on a small slip of paper, stamped it with a red seal, and took the package off the scale. He stamped FIRST CLASS on the top of the package.

"So what's he like? What do you think of him?"

Howard shrugged. "Too early to tell. He seems nice enough."

Doug looked suspiciously at the postmaster as he dropped the package into a large cart. It wasn't like Howard to be so circumspect. He was usually quick and bold in his judgments; this cautiousness and taciturnity seemed out of character for him. Either he liked someone or he didn't, and he did not hesitate to make his opinions known.

But Doug said nothing. The man had just lost his best friend. Who was he to judge behavior in such a situation? "Trish was serious," he said. "We want you to come over."

Howard nodded. "I'd like that," he said honestly.

"How about the weekend, then? Friday or Saturday?"

"Sounds good."

"I'll tell Trish. She'll probably call you about it. She doesn't trust me to handle these things." He opened the post-office door. "See you."

"Later," the postmaster said.

John Smith, Doug thought as he walked down the steps, taking his keys from his pocket. A likely story.

Doug was halfway home before he realized that he had forgotten to buy a lottery ticket. He had been half-joking when he'd said that to Trish, but he had also been half-

serious. He was not a gambler by any stretch of the imagination, but he did buy an occasional lottery ticket when he
remembered. And though he was ostensibly a rational intelligent man, he was not entirely immune to superstition. He
didn't really believe in luck—good or bad—but it wasn't
something he ruled out as being entirely impossible. Besides, he wouldn't mind winning a few million. It would be
nice to be fabulously wealthy. It was something to which he
would gladly adjust.

He turned the car around and headed to the Circle K. He
bought a ticket, letting the machine pick the numbers, and
read over his choices as he walked back out to the car. He
was about to open the door when he saw, near the mailbox
by the curb, the mailman. The postal carrier was kneeling
on the ground, the door to the mailbox open, key and chain
hanging from the lock, and was taking out the deposited
mail. Only he wasn't simply emptying the bin the way Doug
had seen Ronda do; he was carefully examining each envelope, sorting through them. Some he placed carefully in a
plastic tray beside him. Others he shoved unthinkingly into
a brown paper sack.

There was something odd about that, Doug thought. From
the careful way he handled the one group of envelopes and
the casually rough way in which he dealt with the others, it
seemed as though he was planning to hide some of those
envelopes from Howard, as though he had plans for them
other than delivery.

The mailman looked up and stared directly at him.

Doug glanced away, pretending as though he had been
scanning the street and his gaze had accidentally landed for
a second on the mailman as he'd looked around. But in the
brief moment that their eyes locked, he had the unmistakable feeling that the mailman had known he was watching
and that that was precisely why he had looked up at that
moment.

You're being stupid, Doug told himself. The man had
glanced in his direction. That was all. It was a perfectly
ordinary occurrence, a simple random event. There was
nothing strange or sinister about it. But when he looked
again at the mailman, he saw that the man was still staring
at him and that there was a disdainful half-smile on the pale
thin lips.

Doug quickly opened the car door and got inside, feeling

vulnerable, exposed, and slightly guilty, as if he had been caught watching someone undress. He wasn't sure why the mailman's gaze made him feel that way, but he didn't want to stay here and analyze it. He started the car and backed up. The only exit from the Circle K lot was right next to the mailbox, and he hurriedly sped across the asphalt, hoping to pull immediately onto the road. No such luck. The highway was filled with cars and campers coming down from the lake, and he was forced to sit there and wait for an opening. He concentrated on the traffic, looking only to the left, but he could see out of the corner of his eye that the mailman was staring at him, still and unmoving. Then the line of traffic ended and he swung out onto the road. He could not resist the impulse and glanced out the passenger window as he drove by.

The mailman, smiling, waved at him.

4

Billy was on the porch when the mailman came by. There was no warning as there had been with Mr. Ronda, no loud motor or squealing brakes. There was only the quiet purr of a new engine and the soft dry crunch of tires stopping on dirt. Billy put down his BB gun and glanced over at the new mailman, curious, but the windows of the red car were tinted, the interior dark, and all he could see was a thin white hand and the sleeve of a blue uniform reaching out from the driver's window to put a stack of letters in the mailbox. There was something about the sight that bothered him, that didn't sit right. In the darkness of the car he thought he could see a shock of red hair over a pale indistinct face. The mailman did not look friendly like Mr. Ronda. He looked somehow . . . inhuman.

Billy felt a slight chill pass through him, a distinctly physical sensation, though the temperature was already well into the eighties. The white hand waved to him—once, curtly— then the car was off, sailing smoothly and silently down the road.

He knew he should go out and get the mail, but for some reason he was afraid to. The mailbox and the road suddenly looked awfully far away from the safety of the house and the porch. What if, for some reason, the mailman decided to turn around and come back? His dad was in the bathroom at the back of the house and his mom was over at the Nelsons'. He would be stuck out there by himself, on his own.

Knock it off, he told himself. He was just being stupid. He was eleven now, almost twelve, practically a teenager, and he was afraid to get the mail. Jesus, how pitiful could a person get? It wasn't even night. It was morning, broad daylight. He shook his head. What a wuss!

Nevertheless, he was scared, and for all of his self-

chastisement he had to force himself to walk down the
porch steps and up the gravel driveway.

He walked slowly past the pine tree in which they'd hung
the bird-feeders, past the Bronco, over the culvert, and was
at the edge of the road when he heard the car's quiet
engine. His heart pounding, he looked down the road to see
the mailman's car backing up quickly toward him. He stood
rooted to the spot, wanting to run back onto the porch but
knowing how foolish he would appear.

The car pulled to a stop next to him. Now Billy could see
clearly the black interior of the new car.

And the white face of the mailman.

In his chest, Billy's already racing heart shifted into over-
drive. The mailman's face was not ugly, not scary in any
conventional way, but his skin seemed too pale, the features
on his face too ordinary. His hair, by contrast, was so
garishly red as to appear artificial, and this juxtaposition
seemed to Billy somehow frightening.

"I forgot to deliver a letter," the mailman said. His voice
was low and even, smoothly professional, like the voice of a
game-show host or news commentator. He handed Billy an
envelope.

"Thanks," Billy forced himself to say. His own voice
sounded high and babyish.

The mailman smiled at him, a slow, sly insinuating smile
that made Billy's blood run cold. He swallowed hard, turning and walking back up the driveway toward the porch,
concentrating on keeping his feet moving at an even pace,
not wanting the mailman to sense his fear. He kept waiting
to hear the car shift into gear behind him, to hear the
wheels on the gravel as the mailman pulled away, but there
was only silence. He stared straight ahead at the windows of
the house, but he saw in his mind the creepy smile of the
mailman, and it made him feel dirty and slimy, as though he
needed to take a bath.

He was suddenly aware that he was wearing shorts, that
the mailman could see the backs of his legs.

He reached the porch and walked directly to the door,
pulling it open and walking inside. Only now did he turn to
peek through the screen door at the mailman. But the car
was not at the foot of the drive, and there was not even a
cloud of dust where it had been.

"What're you looking at there, sport?"

He jumped at the sound of his father's voice. "Nothing," he said immediately, but he could tell from the look on his father's face that he wasn't going to buy that story.

"What's the matter? You seem a little jumpy."

"Nothing's wrong," Billy repeated. "I just went out to get the mail." He handed over the envelopes he'd been holding.

The expression on his father's face changed from puzzlement to what looked like . . . understanding?

But at that moment there was the sound of tires crunching gravel outside.

They both looked out the window. Hobie Beecham's dented white pickup had just pulled into the driveway, and Hobie himself was hopping out of the cab.

"Okay," Doug said, nodding at Billy. He put the envelopes down on the table and pushed open the screen, walking out onto the porch.

Hobie was striding across the driveway with his patented redneck swagger. He clomped loudly up the porch steps, adjusting the baseball cap on his head. "I was gonna come by yesterday," he told Doug, "but I was on crotch watch." He grinned, taking off his mirrored sunglasses and putting them in the pocket of his Parks and Recreation T-shirt. "It's a tough job, but somebody's got to do it."

Hobie taught auto shop and driver's ed at the high school, but during the summer he volunteered to work twenty hours a week as a lifeguard at the public pool. He was a fair swimmer but certainly no trained lifeguard, and Trish had often wondered aloud why they'd accepted him at all, since it was well known that he spent more time ogling the mothers from behind his sunglasses than he did supervising their kids. She was prejudiced against him, but she had a point, Doug thought. Hobie was big, loud, and unredeemably sexist. Proudly sexist.

Billy, in the doorway, laughed, already feeling better. He liked Mr. Beecham.

"You didn't hear that," Doug told him.

Hobie shook his head, chuckling. "They're startin' 'em young these days."

Billy picked up his BB gun and went to the opposite end of the porch, aiming at the aluminum can he had placed on a tree stump in the green belt, the incident with the mailman already beginning to fade into memory.

Doug and Hobie walked inside, and Hobie took off his baseball cap. He sat down, uninvited, in the nearest chair, wiping the sweat from his forehead. "Got anything cold to drink in here?"

Doug walked into the kitchen and opened the refrigerator. "We have some sun tea, some Coke, some water—"

"Anything more manly?"

"We're out of beer. Besides, it's not even eleven yet."

The other teacher sighed. "Coke, then."

Doug popped open Coke cans for Hobie and for himself and carried the drinks into the living room, handing one to his friend. "So what brings you out this way?"

"The board meeting next Tuesday."

Doug groaned. "Board meeting? We just got out." He sat down on the couch. "Besides, I thought the meeting wasn't until the end of July."

"Well, the bastards moved it up. They figured if they held it while most of the teachers are on vacation, they'd be able to slip the budget through with no opposition. Hell, the only reason I found out is because one of the janitors told me. I saw him at the pool."

"But they have to post the date and time."

Hobie shrugged. "I'm sure they did." His voice took on a sarcastic note. "You know them. They would never do anything illegal." He snorted. "They probably buried it in the classified ads of the paper last week so no one'd see it."

Doug shook his head. "I'm sick of school. I don't even want to think about it until the end of August."

"I just thought you might want to know. If I remember correctly, you were going to petition them for more funds?"

Doug sighed melodramatically.

"For new books?"

He nodded, drinking his Coke. "Yeah," he admitted. "I'm tired of teaching *To Sir, With Love*." He leaned back, his head against the wall. "Some asshole got it into his head a few years ago that teaching popular novels instead of classics would interest kids in reading. So they bought a twenty-year-old novel the kids hadn't even heard of, bought a videotape of the movie, and told me to teach it. It doesn't interest them in reading; all it does is bore them to tears. *The Scarlet Letter* would bore them to tears too, but at least they'd learn from it."

Hobie chuckled. "I kinda liked Lulu, though. She had nice knockers."

"Very funny. It's just that the board and the parents are always harping about how our test scores compare to the rest of the state. Well, other schools are reading *Heart of Darkness* and *Huckleberry Finn*. Our kids are at a disadvantage. I just want them to be able to compete."

"I learned to read from comic books," Hobie said.

Doug sat up straight. "I have nothing against that theory. Of course kids will want to read if they are given interesting reading material. And there is a lot of popular fiction that is worthwhile. I just think that if we're going to operate on that assumption, we should have better material to work with." He shook his head. "Shit."

On the porch Billy giggled.

"Stop spying," Doug called out. "Nixon Junior!"

Hobie grinned. "Sounds like you're going to the meeting."

Doug sighed. "Yeah, I'm going to the meeting."

"Good. We can present a united front."

"A united front?"

"I need a new spray gun for my advanced auto."

"And you want me to back you?"

Hobie looked hurt. "We're brother teachers."

"Okay, but you know how tight the board is. If it comes down to a draw, I'll toss you to the wolves."

"It's a deal." Hobie held up his Coke can. "Cheers."

Walking up the road from the Nelsons', Tritia saw Hobie's truck in the driveway before she had reached the mailbox. She considered turning around and going back, returning after he had gone, but she heard his loud voice carrying on the warm slight breeze and could tell that he was just leaving. She walked across the dirt and turned into the drive.

"Trish," Hobie called out. He laughed loudly and rushed forward, grabbing her around the waist, hugging her. "How's it goin'?"

Tritia put on a strained smile. She didn't like Hobie Beecham, although she tried to get along with him for Doug's sake. She honestly could not understand what her husband saw in the man. He was lewd, crude, and a step above beefwit. She tensed as the hug continued, finally pushing him away. The last time he'd greeted her, he'd taken the opportunity to squeeze her ass, though when she'd told Doug about it he said it was probably an accident. It was no accident, she knew, and she'd told him his friend had better keep his hands to himself or he would find himself with one testicle less.

Billy thought Hobie was great, however, and each time after he came over, the boy walked around the house affecting a swagger, trying to put a southwestern twang in his voice. She wished there was some way to get Billy to emulate and admire some of their more cultured and intellectual friends, but he was at the age when that sort of simplistic macho posturing seemed extremely appealing, and there was no way to effectively dissuade him without pushing him into Hobie's corner completely.

Tritia looked the big man over. "We missed you at the funeral," she said pointedly.

"Yeah, well, I didn't go. I mean, it woulda been kind of hypocritical. I didn't even know the guy. He dumped off my mail, I saw him every once in a while, but we certainly weren't friends."

"A lot of people were there."

He shrugged. "I wasn't. Sue me." He smiled. "Making friends has never been one of my major goals in life."

"I noticed," Tritia said coolly.

Hobie turned to Doug. "Speaking of Ronda, have you seen the new mailman?"

"Yes," he said noncommittally.

"I saw him this morning by the post office. Creepy guy. I don't like him."

Someone else had noticed too! Doug forced himself to remain calm. "Did you talk to him?"

"Don't want to. His job is to deliver the mail, not be my buddy. I don't talk to the meter-reader or the paperboy or the telephone man either. No offense, but that was something I never liked about Ronda. He was always stopping to chat with everyone—"

"Ronda was a good man," Doug said simply.

"And don't you dare say anything bad about him," Tritia ordered. She nailed him with dark stern eyes.

Hobie was about to say something else but apparently thought the better of it and shut his mouth. He gave Doug a

condescending smile of male camaraderie, a smile that all
but said that his wife was being a typical foolish female.
Tritia was right, Doug thought. Sometimes his friend was an
insensitive asshole.

Tritia walked up the porch steps and slammed the door
behind her.

"Anyway," Hobie said, "I don't like the new guy."

"I don't either."

"Weird sucker. He's so pale. And that red hair. Shit, I
wouldn't be surprised if it was dyed. He is kind of faggoty-
looking."

"Well, I don't know about that . . ." Doug said, his voice
trailing off. He wasn't sure what he thought, he realized. He
had no concrete beliefs about the mailman, only an un-
founded dislike, a strong sense of unease sharpened by
impressions gleaned from a few random meetings. He was
not usually given to such impulsive, instinctive judgments,
and he was a little surprised at himself. Ordinarily, he
prided himself on giving everyone the benefit of the doubt,
on believing only the best about a person until shown otherwise. His negative opinion of the mailman, however, had
been born fully formed; he had experienced an instant dislike of the man without knowing a single fact about him.

Dislike and fear.

And fear, he admitted. He was, on some level, for some
reason he could not quite understand, afraid of the mailman. And that too had been instant.

Hobie pulled open the door of the pickup and hopped
onto the ripped seat. He dug into the right front pocket of
his Levi's and pulled out his key ring. "Well, I gotta be
going. You're coming with me to the meeting, though,
right?"

"You got it."

"All right. We'll kick some butt." He slammed the door,
grinning, and started the engine. "I'm on poon patrol tomorrow and Friday, but I'll give you a call before Monday."

"Okay," Doug said. "Have fun."

"I will," Hobie said, pulling his mirrored shades from his
T-shirt pocket, putting them on. "You bet I will." He backed
up quickly and swung about on the road, turning the truck
toward town. He waved once, a short swipe of his hand
above the cab of the pickup, and then was gone.

Doug walked back up the steps.

"Kick some butt," Billy said, putting down his BB gun.

"Don't you repeat that," Tritia called from inside.

"You heard your mother," Doug said. He tried to make his voice sound tough, but he couldn't help smiling. He pushed open the screen door and walked into the house, picking up the mail from the top of the table where he'd put it down.

He glanced at the envelopes in his hand.

Again there were no bills.

5

The next day Doug received a letter from Ford informing him that, due to the outcome of a lawsuit the company recently lost to a consumer-rights organization, the warranty on their Bronco's power train had been extended for another year. There was also a two-dollar rebate check from Polaroid and a letter to Billy from Tritia's mother, with a five-dollar bill in it.

The day after that, the mail consisted of a letter from Doug's mother to Billy—the letter contained a one-dollar bill: she was richer than Tritia's mother but cheaper—and a subscription to the Fruit-of-the-Month Club from an anonymous donor "on this, the occasion of your birthday." The accompanying card was addressed to Tritia, but her birthday was not until January. Doug's was closer, in October, but it was still several months away.

"Who could have sent us this, and why?" Tritia wondered, looking at the small box of red delicious apples.

Doug didn't know, but he didn't like it. He was also starting to worry about the bills. It had been exactly a week since Ronda had killed himself, and while he could not really find any fault with the man who had taken his place—*John Smith*—he did not think it natural that they had received no bills or junk mail in that time. There was something suspicious and unsettling about that. It was strange enough that it had happened once, but for the exact same thing to occur day after day . . . Well! Mail, by its very nature, was neither all good nor all bad. It carried indifferently messages both positive and negative, filtering nothing, making no distinctions. The odds against something like this occurring were probably astronomical.

Besides, he knew that both his water bill and Exxon bill came due at this time each month.

If he didn't get those bills by Monday, he told Trish, he was going to go in and have a talk with Howard.

"Stop being so paranoid," she said. "Jesus, if you're bored, start cleaning up that trash in the back of the house. Start working on your storage shed. Do something useful. Stop thinking up bizarre conspiracy theories."

"What bizarre theory?" he asked. "Some of our mail is obviously getting lost. I'm just going to talk to Howard about it."

"Don't give me that. You've had it in for that new mailman since the moment you laid eyes on him."

She was right, although he had never come out and said as much. He had not, in fact, talked to her at all about the mailman, not specifically, though he had talked about the mail and obviously must have telegraphed to her his thoughts and opinions. What worried him as much as the lack of bills and junk mail, however, was the sheer amount of letters and positive correspondence they were receiving. Under normal circumstances, they did not get this much good mail in a month, let alone in a few days, and that was not something which could easily be explained, which had an alternate, obviously rational explanation. There were too many factors and variables involved. This was not something that could be attributed to the incompetency of a postal worker.

He remembered seeing the mailman carefully sorting the letters he took from the mailbox.

"I'm going to call Howard," he repeated.

Howard himself called the next day, ready to take them up on their dinner invitation. Trish answered the phone, and while Doug knew immediately who it was from the sympathetic tone she adopted and from the sudden understanding in her voice, he did not mention anything about the mail. The postmaster was going through a difficult period, and he did not want to make it even more difficult. He would bring up his complaint next week if nothing had changed, and he would bring it up in a business rather than social environment.

Trish set up a date and Howard agreed to come over on Saturday for roast and potatoes.

"You know what?" Doug admitted to Trish that night before they went to bed. "I think I'm actually starting to miss all that junk mail. I used to toss most of those ads and flyers out without reading them, but now that we don't get them anymore, I feel like we're cut off from society. It's almost like not getting a newspaper. I feel like I'm not up on what's current."

Trish rolled over and turned off the light. "Shut up about the mail," she said. "Go to bed."

6

Lane Chapman lived in a large three-bedroom house on the top of the hill, above the flattened ruins of the old Anasazi village. The house was modern, all wood and glass and angular corners, and the inside looked like something out of a magazine: white throw rugs on white Mexican tile floors, overstuffed white couches, track lights with framed art posters on otherwise bare white walls. Billy stared at the two-story structure as he walked up the paved drive to the front steps. He admired the house, appreciated it, but he didn't like it. It seemed cold, more like an art exhibit than a home, and the two boys usually spent most of their time at the Albins' small but comfortable A-frame.

Although he would never tell this to Lane, Billy also found his friend's parents cold and aloof. Mr. Chapman was hardly ever home, but when he was, Lane stayed well out of his way. He seldom smiled, swore often, and did not like to waste his time talking to kids. Billy was not even sure Mr. Chapman knew his name, though he had been his son's best friend since kindergarten. Mrs. Chapman was always home, but there was something false about her unwavering smile, something phony about her constant niceness. Lane, he knew, adored his mother, but Billy was not sure the feeling was reciprocated. Mrs. Chapman seemed about as warm and responsive as her precious white furnishings.

Before moving here to Pine Top Acres, the Chapmans had lived just down the way from Billy's family in a prefab log home that Lane's dad had built and that he used as a demonstration model for his contractor's skills. Now the Chapmans had an unlisted phone number, and the only people allowed into the house were those few who had been invited.

Billy pressed the doorbell and heard the familiar musical

chime sound dully from the depths of the house. A few moments later, Lane was at and out the door.

"Come on," he said. "Let's hit the road. My dad's home and he's pissed. He just lost a contract to Gagh and Sons, and he's in a bad mood. He's threatening to take me to Crazy Carl again."

Billy laughed. Crazy Carl was the town's oldest barber. A World War II vet, with pictures of the Big One all over his tiny shop, he considered it his patriotic duty to make sure every boy's hair was cut to a length he considered acceptable. No matter what style was requested, Carl would inevitably shave the hair down to a uniform butch. Once, years ago, Billy's dad had taken him to Crazy Carl and had told the old man to just trim a little above the ears. Carl had shaved him almost completely bald, and he had been the laughingstock of his classroom for weeks. Neither he nor his dad had ever gone back again.

"He's not serious, is he?" Billy asked.

"Hard to tell with my dad. He's always threatening to send me off to military school or something." He shook his head. "I'm getting tired of this crap. I swear to God. I'm hitting the road when I'm eighteen, and if my old man tries to stop me, I'll deck him."

Billy hid his smile. Lane was always talking about how he was going to "deck" his dad or "beat his ass." Last week, when they'd found a lottery ticket on the ground, Lane had said that if they had the winning numbers he was going to leave home and send a truckload of dogshit to be dropped on his father's car. Lane's plans and pronouncements were always funny, but there was something sad about them too, and Billy was thankful that he didn't have his friend's parents.

Lane looked around the drive. "Where's your bike?"

Billy nodded toward the edge of the road. "I left it back there. I thought maybe your brother was sleeping. I didn't want to wake him up." The last time he'd come over, he'd called out for Lane instead of knocking on the door or ringing the bell, and Lane's mother, smiling as always, had come out and told him in a polite voice edged with steel that he had awakened the baby.

Lane laughed. "You think your bike was going to wake him up? The doorbell's louder than that."

"Did I wake him up again?"

"No. He's fine. Stop being such a pussy. What do you think my mom's going to do? Beat you?"

It was possible, Billy thought, but he said nothing. He walked down the drive to the bush where he'd stashed his bike while Lane got his own wheels, and soon the two of them were speeding down the road.

Although the land at the top of the hill had been open for development for over two years, few of the acre lots had sold and even fewer had been built upon. There was the Chapmans' house; Dr. Koslowski's house; the house of Al Houghton, who owned Pine Top Acres; and a few expensive vacation homes built by people who never used them. Other than that, the flattened hilltop was home to only trees and rocks and bushes.

Billy and Lane pedaled down the paved road past the dark wood and stone of the doctor's rustic residence. The view from here was spectacular. To the left was the town, white wooden buildings and brown shake roofs peeking up from between summer green trees, and the rugged ridge beyond. To the right was the forest, stretching toward the horizon in an alternating pattern of hill and valley, hill and valley, broken only by the cleared spaces and tiny jumbled patterns of increasingly far-off towns.

They sped along the road. Their plan today was to check out the Indian ruins at the bottom of the hill. A team of archaeology students from ASU had arrived yesterday for their annual summer workshop, and they hoped to be invited to join the exploration.

They had discovered the dig last summer while practicing motocross jumps and maneuvers on the maze of barely perceptible trails that branched outward from the forest service road that dissected the narrow valley. They had seen, from far off, moving swaths of color amid the forest green and had ridden up to investigate. The dig had already been under way for a month by the time they'd arrived, and the sight that greeted their eyes amazed them both. Fifteen or twenty men and women were digging with tiny trowels in square shallow holes precisely outlined with sticks and string. Many of them were examining small rocks and pieces of pottery, dusting the objects off with small black brushes. In the center of the meadow, next to a battered pickup truck, were rows of bones and skulls and Indian grinding stones.

Around the perimeter of this activity, a low stone wall had been partially unearthed.

The two of them had stood with their bikes at the edge of the meadow until someone had spotted them and yelled, "Hey!" Then they'd taken off, pedaling fast and furiously away from the site.

But they had returned the next day.

And came back the day after that.

Gradually, like wild animals, they grew used to the archaeology students and the students grew used to them, and one day, finally tamed, they had gathered the courage to walk into camp.

It had been an eye-opening experience. The two of them had hung around, trying to stay out of everyone's way, until the professor in charge let them chisel out some arrowheads from the hard-packed ground. It had been fun and rewarding, and although they hadn't been able to keep any of the artifacts they'd unearthed, they had both decided then and there that they were going to be archaeologists when they grew up.

The road curved down and they found the trail that led off the pavement through a vacant lot into the forest. Billy jumped the small embankment, Lane followed, and then they were through the lot and into the trees. The trail wound through the underbrush, following the path of a long-dead stream, running down the hill to the valley below. They sped over the sandy earth. Small lizards scattered out of the way of their onrushing tires; birds flew up from the surrounding bushes, squawking into the air. Finally they reached the bottom of the hill, and Billy turned into his stop, sliding across the dirt. Lane skidded to a halt next to him. From off to their right came the faint sounds of conversation and rock music, and they swiveled their bikes around, heading toward the sounds.

Although the low stone outlines of Anasazi buildings stretched across the entire floor of the valley, the university team concentrated on only one small section at a time. Last year, the students had been digging at the north end of the tiny valley, near the meadow, but this year it sounded as though they had given up on that idea and were trying to look for artifacts on the heavily forested south end.

Billy and Lane were at the site almost before realizing it, and they quickly stopped at the edge of the small clearing.

Folding tables and chairs had been set up underneath various trees, and on them were piled books and boxes and assorted work tools. The carpet of brown pine needles that ordinarily covered the ground had been cleared and flat bare dirt shone through, broken in spots by square shallow excavation holes. Bright-blue and red tents were set up about the area, though not enough for everyone to sleep in. The students themselves were grouped around their professor, a balding middle-aged man with an Abe Lincoln beard and a prospector's tan.

The boys parked their bikes in the bushes and walked slowly and shyly forward. A few of the students' faces were familiar from last year, but most of them were new and Billy and Lane weren't sure what kind of reaction they were going to get.

The eyes of the men and women shifted focus from the professor to the two boys trekking across the rough ground. The professor turned to see the new center of attention, and a smile of recognition crossed his face. "I was wondering when you were going to show up," he said. His voice was cracked and hoarse. "Ready to work?"

"That's why we're here," Lane said.

The professor laughed. "Glad to have you aboard. I'm sure we'll be able to find something for you to do." He turned to face his class. "Those of you who are new to our extension course, meet Lane . . ."

"Chapman," Lane prompted.

"And Billy . . ."

"Albin."

"Right." The professor was about to add something else when his attention was drawn to the other end of the clearing. Pressing forward, Billy followed his gaze. He saw movement in the underbrush. A man. A man with a blue uniform and a thin white face.

And bright red hair.

The mailman stepped into the clearing from the other end. He had obviously been walking through the trees and bushes all the way from the control road, which cut across the valley at its southern tip, but his postal uniform was free from all traces of dirt, there were no small dead leaves or branches in his hat, and the gold buttons on his jacket shone brightly, unscratched. He held in his hand a single envelope.

"Dr. Dennis Holman?" he asked in his smooth low voice.

The professor nodded.

"I have a letter for you." He handed the envelope to the professor, then glanced purposefully over at Billy. There was the same suggestive smile on his face that Billy had seen that day by the mailbox, and he felt both sickened and scared. His heart was pounding, and he glanced over at Lane to see if he had noticed, but Lane's attention was focused on a braless woman in the front row of students.

Billy forced himself to stare only at the professor, trying to ignore entirely the creepy insinuating look of the mailman.

Dr. Holman opened the letter and quickly scanned its contents. "Our funding came through," he announced to the assembled group, holding up the letter. "The university has decided to go ahead with our research project."

There was a spontaneous and only partially tongue-in-cheek cheer from the students.

The professor, grinning, nodded at the mailman. "Thanks," he said. "That's the best news I've gotten all semester."

"Glad to be of service," the mailman said.

Ordinarily, Billy thought, that would have been the man's cue to leave, but he showed no intention of doing any such thing. He clasped his hands behind his back and stood there calmly, looking around the camp, taking everything in. His face was purposefully neutral, carefully expressionless, but there was an underlying smugness, an indefinable something that manifested itself in his attitude and that gave Billy the feeling that he was passing judgment on all he surveyed—and that he was happy it did not live up to his standards. He was silent and expressionless, but Billy could tell that inwardly he was gloating.

The mailman's eyes scanned the faces of the students, lingering on none of them, then landed once again on Billy.

Billy was sweating. He could feel twin trickles of perspiration slide in winding paths from beneath his armpits down his sides. His forehead, too, was sweaty, and he wiped it with a palm. It was hot out, but not that hot, and he swallowed hard, wanting to escape, to run, to get the hell out of here. But he could not move. He was frozen in place by that gaze, by the unnatural promises behind that superficially benign smile, so utterly powerless to react that he could not even glance over at Lane.

The mailman nodded at him, a nod of recognition and acknowledgment, a nod that said "I know what you're thinking," then turned away and strode back through the forest the way he had come.

"We got our funding," the professor enthused. "We finally got our funding!" He was holding up the letter proudly. "Now we'll really be able to make some progress."

Billy felt Lane, next to him, give him a nudge with his elbow. "That's great, huh? I guess we'll be able to do more stuff."

"Great," Billy repeated. But his thoughts were not on the professor or on archaeology. His eyes and thoughts were focused on the space between the trees where a moment before he had seen the mailman's white hand wave slowly and lovingly good-bye.

7

Howard pulled into the driveway at seven sharp. It was still light out, but the blue in the east was quietly being usurped by purple, and there was an orange tinge to the pale sky in the west. Billy was sitting on the couch and was right in the middle of a *M.A.S.H.* rerun when Tritia turned off the TV and kicked him upstairs. He complained loudly, but hurried up the steps nonetheless. He was not comfortable around adults, and he usually hid each time they had friends over. Watching him tromp loudly up the stairs, his mother couldn't really blame him. She'd felt the same way herself when she was his age.

"I'll call you when dinner's ready," she said. "You can come on down and get some food."

"Okay."

Doug stood up and went to open the door.

"Don't say anything about Bob unless he brings the subject up first," Tritia suggested. "We're supposed to be cheering him up, taking his mind off his troubles."

He shook his head, pressing past her. "I'm not entirely dim, you know."

She smiled. "Just trying to counteract the Hobie Beecham influence."

"Thanks." Doug pulled open the door while Tritia hurried into the kitchen to check on the food, stepping onto the porch just as Howard started up the stairs. "Glad you could make it," he said.

The postmaster smiled. "Glad you invited me." He was wearing his equivalent of dress clothes: new dark-blue jeans, a starched white-and-rose cowboy shirt, and an agate bolo tie. His boots had been shined and his hair slicked back and held in place with some sort of wet-looking gel. In his hand was a gift-wrapped bottle.

"Come in," Doug said, holding the door open. Howard stepped past him, and both of them moved into the house.

Tritia was taking off her apron, and she moved forward to greet their guest. She, too, had dressed up for the occasion and was wearing a low-cut black dress, matching turquoise bracelet and necklace, and silver antique earrings. Her brown hair was done up in a sophisticated roll. She accepted the proffered present graciously. "Thank you," she said. "But you really didn't have to bring anything."

"I wanted to." Howard looked at her and shook his head appreciatively. "You sure look mighty beautiful today." He turned to Doug. "I've said it before, and I'll say it again, you're a lucky man."

Tritia blushed. She unwrapped the bottle and turned it around to read the label. "Champagne!" She gave Howard a quick peck on the cheek. "Thanks so much. I guess this means we'll forgo the Dr. Pepper." She went into the kitchen, put the bottle down on the counter, and threw the wrapping paper in the garbage sack under the sink. "You two keep yourselves busy for a few minutes. I'll get the hors d'oeuvres ready."

Doug motioned for Howard to sit down in one of the chairs across from the couch, and the postmaster obliged. Doug sat down as well. It was warm. The windows were open, the fan on, but the air still bordered on the uncomfortable. From upstairs came the familiar strains of the theme from *M.A.S.H.* Doug smiled at Howard.

"Excuse me for a moment." He stood up again and walked to the foot of the stairs. "Turn it down," he called out. "It's too loud." The noise of the television faded into a drone, then was silenced. "Billy," he explained, walking back. He settled into the chair. There were questions he wanted to ask, things he wanted to know, but he didn't know how to approach the subject subtly. He cleared his throat, deciding to jump right in, hoping he didn't sound too interested, too curious. "So how're you getting along with the new mailman? Is he still living with you?"

"Yeah," Howard admitted, "but I don't see him much. You know how it is. I'm an old man. I go to bed earlier than he does, wake up later than he does. Our life-styles don't exactly match."

"So what's he like?"

Tritia walked up and placed a plate of cheese crepes on the small table between them. "I'll be back with the champagne," she said sweetly. She fixed Doug with a hard meaningful stare as she turned away from the postmaster, but he pretended not to see it.

Each of them took a crepe and bit into it. "Mmmm," Howard said, closing his eyes and savoring the taste. "That's one thing I miss with Murial being gone: good cooking. You get tired of frozen food and hot dogs after a while."

"Don't you cook?" Tritia asked, bringing them two glasses of champagne.

"I try, but I fail."

She laughed lightly as she returned to the kitchen for her own drink.

"So what's he like?" Doug asked again. "He sure delivers the mail early. Bob used to come by around noon. Now by the time we eat breakfast and clean up a bit, the mail's there."

"John does start early. He's usually gone before I'm even up. He's done with the entire route by eleven, and he stays until four." Howard grabbed another crepe, popping it into his mouth. "He hasn't turned in a time card yet—it's due this week—but when he does, I gotta see what hours he puts down. He's not supposed to be working more than eight. I think it's more like ten or eleven, though."

"Don't you think that's a little weird?" Doug asked. "I mean, delivering the mail so early?"

Trish shot him another withering glance over the postmaster's head as she sat down next to him.

"Yeah, John might be a tad strange. But he's a good worker. He does his job well and gets things done. And he's always eager to do more. That's not something you see a lot of these days. I couldn't ask for a better carrier."

Doug nodded silently. Howard's words were full of praise, but there was an undercurrent of something else in his tone of voice. It was as if he were repeating words he had read and practiced, as if he were saying what he was supposed to say rather than what he actually felt. For the first time since he'd known the postmaster, Doug thought that he was being out-and-out hypocritical, and that was something he never would have thought he'd feel about Howard Crowell. His eyes met Tritia's across the table, and he knew that she'd caught it too.

But Tritia refused to continue this line of conversation, and she deftly changed the topic to something less personal and more neutral, and Doug followed her lead.

* * *

Dinner was excellent, and they ate it slowly. Billy had come down, taken what he'd wanted, and then retreated upstairs to his hideaway. The rest of them ate at the table, enjoying the food at a leisurely pace: Cobb salad, followed by rare roast in wine sauce, served with baked potatoes stuffed with sour cream and chives. To go along with the meal, Tritia had baked some of her homemade bread, which was thick and warm and soft and disappeared almost immediately.

Howard smiled blissfully. "I can't remember when I've had a meal this good."

"Neither can I," Doug said.

"Enjoy it while you can," Tritia told him. "This is our red-meat quota for the month."

"She's very big on eating right," Doug explained. "This is a very health-conscious family."

"You need all the help you can get. If you exercised a little more, we could afford to be more lenient. But you live a completely sedentary life. It's the least I can do to see that you eat properly."

Howard chuckled.

Billy came down with his dishes, smiled shyly at the postmaster, then returned upstairs. They finished off the champagne and Tritia brought Howard and Doug each a beer. She drank ice water.

The conversation grew more somber and less frivolous as the meal progressed, and it was Howard who brought the subject up first. He was already well into his second beer. "I keep wondering why Bob did it," the postmaster said, looking down at his plate, pushing the empty potato skin with his fork. "That's the one thing that really gnaws at me, that I can't understand: why he did it." He looked up at Tritia, his eyes red but his voice even. "You knew Bob. He was an easygoing guy. He didn't let things get to him. He wasn't an unhappy man. He liked his job, loved his family, had a good life. And nothing changed. There was no big catastrophe, no death in the family, nothing that would push him over the edge. Besides, if something was bothering him, he would have told me." His voice trembled slightly and he cleared his throat. "I was his best friend."

Tritia put her hand on his. "I know you were," she said softly.

He wiped his nose with the back of his hand, forcing himself not to give in to tears. "Ellen's taking it really hard. I mean, harder than I thought she would. She always seemed like such a strong woman." He smiled sadly. "Bob used to call her the Rock." He absently fingered his napkin. "She was all drugged out when I went to see her the other day. The doctor's giving her . . . I don't know what all. He says it's the only way to keep her calm. The boys are the ones who have to take care of everything, but you can see that the strain's starting to show. They have questions just like I do, and there just aren't any answers."

"Are they still staying at the house?" Doug asked.

Howard nodded. "I told them to get out, at least for a while. It just stirs up bad memories, and I'm sure it's not doing Ellen any good."

Doug had a sudden picture of the two sons waking up each morning, each of them taking a shower in the same bathtub where their father had blown his brains out, getting their soap from the indented soap dish in which puddles of his blood and pieces of his fragmented scalp had lain. He wondered how Ellen bathed, how she avoided thinking about what she had seen.

"It'll be all right," Tritia told him.

"I miss him," Howard said bluntly. "I miss Bob." He took a deep breath, then the words came out in a rush. "I don't know what I'm going to do with my Saturdays anymore, you know? I don't who I'm going to be able to ask for advice or give advice to or go places with or . . . Shit!"

And he began to cry.

After dinner, they sat on the porch. It was warm, humid, felt like rain. Bats, fluttering shadows of darkness, spun in and out of the illuminated circle generated by the streetlamp. From down the road came the harsh electric sounds of a bug zapper instantaneously frying its victims.

"We used to go bat fishing when we were little," Doug said absently. "We would hook a leaf or something to fishing line and throw it up into the air next to a streetlight. The bats' radar told them that it was a bug, so they'd dive for it. We never caught anything, but we came close a few times." He chuckled. "I don't know what we would've done if we'd've caught one."

"You do stupid things when you're little," Howard said.

"I remember we used to shoot cats with pellet guns. Not just cats that were wild or strays. Any cat." He downed the last of his beer. "Now it's hard for me to remember bein' that cruel."

They were silent for a while, too full and too tired to make the effort at conversation. In the east, above the ridge, lightning flashed, outlining billowy dark clouds. Like most summer storms, it would probably come at night and be gone by morning, leaving behind it a heaviness and humidity that would create a boom business at the air-conditioned movie theater and would send people running to the lakes and streams. They looked upward. The evening was moonless, and though there was obviously a storm approaching, the sky directly above them was an astronomer's dream, filled with millions of pinprick stars.

Doug's chair creaked as he shifted his weight, leaning forward. "Where's, uh, John Smith tonight?" The name sounded ludicrous when spoken. "Is he at your house?"

"Don't know." The beer must have loosened his tongue, for Howard shook his head, a vague movement in the darkness. "He's usually not there this early, though. He goes out at night, but I don't know where he goes or what he does. Some nights I don't think he comes home at all."

"What makes you say that?"

"Well, I been having a hard time sleeping lately. I'm real tired, but I can't fall asleep."

"That's understandable," Tritia said.

"Yeah, well sometimes I get up and walk around, you know, just to have something to do. The other night, I was going out to the kitchen to get a drink of orange juice, and I notice as I pass by that his door's open. I look in there and the bed's made and he's gone. That was around two or three in the morning."

"Maybe he has a girlfriend," Tritia suggested.

"Maybe." Howard sounded doubtful.

"Have you ever seen him sleeping?" Doug asked.

"What kind of question is that?" Tritia frowned.

"Humor me."

"No," the postmaster said, speaking slowly, "come to think of it, I haven't."

"Ever seen his bed unmade?"

Howard shook his head. "But he does stay in his room on

Sundays. Don't even open the door. Just stays in there like he's hibernatin' or something. I think he sleeps then."

"All day?"

Howard shrugged. "I don't know. Maybe not. Maybe he does something else. He always seems real tired on Monday morning."

Doug felt the coldness wash over him. He didn't know why he was pursuing this line of questioning or what he hoped to find out, but there was something about the mailman that bothered him in a way he could not explain. "Have you been getting many complaints about him?" he asked.

"None."

Doug felt more than a twinge of disappointment. He had been half-hoping to hear that there was a ground swell of resentment against the new mailman, that either residual feelings for Ronda or a recognition of the mailman's own obvious peculiarity had brought in a negative verdict from the public.

"As a matter of fact," Howard continued, "people seem to be very happy with the job he's doing. I can't remember the office ever being so busy. People're sending more letters, buying more stamps. I don't rightly know what it is, but the people seem to be more satisfied than they were before." His voice took on an edge of bitterness. "That's all well and good, mind you, and I'm not complaining, but I can't help thinking that this is like a judgment against Bob. I mean, no one's said anything bad about him. In fact, it's exactly the opposite. I hear nothing but praise and good things about him. But on a professional level, people seem to be happier with John." He was silent for a moment, and when he spoke again, his voice was filled with quiet conviction. "Bob was a damn fine mail carrier. The best I've ever known or worked with, and I can't help feeling that he's being betrayed."

Doug and Tritia were silent.

Howard stood up and walked over to the railing, staring out at the green belt. "John's a good worker. He's polite and hardworking. He does a fine job." The postmaster's voice was so low they could barely hear it. "But I don't like him. I don't know why, but, God help me, I don't like the man. I don't like him at all."

Howard left after ten. Doug offered to drive him home, but he said he was not drunk, and indeed he seemed to have no trouble walking in a straight line or speaking clearly. Still, Tritia made him drink a cup of coffee before he left, and both of them watched from the porch as he drove away, red taillights disappearing into the trees.

Doug had asked him about the mail, had told him that he suspected that the new mailman was losing letters, but the postmaster, once again closed off, said that what was happening was common. Mail, like tides, he said, had ebbs and flows, it was never constant. But there seemed to be a pattern here, Doug argued. They were getting no bills or junk mail, nothing negative. Coincidence, Howard said, and although Doug did not believe him, he did not press the point. It was nothing he could prove. Still, he was determined to make out checks for the regular monthly payments on his bills and send them out tomorrow instead of waiting for the bills themselves to arrive.

Locking the front door behind them as they went inside, the Albins decided to leave the dishes until tomorrow. From upstairs, they could hear the rough arhythmic sounds of Billy's snores. Doug smiled. The boy was a regular lumbermill with his log sawing, his snores as loud and deep as those of an old man. Tritia turned the light off in the kitchen and they walked down the short hall to the bedroom.

"Don't you think Billy's been kind of quiet lately?" Tritia asked.

"No more than usual."

"It seems like something's bothering him. He's been, I don't know, distracted. Like today, when he came home from Lane's, I asked him what he'd been doing, and he just shook his head, wouldn't even answer me. Then he sat there and watched TV for the rest of the day."

Doug chuckled. "So what else is new?"

"I'm not joking. Could you just ask him what's wrong? After all, you are his father."

"Okay. I'll talk to him tomorrow. I don't know what you want me to find out, but—"

"Just see if he's in any kind of trouble, find out what's wrong. I'm probably just imagining things, but it never hurts to check. He's almost a teenager, you know."

Doug knew what she was hinting at, but he didn't pursue the subject. "Okay. I'll talk to him."

"Thanks."

They had reached the bedroom. It was dark, and neither

of them turned on the lights. "Of course," he said, "Billy's asleep now."

Tritia was silent.

"Sound asleep," he prodded.

He heard the sound of the bedspread being pulled down. The room was warm, but not nearly as warm as the living room in the front of the house. Far away, thunder rumbled. Doug began unbuttoning his shirt. "It's kind of romantic with the lights off," he said. "Don't you think? I—"

It was then that he felt her hand between his legs. Surprised, he reached forward in the darkness, and his fingers touched smooth rounded flesh. Somehow Trish had silently wiggled out of both her dress and her underwear. Their lips met, and he felt her warm wet tongue slide lovingly into his mouth. Her hands slowly unbuckled his belt, unzipped his zipper, pulled down his pants and shorts. He kicked off his shoes, stepped out of the clothes bunched around his ankles, and the two of them moved silently over to the bed. She pushed him onto his back without speaking, and he stretched out straight on the mattress. Her fingers, soft and gentle, grasped his penis, massaging it, making it hard. The bed creaked and jiggled as she moved into position, and he could smell the musky scent of her arousal as her pubic hair brushed his face. He moved his head upward, and his tongue touched moisture. He could taste her, sweet and sour, and as his tongue slid into her ready opening, he felt the warmth of her mouth engulf his penis.

It was nearly an hour later before they were through. It had been a long time since they'd both enjoyed it this much, since they'd allowed themselves to enjoy it this much. In the past year or so, their lovemaking had consisted of commercials rather than feature films, short quick trysts taken when they were sure Billy was asleep or would be gone for a long period of time. Ever since Doug had explained to his son the facts of life, they had both been careful that no clues to their lovemaking could be spotted by the boy. But this had been like the old days, long and unhurried and giving and wonderful.

Exhausted, sated, they fell asleep in each other's arms, still naked, still clutching each other.

8

Billy stood outside the theater, waiting for his dad to pick him up. The movie had ended early nearly twenty minutes ago, and everyone else was gone. The parking lot was deserted. Even the ushers and other theater workers had finished cleaning up and were leaving.

Where was his dad?

He'd called home about ten minutes ago, once Brad and Michael's parents had come to pick them up, and his mom had said that Dad had just left and was on his way.

So where was he?

The last of the theater workers' cars left, loud rock music blaring distortedly from speakers that were not meant to handle such volume, and now the parking lot was empty save for an abandoned pickup at the far end. The overhead lights, one mounted on a telephone pole, the other on an actual lamppost, blinked simultaneously off.

And now there was only darkness and silence.

No, not quite silence.

There was a soft purring.

The sound of a new car engine.

Billy's heart began pounding. He stepped across the sidewalk and looked up and down the street, desperately searching for his dad, but his dad was nowhere to be seen.

There was only a new red car cruising slowly down the street toward him.

Panic gripped his chest, and he looked around for some place to hide. But the outside of the theater was flat and featureless, with no alcoves or indentations in which to conceal himself. There were not even any bushes behind which he could duck. The people who had built the theater had torn out all trees and bushes and had paved over the bare flattened ground for their parking lot. He was stuck. There was nothing he could do, no place he could go.

The car pulled into the parking lot. The passenger window slowly lowered, and against the darkness of the interior he saw the mailman's milk-white face and bright-red hair.

The car stopped next to him. "Need a ride?" The smooth voice was seductive, suggestive.

"My dad's coming to pick me up," Billy said. His heart was pounding so crazily that he thought he might have a heart attack.

"Your dad's not coming," the mailman said. His voice was still silky, but there was an undercurrent of menace in it. The passenger door opened. "Get in."

Billy backed away.

"Your dad's not around anymore," the mailman said, and chuckled. There was something about the way he stretched out the word "around" that sent a chill of goosebumps down Billy's arms. "Get in."

"No," Billy said.

"You'll get in, and you'll like it." The mailman's arm stretched out through the open door.

And continued to stretch.

And continued to stretch.

Until his cold white fingers were clamped around Billy's throat.

And Billy awoke screaming.

9

It was Doug's turn to make breakfast, and he plugged in the waffle iron and mixed the batter while Tritia went outside to do her morning watering. He stirred the waffle mix absently. The screaming bothered him. Billy had never had a nightmare of that magnitude before. Even after they had calmed him down, convinced him it was only a dream, he was still pale and trembling and he seemed reluctant to let them leave. But he refused to tell them what the nightmare was about. Doug had pressed him, but Tritia had told him with a slight tug on the arm that the questioning could wait until a more opportune time.

Billy had slept the rest of the night on the couch downstairs.

The batter mixed, Doug moved into the living room and peeked out the window. He had placed a letter in the mailbox late yesterday afternoon before Howard came over, a long detailed answering letter to Don Jennings, catching him up on the milestones of his life over the past decade. The red flag on the box was down now, and he glanced over at the clock. Six-thirty-three. The mail was being delivered earlier every day. And on a Saturday. He thought the post office had discontinued Saturday service.

He walked outside onto the porch, down the steps, and up the drive. Last night's storm had not materialized, passing over Willis without even bothering to say hello, but it had left behind it some hellacious humidity. By the time he reached the mailbox, he was already starting to sweat. He opened the metal door. His letter was gone and in its place was a thin white envelope with striped blue trimming addressed to Trish.

"My tomatoes!"

He could hear Trish's cry from the road. He hurried up the drive to where she stood in the garden, hose in hand. She looked at him and pointed to the plants at her feet.

"The javelinas got my tomatoes again!" She kicked the ground. "Goddamn it!" Javelinas had eaten her tomato plants each summer for the past three years. Last year, the tomatoes had been greenish red and almost ripe when the wild pigs had raided the garden. This year, Doug had made a little chicken-wire fence around the garden to keep the animals out, but apparently it hadn't worked.

"How are the other plants?" he asked.

"Radishes are okay, zucchini is salvageable, cucumbers are all right, cilantro and the herbs are untouched, but the corn is completely ruined. Damn!"

"Need some help?"

She nodded disgustedly. "We'll redo what we can after breakfast. I'll just finish watering right now."

"We could set traps if you want. Hobie knows how to do it."

"No traps," she said. "And no poison. I hate the little bastards and I want them to die, but I don't want to be the one to kill them."

"It's your garden." He walked around to the front of the house and went up the porch, hearing the sound of slow tired footsteps on the floor as he stepped through the door. He stood unmoving, mouth open in mock incredulity, as Billy headed away from the couch toward the kitchen. "I don't believe it," he said. "Miracle of miracles!"

"Shut up," Billy said.

"You actually got up on your own."

"I have to go to the bathroom," Billy mumbled, making his way down the hall.

"Wait a minute," Doug said seriously.

Billy turned around.

"Are you all right?"

The boy stared dumbly at him for a moment, then recognition registered on his face. He nodded tiredly and walked into the bathroom, slamming the door and locking it.

Doug deposited the envelope on the coffee table in front of the couch and opened the refrigerator, taking out the butter and jam. From the cupboard he withdrew honey and peanut butter, setting them all on the counter next to the plates. The dirty dishes from last night were still in the sink, but he figured he'd do the dishes all at once after they finished breakfast. He opened the now hot waffle iron and ladled in some batter, closing it and listening to the quiet sizzle, smelling the familiar rich buttermilk odor.

The toilet flushed and Billy came out, walking straight through the kitchen to the living room, where he automatically turned on the television.

"TV on Saturday morning?" Doug said. "That's sickening."

Billy ignored him and turned on a cartoon, settling back into the couch to watch.

Tritia came in, looking hot and angry, as he pulled the first four waffle squares from the iron. "You want these?" he asked.

She shook her head. "Give them to Billy."

"Why don't we go on a picnic today?" Doug suggested, dropping the waffles on a plate. "We haven't done that for a while. It's going to be hot and horrible anyway. We'll go to Clear Creek."

"Sounds good," Billy said from the living room.

Tritia looked at her son, pushed the hair back from her forehead, then nodded her assent. "All right," she said. "Let's do it."

They decided to hike down the path through the green belt rather than drive or walk along the road. It was faster, more fun, and would take them to a less-populated section of the creek. Tritia made them salami-and-cheese sandwiches on homemade bread, and Doug carried the ice chest while she and Billy hauled the folding chairs. To their right, the low gentle slope of the land graduated into a steeper rise, dirt and light sandstone giving way to darker granite. The vegetation changed from pine and manzanita to aspen and acacia, with long vinelike tendrils of wild strawberries growing parasitically over the rock face, intermixed with ferns and bottlebrush and poison sumac. The trail itself was lined with the tiny red flowers of Indian paintbrush. To their left, the level ground swooped downward to meet the creek, and the path followed this descent in its own late unhurried way.

They heard the creek before they saw it, a low continuous gurgle that sounded remarkably like the peal of distant thunder. As they grew closer, the amalgam of sounds became differentiated and they could hear birds and bugs as well as water. This section of the creek was flanked by saplings—aspen and cottonwood and sycamore—that grew

in chaotic abundance between the boulders that ran like a
second stream along the side of the creek, and they had to
walk quite a ways past the bend before finding a flat spot of
dirt close enough to the water to set up camp.

They set down the ice chest between their chairs. Billy
had worn his cutoffs and, after grabbing a can of Coke,
immediately jumped into the creek, splashing wildly to cool
himself off. The water level was low, but still deep enough
for him to swim. He dogpaddled for a few moments, dunk-
ing his head and pushing from rock to rock, then, bored,
stood up and began wading upstream.

"Don't go too far!" Tritia called out.

"I won't!" he yelled back.

Doug sat down on his chair. He had brought along the
latest Joyce Carol Oates novel to read. He found Oates, as
a person, unrelievedly pretentious and phony, and most of
her books boring and much too long, but there was something compelling about her as an artist, and he found himself inevitably reading her novels and short-story collections
as soon as they came out. He didn't like either her or her
work, but he was a fan.

Strange how that worked, he thought. Hobie was a hardcore
Clint Eastwood fan, and he was not. Yet when it came
down to it, he liked more Clint Eastwood movies than
Hobie did.

Life was full of paradoxes.

The mailman was a paradox. Doug hated the man, but as
he had told Howard, the man had been delivering the most
consistently good mail they had ever received. Of course,
the carrier had nothing to do with the contents of the
mail—if the messenger was not to be blamed for the message, he was not to be congratulated either—but it was hard
not to associate the two.

He glanced over at Tritia, peacefully looking out over the
creek at the cliffs beyond. He was surprised that she had not
felt any real dislike for the mailman, that she had not picked
up on the unnaturalness that seemed to be an inherent part
of his makeup. Ordinarily, she was by far the more sensitive
of them, noticing instantly any behavioral aberrance, making snap judgments based on intuition, which were usually
correct. He did not see how she could be so blind this time.

He opened the book on his lap. Why had he been thinking about the mailman so much lately? It was beginning to

border on the obsessive. He had to force himself to stop it. He had to quit sitting around, worrying, fretting, and find something else with which to occupy his time. Instead of thinking about the mailman, he should be getting to work on that damn storage shed.

But Howard didn't like him either.

That meant nothing. Two negative reactions to a person's personality did not mean that that person was evil.

Evil.

Evil.

There. He had thought it, if not actually said it. For that was the word that had been floating in the back of his mind since the day at the funeral when he had first seen the mailman. It was a simplistic word, almost cartoonish in its romantic-pulp implications, but much as he hated to acknowledge or recognize it, it was the word that best described what he felt about the mailman.

The man was evil.

"What are you thinking?" Tritia asked.

He looked up, startled and embarrassed to be caught in his ruminations. "Nothing," he lied, turning back to the book in his lap.

"Something."

"Nothing." He was aware that she was staring at him, but he chose not to acknowledge the fact. Instead, he concentrated on the words in front of him, on the meaning behind the words, on the thoughts behind the meaning, trying to lose himself in the prose. Eventually, he succeeded. Just as he used to fall asleep as a child while pretending to be sleeping as his parents checked in on him, he now began reading while pretending to read.

Ten or fifteen minutes later, he heard Billy's voice, only a fraction louder than the creek song but rapidly gaining in volume. He looked up from his book.

"Dad!"

Billy came splashing through the center of the creek toward them, holding in his hand a wet and soggy envelope. Water was dripping from the uneven ends of his bangs and from his bare arms. There was a look of excited discovery on his face, as though he had just found the Lost Dutchman gold mine or had just unearthed some long-buried treasure. "Dad!"

Doug marked his place in the book and put it down on a large dry rock next to him. "What is it?"

"Come here. You have to come here."

He looked at Tritia questioningly.

"Oh, do something with your son for a change," she said. "Remember what we talked about? Besides, it's a beautiful day. Don't sit here and waste your life reading."

Doug stood up. "That's where he gets it," he said, wagging an admonishing finger in her direction. "It's a part of the rampant anti-intellectualism that's sweeping this country."

"Pedant."

"Fine. But if he turns out to be a gas-station attendant, it's your fault. I tried my best." He took his wallet out of his pants, placing it on top of his book, then walked over the weeds and rocks toward his son. Scores of tiny brown grasshoppers sprang up at each step, moving frantically from one clump of grass to another. "What is it?" he asked Billy. "And why do you have that letter in your hand?"

"I can't tell you, I have to show you."

"Where is it?"

"Just down the creek aways."

"Do I have to get wet?"

Billy laughed. "Don't be such a baby. Come on."

Doug took one tentative step into the water. It was cold.

"Weird stuff," Billy promised. He waved the envelope tantalyzingly in the air. "There's more where this came from. That's your only hint."

Doug stepped fully into the water. The creek was cold, but it was shallow and came up only to midthigh. Billy began moving away, motioning for him to follow, and he waded after his son.

They rounded a bend and then another one, the cliffs growing steeper on the sides. The water was a little deeper here, the rocks at the bottom slippery. On the floor of the clear creek he could see small black spots on some of the stones. Leeches. "I didn't know you were walking through this kind of area," he said. "I don't like it. It's dangerous. From now on, you stay closer to us."

"It's not that bad."

Doug nearly slipped, and he caught himself on a rock with his hand. Billy, however, was wading straight through the water like an expert. "Well, at least make sure someone's with you if you go out of sight. You could break your head and we'd never know."

Billy had stopped at another bend, pointing around the curve. "There it is," he said.

Doug caught up to him.

And stopped.

Both sides of the creek were littered with envelopes, white and brown and tan and beige. Hundreds of them. They were everywhere, like rectangular patches of snow or some bizarre form of fungus that grew in precise geometrical patterns, covering everything, caught on bushes, sticking out from between rocks. Most of them were wet and waterlogged, in the mud at the edge of the creek. Still others were perched in the branches of nearby trees.

"Weird, huh?" Billy said excitedly. He pulled an envelope from the branches of a sapling next to him.

Doug picked up the two nearest envelopes. Bills. He recognized them immediately from the preprinted return address and the clear window with the name, number, street, city, state, and zip code of the intended recipient. He looked around him. Nearly all of the envelopes seemed to be of the short squarish type that ordinarily housed bills or bad news. Very few were of the long less formal variety or were the small cute envelopes of personalized stationary.

He stared, stunned, at thirty or forty envelopes that looked like they were growing on a tree.

The mailman had been dumping mail at the creek.

It was an inescapable conclusion, but it still gave Doug a strange feeling to acknowledge it. Why would the mailman do such a thing? What was the point? What was the reason? The very strangeness of it was frightening, and he could not understand what the mailman hoped to gain. It was crazy. If he had simply wanted to get rid of the letters, he could have burned them or buried them or dumped them someplace more convenient. He looked around. The spot was so far off the beaten track that Doug did not see how the mailman could even have known about it. He would have had to hike in a mile and a half from the road to get here, carrying the mailbags, since there was no path to this location that was wide enough to drive upon.

He glanced over at Billy. His son must have seen the expression on his own face, for he had dropped the envelope he was holding. The excitement was disappearing from his eyes and was being replaced by what looked like understanding.

And fear.

Tritia sat in her chair, head tilted back, staring up at the sky. She loved to watch clouds, to lay back and enjoy their billowy transformations, ascribing concrete form to their temporary shapes. And nowhere were the clouds more visually dramatic than in Arizona. As a young girl growing up in Southern California near the Pacific Ocean, she'd had her share of clear days, of blue Rose Parade skies, but in California the cloud situation was either feast or famine. Either they were nonexistent or they covered the entire sky from horizon to horizon with a monochrome ceiling. Rarely did she see the huge shifting shapes she saw in Arizona, clouds so white against sky so blue that they looked fake.

"Trish!"

She sat up straight at the sound of Doug's voice. His tone was unexpectedly serious, and her first thought was that he or Billy had slipped and fallen and broken something, but she saw with relief that they were both walking normally through the water toward her, not holding arms or wrists or fingers. She relaxed a little, though she noticed that Billy was not as excited as he had been earlier.

He looked . . . scared. She pushed the thought from her mind. "What is it?" she asked.

"You have to see it. Come here." Doug stepped out of the creek toward her.

She stood, adjusting her shorts. "Do I have to?" she asked teasingly, but the only response she received was a slight attempt at a smile. Something was definitely wrong. "What is it?"

"Nothing. Well, not nothing, but nothing serious."

"What is it?"

"I have to show it to you. Come on."

Feeling increasingly apprehensive, she followed Doug into the creek, holding tightly to his arm as the three of them walked over the slippery rocks upstream, moving through small banks of rapids, around bends. Tree branches swiped at her face as the creek narrowed.

"I'm not crazy," Doug said as they rounded a curve, and before she could figure out what the hell he meant by that enigmatic remark, she saw what they had brought her here to witness. Her heart gave a small leap in her chest as she stared at the envelopes, seemingly thousands of them, scattered about both sides of the creek, on the rocks, on the trees, in the weeds, in the mud. It looked almost like a fairy-tale land, this section of the creek, a place that had been either blessed or cursed by magic. She stood rooted to the spot, water coursing over her tennis shoes and ankles. The sight before her was so crazy, so wrong, that she did not know what to think. She looked over at her husband. She had caught his fear, she realized, and though it was not a pleasant feeling, at least she knew she was not alone. The two of them stood next to each other, holding hands. Billy, in front of them, was silent, and she knew from the expression on his face that he too understood that something here was definitely not right.

"There's no road to this spot," Doug said. "He had to walk here, to carry all those sacks, however many there were." He pointed up at the cliff beside them. "I figure he dropped them from up there. It's the only way they could be so scattered and the only way they could get into those top branches."

"But why?" Tritia asked.

He shook his head slowly. "I don't know."

A slight breeze stirred the trees, several envelopes falling from the branches on which they were perched into the creek, and the three of them stood there, silent, unmoving, as the envelopes swirled around their legs and continued downstream.

10

Doug tried to call Howard after they returned home from the picnic, but he wasn't at either his house or the post office. Or, if he was, he wasn't answering the phone. Doug let the phone ring fifteen times before hanging up. "That mailman'll be fired for this once Howard finds out," he told Tritia. "It's a federal offense to tamper with the mail. He'll probably go to prison."

He hoped the mailman would go to prison.

They had picked up several envelopes from the creek and had brought them home. They'd looked for mail addressed to themselves but hadn't been able to find any, so they'd settled for envelopes addressed to people they knew. The rescued mail was still in the car. He was planning to show it to Howard as proof.

Doug spent the rest of afternoon trying to call Howard, trying to read, trying to listen to the radio, trying to start on the storage shed, but he was anxious, hyper, and could not seem to settle down enough to concentrate on any one thing.

They had spaghetti for dinner that night. Billy complained because it was homemade, with herbs and vegetables from the garden, but he ate it anyway. "Next time," he advised, "let's just have Ragu like normal people."

"This is better than anything you could buy at the store," his father told him.

"And healthier too," his mother added.

Billy grimaced as he swallowed the food.

Doug tried to call Howard again after dinner, but when he picked up the phone, it was dead, no click, no dial tone. He jiggled the twin buttons in the cradle but to no avail. "Something's wrong with the phone," he said. "Did either of you call anyone recently?"

"No one's touched it since the last time you tried to call Howard," Tritia said, clearing the table.

"I'll try the one in the bedroom." He walked into the bedroom, picked up the receiver, but this phone was dead too. He hit the receiver once, hard, against the nightstand and put it to his ear, listening. Nothing. "Damn," he muttered, slamming it down. He'd have to stop by the phone company as well as the post office tomorrow. He stared at the white plastic telephone. He hated dealing with the phone company. Every time he went into their office he saw four or five workers lounging around, trying to pick up on the receptionist, but whenever he asked for someone to stop by his house to investigate a problem, it took at least three days to schedule the call, no matter how simple the problem was, no matter how great the rush.

"Nothing?" Tritia asked as he came back down the hall.

He shook his head. "It's dead."

"Well, there's nothing we can do until tomorrow." She finished putting the dishes into the sink. "You want to wash or dry?"

"Dry," he said tiredly.

She handed him a towel.

There was nothing to watch on either regular TV or cable, and after doing the dishes they decided to put in a videotape. "Something we can all agree on," Tritia said.

Billy trudged upstairs. "I'm watching regular shows."

"I said we're going to watch something we can all agree on," she called after him.

"TV shows are better than movies," Billy called back.

She looked at Doug. " 'TV shows are better than movies.' Did you hear that? Somewhere we went drastically wrong with that child."

He chuckled. "Okay, what's it going to be, then? *Deep Throat*? *Love Goddesses*?"

She hit his shoulder. "Be quiet. He can hear you."

"Yes I can," Billy called from upstairs.

"See?" She picked up the list of their videotapes from the table, scanning it. "Let's watch *Annie Hall*," she said finally. "I haven't seen that for a while."

"Sounds good." Doug got up and went over to the bookcase, turning his head sideways to read the titles on the videotape boxes until he found the right one. *Annie Hall* was on the same tape as *The Haunting* and *Burnt Offerings*, sandwiched in between the two horror movies, and he had to fast-forward the tape to get to it.

"Last chance," he called upstairs as the credits began.

Billy did not even bother to respond.

The movie was as funny, and as on-target, as ever, and Doug was glad that they'd decided to watch a comedy. It helped take his mind off everything else that was going on.

Woody was just entering Christopher Walken's room to talk about night driving when the lights in the house suddenly dimmed into darkness and the television blinked off with a crackle of electronic static. The VCR hummed as it slowly powered down.

"Blackout," Tritia announced. She stood up and felt her way to the kitchen, where she took a flashlight from the junk drawer. She also withdrew a book of matches and two candles. "Are you coming downstairs?" she yelled to Billy.

"No. I'm going to bed."

"At eight-thirty?"

"There's nothing else to do."

"You could come downstairs and read by candlelight with us," Doug suggested facetiously.

Billy loudly snorted his derision.

Tritia lit the candles, placing them in candle holders, while Doug moved over to the front windows. "It's kind of weird to have a blackout with no storm," he said, pushing aside the curtains. He peered into the darkness, toward the other homes down the road, and thought he saw yellowish light filtered through the branches of the trees. "That's strange," he said.

"What?"

"I think the Nelsons still have power."

"I could call them—"

"No phone," he reminded her.

She laughed. "It's a conspiracy."

"It's an adventure. We're cut off from the world, all alone. Kind of exciting, don't you think?"

"And romantic," she added, moving next to him. She put a candle on the windowsill.

"I'm still awake!" Billy yelled. "Don't do anything that'll embarrass you later."

They both laughed, and Doug felt Tritia's arm snake

around his waist. She drew him closer, giving him a light kiss that barely missed his mouth. "We'll wait until he's asleep," she whispered, promised.

Tritia woke up in the middle of the night to go to the bathroom. Doug was asleep next to her, breathing regularly and half-snoring, and she quietly, carefully, pushed the sheet from her body and swung her legs off the bed, glancing at the digital clock on the dresser. The blue liquid quartz numbers said it was three-fifteen. She had put on her panties and nightdress after they'd made love, but she still slipped on a robe before padding across the hall to the bathroom. She'd never felt comfortable walking around the house undressed. The full moon shone through the opaque window above the bathtub like a streetlight, partially illuminating the small room. She pulled up her robe and nightdress, pulled down her panties, and sat down on the toilet to pee. When she was through, she pulled up her panties, flushed the toilet, and went into the kitchen to get a drink.

The night was quiet, but not as quiet as it should have been. Below the melodic chirping cricket music and the occasional cry of a nocturnal bird was another, less natural, noise. A low even rumbling that started and stopped and grew ever closer.

A car engine.

Tritia moved into the living room and bent forward to peek through a slit in the closed curtains. Who would be driving around here at this hour? Certainly not the Nelsons or the Tuckers or any of the other people who lived around them. She pulled the curtain opening wider.

The red car of the mailman pulled up on the road in front of the house.

Tritia sucked in her breath. She could hear the faint sound of a rock-'n'-roll song from the car's stereo. As she watched, a thin pale hand reached out from the driver's window and pulled open the gate of the mailbox, the other hand depositing several envelopes. The mailman's face appeared at the car window, white against the black background. He looked in her direction, seeming to know right where she was, though he could not possibly have seen the thin crack between the curtain halves in this darkness. He smiled, a slow sly corrupt smile that promised things she did

not want to think about, things that made her blood run
cold.

She wanted to look away, to move out of his sight, but
she was afraid to let him see the curtains fall, and she
remained completely still, unmoving. Although only one
eye and a portion of her right cheek was next to the narrow
opening, she was acutely aware of the fact that she was
almost naked, that her nightdress had ridden up above her
panties as she bent forward, and she felt as embarrassed and
humiliated, as if she had been caught masturbating.

The mailman waved once, smiling broadly at her, then
pulled away, into the darkness, the sound of his engine
fading.

She realized only now that she'd been holding her breath,
and she closed her eyes, breathing deeply, relaxing, as the
car drove down the dirt road.

She let the curtain fall and stood there for a moment,
holding on to the table for support, before finally retreating
to the bedroom, climbing into bed, and snuggling under the
safety of the sheets. Next to her, Doug's body felt warm and
strong and reassuring.

The night was completely silent now, even the crickets
making no noise, and she lay awake for what seemed like an
eternity before finally falling asleep.

She dreamed of the mailman.

He was delivering the mail, but instead of stopping at
their mailbox, he pulled into the drive and parked next to
the house. Through the window, she saw him getting out of
the car. He was smiling. She ran through the house, into the
bedroom, the bathroom, the loft, looking for Doug or even
Billy, but she was all alone. The house was empty. She tried
to escape through the back door, but it would not open.
Behind her, she heard the mailman's footsteps crossing the
living room and then the kitchen. She ran into the bedroom,
intending to shut the door and barricade it, but she discovered that there was no door.

The mailman stepped into the room, grinning hugely.

He was wearing no pants.

And then he was on her and in her, his unnaturally long
penis hot and burning, like a curling iron or a soldering gun,
and she could feel the cauterizing pain as he pumped away
inside her. The agony of it caused her to scream—primally,

uncontrollably—but she was aware with a sickening feeling of revulsion that there was pleasure mixed in with that horrible burning pain, that on some gross physical level a part of her body was enjoying this.

She awoke drenched in sweat, hair and pillow damp, and she cuddled close to Doug to push away the fear, holding him tightly. Outside, far away, she thought she heard the low smooth purring sound of the mailman's car retreating into the forest.

11

Doug was taking a shower when the water went off; he was washing his hair, the top of his head covered with shampoo lather, as the water disappeared in midspray. "Hey!" he yelled.

"Water's off!" Tritia called from the kitchen.

"Great," he muttered. Eyes still closed, the shampoo beginning to drip onto his nose and cheeks, he drew aside the shower curtain and felt along the wall for the towel rack. His fingers closed around terry cloth. It felt like one of Tritia's good towels, the ones that hung in the bathroom for decoration and were not to be used, but this was an emergency and he used it to wipe the shampoo off of his face and out of his eyes. The bathroom was dark. The power had not come back on since last night, and the only illumination came from the small window. He quickly toweled off his hair, then stepped out of the tub. He pulled on his underwear and pants and opened the door, walking out to the kitchen, still dripping. "What happened?"

Tritia was standing in the center of the kitchen, hair sticking out at odd sleep angles, staring at the half-filled coffeepot in the sink. She shook her head. "I was filling the pot and the water shut off."

"Did you check under the sink?" He opened the bottom cupboard, but the garbage sack and the boxes of cleanser and detergent were all dry. None of the pipes was dripping.

"I'll go outside," he said, "see if I can find anything."

He went out through the back door. The rocks and pine needles hurt his feet, but he walked across the dirt to the side of the house where the pipes connected with the meter. He looked at the numbers through the yellowed glass.

There was no water pressure at all.

He bent down and opened the runoff faucet but nothing came out.

"What the hell . . . ?" He turned the handle at the junction of the water main and house pipes, but nothing registered on the meter.

"What is it?" Tritia asked as he came back in the house.

"Hell if I know. The water doesn't seem to be turned on." He ran a hand through his hair, feeling the stickiness of the shampoo against his fingers. "I'll go find out about the water and electricity after breakfast."

"And the phone," Tritia reminded him.

He shook his head disgustedly as he walked back into the bathroom. "And the phone."

The department of water and power was located in a small brown prefab building adjoining Town Hall. Doug drove slowly over the speed bump that separated the parking lot from the street, and pulled into a marked space next to one of the town's three police cars. He got out of the Bronco without bothering to lock it and strode across the asphalt to the glass doors of the front entrance. The top of his head felt strange and he realized that he could still sense the subtle stiffness of dried shampoo in his hair.

The girl behind the counter seemed young enough to be one of his students, but her face didn't look familiar. She was bent over the keyboard of an Apple computer, studiously watching her fingers hunt and peck through the alphabet, not even bothering to look up when he entered the office.

He cleared his throat loudly. "Excuse me."

"Be with you in a sec," the girl said. She examined the screen before her, then pressed a series of keys, intently watching their effect.

Doug looked around the office. It was small and poorly furnished, the walls covered with cheap paneling and framed documents. An empty desk across from the girl's was covered with layers of paperwork. Against one wall was a series of gray metal file cabinets.

The girl pressed another key, then, nodding, stood up and approached the counter. She was pretty and her smile appeared to be genuine, but the expression on her face was terminally vacuous. "How may I help you, sir?"

"Last night, around nine o'clock, our electricity went out. We thought at first that it was just a blackout, but the power never came back on. Then, this morning, our water was shut off. I went out to check the pipes, but there was nothing wrong. The meter said we had no water pressure at all. I want to get both our water and electricity turned back on."

The girl retreated to her computer. "Can I have your name and address?"

"Doug Albin. Lot Four-fifty-three, Trail End Drive."

One key at a time, the girl punched his name and address into the computer. She examined the screen before her. "According to our records, you notified us that you wished to discontinue service."

"Discontinue service? Why the hell would I do that?"

"I don't know, sir." She stood up. "Here, let me check. We should have your letter on file."

"My letter?"

"According to our records, you sent us a letter last Thursday." She walked across the office to the file cabinets. After a few moments of searching through a row of forms and papers, she pulled out a single sheet of typing paper stapled to a business envelope. "Here it is." She returned, handing him the paper.

He scanned the typed text, reading aloud: " 'Dear Sirs, On June 12, my family will be moving to California, where I have taken a job with the Anaheim Unified School District. Please disconnect my electricity on June 11 and my water on June 12. Thank you.' " He glanced up sharply. "What is this?"

The girl looked confused. "I don't know what you mean, sir. You didn't send us that letter?"

"I most certainly did not. Now I want my electricity and water turned back on, and I want you to find out who did send it."

"Well maybe it was a joke. Maybe one of your friends—"

"It's not a joke, and I don't think it's funny." His hands were shaking, and he put them up on the counter. He realized that he was being unnecessarily harsh with this girl, that he was taking his anger out on her though she obviously knew nothing, but there was a sickening feeling beginning to form in the pit of his stomach, a feeling of helplessness, a feeling that he was being dragged into something he could not hope to fight against, and it made him want to yell at someone. He closed his eyes and forced himself to calm

down. "I'm sorry," he said. "Just turn my water and electricity back on."

"It'll be this afternoon before we'll be able to put a man
on it," she said. "There's a five-dollar hookup charge—"

"Look," Doug said, keeping his voice intentionally low
and even, "you guys screwed up. You turned off my water
and electricity without me asking you to, and I'm sure as
hell not going to pay for your mistake."

The girl stiffened, her manner suddenly defensive. "It's
not technically our mistake. We received a letter—"

"I'm not going to waste my day playing word games,"
Doug said. "Let me speak to your supervisor."

"The manager's out of the office right now, but I can
leave your name and number and have him call you when
he returns."

"Do that. And do you think you could have my water and
power turned back on? My wife and son would like to take
a bath sometime today, and it would be nice if we could
cook our dinner tonight."

The girl nodded. "We'll get this straightened out. I'm
sorry for any inconvenience." Her voice was conciliatory,
with a hint of worry in it, and he realized that she was
worried about what he would say to her supervisor.

"It's not your fault," he told her. "I don't mean to take it
out on you. I'm just frustrated right now."

"I understand. And I'll have the manager call you as soon
as he returns," she promised.

"Thanks." He turned and walked out the door, reaching
into his pocket for his car keys.

His hands were still shaking.

His anger grew stronger after his trip to the phone company. Here, again, they had received a letter supposedly
from him telling them to discontinue service, but when he
asked them to reconnect his phone, they told him there
would be a twenty-dollar charge and that the earliest phone
service could be reinstated would be Thursday. He went up
the office hierarchy, telling his tale to increasingly authoritarian men until he had reached the district manager, who
told him, unequivocally, that service would be reinstituted
only after he paid the charge and that the earliest possible
hookup date would be Wednesday. He could, if he so de-
sired, file a refund request explaining the particulars of his

situation. The request would be sent to Mountain Bell head-quarters and its merit judged there.

He angrily pulled out of the small parking lot and nearly backed into old Mrs. Buford, who honked her horn at him. She yelled something he could not understand through her closed window. He waved his apology.

Letters.

Who would send letters to the phone company and the water and power company asking them to discontinue his service?

No, not who? Why? He already knew who had sent the letters, or at least had a good idea who'd done it.

The mailman.

John Smith.

It was not logical, and he had no idea why the mailman would do such a thing, but there was no doubt in his mind that it had been he who'd sent the false messages. There was something about the almost perfect calligraphy of the forged signature that reminded him of the professional-caliber speaking voice of the mailman. There was fear mixed in with his anger, but anger definitely had the upper hand, and he drove directly to the post office, intending to voice his opinions, his suspicions, his accusations to Howard.

The parking lot was crowded, but a Jeep was pulling out just as he arrived, and Doug quickly drove into the spot. He picked up the envelopes from the seat next to him. They were still damp, the paper smooth and softly pliable against his fingers. He nodded politely to the old men seated on the bench outside the building, then pushed open the door.

The first thing he noticed was the heat. It was warm outside, but it was absolutely hellish in here. The air was humid and stagnant; nothing came out of the ceiling vents, and the familiar low whistle of the swamp cooler was absent. The office was crowded anyway, though. Six or seven people stood in line, letters and packages in hand, and he could smell the sickeningly tart odor of women's perfume and men's deodorant mixed with the scent of freshly flowing sweat. He glanced toward the counter, but Howard was not there. Instead, the mailman stood behind the front desk, talking in low patient tones to the elderly female customer before him. There was sincerity in his voice and on the expression of his face, but it was a false smarmy sincerity, the superficial interest shown by a salesman to a mark, and

Doug found the mailman's attitude both condescending and offensive.

The mailman was not sweating.

Doug tried to peek behind the paneled partition in back of the mailman to find out if Howard was somewhere in the rear of the post office, but he could not see anything. He was surprised that Howard would let the new man take charge of the front counter, particularly after what the postmaster had revealed to them the other night. He could not remember ever seeing Ronda within the post office unless it was to pick up or drop off a batch of mail, and he had never seen anyone besides Howard working behind the counter.

Somehow that made Doug even angrier.

The old woman accepted the change given to her by the mailman, put it in her purse, and turned to walk away. Doug quickly stepped past the other patrons up to the counter. "Excuse me," he said shortly. "I'd like to talk to Howard."

The mailman looked at him, with a hint of a smile playing about his thin lips. "There were other people in line before you, sir. Please wait your turn." His eyes rested for a second on the soggy letters in Doug's hand. He said nothing and his eyes betrayed no recognition, but his smile grew broader.

"Could you just call him out here for a moment?"

"I'm sorry, sir. Please wait your turn."

He was about to argue, but when he turned to look at the people behind him, he saw them gazing at him with impatience. "Fine," he said. He moved to the rear of the line.

Ten minutes later he finally moved up to the counter. He had been watching the mailman constantly, studying him, looking for a trace of anything out of the ordinary, but aside from his air of natural superiority there seemed to be nothing amiss. The mailman did not look at him once.

The fear and the anger were in about equal portions now.

He stepped up to the counter, wiping the sweat from his forehead with his palm. "I'd like to talk to Howard."

"Mr. Crowell is not here today."

The words were so simple yet so totally unexpected that they caught him off guard. Howard wasn't here? Howard was always here. "Is he sick?" he asked.

"Yes he is. May I help you?"

Doug glared at the man. "Maybe you can. My family and

I went on a picnic by Clear Creek yesterday, and we found unopened, undelivered mail strewn along the banks of the creek."

A light smile played across the mailman's lips. " 'Strewn?' "

His mocking intonation was so much like Tritia's that Doug faltered for a second. But he recovered almost immediately and put the envelopes on the counter. "Here are a few pieces of mail we rescued."

The mailman reached for the envelopes, but Doug drew them back. "I'm going to give these to Howard."

"I'm sorry. It is the duty and responsibility of the postal service to deliver mail. It is against the law for you to retain undelivered items."

Doug could feel the adrenaline rushing through his veins. He was sweating profusely now and again he wiped his forehead. "These all seem to be bills," he said. "And there were hundreds of more bills at the creek. Now, I haven't been getting my regular bills lately. In fact, I don't think I've gotten a bill since your predecessor died. I don't know what's going on, but a large chunk of my mail seems to be disappearing."

"I haven't gotten my bills lately either," the man in back of him said.

Doug watched the mailman's face for a reaction, for a sign that he had hit a nerve. He'd expected the mailman to glare at him, to get angry, to somehow tip his hand and admit that he'd been dumping the mail at the creek, but the mailman's face remained serenely neutral.

"I promise that we will look into these complaints as soon as possible," the mailman said. His voice was pleasant, unperturbed, calmly reassuring. "Do you have anything else, Mr. Albin?"

"Just that someone's been sending letters to the department of water and power telling them to cut off my water and electricity. The same person sent a letter to the phone company telling them to disconnect my phone. I believe that's mail fraud."

"Yes it is, Mr. Albin. And I assure you we will look into it immediately. I will tell Mr. Crowell of your concerns."

Doug looked into the mailman's eyes and saw in them a blank hardness that bored right through him and made him want to glance away, but he forced himself to hold contact.

The sweat felt cold on his body. "Thank you," he said tersely.

The mailman stretched out a thin pale hand. "Now would you please hand over the undelivered mail in your possession?"

Doug shook his head. "Take me to court. I'm giving these to Howard."

"Fine," the mailman said, his voice eminently reasonable. "Now, would you please step aside? There are other people waiting behind you, Mr. Albin."

Doug turned away from the counter and strode out of the post office to his car. It was not until he was halfway home that he remembered that he had not told the mailman his name.

The mailman had simply known.

12

Hobie arrived home feeling good. The pool had been crowded today, and not just with kids. A gaggle of women in their early to mid-twenties had arrived in the afternoon and had taken up residence near the deep end of the pool, far away from the children and their mothers. Before their arrival he had been casually scoping out Mrs. Farris, who was trim and fit and wore a pinkish-peach bathing suit that became nearly see-through when it was wet, but his attention shifted as the new group set up their towels and broke out the tanning lotion. They all had the brown smooth bodies of aerobic instructors, and they all had incredibly great tits. One of them, a brunette, was wearing a modified string bikini, and when she bent over, he could see almost up the crack of her perfectly formed ass. The others wore brightly trendy swimsuits cut so close to the crotch that he knew they had to shave.

It had been a damn good day.

He pulled out his keys and opened the door, taking his mail out of the box before walking inside.

Although Hobie lived in a large brown-and-white mobile home near the center of town, just down the road from the shopping center in what was admittedly not the best section of Willis, he was comfortable with his place of residence. The houses here were close together and not as nice as those in the rest of town, but that suited him just fine. No one bothered him, no one told him to turn down his stereo, no one told him to clean up his yard or get rid of his automobiles. He knew that his property looked like a miniature junkyard. There was no lawn to speak of, only flat dirt, and there was a 1974 Vega and a 1979 Datsun parked in the front and a 1965 Mustang on blocks in the back. His carport was littered with various auto parts and two old engine blocks. But he didn't mind it, and neither did his neighbors.

The inside of the trailer was nicer. He kept it up, even though he lived alone, and it wasn't bad, if he did say so himself. He tossed his shades on the front table and went into the kitchen, grabbing a beer from the fridge. He popped open the tab, took a swig, and glanced at the return addresses on the envelopes in his hand: his mother, the Classic Mustang Club, his paycheck from the district.

One piece of mail, a long yellowish envelope, had no return address at all, and he turned it over in his hand. Both the front and back were covered with smeared brownish red fingerprints. Frowning, he put down his beer and tore the envelope open. Inside were two photographs paper-clipped together. The top one showed a nude Oriental girl of fifteen or sixteen lying on a flat straw mat. He stared at the picture. The girl was beautiful, with large almond-shaped eyes and a full sensuous mouth. She was spread-eagled, legs in the air, the dark folds of her vagina clearly visible through her sparse black pubic hair.

He unfastened the paper clip. The bottom photo showed the same teenage Oriental girl on the same straw mat.

But her head had been cut off and placed on top of her stomach.

On the photo were the same smudged brownish red fingerprints as on the envelope.

He felt suddenly sick to his stomach. Against his will, he had been aroused by the first picture of the girl. She was young, but she was gorgeous and her body looked luscious, inviting. But the second photo was like a punch to the gut. He closed his eyes, turning the picture over so he wouldn't have to look at it, but he could still see in his mind the girl's dead staring eyes and round-O mouth, the twisted veins and tubes protruding like spaghetti from her open throat, and the puddle, no, *pool* of blood spreading outward from her neck across the mat.

Who would have sent him such a thing? Who could have sent him such a thing? And why?

And what about those fingerprints?

He quickly crumpled up the photos and the envelope they'd come in and dropped the whole thing in the trash. He washed his hands off in the sink, scrubbing them with Lava the way he did when trying to get grease off his fingers. The kitchen seemed darker than it had before, although the sun would not set for another two hours, and he flipped on the lights, grabbing another beer after downing the first in three large successive swallows. He sat down at the table, forcing himself to read the other letters, but even the message from his mother could not cheer him up, and when he tried to recapture his earlier good mood, tried to think again of the bathing beauties at the pool, he saw them lying on the hard concrete, decapitated, their heads placed on their tan stomachs and staring at him with dead open eyes.

13

Hobie came over just after breakfast, knocking once, perfunctorily, on the doorjamb before pulling open the screen and walking into the living room. He cocked a finger at Billy, sprawled on the couch. "Hey, sport."

Doug was putting away the last of the breakfast dishes, and he glanced at his watch as Hobie headed toward the kitchen. "It's only eight-thirty."

"Yeah, well, the meeting starts at ten, and I figured we should get there ahead of time and discuss things, plan what we're going to say. I tried to call yesterday after I finished at the pool, but a voice kept saying your line had been disconnected."

Doug shook his head. "Someone forged a letter from me and sent it to the telephone company, telling them I was moving and wanted my phone service stopped."

Hobie laughed. "Really?"

"They sent a letter to the department of water and power, telling them to cut off my water and electricity too."

Hobie's smile faded. "That's a little more serious. One letter might be a joke, but two . . ." He shook his head. "Who do you figure it was?"

The mailman, Doug wanted to say, but he shrugged instead.

"You think it was a student? Who did you flunk this year?"

"No one. Besides, I don't think I had any students who hated me this time. The closest I can figure is Duke Johnson, but even he didn't dislike me that much."

"And even if he did, he wouldn't be smart enough to think up something like this."

"Exactly."

"Did you call the cops?"

"I told them everything and gave them copies of the

letter, but they said there wasn't a whole hell of a lot they could do."

Hobie snorted. "What else is new?"

Doug wiped the counter and hung up the dishtowel. "You want to head over there now?"

"Yeah. I called Mark Pettigrew, and he's going to meet us there. I tried calling the coach and Donovan, but neither of them was home. I think they're on vacation. I heard Donovan say something about going up to Durango."

"All right, let's get it over with, then." Doug stepped into the hall and knocked on the bathroom door. "Hobie's here. I'm going."

"Okay," Tritia said through the closed door. "Good luck. I hope you get your books."

"I'm not holding my breath." He returned through the kitchen into the living room. Hobie opened the screen door and stepped outside. Doug turned to his son, still on the couch. "I'll be back around lunch. Mind your mother."

"I always do."

Doug laughed. "That'll be the day." He followed Hobie onto the porch and the two of them walked out to the auto teacher's truck.

"Speaking of water and electricity, I didn't get my utilities bill this month," Hobie said.

"We haven't gotten any bills at all."

"Come to think of it, I haven't either. Ain't that weird? I shouldn't say anything bad about this new guy—I mean, he's just getting started, just learning the ropes and all—but I think he's losing a lot of mail. I usually get a ton of mail every day. Lately, though, I've been getting two or three letters at the most, some days nothing at all."

Doug climbed into the cab and slammed the door, digging his safety belt out of the crack of the seat. "Bills and junk mail, right? You're missing bills and junk mail."

"Yeah." Hobie seemed surprised. "You too, huh? Maybe I should go in and talk to Crowell and bitch about this, find out what's going on." He started the truck and backed up the drive, swinging around on the road.

They took off, a spray of gravel shooting up behind them. Doug held on to the dashboard with one hand for support. Although he taught driver's ed, Hobie himself was a scary driver and Doug needed as much reassurance as possible whenever he went someplace in his friend's truck.

As they drove through the trees toward town, he told Hobie of their picnic at the creek, of the dumped and scattered letters. He reported the facts objectively. He didn't come out and say that he thought the mailman had been stealing and dumping mail, that he thought the mailman had sent the fake letters to the telephone company and department of water and power, but the implication was unmistakable. The other teacher's face became more serious and more set as he spoke.

Hobie was silent as they drove past the trailer park and turned left onto the highway. "There's a lot of weird things going on," he said finally. "A lot of weird things."

Doug asked him what he meant, if he had experienced anything unusual connected with the mail, but he frowned and shook his head and refused to answer, and they were both silent as they drove through town toward the school.

Willis High was separated from the town proper by an especially large stand of oaks and acacias and ponderosas, and was located next to the Edward G. Willis Memorial Park. The football field had been constructed at one end of a natural meadow, and the pool, which was shared jointly by the school and the park, was located at the opposite end.

There was a crowd at the school when they arrived, a large group of people standing near the open door of the gym. In the faculty parking lot were two police cars and an ambulance, lights flashing, although neither Doug nor Hobie had heard a siren all morning. Doug glanced over at his friend, then out the window at the scene before them. A strange feeling had come over him. He was at once surprised and not surprised, tense and numb, as he looked at the crowd. He knew this was going to be bad.

"Something happened," he said simply.

Hobie pulled the truck under a tree for shade, and they got out, hurrying across the dirt to the gym. Several other teachers were there, as well as nearby residents and one of the school-board members.

Doug walked up to Jim Maxwell, who taught ninth-grade social studies. "What is it?"

"Bernie Rogers hung himself in the gym."

Doug looked at Hobie, shocked, feeling as if someone had just kicked him in the stomach. He did not know what he had been expecting, but it had not been this. A senior who had graduated with honors, Bernie Rogers had been one of those rare students who was into both academics and athletics. The basketball team's star forward, he had scored in the top 10 percent nationally on his SATs and was the only senior this year to have passed the Advanced Placement tests for both history and English. He was also the only student Doug could remember who had taken both his American Literature class and Hobie's Advanced Auto, and had excelled in each.

"Lemme see," Hobie said, pushing his way through the crowd toward the door. Doug followed, jostling past people until he was through the door and inside the gym.

Bernie was naked, his body bluish and bloated, blackened blood dripping in uneven rivulets from where the rope had cut into his neck. It looked as though he had been there for several days. Below him on the smooth wood of the gym floor was a puddle of hardened urine and feces, some of which had run down the inside of his thighs and now hung like stalactites from his feet. The boy's eyes were wide open and staring, focused on nothing, surprisingly white against his darkened skin.

Doug felt sick to his stomach, but he could not look away. A note was pinned onto Bernie's chest, the pins shoved deep into his skin, dried blood dripping down the page in a jagged wave, obscuring whatever words had been written. The boy had obviously put the noose around his neck and leapt from the top of the closed bleachers, and Doug found himself staring into the rafters high above, wondering how Bernie could have possibly tied the end of the rope up there without the aid of a ladder. Two policemen, a photographer, and a medical examiner stood off to the side of the gently swinging body in a tight group, talking among themselves. Two ambulance attendants stood next to the far wall, waiting. Another policeman kept the crowd from getting too close.

"Jesus," Hobie breathed. The usual bravado, aggressiveness, was gone from his voice, and his face was bleached, pale. He stepped aside as two other policemen, one carrying long-handled shears, the other a retractable stepladder, pressed through the gym door behind him. "I knew Bernie," he said. "He was a good kid."

Doug nodded. He watched silently as the policemen set up the ladder and cut down the body. Apparently, the photographer had taken his pictures before they'd gotten there. Bernie's form was stiff, unmoving, legs and arms still frozen in the position in which they'd been hanging, but the men laid him down as carefully as they could on the floor, on top of a white plastic tarp spread by one of the ambulance attendants. The medical examiner moved forward to have a look, crouching down on one knee and opening his black bag.

"I was just talking to him last week," a man said. "After school got out."

Doug looked to his right, to the source of the voice. It was Ed Montgomery, the coach. The portly man's natural hangdog expression had been intensified and cemented with shock. He shook his head slowly back and forth, talking to no one in particular. "He was saying how he was going to get a part-time job at the post office this summer to help pay for his schooling in the fall. His scholarship didn't cover books and rent, only tuition."

Doug's ears pricked up at this, and he felt a familiar chill creeping down his back. He moved next to the coach. "He was going to get a job where?"

Ed looked at him blankly. "At the post office. He'd already okayed it with Howard." He shook his head. "I can't understand why he'd do such a thing. He had everything going for him." The coach stopped shaking his head and looked into Doug's eyes, his troubled gaze focused, as if he'd just thought of an idea. "You think maybe he was murdered?"

"I don't know," Doug said. And he didn't. He suddenly wanted very badly to see what was written on that note pinned to the boy's chest. He took a step forward.

"Stay back please," the policeman warned, holding his hand palm-up in Doug's direction.

"I have to see something. I was his teacher."

"Only official personnel and family members are allowed near the body."

"Just for a second."

"Sorry," the policeman said.

Doug turned away from the gym and pushed his way out the door, into the fresh air, needing more room, more space in which to breathe. The blood was pounding in his temples.

Bernie Rogers had been planning to work part-time at the post office.

The post office.

It didn't make any logical rational sense, but in some twisted way it fit, and it scared the hell out of him.

He moved through the small crowd and leaned against a tree, gulping in the fresh air. He looked up, toward the road, and thought he saw, through the pines, a red car moving slowly away from the park toward the center of town.

14

Tritia sat alone on the porch, feeling uncharacteristically depressed. Both Doug and Billy were gone, Doug to his meeting and Billy off somewhere with Lane, and she was all alone. Usually she liked being by herself. She so seldom had time alone anymore that, when the opportunity presented itself, she was grateful. But today she felt different, strange.

The cassette player was next to her on the slatted wooden floor of the porch. It had been barely working the last time she'd used it, but she'd scavenged three batteries from one of Billy's old remote-controlled cars and had found a fourth in a drawer in the kitchen, and now it was playing perfectly. She had the tape player turned loud. George Winston. Ordinarily, she liked to match the music to the day, choosing sounds to complement her feelings, but today the music seemed totally inappropriate for a sound track to her life. The soothing impressionistic piano, the deliberate spacing of clear notes and silences, went perfectly with the summer sky and green forest, but she herself felt hopelessly out of sync.

She stared out at the trees, at the hummingbird-feeders hanging from the branches, seeing them but not seeing them, her eyes using the feeders as a focal point, though her mind was off in space somewhere, thinking about something else.

Thinking about the mailman.

She had not told Doug about seeing the mailman last night, nor about her nightmare afterward, although she was not sure why. It was not like her to be secretive, to keep things from him. They'd always had a close, honest relationship, had always confided in each other, shared their hopes, fears, thoughts, opinions. But for some reason, she could not bring herself to talk to him about the mailman. She had made excuses, rationalized, tried to convince herself, and all of her excuses sounded logical, reasonable—Billy was awake and listening, Doug had left too early and she'd had no time to talk to him—but the truth was that she didn't want to talk to him, didn't want to tell him what had happened. She had never felt that way before, had never experienced anything like it, and it scared her more than she was willing to admit.

Doug had not picked up the mail this morning before he left, and she'd been too afraid to go out to the mailbox and retrieve it herself, so she'd sent Billy out to get it, watching him from the porch to make sure he was all right. He came back with three letters: two for Doug, one for her. The letter was sitting next to her right now, on the small table on which she'd put her iced tea. She hadn't wanted to open it right away, though it was from Howard and she had no real apprehension about its contents, and she'd set it aside until she felt like looking at it. Now she picked it up, tearing open the envelope. The letter was addressed to her, but the first line of the message read, "Dear Ellen." She frowned. That was strange. But then Howard had been under a lot of stress lately, a lot had happened to him. It was bound to show up in some way or other. She continued reading:

Dear Ellen,
    Sorry I couldn't come by Saturday night, but I was forced into dinner at the Albins'. What a horrible time. The food was awful, the kid was a brat, and Albin and his wife were as boring as ever. That phony bitch Tritia . . .

She stopped reading, feeling as though all of the air had been sucked out of her lungs, a sudden emptiness in the pit of her stomach. She looked at the letter again, but the words were blurry, liquid, running. Her eyes brimmed with tears. She was surprised by the vehemence of her reaction. She had never been an overly sensitive person about either herself or her cooking, had never really minded constructive criticism, but this type of cruel betrayal, particularly in regard to her family, particularly coming from a friend like Howard, hurt a lot. A hell of a lot. She wiped the tears from her eyes angrily, refolding the letter and putting it back in the envelope. Howard had obviously intended to send a letter to both her and Ellen Ronda and had unthinkingly placed the letters in the wrong envelopes.

Ellen was no doubt reading about the lovely time and dinner Howard had had.

She was not usually this emotional, this easily hurt, but dammit, she had been trying to help Howard through a difficult period, and this backhanded back-stabbing cut deep. She and Doug had always considered him a friend. Maybe not a close friend, but a friend nonetheless, a man whose company they both enjoyed. Why would he do something like this? And how could he be so two-faced? He had never been a deceitful or duplicitous man. Outspoken honesty had always been his greatest strength and greatest weakness. He had never hesitated to speak his mind, no matter what the consequences. It would be one thing if he had just come out and said he didn't want to come over for dinner or didn't enjoy their company or didn't like the food they served him, but to sit there and lie to them, to—

The phone rang. Tritia dropped the letter on the small table, pushed herself out of the butterfly chair, and hurried across the porch into the house. She caught the phone on the fifth ring, clearing her throat to purge the emotion from her voice. "Hello?"

"He's after me!" The whisper on the other end of the line was frantic and borderline hysterical, and Tritia did not at first recognize it. "He's here now."

"Excuse me?" Tritia said, puzzled.

"I think he's in the house now," the woman whispered.

Now she recognized the voice. Ellen Ronda. She was shocked at how different Bob's wife sounded. Gone was the cool-as-ice voice Tritia had heard for as long as she could remember; gone, too, was the grief-stricken wildness she'd heard on the day of the funeral. In its place was fear. Terror.

"Who's after you?" Tritia asked.

"He thinks he's being tricky, but I can hear his footsteps."

"Get out of the house," Tritia said. "Now. Go someplace and call the police."

"I already called the police. They refused to help me. They said—"

Ellen's voice was cut off, and a man's deep baritone came on the line. "Hello?"

Tritia's heart leapt to her throat. It took all of her courage, all of her inner strength not to hang up the receiver. "Who is this?" she demanded in the most intimidating voice she could muster.

"This is Dr. Roberts. Who is this?"

"Oh, it's you." Tritia relaxed a little, breathing an audible sigh of relief. In the background, she could hear a male and female voice arguing. "This is Tritia Albin."

"Tritia. Hello. I heard part of your conversation from this end. Ellen told you she was being chased, did she?"

"Yes."

"I'm sorry she disturbed you. Her sons have been trying to keep an eye on her, but they can't monitor her twenty-four hours a day, and lately each time she has a chance she calls someone and tells them she's being stalked." He breathed deeply, the heavy intake of air thick and rough over the phone. "I don't know what we're going to do. The boys don't want to even consider it, but I told them that their mother's going to have to seek some kind of counseling. I refuse to treat her by simply pumping drugs into her body, and her emotional situation is far worse than I am equipped to handle. She may even have to be institutionalized for a short period of time. Who knows? I'm certainly no expert in these matters."

"What's happened to her?" Tritia asked.

"Grief. Repressed, pent-up emotions suddenly finding an outlet. As I said, I'm no expert, but it's clear that Bob's sui—uh, death, triggered this whatever-it-is, acted as the catalyst." The arguing in the background grew louder, more heated. "Sorry, but you're going to have to excuse me. I think we have a slight emergency developing here. Thank you for your patience and cooperation. I'll be in touch."

He hung up before Tritia could say good-bye. She lowered the receiver slowly into its cradle. For some reason, she felt guilty, as though she had somehow betrayed Ellen's confidence. It was a strange thought, not at all logical, but then the entire conversation had been more than a little surrealistic. She had been relieved when the doctor had picked up the phone, grateful to hand over the reins of responsibility and decision, but she had not been able to do so wholeheartedly or with a clear conscience, though she trusted the doctor completely. She walked out of the house, back onto the porch, and sat down numbly in her chair. Ellen was obviously disturbed, obviously having some serious emotional/psychological problems, but for a moment there, before the doctor had come on the line, Tritia had actually believed that someone had been after Ellen, that someone had been in her house.

And she knew exactly who that someone was.

"Wow, look at the tits on that one." Lane grinned hugely.

Billy smiled wanly back. They were on the floor of The Fort, going through the *Playboy*s. Ordinarily, Billy would have been just as caught up in their reading as Lane, but today was different. He felt restless, ill at ease, bored. He stared down at the magazine on his lap, at the photo of the woman in the postal cap. She was without a doubt the most gorgeous, most perfect woman in all of their *Playboy*s, but today he didn't feel excited looking at her. He felt uneasy. Was there something familiar about her eyes? Did her mouth look like . . . *his?*

Stop that, he told himself. He forced himself to look at her boobs, at the huge pinkish-brown nipples on the tips of her perfectly formed breasts. There was nothing about her tits that reminded him of the mailman or that was the least bit unusual or masculine. They were normal, healthy, good old American female breasts.

Still. . . .

"Guess what?" Lane said. His voice was casual, nonchalant, but it wasn't a natural nonchalance. Billy had known Lane for most of his life, and he could tell when his friend was lying and sometimes even what he was thinking just by the tone of his voice. This was not spur-of-the-moment. This was a purposeful, intentional casualness, something Lane had planned and practiced.

"What?" Billy said, equally cool.

Lane glanced slowly around, as if making sure that no one was peeking into the HQ from the outside or from the Big Room. He withdrew a crumpled folded envelope from his pants pocket, handing it over. "Check this out."

Billy glanced at the outside of the envelope. It was addressed to Lane at his house, and the return name in the upper left corner was Tama Barnes.

"Look inside," Lane prodded.

Billy took out the folded paper inside. It was a letter, written in an obviously female hand. He turned the letter over. Underneath the flowery cursive characters was a Xeroxed photo of a nude Hispanic woman. She was smiling, hands cupping her ample breasts, legs spread wide. The photocopied picture was too smeared and dark and blurry to provide details, but Billy had seen plenty of details in the magazines on the floor, and his mind filled in what his eyes could not see.

"Read it," Lane said. He was grinning.

Billy turned the letter over and read. The letter started out with a standard salutation but quickly began describing in detail all the forms of pleasure that Tama was willing to give to Lane, all the sexual techniques at which she was an expert. Billy couldn't help smiling as he read what Tama wanted to do to Lane's "love pump."

"What are you laughing at?" Lane demanded.

"I bet she doesn't know you're eleven years old."

"I'm old enough," he said defensively. "Besides, I already sent her a letter back."

"You what?" Billy stared at him.

"Read the end of the letter."

Billy turned the paper over. His eyes flew down the page to the last paragraph:

. . . Maybe we could get together some time. I think we'd have fun. If you send me $10, I'll send you some intimate pictures of me and my sister, along with our address. I sure hope I hear from you soon. I'd love you to <u>come</u> and visit me.

Billy shook his head, looking up from the letter. "What a dick. Can't you tell it's just a rip-off to get your money?" He pointed toward the Xeroxed photo. "They probably cut this out of a magazine."

"Oh, yeah?"

"Yeah. Besides, look at where that P.O. box is. New York. Even if she does send you her real address, what are you going to do? Go to New York?" He handed Lane the letter. "You didn't send ten dollars, did you?"

Lane nodded. "Yeah," he admitted.

"That was dumb." He looked at his friend curiously. "Where'd you get the money anyway?"

Lane glanced away. "My old man."

"You stole it?" Billy was shocked.

"What am I gonna do? Tell him I want ten dollars to send to Tama Barnes so I can get her pictures and address?"

"You shouldn't've stole it."

"Fuck you. My old man has plenty of money. He didn't even notice it was gone."

Billy looked down at the open magazine on his lap, saying

nothing. He and Lane often fought, often argued, often insulted each other, but there had been something else in his friend's voice just now, a hardness, a belligerence, a seriousness that said this was not a subject for argument, at least not for their usual temporary playful form of argument.

They were silent for a while, the only sound in The Fort the quiet whisk of turning pages.

"You're probably right," Lane said finally. "I probably won't get anything. I probably won't even get my pictures. But who can tell?"

"Yeah," Billy said.

"I bet she has a nice beaver, though."

Lane's voice was normal again, but underneath the superficialities something had changed, something that could not change back, and Billy somehow knew that this mundane moment was a turning point in their relationship. He and Lane might never again be as close as they had been, or even as close as they were now. It was a sad realization, a depressing discovery, and though Lane soon tired of looking at the *Playboy*s and wanted to ride down to the dig and see what was happening there, Billy convinced him to stay in The Fort, as if by remaining within its boundaries they could stop the change from occurring and freeze everything exactly as it was now.

The two of them remained within the HQ for the rest of the morning, talking, looking at the pictures, reading aloud the party jokes, like the friends they had always been and had thought they always would be.

15

The entire town was talking about The Suicides. For that was how they thought of them now. The Suicides. In big capital letters. It had been easy in the aftermath of the funeral and the outpouring of public sympathy for Bob Ronda's family to focus on the mailman's life rather than his death, to dwell on his good points. But the fact remained that he had killed himself. He had blown his brains out with a double-barreled shotgun and had, in the process, pushed his wife over the edge of sanity and let down an entire town that had loved him, cared about him, believed in him.

And now Bernie Rogers had done it as well.

It was all Doug and Tritia heard about at the grocery store. The Suicides. Willis had had suicides before—Texacala Armstrong had shot herself last year just after her husband had been finally taken by cancer—but the deaths had been isolated and understandable: people dying of disease, people who had recently lost a loved one, people with no hope. Never, in anyone's memory, had there been two suicides within two weeks of each other. And by seemingly normal people for no good reason.

The bizarreness of the coincidence was not lost upon anyone, and shocked grief was mixed with both morbid curiosity and superstitious fear as people talked in hushed whispers about what had happened. Even the worst gossips in town seemed to approach the subject reverently, as if suicide was a communicable disease and by not trivializing or sensationalizing the deaths they could somehow vaccinate themselves against it.

The afternoon before, after returning from the meeting, Doug had told Tritia about Bernie Rogers, about seeing the body, about his suspicions. She, in turn, had told him about the call from Ronda's wife and about the letter from Howard, although she still, for some reason, could not bring

102

herself to tell him of her nocturnal experience with the mailman. He wanted to go immediately to the police, to explain to them that he thought the mailman was somehow behind or responsible for both deaths, but she convinced him, after a heated name-calling argument, that as a teacher and supposedly respected member of the community, he could not afford to damage his credibility by making wild accusations. He still had the envelopes they'd retrieved from the creek, but he realized that everything else was entirely unsubstantiated and required not only a tremendous leap of faith but also a belief in . . . what?

The supernatural?

Maybe he was crazy, but he didn't think so, and he knew that behind Tritia's logical arguments she didn't either. He still thought he should go to the police and tell them what he knew, or what he suspected, but he was willing to hold off for her sake. She was right. News spread in a small town, and if he happened to be wrong, if the mailman was just a normal man with pale skin and red hair, he would forever be branded a nut. In the back of his mind, though, was the nagging thought that someone else might be in danger, that by remaining silent and passive he might allow something else to happen, and he was determined to keep his eyes and ears open for anything unusual, anything out of the ordinary, and to report everything to the police if he suspected that anyone was going to be hurt or injured. Or killed.

They moved up and down the aisles of the store, Tritia going through the coupons, reading aloud from the shopping list, Doug taking the items from the shelves and putting them into the cart.

"Mr. Albin!"

Doug put a box of cornflakes into the cart and looked up. A tan young woman wearing tight shorts, a tight T-shirt, and no bra waved at him from down the aisle. She smiled, radiant teeth lighting up her pretty face. He knew she was an ex-student, though he could not immediately place her, and he tried desperately to connect a name with the face as she walked up the aisle toward him.

"Giselle Brennan," she said. "Composition. Two years ago. You probably don't remember me—"

"Of course I remember you," he said, and now he did, although he was surprised at himself. Giselle had been one of those fringe students who had shown up for class only when she felt like it and had barely eked out a C for the semester. Not the type of student he ordinarily remembered. "How are you doing?"

"Fine," she said.

"I haven't seen you around for a while."

"Yeah, well, I moved to Los Angeles, worked as a temp in a law office while I went to school part-time, but I didn't really like it much. Los Angeles, I mean. Too crowded, too smoggy, too everything. I'm back here visiting my parents right now." She smiled brightly at him. "The place seems to have weirded out since I left."

Was it that obvious? Doug wondered. Could even an outsider sense it?

Giselle gestured toward Tritia. "Is this your wife?"

"Yes. This is Tritia."

Tritia nodded politely. "Hello."

"Hi." Giselle beamed. "You know, your husband's a really good teacher. I bet you're really proud of him. I never liked English much—I was always more of a math person—but I sure enjoyed his class."

"But did you learn anything?" Doug joked.

"I did. I really did. I learned the difference between 'that' and 'who.' "

Doug chuckled.

"Don't laugh. I'm serious. That's something that always stuck with me. Before I had your class, I used to say, 'The person that went to the store,' or 'The guy that sold me the car.' But ever since you gave us that lecture, I say 'The person *who* went to the store,' 'The guy *who* sold me the car.' "

"I'm glad I got through to somebody."

"You did. And it's helped me a lot. Now I'm a real snob about it, in fact. Once I went to this party and there was a guy in really trendy clothes playing the serious intellectual. Only he kept saying 'that' when he should have said 'who.' It made me feel so superior! Here was this man who should have intimidated the hell out of me, and I wasn't intimated by him at all. I felt sort of embarrassed for him, if you want to know the truth. It was great!"

Doug wasn't sure what to say. "Thank you, I guess."

"You're welcome."

"You're giving him a swelled head," Tritia said. "Now it's going to be even more impossible to live with him."

Giselle didn't pick up on the humor. "He's the best teacher I ever had," she said seriously. "Even though he gave me a C." She looked toward her shopping cart at the end of the aisle. "Well, I've got to get going. I'll be around for a while, though. Maybe we'll run into each other in town somewhere." She looked shyly away. "Maybe we can meet for lunch or something."

Doug nodded. "Maybe. Nice seeing you again."

The girl returned to her cart, retreating down the aisle, and Tritia raised her eyebrows. "Ha," she said.

"What does that mean, ha?"

"You know exactly what it means."

"The poor girl obviously came to the store to get herself a quarter-pound Hoffy, and you're picking on her."

"You're nasty!" Tritia laughed and hit his shoulder, and he felt a little better. He put an arm around her waist. They continued down the aisle and up the next one to the produce department and didn't hear a single word about The Suicides. When they reached the checkout stand, however, he heard snatches of words from various conversations, and the words "killed himself" and "death" seemed to pop up an awful lot. His eyes rested on the *Willis Weekly*, displayed on its stand next to the counter, and he thought of Ben Stockley, the editor of the paper. He didn't know why he hadn't thought of the editor before. If anyone in town would listen to him, hear him out, perhaps even believe him, it would be Stockley. He said nothing to Tritia, but he decided then and there that he was going to pay the editor a visit later in the day.

They moved forward in line.

The Bronco seemed to hit every bump and chuckhole on the road home. There were eggs and other fragile food items in the back of the vehicle, and Doug tried to drive slowly and carefully down the dirt road. They drove over the creek and around the turn, and were heading along the straight stretch toward home when they saw, in the distance, what appeared to be two figures kneeling in the middle of the road. As they drew closer, they saw that the figures were Ron and Hannah Nelson and that they were crouched on the dirt before the unmoving form of a German shepherd.

"Oh, my God," Tritia said. "It's Scooby. Stop."

Doug pulled the car over to the side of the ditch just in front of the couple. They could see, this close, that Hannah Nelson's face was streaked with tears. Both of them hopped out of the car, hurrying forward. Ron stood up as they approached.

"What happened?" Doug asked.

"Scooby's dead." Ron's voice was choked and halting, and it seemed as though he too was about to cry. "I think he was poisoned. There's not a mark on him, but there's, like, saliva still dripping from his mouth. The saliva's kind of red."

"Do you need some help? Do you want me to take him to the vet?"

"No. We'll take him. There's nothing that can be done now."

Doug looked down at the dog. There were, indeed, no marks on him, but the animal's eyes were open wide in an expression of terror and agony. The drool that hung in threads from his open mouth had pooled on the dirt in a muddy, bloody mixture. He met Tritia's glance and saw in her eyes disgust and pity and anger.

"Who could've poisoned him?" she asked. "Do you have any idea?"

Ron swallowed hard. "No. But the Wilkersons' dog was poisoned yesterday, and someone told me that two or three dogs in town have been poisoned the last couple days."

"But how could they have gotten Scooby? I mean, you always have him tied up."

"Actually, he broke his chain yesterday and ran off," Hannah said. She closed her eyes, took a deep breath, obviously willing herself not to cry. "It took us a few hours to find him."

"He was up past your place," Ron added.

Hannah began sobbing again, turning away from them.

Doug put a comforting arm around Tritia. "You sure there's nothing we can do?"

Ron shook his head. "Thanks, though."

"Let us know what you find out." Tritia moved forward and put a hand on Hannah's shoulder. "Call me."

The other woman nodded silently, and Doug and Tritia made their way back to the Bronco. Doug put his key in the ignition, started the engine, put the car into gear, and they pulled away from the ditch, moving slowly around the Nelsons and heading toward home. Glancing in the rearview mirror, Doug saw Ron pick up the dog and carry him toward the driveway.

Neither of them said a word as they pulled into their own drive. Doug parked next to the house and got two sacks of groceries from the back of the vehicle. Tritia carried the other sack. They walked into the living room. As usual, Billy was sprawled on the couch, watching TV. *The Brady Bunch.* Doug put his sacks down on the kitchen counter. Next to the sacks was this morning's mail. It had been delivered before breakfast, before they had even awakened, but neither of them had been brave enough to open the envelopes.

Now Doug shuffled through the mail and set aside the three envelopes addressed to himself. As Tritia put down her sack, he tore open the first one and unfolded the enclosed letter: "Dear Tim . . ."

His name wasn't Tim. He frowned, reading on:

You missed the meeting, so I'll fill you in on the details. We passed resolutions five through nine unanimously and hired the new custodian. That asshole Albin gave us a sob story about books and we told him we'd find the funds just to shut him up, but to be honest, there are several more important items we could be spending the money on. I'd like you to write him a letter explaining that our budget for this fiscal year does not allow for new curriculum expenditures other than those already approved, etc. etc. . . .

His eyes jumped to the bottom of the letter. It was signed by Willard Young, the president of the school board. "Tim" had to be Tim Washburn, the only board member who hadn't attended the meeting.

"Those sons of bitches," he swore softly.

"What?" Tritia asked.

"They're not going to give me my books."

"But I thought you said—"

"They lied to me." He handed over the letter. "I can't believe it."

"I can." She read the letter, then threw it down on the counter. "What else is new? They've been screwing the

teachers every year since we've been here. What made you
think they were going to change?"

Doug picked up the second envelope. As he'd suspected,
it was an official letter from the board, apologizing for not
having enough money in the budget to buy his requested
copies of *Huckleberry Finn*.

He tore the letter up and opened the cupboard under the
sink, throwing the pieces into the garbage sack.

Tritia was starting to unload the grocery sacks, but Doug
handed her the single envelope addressed to her. "Open it,"
he said.

"Now?"

"I have a theory."

Tritia took the envelope from him and carefully opened
it, reading the short enclosed note. No, she thought, this
can't be real. She read over the letter once more:

> What makes you think I would want to meet with you?
> You were always a smug self-satisfied bitch, and I have
> no reason to believe that you have changed . . .

Smug self-satisfied bitch.

It was a phrase Paula had often used to describe women
she did not like, and it lent the message an authenticity not
found in the stilted phrasing of the rest of the letter. Tritia's
lips suddenly felt dry. Of course, she had never told Doug
of her last meeting with Paula, of what had been said on
both sides. She had let him believe that they had simply
drifted apart after the move and she had kept up the pre-
tense of a friendship long after contact had been cut off.

But after all these years, and after reading that letter, she
had honestly thought that Paula might want to get together
again. Lord knows, she had often thought of Paula in the
intervening years, had often regretted the things she'd said.
The two of them had been such good friends and their
falling out over such a relatively minor item that she'd had
no trouble believing that Paula wanted to meet.

Smug self-satisfied bitch.

"What is it?" Doug asked.

She quickly folded the letter, not wanting him to see.
"Paula's not going to be able to come," she said. "She
changed her mind."

"Apparently so did Don," Doug said dryly. He handed

her a letter from Don Jennings. There were only two words between the salutation and the signature: "Fuck you."

Tritia blinked, not believing her eyes. She could not recall hearing Don ever use profanity. Not even "shit" or "hell" or "damn." She glanced up at Doug. "That's not like him," she said. "Not unless he's changed an awful lot since we knew him."

"I don't think it's from Don."

"Do you—"

"I don't think the first one was either," he said, anticipating her question. "I don't think Don got a job in Phoenix, I don't think the Jennings are moving to Arizona, I don't think he wrote to me at all."

Tritia felt a tremor of fear pass through her. "That's an awful lot of trouble for someone to go through just to play a practical joke," she said. "That first letter was so detailed. Whoever wrote it either knew Don or knew you, because there were things in there that a stranger couldn't possibly've known."

"It wasn't a joke," Doug said. "I don't know what it was, but it wasn't a joke." He held out his hand. "Let me see your letter."

She didn't really want him to read the letter, but she handed it to him anyway. She watched his eyes dart quickly from left to right as he scanned the words.

"That's what I thought."

They were silent for a moment. Tritia looked over at Billy, who was watching TV, pretending he hadn't heard what they were talking about. He'd heard, she knew. But she was glad he was pretending he hadn't. She didn't want to talk to him about this, didn't want to explain what she couldn't explain.

She turned away from Doug. She didn't want to talk about it to him either. She didn't want to talk about it at all. She began unpacking groceries.

16

"That's a very interesting theory," Stockley said. "Very interesting." He broke open a fortune cookie, reading his fortune, throwing the slip of paper away and slowly chewing the cookie as he mulled over what Doug had just told him.

A slovenly paunchy man in his mid-fifties, Ben Stockley looked like a stereotypical reporter. His pants were always black, his shirt always white, and both were always wrinkled. His hair was gray and thin, combed back over his scalp, and was slightly too long for both his age and contemporary fashion. Stockley's face was rough and leathery, with blunt Broderick Crawford features, and he always seemed to be sweating, no matter what the temperature. In his lower right desk drawer, the editor kept a box of risqué fortune cookies he ordered directly from some company in New York. He bought the fortune cookies because he loved them and said he didn't want to have to pay for a whole meal just to get one, but he also enjoyed giving the cookies to unsuspecting visitors and watching the reactions on their faces as they read their usually obscene fortunes. He particularly liked giving the cookies to bashful young women and prim old ladies.

"Well, what do you think?" Doug asked.

"You going to blame the mailman for poisoning dogs, too?"

Doug slumped in his seat. "You don't believe me."

"I didn't say that."

Doug looked up at him hopefully.

The editor broke open another fortune cookie. "Have you gone to the police with any of this?"

"Well, I told them about the letters to shut off my phone, water, and electricity. I even gave them copies. But I haven't told them anything else."

"Maybe you should go to them." Stockley raised his

hand. "I'm not saying I believe you, but if you're right, this is definitely a matter for the police."

"I don't know if I'm right either. That's why I came to you. If I walk into the police station and tell them what I just told you, they'll probably think I'm crazy."

The editor chuckled. "You didn't want publicity, so you came to a newspaper. That's a good one." Doug started to protest, but Stockley cut him off. "I understand. I know what you're trying to do, but the problem is that a newspaper deals with facts. If a story doesn't have the five Ws, I don't print it. I could do a feature on you, let you put forth your ideas, but everything would be attributed to you, and I don't think that's what you want."

"Actually, I'm not really looking for an article, although I think people probably do need to be warned. What I really came in for was confirmation. I mean, you know what goes on in this town. If someone stubs his toe or catches a cold, you're aware of it. I just thought that if anyone had noticed something unusual lately, it would be you. Am I right?"

Stockley was silent, chewing.

"Just tell me what, if anything, is going on. What have you heard?"

The editor's gaze was troubled. "The relationship between a journalist and his source is very sacred," he said finally. "It's analogous to a lawyer/client relationship, a doctor/patient relationship, a priest/confessor relationship. I could pussyfoot around this, but I'll be honest. Yes, I have heard some talk. Nothing specific, nothing like what you've told me, and nothing that anyone would admit to if questioned, but other people have noticed odd things occurring lately. And I think they'll notice even more after Bernie Roger's suicide. I should remain neutral, objective, and impartial, but I'll tell you the truth. Yes, I think something strange is going on around here. And I think it's centered around the mailman."

Doug felt relief flood through him. He hadn't realized how good it would feel to have an ally, to hear someone, a third party, say that he was not crazy, that he was actually on to something. At the same time, it made everything that much more frightening. If all of this was true, the mailman was at the very least dangerously unbalanced and deranged.

Stockley was right. He should go to the police and tell them everything.

The editor opened a drawer, drawing out a stack of mail. "Newspapers always get a lot of mail. A lot of weird mail. We get put on every crackpot mailing list imaginable. Nazis want us to give them free publicity, communists want us to cover their causes, religious fanatics want us to explain to people how the anti-Christ has infiltrated the government. For two weeks—the two weeks after Ronda died—we got nothing but good mail, like you said. Subscriptions were up, letters of praise rolled in, even the chronic cranks stopped harassing us. That was weird enough in itself. Then, a few days ago, we began to get these." He picked up the top letter from his pile. "Here, read this."

Doug took the letter and quickly read it over. It described in detail the sexual torture and mutilation of someone named Cindy Howell. He grimaced. The description was so grisly and so disgusting that he could not finish reading it. "Who is Cindy Howell?" he asked.

"My daughter," Stockley replied.

Doug looked immediately up.

"She's fine. Nothing's happened to her. She lives in Chicago, and I called her right away. I called the Chicago police and told them, sent a photocopy of the letter to them, in fact. They're keeping a surveillance on her house as a favor."

"I didn't know you had a daughter."

"That's because I never told anyone in town. She was from my first marriage, and I never told anyone about that, either."

"How do you think the mailman found out?"

"I'm not sure it is the mailman. Read the postmark. It's from Chicago. It could be from enemies I made there or from some crazy who's after my daughter. Or it could just be a harmless threat from some crank. Notice that it's written in the past tense. These are all things that're supposed to have happened already."

"But you said you thought the mailman was—"

"I don't know. I'm not sure of anything." He hefted the pile of letters. "These are all similar. They're postmarked from cities all over the country and involve people I've known throughout my life. They're not all sexually explicit like that one, but they're all equally sick. They could all be part of some organized effort to harass me, although I can't see a reason why; or they could all be part of some outrageously unlikely coincidence. I'm inclined to believe you about the mailman because I've noticed the same pattern in my mail as you have. And because other people have hinted about it to me as well. I don't know exactly what's going on here, but it does seem to be centered around the mail and it does seem to have started after this John Smith took over."

"Will you come with me to the police, then? They'll believe both of us."

"Believe us? Believe that one man sorts through and readdresses mail, writes forged letters to people all over town, well-researched letters at that, is responsible for two suicides as well as God knows what else? I'm not sure I believe it. I think that the mailman is somehow involved in this, but I don't know what the connection is. We're edging into *Twilight Zone* territory here."

"You think I should tell the police what I know?"

"What you know?"

"What I think, then."

"I don't know how much good it will do at this point, without any proof—"

"I have the letters from the creek."

"That's true." The editor leaned back in his chair. "Yes," he said. "I think you should talk to the police. I won't go with you, because my credibility's not my own, it's tied to the paper's as well, and that is something I will not jeopardize. You know Mike Trenton?"

"He was in my class several years ago."

"He's a good kid, and a good cop. Talk to him. He has an open mind. He might listen. Stay away from Catfield."

"Mike Trenton. Can I tell him about your letters?"

Stockley nodded. "Tell him." He sighed and leaned forward, withdrawing another fortune cookie from his desk. "I shouldn't be getting involved in this. I'm supposed to report stories, not be part of them, but to be honest you've scared the hell out of me."

Doug smiled wanly. "I've been scaring the hell out of myself for a week."

"It's time to do something about it," the editor said. He bit into his fortune cookie.

Doug sat on the low Naugahyde couch in the waiting room of the police station. Behind the counter, uniformed clerks and officers answered phones and completed paperwork. He felt old. Three of the five employees in the office had

been his students at one time or another. That wasn't unusual. In a town as small as Willis, he was always running
into ex-students. But seeing ex-students in positions of authority, their young faces hardened into adulthood, made
him feel hopelessly old.

Mike Trenton emerged from one of the back rooms,
smiling broadly. His hair was shorter than it had been in
high school, but aside from that, he had hardly changed at
all. His face was still openly honest, naïve, and even in his
dark-blue uniform, he seemed young. "Long time no see,
Mr. Albin."

"Call me Doug."

"Doug." He shook his head. "It feels weird calling a
teacher by his first name." He chuckled. "Anyway, what
can I do for you?"

Doug glanced around the crowded office. "It's kind of
busy in here. Is there someplace we can talk that's more
private?"

"If this is about your case, you'd have to talk to Lt.
Shipley. He's trying to track down those letters—"

"Well, it's related to that, but not exactly." He motioned
with his head toward the hall. "Can we talk in your office or
something?"

"I don't have an office, but I suppose we can use the
interrogation room." He waved to one of the clerks. "I'll be
in the exam room," he announced.

The clerk nodded, and the two of them passed through a
small security gate and into the hall. Doug followed Mike
into the interrogation room, a small cubicle with barely
enough room for two chairs and a table.

Now that he was here, Doug did not know where to
begin. The chronology he had developed, the arguments he
had worked out in his mind, withered in the just-the-facts
environment of the police station. He had no proof, not
really, only some strange occurrences and tentative connections. Connections that, it was obvious now, required great
leaps of faith. The confidence he had felt while talking to
Stockley in the newspaper office had vanished entirely. He
had not been expecting to get from the police the type of
reception the editor had given his ideas, but he still had not
been prepared for the lack of belief he now knew would
greet his story. He had been stupid to come here at all.

Still, as he looked across the bare table at Mike Trenton,

he saw not cynicism and disinterest in the young officer's eyes but an open willingness to hear him out.

This had better be good.

He started at the beginning, with Ronda's unlikely suicide and his initial impression of the new mailman at the funeral. He had an impulse to speed his story up, to relate it in the shorthand manner in which he'd seen witnesses talk on television, but he forced himself to take his time, to carefully go over every small detail, every emotional impression, believing that it would lend verisimilitude to his theory.

Mike stopped him before he was halfway through. "I'm sorry, Mr. Albin. No offense, but this has been a pretty hectic week around here. This isn't a big-city police department. We have twelve cops working in two shifts. There's been a series of dog poisonings, a suicide we're still investigating, and the usual fights in the cowboy bars. We're seriously undermanned at the moment. I know we've been having a lot of trouble with the mail, but to be honest, you should be talking to Howard Crowell—"

"Look, you may think I'm crazy—"

"I don't think you're crazy, Mr. Albin."

"Doug."

"Doug."

"I don't know exactly what's going on around here, but it seems to me that John Smith, if that is his real name, has the ability to . . . to somehow channel the mail in the way he wants it to go. He can separate letters from bills, good letters from bad. He can redirect a letter from its intended recipient to the person the letter is about. We got a note from Howard the other day that was supposed to be for Ellen Ronda. But the envelope was addressed to us. And this has happened to other people."

"So you're saying that Mr. Smith somehow opens all these envelopes, reads all these letters, and redirects them as some sort of perverse practical joke?"

"I don't know what I'm saying."

"Assuming that he would want to, do you know how long it would take for one man to do such a thing, even in a town this small?"

"I'm not sure he sleeps. Hell, I'm not sure he's even human."

"You lost me, Mr. Albin. I respect you and all, and I

admit that strange things have been happening to the mail lately, but this sounds a little off the deep end."

Doug smiled wryly. "You haven't heard it all. I also think he's connected with Bernie Rogers' death and Bob Ronda's."

"This is a joke, right?"

"No joke. Just hear me out." He went on to explain his discovery at the creek and the increasingly bizarre nature of the mail both he and the newspaper had been receiving.

Mike frowned. "How come Ben didn't tell me this himself?"

"He didn't even want me to tell you."

"So what about Ronda and Rogers?"

Doug explained their connections to the post office and the unlikely nature of their suicides.

"We have been wondering how Rogers tied that rope," Mike admitted.

"So, what was written on the note pinned to Bernie's chest?"

The policeman shook his head. "Sorry. Confidential."

"But you don't think I'm totally crazy?"

Mike looked at him silently for a moment. "No, I don't," he said finally. "God knows why, but I don't. I don't entirely believe you, but I don't disbelieve you either."

"Good enough for now. I know there's no proof against the mailman. There's no way you can haul him in. Yet. But I just want you to keep your eyes and ears open. Be on the lookout. Just be prepared."

The young officer shook his head, grinning ruefully. "If anyone else finds out about this, I'm dead meat. But okay."

Doug stood up, pushing his chair back. He looked at the policeman curiously. "You got something, didn't you?" he asked. "In the mail?"

Mike stared up at him, then nodded slowly.

"I could tell. You dropped that cop routine pretty fast and hopped aboard the bandwagon, no questions asked."

"I got a letter from my fiancé in Phoenix, telling me she wanted to break up. I called her, but her phone was out of service. So I took a sick day and drove down to ASU. She'd never sent me the letter. Her phone had been left off the hook accidentally on the day I tried to call." He scratched his nose. "Maybe I'm just looking for an easy excuse, but I think there might be something to what you say. I think there's something going on with the mailman. I still don't entirely believe you, and I hope we're not turning Mr.

Smith into a scapegoat for our problems, but I'll keep a watch out."

"That's all I ask. I'll let you know if anything comes up."

"And we'll let you know if anything happens with your water and power and phone letters."

Doug thanked Mike and returned down the hall. The young policeman let him through the security gate into the lobby, and walking out to the car, Doug felt better than he had in quite a while. It was nice to be able to share some of the burden.

He got in the Bronco and took off.

On the way home, he passed the mailman, unloading mail from the box in front of Circle K, sorting the envelopes, carefully putting some into his plastic tray, shoving the others into a brown paper sack.

He waved as Doug drove by.

17

The next day the mail was normal. It had still been delivered at some odd hour before they woke up, but the mail itself was neither unnaturally good nor unnaturally bad. There was a subscription notice from *Newsweek*, a Visa bill, some junk mail. Nothing out of the ordinary, though that itself was out of the ordinary.

Doug tried to call Stockley at the paper, but the secretary said he was not taking any calls. He told her to give the editor his name, and after a great deal of convincing she agreed to do so, but when she came back on the line, she informed him that it was paste-up day and that the editor refused to be interrupted by anyone. She said he'd call Doug back when he got the opportunity.

The mail was normal the next day as well, and Doug began to think that maybe he had jumped to conclusions, that he had overreacted, that he had been wrong. Tritia said nothing, but he could tell that she was thinking the same thing, and he could tell that she was relieved.

The next morning the mailbox was filled with letters. Doug went out to the mailbox before breakfast, while Billy was still asleep and Trish was watering her garden. There were ten envelopes all together, and the sheer bulk of them in the mailbox was somehow ominously threatening. Glancing quickly at their faces, he saw that few of the envelopes bore familiar addresses, and he stuffed them down the back of his pants, letting his shirt hang over the top half of the stack. Inside the house, he tore up the envelopes one by one, without looking at their contents, shoving the pieces in an empty milk carton in the garbage.

Trish walked in just as he closed the top of the carton. "Any mail?" she asked, wiping her wet hands on her jeans.

"None," he lied.

The next day there were no letters at all, nor any the day

118

after that. It was almost as if he was being punished for tearing up the mail when it had arrived, as if he had rejected an offering and was to receive no more as punishment.

But that was crazy thinking.

Still, the absence of mail was somehow just as perturbing as its presence, and it made him feel strangely on edge. He had probably seen too many movies and read too many books, but he could not help ascribing a malevolent intent to this temporary respite. It felt to him like the calm before the storm, and he kept waiting for the storm to hit. He tried to finish the first wall of the storage shed, but he could not seem to concentrate and he gave it up after only an hour's work.

At the store that afternoon, he noticed that many of the people with whom he came in contact seemed tense and testy. Todd Gold, owner of the deli next door to Bayless, did not even acknowledge his greeting. When Doug waved and called out "Hi," Gold turned curtly away and retreated into his store.

But he told Trish none of this. She seemed to be much happier since the mail had stopped coming, and though this out-of-sight-out-of-mind mentality was not typical for her, was indeed entirely out of character, he did not want to drag her into what might simply be his own delusion. After all, perhaps there had been nothing strange going on, nothing out of the ordinary. Perhaps his imagination had overreacted to a bizarre series of seemingly interconnected occurrences that had really had nothing to do with one another.

Perhaps.

But he didn't think so.

18

Tritia felt a little better today. For the third day in a row they had received no mail, and for some reason that cheered her up. The old no-news-is-good-news theory. Besides, she was going to see Irene Hill, and a visit with the old woman never failed to lift her spirits.

She turned off the highway and drove down Pine Street. She passed the Willis Women's Club and sped by the brick building guiltily. She had made a commitment to attend Weight Watchers meetings there every afternoon for six months but had not shown up since the third meeting. She had adhered to the strict diet for the first two weeks and had lost five pounds, half of her goal, but the pressure had been too much. The weigh-ins, the pep talks, the lectures, the journals, the propaganda, had all made her feel too constrained. Besides, although she could afford to lose a little on the thighs, she still had a shapely figure and she knew she looked a hell of a lot better than some of the women in town who had not signed up for Weight Watchers at all.

She saw one of those women now, Beth Johnson, pulling out of the post-office parking lot. Beth waved at her, a false plastic smile on her face, and Tritia waved back.

She continued down Pine, then turned off on the dirt road just before the golf course. She continued around the small hill until she came to the small cluster of homes adjacent to the old ranger station.

She pulled into Irene's driveway. She had first met Irene Hill when they had both worked as volunteers for the annual library book sale a few years back. Irene had been one of the original founders of the library, back in the days when few people in the town read or wanted to read, and she had, by all accounts, been one of the major civilizing forces in the community. Even after retiring, Irene had continued her association with the library, spearheading fund-raising efforts and volunteering for book drives, patron-membership drives, and book and magazine sales. It was Irene herself, in fact, who initially called Tritia, soliciting her help.

The two of them had hit it off instantly. They were of different generations, of course, but Irene was up on current politics and cultural events, and with her outgoing personality and boundless enthusiasm for everything, she seemed to have more in common with Tritia than with the fossilized volunteers her own age.

Tritia got out of the car and walked up the faded wood steps to the screened porch. She knocked on the door and Irene's voice sounded from the kitchen, "Come on in. Door's unlocked."

Tritia pushed open the door and walked inside. Irene's house was decorated with antiques, though they had not been antiques when originally purchased. The foyer was dominated by a large halltree, and the living room contained not only antique bookcases and china cabinets but a pristine Victrola and a beautiful baby-grand piano. Tiny porcelain figures, collected for the past half-century, lined shelves on the wall. The house was warm and comfortable, filled with healthy plants, and Tritia always felt good here, happy, as though she were in some sort of sanctuary protected from the outside world.

Irene was in the kitchen, plucking leaves from a tied bunch of dried plants. She often made her own tea from a mixture of mints and flowers she grew in her garden, a wonderful brew that Doug and Billy both said tasted like dirt. The old woman turned around as Tritia entered the room, her fingers continuing to skillfully defoliate the dried herbs as if they worked on their own, disassociated from the rest of her body. "How've you been, sweetie?" she asked. "Haven't seen you in, what, two or three weeks?"

Tritia smiled. Irene was the only person she'd ever met, young or old, who could say words like "sweetie" or "honey" without making them sound either cloying or condescending. "I'm okay," she said.

"You don't sound okay. You sound kind of tired. In fact, you look a little peaked as well."

"Stress," Tritia said.

The old woman stopped tearing leaves and used a corner

of the apron she was wearing to wipe sweat off her forehead. "Doug?"

"No, nothing like that. It's just . . ." Her voice trailed
off. "I don't know what it is."

"I got your card this morning."

"Card?" Tritia felt a warning light go off in her brain. She
had sent Irene no card.

"Yes. It made me laugh, but I don't know why you sent
it. I'm not sick."

Tritia felt the stability she'd begun to recapture the last
few days recede, a familiar fear welling within her. She
looked around the kitchen and suddenly the room itself
seemed strange, the light coming in through the window not
quite right. "I didn't send it," she said.

The old woman's face clouded over. She was silent for a
moment, though her fingers continued to work. "I was
afraid of that." There was no surprise in her voice, no
emotion at all. It was a statement of fact, delivered straight.

Tritia moved over to the breakfast nook and sat down.
"You know, too."

"Know what?"

"About the mailman."

Irene stopped working and sat down across the table from
Tritia. "I haven't seen him. But how could I not know
what's been happening to the mail? I've been getting letters
from people I haven't seen for years. Decades, even. People
I thought were dead. I got a letter from Sue at the library
that Sue never sent."

Tritia nodded. "It's been happening to everyone."

"Well, no one's talked to me about it. I called Howard up
the other day to complain, but he seemed real distracted
and didn't seem to pay much attention to me. I went over to
the post office that afternoon, but that new man was there,
and he told me that Howard had gone home sick." She
shook her head. "I've never known Howard Crowell to be
sick."

"Neither have I," Tritia said.

"The past few days, I've been getting get-well cards from
people." Irene smiled. "At first I thought the doctor was
telling everyone else something he wasn't telling me. But
then I thought that this wasn't a joke. Friends sent me cards
as though they thought I'd suffered a heart attack. I called

to let them know I was all right, and they said they hadn't sent me anything."

"I didn't either."

"I know." Irene looked out the window. A hummingbird alighted for a moment on a honeysuckle branch next to the window, then zoomed off above the trees. "I've decided to just ignore it. Hopefully it will all go away."

Tritia frowned. It wasn't like Irene to simply "hope" that something would go away. She had never been the passive type. "Have you talked to Howard since then?"

Irene shook her head. "Have you?"

She hadn't, but she was not sure why. It was obvious to her now that Howard had not sent that letter to her, but she had still been harboring some residual anger and had not been able to quite shake her duplicitous image of the postmaster. She would force herself to see Howard today, on the way home.

"Let's talk about something else," Irene said, standing up. "We have quite a bit to catch up on."

This wasn't like Irene either. Tritia looked into her friend's face and saw in her expression a woman she didn't know. A frightened woman. The warning light was now flashing, accompanied by a buzzer. "Have you told anyone?"

"Let's talk about something else," Irene said firmly.

Tritia drove around the block once, twice, then finally gathered up enough courage to pull into the post-office parking lot. She sat for a few moments in the car, then forced herself to get out and walk inside.

The parking lot was virtually deserted, only one car and one pickup in the spaces next to her. That was unusual but not completely unheard of for this time of day, but what was weird was the fact that no one was sitting on the benches outside the building. The old men who usually wiled away their days in front of the post office were nowhere to be seen.

She stepped inside. The mailman was alone behind the counter, helping an elderly man with a white mustache. This close, his sharp red hair seemed somehow threatening, particularly when paired with the blandness of his pale features. Howard was nowhere to be seen. She tried to catch a glimpse of the room behind the partition in back of the counter, to see if the postmaster was working in the back, but she could see nothing from this angle.

She looked around the lobby. She had not been here in several weeks, and the room had changed. In place of the Selective Service poster that had been prominently displayed on one wall—a poster featuring a benign young man seated on a stool next to his pretty girlfriend—was a poster filled with the grimacing sweaty head of an ugly marine, flecks of blood on the collar of his uniform, aggressive words printed over his photo, demanding, ordering that all eighteen-year-old males register upon reaching their birthdays. The entire character of the post office seemed different. Even the stamp posters on the walls had changed. Where once had hung beautiful posters for the most recent nature stamps and wildlife philatelics were now three identical signs for a new stamp celebrating the anniversary of the invention of the hydrogen bomb.

The room seemed very hot, almost oppressively so. The day was not particularly warm or humid, was in fact uncharacteristically cool for this time of year, but the inside of the post office was roasting.

The man at the counter finished his business, turning to go, and Tritia realized with something like panic that she was the only other patron in the post office. She, too, turned quickly to leave, but the mailman's smooth professional voice held her. "Mrs. Albin?"

Tritia turned around. The mailman was smiling kindly at her, and she thought for a second that she and Doug were wrong, they'd both been paranoid, there was nothing wrong with the mailman, nothing unusual. Then she moved forward and saw the hardness of his mouth, the coldness of his eyes, remembered the creek, the letters.

And the night-time delivery.

The mailman continued to smile at her, although it was really more of a smirk than a smile. "May I help you?"

She was determined to remain strong and confident, to not show her fear. "I'd like to speak with Howard."

"I'm sorry," the mailman said. "Howard went home sick this morning. Is there something I can help you with?"

The words he spoke were innocent enough, straightforward enough, but there was something about the way he said them that made her flesh creep. She shook her head, beginning to back slowly out of the office. "No, that's okay. I'll come back later when he's in."

"He may not be in for a while," the mailman said.

Now both his words and his manner had taken on a distinctly threatening edge, though he continued to hold his plastic smile in place.

She turned to go, her skin prickling with cold despite the oppressively warm air.

"You're nice," the mailman said, and his voice took on a sly suggestive quality.

She whirled around, feeling both the anger and the fear coursing through her veins. "You stay away from me, you slimy son of a bitch, or I'll have you in jail so fast your head will spin."

The mailman's smile grew wider. "Billy's nice too."

She stared at him, unable to think of a retort, the words reverberating in her head to the rhythm of her furiously pounding heart, *Billy's nice too Billy's nice too Billy's nice too*, the fear, now on the surface, taking control, no longer something she could contain. She wanted to run from the building, hop in the car, and take off, but some inner reserve of strength came to her rescue and she said coldly, "Fuck you, I'm going to the police." Walking slowly, assuredly, confidently, she left the building and got into the Bronco.

But she did not go to the police. And it was not until she was well off the highway and almost to the first crossing that she had to pull over and park the car until she had stopped shaking enough to continue driving.

19

Billy was watching TV when Lane came over. Well, not really watching. The television was on and he was looking at it, but it was merely background to him, white noise and white light. He was thinking about Lane. Ever since the other day at The Fort, his friend had seemed altered, different. It was nothing he could put his finger on, no change in outward action or appearance, but the difference was more profound and more disturbing than the schism he had sensed when he and Lane had argued over the letter, much more than the seeds of a gradual drifting apart. No, this was something else. He and Lane had gone down to the dig yesterday, had helped unearth an extremely well-preserved group of primitive cooking utensils, and Lane had acted, for all intents and purposes, the same way he always had. But there was a new secretiveness to his manner, a not-quite-definable quality that made Billy extremely nervous. Lane reminded him of a man he had seen in a movie, a man who had for years been killing young children and burying their bodies in his basement, waiting patiently for the right time to spring his secret on the world, to proudly announce his deeds to everyone.

But that was stupid. There was no way Lane could be harboring such a horrible secret. Still, his friend seemed changed in a way he found impossible to understand.

He reminded Billy of the mailman.

That was what it came down to, really. There was no resemblance at all, not in actions or attitude, but on some gut level, he had made the connection and it stuck. He was not simply worried about his friend, he was afraid of him.

Lane's familiar shave-and-a-haircut knock rattled the screen, and Billy called for him to come on in. Lane was dressed in old jeans and a black rock T-shirt. He had combed his hair

126

differently than usual, parting it in the middle, and it made him seem older, harder.

"Hey," Billy said in greeting, nodding at his friend.

Lane sat down on the couch. He was grinning hugely, a sincere grin of happiness that for some reason struck Billy as wrong and unnatural, and he looked toward the back of the house. "Your mom here?"

Billy shook his head.

"Too bad."

Billy tried not to let his puzzlement show. When had Lane ever expressed disappointment that a parent was absent from either of their houses? On the verge of adolescence, eager to prove their adulthood, both of them ordinarily tried to avoid parents as much as possible.

The two of them stared silently at the TV for a few minutes. Finally, Billy swung his feet off the coffee table and stood up. "So what do you want to do?"

Lane shrugged noncommittally, a gesture that somehow rang false.

"Want to go down to the dig, see what's happening?"

"Why don't we check out The Fort?" Lane said. "There's something I want to show you."

Billy agreed, though he was not at all sure that he was ready to see what his friend wanted to share with him. He walked outside and around the side of the house, where his dad was sitting on the porch, reading. "We're going," he announced.

His father looked up from his book. "Who's 'we?' And where are you going?"

Billy reddened a little, embarrassed by this verbal recognition of his not-yet independent status. "Me and Lane," he said. "We're going out to The Fort."

"Okay."

"See you later, Mr. Albin," Lane said.

The two boys walked across the slatted and recently stained two-by-fours to the front of the house, stepping off the porch and moving past the garden. They followed the path through the green belt, into the trees, and the house was lost from sight. Small branches and dried pine needles crackled beneath their feet. "So what is it?" Billy asked. "What do you want to show me?"

Lane smiled enigmatically. "You'll see."

They reached The Fort, hopping easily up on the roof and

shimmying down through the trapdoor into the Big Room. Lane strolled casually into the HQ, sat down, picked up a *Playboy*, and began thumbing through it. Billy grew angry. He knew that his friend was drawing out the tension, making him wait, wanting him to beg to see whatever it was he wanted to show him, but he refused to give Lane the satisfaction. He remained in the Big Room, pretending to straighten one of the posters on the wall.

Lane tired of the charade first, and he put down the magazine, standing up. "I got a letter back," he said simply.

"From that woman?" Billy was surprised.

Lane smiled, a cunning, knowing smile that should have been conspiratorial but was not. "Want to see it?"

Billy knew he should say no. The smug self-satisfied expression on his friend's face was so unlike Lane that it seemed almost frightening, particularly in the dim half-light of the clubhouse. That smile had awakened within him a growing feeling of dread, but he found himself nodding assent.

Grinning, Lane handed over the envelope.

Billy took out the letter, unfolding it slowly. Lane's eyes were on him, hungrily taking in every move, studying his face as if waiting for a reaction. He pulled open the final fold and felt his stomach contract as if it had been hit with a softball.

His mother, completely naked, sitting in a chair with her legs in the air and her pubic area thrust outward, was grinning up at him from the Polaroid photo attached to the letter. He could clearly see, even through the blurred focus, the glistening folds of her wet vagina, the tiny puckered hole of her anus.

The handwriting on the letter was not that of his mother, but his eyes focused anyway on an underlined phrase in the middle of the page:

<u>I love dick.</u>

It was hard to breathe. His lungs did not seem to be working properly. He tried to suck in air, but his mouth was so dry that the inhalation tasted dusty and harsh and almost made him throw up. The paper was shaking noisily in his trembling hand and he let it fall to the dirt. He looked up at Lane. His friend was grinning hugely, his face filled with a sickening expression of smugness.

And lust.

Billy said nothing, but lashed out. His fist struck Lane full on the face, and unprepared, the other boy fell backward onto the ground. Billy kicked him in the side. His eyes were stinging and it was difficult to see, and it took him a second to realize that he was crying.

Lane scrambled to his feet. He was obviously in pain, his face red, nose bloody, eyes watering, but he was grinning crazily. "She said she wants it, and I wrote her back and said I'd give it to her. I'll fuck her all she wants."

Billy struck out again, but this time Lane was prepared. He punched Billy hard in the stomach, and Billy went down, doubling over, clutching his midsection.

Lane scrambled up the rope, through the trapdoor. "I'm gonna show this to everyone," he said. "Maybe other people'll want to try your mom too."

And Billy lay crying on the ground as he heard his ex-friend's footsteps run over the twigs and leaves toward home.

20

Doug crouched on the porch, looking through the telescope at the trees on the ridge. Tonight would be a full moon, and he had brought the telescope outside so he could see the craters. They had gotten the telescope for Billy last Christmas, and the boy's interest in astronomy had waxed and waned since then in cycles roughly corresponding to those of the moon. The last time he'd used the telescope the high-powered setting had seemed somewhat blurry, and he'd asked his dad to check it out, but Doug had not had a chance to do so until now.

He focused the eyepiece until he could see the individual needles of a pine tree atop the ridge. Billy was right. The magnified view was a little blurry, but it probably wasn't enough to hamper anyone's enjoyment. They would still be able to see craters fairly clearly.

He swung the telescope over until he was looking at the Ridge Road. It was after seven and the sun was setting fairly fast. The dirt road winding up to the top of the cliff appeared orange in the fading light. He was about to use the telescope to look at something else when he saw movement at the bottom of his field of vision.

A red car moving slowly up the road.

Doug's heart skipped a beat.

The mailman was driving up to the top of the ridge.

A wave of cold passed over him. Ridge Road ran parallel to the highway through town before swerving up to the top of the cliff and unceremoniously dead-ending in an empty field strewn with boulders. The road intersected Oak right next to the school and was used as a lovers' lane by many of the high-schoolers, but no one lived on top of the ridge.

There was no place on its summit to deliver mail.

The car passed over the top and Doug looked up from the telescope, standing. Even with his naked eye, he could clearly see the road from here, a light slice curving through the darkness of the ridge. He could not make out the detail he could through the telescope, but he would have no problem seeing a car go up or down the road.

He stared, waiting.

Waited, staring.

The sun sank lower in the west, throwing the face of the ridge into shadow until he could no longer differentiate between trees and cliff and road. Although he would have no trouble seeing the mailman's car descend if its lights were on, there was no way he'd be able to spot the car with its headlights off.

He had a gut feeling, however, that the mailman was still up there on top of the ridge and would be for some time.

What could he be doing? Doug opened the screen door quickly and sneaked inside the house before the bugs hovering near the porch light could follow. Tritia was putting away the last of the dinner dishes and Billy was already upstairs.

"I'm going to cruise down to Circle K," Doug announced.

Tritia closed the cupboard. "What for?"

He had no lie handy, but his voice didn't falter as he made up an excuse on the spur of the moment. "I just had a sudden urge for a candy bar. You want one?"

She shook her head. There was a suspicious look on her face, but she said nothing.

"Big Hunk!" Billy called from upstairs.

"What if they don't have any?"

"Reese's!"

"Okay." He turned back toward Tritia. "Anything for you? Granola bar maybe?"

"No." She was quiet for a moment and looked as though she was about to say something, but she remained silent.

"I'll be back in fifteen minutes or so." Doug opened the screen door and stepped out, closing it behind him.

Tritia followed him onto the porch. "Be careful," she said quietly.

He turned to look at her. She knew something or sensed something. He could tell she was worried. He wanted to talk to her, to let her know what he was going to do, but somehow the words wouldn't come. He nodded, saying nothing, and walked down the steps to the Bronco.

He drove quickly, once he was out of eyesight and earshot of the house, eager to get over to the ridge, though he had the feeling the mailman wasn't going anywhere.

It was strange. The mailman had never, to Doug's knowledge, been seen shopping, buying gas, eating, or doing anything other than official postal work. It was hard, in a town this small, to remain completely to oneself, to remain a mystery, and before this, he would have thought it impossible. Even if a person was pathologically antisocial, his neighbors would notice his comings and goings, his personal habits, and would report to their friends, who would report to their friends, and so on until the entire town was informed of his movements. A small town was no place for an individual who craved anonymous privacy, no place for a recluse. But the mailman seemed to be pulling it off.

Now, however, he had the opportunity to see the mailman after hours.

And Doug had the feeling he was doing something other than postal work.

He swung onto the highway and sped through town, braking to thirty-five just before the speed trap next to the bank. He turned off on Oak and followed it to the Ridge Road, hands growing increasingly sweaty on the steering wheel. There were no streetlights here and the road was dark. He slowed to a crawl as he reached the top of the ridge, not sure of what he would find, not wanting to give himself away.

The land at the top was flat, tall grass and weeds punctuated by boulders of various sizes but without any significant foliage to hide behind. He cut the headlights and pulled to the side of the road, turning off the engine so as not to attract attention to himself. He was scared, but he had to go through with this. He rolled down the Bronco's window. The moon in the east was starting to rise, casting long shadows on the ridgetop. The road, he knew, ended just a mile up ahead, and unless the mailman had left while Doug was driving over here, he was somewhere in between these two points.

Doug sat in the car for a few moments longer, gathering his courage, giving his eyes time to adjust to the gloom. There was a slight breeze blowing, a wispy, barely perceptible current of air that animated the blue-lit grass stalks and whispered sibilantly. Only . . . only there was another noise besides the wind whispers. A low faint murmur coming from somewhere up ahead, rising and falling with the tides of the breeze.

The mailman.

Goose bumps rippled down Doug's arms. Slowly, carefully, quietly, he opened the car door and got out, closing it softly. He began walking forward, keeping to the side of the road, grateful he was wearing dark clothes that would allow him to blend in with the night.

The ridge was not entirely flat, he saw now. It appeared so from a car, but walking, he noticed that a slight rise continued imperceptibly forward, the grade just enough to shield the center of the ridge from view.

The murmuring grew slightly louder.

Doug continued walking. His keys and change were jingling in his pants and he put his hand in his pocket to muffle the noise. The road curved slightly, the land leveling off, and he came to an abrupt stop, his heart thumping loudly in his chest. The mailman was about half a mile directly ahead of him, off the road, in the middle of the field. Even from here, he could see the lithe thin figure dancing madly amid the rocks and boulders, arms flailing with wild abandonment. He knew who it was without moving closer, but he wanted to be near enough to see everything, and he left the road, ducking through the grass, creeping forward, the fear a palpable presence in his body. Behind him, the moon was rising, full and bright, throwing the top of the ridge into phosphorescent relief, casting a soft light on the entire scene.

He moved silently forward. The sounds grew louder. The mailman was chanting something. At first it sounded like a foreign language, so strange and alien were its rhythms and cadences. But, listening closer as he approached, Doug realized that the words of the chant were English.

"Neither rain nor snow nor sleet nor hail. . . ."

He was chanting the motto of the Postal Service.

The skin on the back of Doug's neck prickled, peach fuzz standing on end. He crept behind a large irregularly shaped boulder and peeked out from behind its bulk. The mailman was leaping in the air, twirling joyfully, not following any steps or preplanned moves, dancing wildly and impulsively. This close, Doug could see that the mailman was dressed in his full postal uniform: shoes and pants, shirt and cap. Brass buttons glinted in the moonlight. Blue-blackness was reflected off the spit-shined shoes.

Doug's mouth was dry and cottony, his heart pounding so loudly that he was sure the mailman would be able to hear it. He had known there was something odd, something strange, something evil about the mailman. But he realized now that he was in far over his head. The mailman's dance was spontaneous and celebratory and could very well have had something to do with witchcraft or satanism, but he had an intuitive feeling that the dance was related to something much worse, something much more primal and unfathomable, something he did not and perhaps could not understand.

The mailman stopped chanting and grinned crazily, perfect teeth seeming to glow in the moonlight, staring raptly up at the sky as his legs moved in impossible steps, his arms mirroring each foot movement. He began to chant again. The Postal Service motto.

The mailman had been dancing for at least the five minutes that Doug had been watching, dancing at full throttle, using all of his strength and all of the energy at his disposal, but he showed no signs of tiring. Indeed, he did not even appear to be sweating.

Doug had no doubt that the mailman could keep this up until dawn.

He began backing away the way he had come, retreating behind the boulder, into the gras s For a second, he thought he saw the mailman look directly at him and laugh, but then he was running, hurrying through the grass and down the road to the Bronco.

He turned around without flipping on his headlights and sped down the Ridge Road toward home.

He had forgotten all about Billy's Big Hunk and his supposed trip to Circle K, but neither Tritia nor Billy said anything to him when he arrived back, and he knew that they knew he'd been lying.

In bed that night, he stared up into the darkness, listening to Tritia's deep even breathing and to the sounds of nocturnal nature. Somewhere near the house a cricket chirped tirelessly, and from the trees in back came the intermittent hooting of an owl.

Usually, he had no trouble falling asleep. He had needed a lot of rest as a child, and even as an adult had always been able to dive into dreamland soon after hitting the sheets. But tonight he lay awake with his eyes closed through Carson, through Letterman, then got up to turn off the TV, thinking perhaps that the noise was keeping him awake, though it had never bothered him before. But the outside noises also seemed to shut off at the same time as the television, and as he lay there in bed, staring up into the darkness, he imagined he heard on the slight breeze the sound of distant chanting.

21

Hobie was awakened by the noise of clanking metal, and it took his sleep-numbed brain a moment to identify the sound. His mind was still half-trapped in his dreamworld, a wonderful place where there was a gigantic swimming pool and he was lifeguard and all the women swam naked. He had taken off his trunks and was just about to join one blond lovely on a beach towel when the noise had intruded on his sleep and returned him to the real world.

The sound came again, a metal clanking, and this time he recognized it. The lid of the mailbox. He frowned, glancing over at the alarm clock next to his bed. Jesus, it was three in the morning. Why the hell was his mail being delivered at three in the morning?

He pushed off the covers and started to get out of bed when he suddenly stopped himself. How had he been able to hear the opening and closing of the mailbox lid? The mailbox was at the far end of the trailer, and the sound it made could be heard only when standing right next to it. And how had the sound woken him up? He was a heavy sleeper and ordinarily he slept through the night without awakening. Even his alarm usually had a difficult time rousing him.

He felt a sudden chill, and he quickly stood up and put on his robe. Something strange was going on here. If the mailman was still outside, he was going to ask that queer little son of a bitch . . .

How had he known it was the mailman?

The chill grew, coldness creeping up his spine. It was such a bizarre thought to begin with, why had he assumed—no, *known*—that the mailman had just made a delivery in the middle of the night? Why hadn't he thought that vandals were tampering with his mailbox? That kids were dropping eggs in there?

136

Hobie walked out to the living room in the front of the trailer. He was not a timid man, but he had to force himself to move forward across the carpet. What he really wanted to do was return to bed and hide his head under the covers.

He opened the door. The street was empty. Moonlight shone on the hoods of his cars in the front yard. He put his hand in the mailbox and withdrew an envelope. It was thick, stuffed. He closed and locked the door behind him, turning on the lamp in the living room and looking at the envelope in the light. There was no return address, but the postmark was Vietnam.

Vietnam?

He examined the postmark more carefully. It was dated June 4, 1968.

A cold sweat broke out on his body. The temperature in the trailer seemed at once too cold and too hot, and he sat down heavily on the couch, staring at the envelope in his hand, not having the nerve to open it.

Vietnam. 1968.

It wasn't possible. A letter could not have been lost for over twenty years and then found and delivered. Could it? He fingered the envelope nervously. Maybe Doug was right. Maybe it was the mailman himself doing this, sending these fake letters to people. Why else would he be delivering them in the middle of the night?

But why would he do such a thing? What could he possibly hope to gain? It was a felony to tamper with the mails. If he got caught, he would go to prison.

Hobie tore open the envelope.

Four photos fell out. As before, they were before and after shots. An Oriental girl, fourteen or fifteen, head and vagina shaved bald, on all fours in a dark and dirty room. The same girl, legs amputated and propped in back of her head, face screaming with agony and terror. An even younger girl, possibly Asian, possibly white, tied spread-eagled to stakes embedded in the dirt, dark-green jungle behind her. The same girl, eviscerated, eyes wide and unseeing, mouth frozen in a rictus of tortured pain.

Hobie felt his bowels contract. The fear was strong within him. His palms were sweaty, his hands shaking, and the paper rattled noisily as he held up the letter, but he forced himself to read it:

Bro,

Things here are getting pretty hairy. We're out of the cities and into the villages. The damn jungle is really thick, green everywhere as far as you can fucking see. Even the sky's starting to look kind of greenish. We don't know where the VC is or when they're going to attack. It's a tense scene. Everything here makes you jump. We've been waiting on edge for something to happen just like we were told, but the sergeant decided that the best defense is a good offense and the other day we went out on our own. You can see the pictures. A guy named Mac took them and developed them. It was a VC village. The men were all gone, but their wives and daughters were there and you know what they wanted. Lots of good healthy American dick. We couldn't just leave them, though. They'd be able to tell the others which way we'd gone, so after we were finished with them we silenced them. You can see the pictures. Gotta go. You can tell Dad, but don't tell Mom. I'll write her a letter when I get a chance.

Dan

Hobie stared at the letter a long time after he'd finished reading it. It was from Dan. There was no doubt about that. Even after all these years, he still recognized his brother's handwriting. But the hardness, the insensitivity, the casual approach to raping and killing, that was something entirely unlike Dan.

He found himself thinking for some reason of a time when he was eight or nine and he and one of his friends had been pouring salt on a snail, watching it dissolve. Dan had seen them and had burst into tears, crying for the snail and its now fatherless family, and it had taken both their mother and father to console him.

Hobie wanted to cry now, out of sadness for the loss of his brother, which even this tentative connection made once again real and immediate, and out of sadness for the change that had occurred within the boy before he died, a change that neither he nor his parents had ever seen.

What would Dan have been like had he come back?

Hobie put down the letter and scooped up the photographs. His gaze fell upon the eviscerated pubescent. The fear which had receded for a moment returned full-force, and he quickly reached over and turned on the lamp next to the couch, clicking the switch until the bulb was on the third and highest wattage. The light successfully evaporated the shadows in the room but could do nothing to dim the shadows stalking him from within.

He'd had enough of this. Doug was right. Something was definitely screwy here, and tomorrow morning he was going to go over to the post office and find out what it was. Find out why he was getting twenty-year-old letters and photographs, and why they were being delivered in the middle of the fucking night. He'd demand that Howard do something, and if the old man didn't want to, well, then, he'd damn well better have his insurance paid up.

Hobie folded the letter and put it back in the envelope, shoving the pictures in with it. Half of him wanted to crumple up the letter, rip the photos, and throw the whole thing away, but another part of him wanted to save it all, to keep this last memento of Dan, and he put the envelope on the coffee table. He'd think about it later, decide what to do in the morning.

He was about to get up, turn the light off, and go back into the bedroom when he heard the sound of footsteps shuffling outside the door. Fear flared within him, and he sat unmoving, afraid even to breathe. A low metal clanking told him that the mailbox had been opened and closed.

Another letter delivered.

He knew he should jump up and confront the mailman, rush outside and beat the crap out of the scrawny faggoty bastard, but he was afraid to so much as acknowledge his presence. He shut his eyes, muscles tense, trembling within, until he heard the sound of retreating footsteps, the purring sound of a fading engine.

He sat there until dawn, afraid to return to bed, afraid to look into the mailbox, afraid to move, and it was only the sound of his alarm ringing at six o'clock that forced him to finally leave the couch.

22

Doug sat in the hard-backed chair, glaring at the police chief. "I saw it!"

"Okay, let's assume that the mailman was dancing in the dark. So what? It's not against the law to dance. Dancing is considered a legitimate form of self-expression."

"Don't play games with me. There're some weird fucking things going on in this town, and you're giving me this piddly-ass bullshit."

The chief eyed him coolly. "The law is not 'piddly-ass bullshit,' Mr. Albin. I am well aware of your opinions on this subject, and I'll be honest and tell you that we are pursuing all avenues in our investigations."

Mike Trenton, next to the chief, stared silently down at the table.

"Don't patronize me with that Jack Webb crap. You know as well as I do that something strange is going on here."

"I don't tell you how to teach; don't you tell me how to do my job." The chief stood up. "I would appreciate it if you would stay out of police business. We are fully capable of handling—"

" 'Fully capable?' "

"That is all, Mr. Albin." The chief put his hands on the table and leaned forward. "I've wasted enough of my morning talking to you and listening to your theories. Please do not harass this department again or you'll find yourself charged with obstruction of justice. Do I make myself understood?"

Doug looked across at Mike, but the young cop was still looking down at the table, refusing to meet his gaze. "Perfectly," he said.

Doug spent the rest of the day the way he'd wanted to spend the entire summer—sitting on the porch, reading. But try as he might, he could not relax and enjoy himself. He knew he had screwed things up royally at the police station, and the knowledge that he might have lent the mailman legitimacy in the eyes of the police gnawed at him. He should have known better. He should have been more cautious, should have at least maintained the appearance of calm rationality. Instead, he had ranted and raved like a fanatic.

He put down his book and stared out at the trees. Was it possible that he was reading into events interpretations that weren't there? That he really was suffering from some sort of obsessive delusion?

No.

He had seen the proof with his own eyes.

A bluebird flitted from tree to tree, searching for food, and he watched it impassively. Many of his fellow teachers, he knew, lived in little academic worlds of their own, completely disassociated from the life around them. He could not do that. It would be nice if he could, but fortunately, or unfortunately, he lived in the real world. He was affected by politics, by economics, by the weather.

By the mailman.

That was one thing he'd learned the past two weeks: how much he was affected by the mail, how much the mail intruded on all aspects of his life.

"Doug!"

He looked up. Trish was standing in the doorway, holding open the screen.

"You want to have lunch on the porch or inside?"

He shrugged noncommittally and picked up the book from his lap.

A moment later, he felt Trish's hand on his arm. "Why don't we go to Sedona for the day, get away from all this? We're both letting it affect us far too much."

He nodded slowly. "You're right."

"It would do us good to get away."

"Yeah. We can go up Oak Creek Canyon to Flagstaff. They have a real post office there. Maybe I can talk to—"

"No," she said firmly. "I mean, get away from *this*. All this craziness. It seems like the mail's the only thing we think about or talk about anymore. Let's just take Billy and go to Sedona and have a nice day's vacation, like we used to. We'll eat, shop, and be typical tourists. How does that sound?"

"It sounds good," he admitted.

"Are you willing to give it a try?"

He nodded.

"So, do you want to eat inside or on the porch?"

"On the porch."

She headed back toward the open door. "Food's on its way."

They left early the next morning, stopping first by the bakery for donuts, coffee, and chocolate milk. Trish was right, Doug thought as he drove out of town. Maybe they needed a short vacation, needed to get away in order to gain some perspective. The trees sailed by as he kept pace with the speed limit. Already he felt easier, happier, more relaxed than he had in weeks. It was as if the mantle of responsibility he had placed upon himself had been left behind at the town limits. Although he knew it would be waiting for him when he got back, he was grateful to be rid of it even temporarily and was determined to enjoy the day.

The forest grew thicker as they headed north. The narrow highway wound between cliffs and into gorges, following the lay of the land. Subforests of small saplings grew in the shade of huge ponderosas. Low bushes covered all available space. Here and there, they could see the stark leafless skeletons of trees hit by lightning, bare branches contrasting sharply with the surrounding lushness. Once, near a small pond in a grassy meadow, they saw a deer, frozen in place by the terror of seeing their car.

Then the trees tapered off, segueing from forest to high desert, and after another hour, the road hit Black Canyon Highway.

"Burger King," Billy said as they passed a sign that said it was forty miles to Sedona. "Let's eat at Burger King."

It was the most interest he'd shown in anything all day, and Doug was about to say okay, but Tritia said firmly, "No, we're going to eat at Tlaquepaque."

"Not that place again," Billy groaned.

"We haven't been there in over a year," his mother told him.

"Not long enough."

"You be quiet."

They were all silent after that, listening to the hum of the Bronco's wheels and the sounds of static and country music

from the station in Flagstaff. Fifteen minutes after they
passed the turnoff for Montezuma's Castle, Doug pulled off
Black Canyon Highway and headed down the two-lane road
that led to Sedona. Of the three approaches to the town,
this was the most spectacular. There was no gradual shift in
the color of the rocks as there was coming in from Camp
Verde, and there were no obscuring plants and trees as
there were along the road through Oak Creek Canyon. The
land here was tailor-made for western movies: great open
expanses strategically broken by the dramatic shapes of the
red rock cliffs. The colors were vivid: blue sky, white clouds,
green trees, red rocks, sharp contrasts that could not be
captured by any camera.

They drove past Bell Rock and past Frank Lloyd Wright's
Church of the Holy Cross, the road gradually hugging closer
to the creek and the cliffs as the first shops and resorts
appeared.

They went directly to Tlaquepaque, a Spanish-styled com-
plex of galleries, shops, and boutiques located in a wooded
spot at the edge of Oak Creek. They strolled through the
shops, taking their time. Billy soon grew bored and ran
ahead, checking out the tiled fountains that seemed to be in
every courtyard and counting the coins in the water while
surreptitiously examining the bathing-suited mannequins in
the clothes store windows. Tritia fell in love with a Dan
Namingha print she saw in one of the galleries, and while
she and Billy continued on ahead, Doug doubled back on
the pretext of going to the bathroom and bought the print,
hiding it under a blanket in back of the car.

As Tritia had promised, they ate lunch in the outdoor
patio of the small Mexican restaurant, listening to the bur-
ble of the creek. Their view was limited by the trees and the
courtyard, but they could still see hills of red rock, the color
made more brilliant in contrast with the green foliage.

It was a relaxing lunch, and for a moment Doug was
almost able to forget about the mail, to forget about everything that had happened recently in Willis. Then a blue-
suited postal carrier, brown bag slung over his shoulder,
stopped off and handed a stack of envelopes to the girl
behind the cash register. The mailman smiled at the girl,
seemingly normal and friendly, but for Doug the mood was
spoiled, and as he ate his chili relleno, he watched the
mailman make the rounds of all the shops.

*   *   *

The trip home was uneventful. Billy slept in the back seat while he and Trish stared out at the passing scenery and listened to an old Emerson, Lake & Palmer tape. They passed the green sign that announced the Willis town limit a little after four, and Doug drove past Henry's Garage and the Ponderosa Realty office, but just beyond the Texaco station, the road was blocked by two police cars with flashing lights. A single policeman stood next to each car, along with a crowd of motorists who had not been allowed to pass the barrier. Several local residents milled around nearby. Doug saw at the edge of the crowd the brown uniform of a member of the sheriff's posse.

He pulled to a stop in back of a battered jeep and told Trish and Billy to wait in the car as he got out to investigate. As he approached the makeshift blockade, he realized that one of the policemen was Mike Trenton. He strode up to the young cop. "Mike, what happened?"

"Please stay back, Mr. Albin. We can't let you through."

"What happened?"

"Ben Stockley went crazy. He took a pistol into the bank about an hour ago and started shooting."

"Oh my God," Doug breathed. "Was anyone hurt?"

The police officer's face was pale, tense. "Fourteen people are dead, Mr. Albin."

23

The murders made national news. All three of Phoenix's network affiliates sent vans and reporters to Willis, and their stories were picked up for the national nightly newscasts. Channel 12 seemed to have the best coverage, and before going to bed Doug watched again as the cameraman's tele-photo lens caught the white flash of Stockley's gun behind the smoked bank window at the precise moment that the editor killed himself. The suicide had happened live during the five-o'clock broadcast, and even the reporter had stopped talking as the sound of the shot echoed with a grim finality. Doug had known then that Stockley was dead, that he was not merely wounded or injured, and he'd watched with increasingly blurred vision as the remaining hostages ran out of the building and the police swarmed in.

By the time the commercial came on, he was openly crying.

He and Stockley had not exactly been friends, but they were closer than acquaintances, and the man's death had affected him strongly. He had respected the editor. And he had liked him. It was strange watching it all on TV, seeing places he knew and people he knew in such a distanced and depersonalized form, and somehow it made him feel more depressed.

In an update, over a shot of Stockley's covered body being wheeled across the bank parking lot to an ambulance, the anchor said that a series of letters had been found in the editor's desk that police believed would give them a clue as to why he had suddenly gone on the killing rampage.

Letters.

Doug shut off the television and walked down the hall to the bedroom, where Trish was already asleep and snoring.

Letters.

The connection was so damn obvious that even that dolt-

145

ish police chief would have to see the pattern. But, no, he remembered seeing news coverage of similar events, friends and neighbors uniformly repeating how they couldn't believe the kind, considerate, normal person they knew could have committed such horrible acts. The man who suddenly went crazy and murdered innocent bystanders was becoming a regular feature of the nightly news; there was nothing really unusual about it anymore.

Of course, Doug himself was one of those people who could not imagine how Stockley could have done such a horrible thing. He had no doubt that the mailman was at the bottom of this, behind it all, but try as he might, he could not imagine anything written in a letter that could so completely send a person around the bend, that could make an ostensibly sane man start killing innocent individuals. Much as he hated to admit it, much as it hurt him to admit it, there probably had been something wrong with Stockley to begin with, some breaking point, some button the mailman had known how and when to push.

There was something even more frightening about that, for just as it was said that everyone had a price, everyone probably also had a breaking point.

Maybe he'd been wrong before. Maybe the mailman hadn't killed Ronda and Bernie Rogers. Maybe they'd killed themselves because the mailman had known exactly what to do to set them off, to push them over the edge. Maybe the mailman knew what that point was for all of them, for everyone in Willis. For himself.

For Tritia.

For Billy.

It was long after midnight when Doug finally fell asleep, and his dreams were filled with white faces and red hair and envelopes.

The next day was hotter than usual; the sky clear, without a trace of cloud to offer the earth temporary shade from the hellish sun. Hobie dropped by just before lunch, dressed in his lifeguard uniform, though it was Wednesday and the pool was closed for cleaning. He came up on the porch, accepted Doug's offer of iced tea. He seemed distracted and ill at ease, unable to concentrate. Doug talked to him about the murders, but though his friend nodded in all the right places, even volunteering an occasional comment or opinion, he seemed not to be listening, the conversation going in one ear and out the other.

Facing Hobie, Doug noticed food stains on the black swimming trunks, and this close he saw that his friend's T-shirt was wrinkled and not as white as it should have been, as though he had been wearing it for days, sleeping in it.

Even Tritia must have noticed something odd about Hobie, for she was not as hostile to him as she usually was. Indeed, as the three of them ate Italian sandwiches on the porch, she seemed downright sympathetic toward him, going out of her way to bring him into the conversation, and for the first time that day he relaxed a little, though he was by no means his usual talkative overbearing self.

After lunch, Tritia returned indoors, and the two men remained on the porch. "So, whatever happened with your books?" Hobie asked, belching loudly. "Ever get an official no from the district?"

Doug nodded. "I sent them a letter back, though, complaining."

"What'd they say?"

"Nothing." Doug smiled wryly. "I guess their reply got lost in the mail."

"Willard Young. Shit, he's nothing but a dick with feet."

"Wrong side of the body. I'd call him an asshole."

"That too."

They were silent for a moment. From inside came the muffled clink of china as Tritia washed their plates.

"Something's happening in this town," Hobie said finally. His voice was low, serious, totally unlike his usual loud bluster, and Doug realized that for the first time he was hearing the sound of fear in his friend's voice.

The emotion had to be transferable, he thought, for he could feel the cold prickling of peach-fuzz hair on his own arms and neck. "What is it?" he asked, keeping his voice neutral.

"You know damn well what it is." Hobie looked at him. "The mailman."

Doug leaned back in his chair. "I just wanted to hear you say it."

Hobie licked his lips, ran a hand through his already tousled hair. "I've been getting letters from my brother," he said.

"You never told me you had a brother."

"He was killed in Vietnam when he was nineteen." Hobie took a deep breath, and when he spoke again, his voice was filled with an uncharacteristic bitterness. "He was only nineteen years old. Richard Nixon's going to burn in hell for that one. He'll join Lyndon Johnson, who's already down there." He looked at Doug. "But the point is, these are letters Dan wrote when he was over there. Letters we never got. Letters that somehow got lost."

Doug didn't know what to say. He cleared his throat. "They might not be real letters," he said. "We've been getting . . . fake letters, letters supposedly from friends but written by the mailman himself. I don't know how he does it or why he does it, but—"

"They're real. They're from Dan." Hobie stared silently out at the trees, as if watching something. Doug followed his friend's gaze, but could see nothing there. When he turned back, he saw that Hobie was on the verge of tears. "I don't know where the mailman found those letters, but they're in Dan's handwriting and they have things in them that only he could know. The only thing is . . . I mean, I'm not a religious guy, you know? But I keep wondering if maybe those letters were supposed to be lost, if we weren't supposed to get them because . . ." He shook his head, wiping his eyes. "I'm learning things about my brother that I didn't want to know. He's a completely different person than I thought he was, than my parents thought he was. Maybe he changed in Vietnam, or maybe . . ." He looked at Doug. "You know, I wish I'd never seen those letters, but now that I got them, now that I'm getting them, I have to keep reading. It's like I don't want to know, but I have to know. Does that make any sense to you?"

Doug nodded. "How many have you gotten?"

"I get one a day." Hobie attempted a halfhearted smile. "Or one a night. They come at night."

The two of them were silent for a moment.

"The mailman's responsible for Stockley," Doug said quietly. "I don't know what he did or why or how he did it, but he did it. He drove him to murder. He somehow got him to go into that bank and start shooting. It sounds crazy, I know. But it's true."

Hobie said nothing.

"I'm not sure if Bernie Rogers killed himself, but I do

know that if he did, he was pushed into it. The same goes for Ronda." He reached over and put his hand on Hobie's shoulder. The gesture felt strange, uncomfortable, but not unnatural. He realized that, in all the years he had known him, this was the first time he had ever touched his friend. "I'm worried about you," he said. "I want you to be careful. I don't know what's happening here, but it seems like the mailman's picking on you for some reason, that—"

"That what? I'll be next?" Hobie snorted derisively, and for a moment he seemed like his old self. "You think I'd actually kill myself? Shit. You got another think coming."

Doug smiled. "I'm glad to hear you say that."

"I'll admit, this thing's got me a little worked up, but I'm still playing with a full deck here. I'm not about to let a little mail drive me over the edge."

"Okay."

"But we gotta do something about that fucker, you know?" Hobie's voice was serious, intense. He looked directly into Doug's eyes, and what Doug saw there as he looked back frightened him. He glanced quickly away.

"You're with me on this, right? I mean, you're the one who first found out about him."

"Yes," Doug said. "But . . ."

"But what?"

"Just don't do anything stupid, okay? We'll get him, but just don't do anything dangerous. Be careful."

Hobie stood up. "I have to go. I have to get back to the pool."

"The pool's closed today," Doug reminded him gently.

"Yeah," Hobie said. He shook his head absentmindedly as he walked across the porch and down the steps. "I been forgetting a lot of things lately."

"Be careful," Doug said again as his friend got into the truck. Tritia came out on the porch and stood next to him, wiping her hands on a dishtowel. Both of them waved as Hobie backed up and swung onto the road.

Hobie did not wave back.

24

Doug and Tritia walked out to the mailbox together.

It was strange how such a benign object, an inanimate hunk of hollow metal, could within such a short time have taken on such a malevolent, threatening quality. They walked across the crunching gravel slowly, solemnly, with trepidation, as if approaching a gallows or guillotine. They said nothing, not speaking, almost afraid to speak.

The morning was overcast, unusual for late June, and Doug wondered if perhaps the rains would come early this year. The thought disturbed him somehow. It was not unheard of, not even that unusual, but the fact that all of this strangeness was accompanied by a shift in traditional weather patterns gave the entire situation a broader, more cosmic quality. Ordinarily, he would have dismissed such an obviously ludicrous idea, but these were not ordinary times. Both Trish and Billy had been withdrawn and uncommunicative the past few days, Billy downright sullen, and he suspected that each of them had seen something, though neither would admit it.

That was scary, Doug thought. They had always been a close family, had always shared everything, but now they were drifting apart, becoming more private, more closed with one another. And he didn't know what to do about it.

They reached the mailbox. As if it was a ritual they had performed before or an act they had practiced and worked out ahead of time, Doug opened the box and Tritia withdrew the envelopes.

There were two of them, one for each.

Tritia looked at him questioningly, handing him his envelope.

In answer, Doug tore it open. The envelope was empty.

Tritia's face was pinched, tense, as she opened hers. There was a letter inside and she took it out, unfolding it. She scanned the page, face blank, unreadable, then looked up at him. "Who," she asked, "is Michelle?"

Doug was puzzled. "Michelle?"

She handed him the letter and he read it over. Halfway down the page, he knew the Michelle to whom she was referring. Michelle Brunner, an old girlfriend from college, the only woman besides Tritia with whom he'd ever had what could be legitimately termed a sexual relationship. He frowned as he continued reading. The letter made it sound as though he and Michelle had been carrying on a hot and heavy affair for years, seeing each other whenever they could, though in reality he had not seen her since his Junior year in college, two semesters before he'd met Tritia.

"It's fake," he said, folding the letter.

"Who's Michelle?"

"Michelle Brunner. I told you about her. The crazy one?"

"The slut?"

Doug smiled wanly. "That's her."

"She still writes to you?"

"You know who wrote this," he said, his smile fading. "And it wasn't Michelle."

She nodded tiredly. "So what are we going to do? This is just getting worse."

"We've got to put a stop to this. After breakfast, I'm going to talk to Howard. And if I can't get him to do anything, I'm going to call the main post office in Phoenix. I don't know why I didn't do it before. I should have called them the first thing. I should have sent them samples of the letters we found in the creek—"

"They never would've got there."

"That's true."

"And how are you going to tell them everything? You think they'll believe you? They'll just think you're some paranoid crank."

"No, I won't tell them everything. But I'll tell them about the mail delivery. At the very least, they'll transfer the mailman somewhere else."

"And if he won't go?"

The question hung, unanswered, between them.

"Come on," Doug said. "Let's go have breakfast."

The line in front of the post office was long, the patrons irate. Doug walked slowly across the parking lot. The peo-

ple in line looked different than usual. Shabbier, seedier.
They were dressed not in the nice clothes they usually wore
when going into town but in older dirtier garb—painting
clothes, work pants, torn undershirts. There was grease on
the arms and faces of some of the men, and few of the
women had bothered to comb their hair or take it out of
rollers. One old woman was wearing a bathrobe and slippers.

Even from here, Doug could hear the menacing tone of
the crowd's conversational buzz. The people in line were
not chatting of the news, sports, or weather, not catching up
on local gossip. They were not even sharing complaints or
grievances. They were venting their anger, telling and retell-
ing the same events in order to keep that anger fueled,
speaking of canceled insurance, threatened lawsuits for non-
payment of bills, problems caused by the mail.

Instead of standing outside of the post office in line, Doug
walked through the second of the double doors into the
building. He looked around. Things had changed since the
last time he'd been here. The place seemed darker, dirtier.
The blinds over the windows were drawn, and one of the
recessed bars of fluorescent light had burned out. The swamp
cooler was off again, and the room was sweltering, the
humid prestorm air augmented by the sour odor of mingled
sweat and breath. The posters on the walls were different as
well, he noticed. The Love stamp poster that had hung
forever on the wall above the forms table had been replaced
by a poster for a new fifty-cent commemorative guillotine
stamp. The poster, white against a black background, de-
picted a large wooden guillotine, metal blade gleaming as
hordes of vicious-looking people crowded around it. On the
side wall, where Howard had traditionally hung advertise-
ments for upcoming stamps featuring famous people, was a
large poster of an Adolf Hitler stamp and, next to that, a
stamp featuring the demented visage of Charles Manson.

At the counter was the mailman, red hair practically
glowing in the dim room.

The hair was prickling at the back of Doug's neck, but he
refused to let the mailman see his fear. He walked up to the
front counter. "I want to talk to Howard," he said as
forcefully as he could.

The mailman eyed him coldly. "I'm helping someone else
right now. If you'll just wait your turn in line—"

"Just tell me whether or not Howard's here."

"You'll have to wait your turn."

"Yeah," several people echoed.

"He's not here," a man in line said. "I heard Mr. Smith tell someone else he's not here."

Doug turned to look at the owner of the voice. It was a person he did not know, a small timid man sandwiched between a scowling woman and a blank-faced teenager. The man was obviously not used to speaking up or speaking out. He had the naturally apologetic features of the perpetually frightened, but there was determination in his face, anger in his eyes, and at that moment he looked to Doug almost heroic. Someone else was willing to fight back against the tyranny of the mailman.

"Thank you," Doug said.

The small man grinned. "No problem."

The mailman was already helping the customer in line, pretending as though nothing had happened. Doug walked out the door and back outside. He crossed the small parking lot, taking his keys out of his pocket. He would go to Howard's house and catch up with him there. It was obvious to him now that, like the rest of them, the postmaster was afraid of his underling, but maybe he'd be able to talk Howard into taking some action. Something sure as hell had to be done.

He opened the door of the car and got in. He hadn't noticed it from the outside, but his windshield, he saw now, was covered with spit. Saliva dripped from several spots on the glass. He looked over at the line outside the building, trying to determine who had done it, but no one glanced in his direction at all.

He turned on the wiper/washer and backed out of the parking lot, pulling onto the street. He headed toward Howard's.

The postmaster lived on a low hill in one of the nicer sections of town. His house was in what passed for a subdivision in Willis, and was not far from the post office. Unlike the area in which Hobie lived, the single-story homes on Howard's street were all well kept up and well taken care of.

Doug parked the car on the street in front of the white clapboard house. He turned off the ignition. There was no sign of Howard's car, but that meant nothing. It could very well be parked in the garage.

He got out of the car and headed up the front walk. The grass, he noticed, was yellowish brown, not green like the lawns in front of the other houses. Not a good sign. Like many older people, Howard had always been a fanatic about maintaining his yard.

He stepped onto the front stoop and rang the bell, listening for the ring. Nothing. He knocked on the door instead. He waited for a few moments, then pounded again. "Howard!" he called, "are you home?"

There was no sound from within the house, and after three more tries and five more minutes he stepped off the stoop and moved over to the large living-room windows. The curtains were closed, but they were sheer and he figured he'd be able to see something inside. No such luck. Through the material he could see nothing. The interior of the house was much too dark and monochromatic for individual elements to be differentiated. He moved around the side of the house to the dining-room window, then to the kitchen, then around to the back bedroom, hoping at least that a drape would be parted, open wide enough for him to see inside, but the curtains were all firmly and carefully shut. He tried the back door, but it was locked.

"Howard!" he called, knocking.

No answer.

There were other houses flanking Howard's, but their owners were either inside or at work, and the entire neighborhood seemed empty and abandoned. It gave Doug the creeps. He felt as though he was in one of those movies where the sun flared or some other pseudo-scientific catastrophe had occurred and he was the last man on earth, left alone to wander through the perfectly preserved artifacts of an otherwise untouched world.

A dog barked a few houses away, and Doug jumped. Jesus, he was getting skittish.

"Howard!" he called again.

No answer.

Either the postmaster wasn't here, or he was so sick he couldn't answer the door, or he was hiding.

No matter what, he would give the front door one more try, and if he didn't get an answer, he would call the post office in Phoenix. He walked back around to the front of the house and was about to knock on the front door one last time when he saw a white envelope on the brown straw mat at his feet. It had not been there before. Of that he was certain.

He picked up the envelope. His name was on the front, written in a shaky, childish scrawl. He tore the envelope open and pulled out the piece of paper inside. On it were written two words in that same shaky hand:

Stay Away

He pounded on the door. "Howard!" he called. "Let me in. I know what's happening. Howard!"

But the door remained stubbornly closed, the curtains unmoving, and for all of his effort he heard no sound from inside the house.

He got the number of the main branch of the post office from Directory Assistance and dialed from the bedroom. He closed the door with his foot. Billy was in the kitchen with Tritia, helping her to make bread, and he didn't want the boy to hear the conversation. A woman's voice came on the line. "United States Postal Service Information, how may I direct your call?"

"I want to complain about one of your mailmen."

"Just a moment, sir. Let me transfer you to our Personnel department."

Doug listened to a few seconds' worth of innocuous Muzak before a man's voice came on the line. "Hello, this is Jim. How may I help you?"

"I want to complain about one of your mailmen."

"Could I have your name and zip code?"

"My name's Doug Albin. My zip code is 85432. I live in Willis."

"Willis? I'm sorry, sir, but if you have any complaints you should direct them to the postmaster in your area."

"That's the problem. I can't get a hold of my postmaster. Besides, our mail service has deteriorated so much that I think it's time you knew about it."

"Let me connect you to my supervisor."

"I'd—" Doug began, but there was a click. More Muzak. Mantovani Beatle songs.

A minute or so later another man came on the line. "Chris Westwood."

"We're having a lot of problems here with our mail. I want someone to do something about it."

"You're in Willis?"

"That's right."

"What exactly is the trouble?"

"Our mailman is dumping our mail by a creek instead of delivering it."

Westwood's voice became more concerned. "That is a serious charge, Mr.—"

"Albin. Doug Albin."

"Mr. Albin. That doesn't sound very likely to me—"

"I don't care if it's likely or not," Doug said, an edge of exasperation creeping into his voice. "That's exactly what has happened, and there are many witnesses."

"Well, there's nothing really that I can do, but I can fill out a complaint form for you if you wish. Once the complaint is processed, an investigator will be sent out to look into the problem."

"That's fine," Doug said.

Westwood asked his full name, address, occupation, and other personal information that he supposedly wrote onto the complaint form. "Now do you happen to know the carrier's name and number?"

"His name's John Smith. That's all I know."

"John Smith. John Smith. Let me check." Doug thought he heard the soft clicking of computer keys. "I'm sorry, but we have no John Smith working in Willis. I have listed here Howard Crowell as postmaster, and Robert Ronda, carrier."

"Ronda committed suicide over a month ago."

"I'm sorry. We have no record of that here. It's not listed on our computer."

"Well, he was transferred here from Phoenix. Could you just see if you could find any John Smiths working in the Phoenix area?"

"Just a minute. I'll browse by name instead of zip code." There was a pause. "No, Mr. Albin. There is no John Smith working for the post office anywhere in Arizona."

Doug said nothing.

"Did you hear me, Mr. Albin?"

He hung up the phone.

25

The town was unusually subdued for the Fourth of July. Fewer than a third of the people who usually came to the annual Picnic in the Park showed up this year, and even the Jaycee's fireworks display was sparsely attended. Doug made Trish and Billy stay for both the daytime celebration and the fireworks, though neither of them wanted to, and while he pretended to have a good time for their sakes, he noticed a definite attitude change among their attending neighbors and acquaintances, and it unnerved him more than he was willing to admit. People he'd known for years, even other teachers and ex-students, seemed cold and distant, almost hostile. No one seemed to be having a good time.

He wasn't feeling that good himself. He'd gone to the police yesterday with his new information about the mailman, but they had treated him as if he was a chronic complainer, someone who consistently came to them with false information based on his own paranoid delusions. He had asked to see Mike but was told that the young policeman was off for the day, and instead he told his story to Jack Shipley, who humored him with the sort of condescending agreement usually reserved for drunks and crazies. As patiently and rationally as he knew how, he explained the facts, told Shipley that he believed impersonating a postal worker was a punishable crime and that everything he said could be verified by calling the main branch of the post office in Phoenix. The officer had said he would follow up on the information Doug had given him, but it was clear that he probably would not.

What could he do when the whole town was going to hell in a handbasket and the damn police were too blind to see it and too dumb to act on it when it was pointed out to them?

He could not help wondering how the mailman was spending his time today, what he was doing for the Fourth. There was no mail delivery on the holiday, but somehow he just couldn't see the mailman eating hot dogs and apple pie and participating in patriotic celebrations.

The day was hot and at the afternoon softball game the mood was ugly. There were barely enough men for two teams, and it was clear that most of those who had volunteered to play had done so out of obligation. The game was hard and dirty, with balls thrown intentionally at batters, hits aimed purposefully at pitchers. The spectators seemed to thrive on the nastiness and were soon yelling for blood. In the past, the competition had been light and friendly, with neighbors and families good-naturedly cheering on their teams. But today it was a cutthroat crowd, bent on violence. A fistfight broke out among two of the players, another among members of the audience. No one moved to stop either brawl.

Doug, Tritia, and Billy stayed for only a while, then moved on to the barbecue. The food was bad: hot dogs and hamburgers dry and burnt, Cokes flat and warm. The familiar sight of Ben Stockley, intruding on family get-togethers with his camera, bothering the town officials with detailed questions they could not answer, conspicuously doing his job on a day when all others were having a holiday, was also missed; it contributed to the rather grim atmosphere that prevailed over this Fourth.

Irene showed up late in the afternoon, as she always did, and Tritia motioned her over. The old woman alone seemed to be in good spirits, and she helped cheer the three of them up, telling tall tales about holidays of the past as the four of them sat together at a picnic table under the pines.

That night, in the parking lot after the fireworks, Bill Simms and Ron Lazarus got into a shouting match and then a fight as their respective families looked on. They were rolling in the dirt, kicking and punching and screaming obscenities, and it took Doug and two other men to pull the two apart.

"You killed my dog!" Simms screamed. "You fucker!"

"I never touched your goddamn dog, you asshole!" Lazarus spit at the other man, a glob of saliva that landed harmlessly in the dirt at his feet. "But I wish I had."

Doug held on to Simms. He could feel the man's muscles straining as he struggled to break free. The other men held Lazarus. One of the women ran to get a policeman and returned with Mike Trenton, who warned the two fighters that their butts would be thrown in jail if they didn't knock this crap off right now.

The men angrily stomped off to their respective cars, the crowd dispersed, and Doug and the young cop stood looking at each other. The policeman looked away, unable to meet Doug's eyes.

"I guess they told you I came by."

Mike nodded. "I tried to call you this morning, but there was no answer."

"I was home. We were all home."

The policeman shrugged. "I called twice. No one answered."

"Why did you call?"

"I wanted to tell you that I'd interviewed Mr. Smith and that I called Phoenix."

"And?"

"And he denies everything. I didn't use your name, of course. I—"

"What about the post office? What did they say?"

"We couldn't verify what you said. Their computers were down. They'll call us back when they can access the information."

"What do you think?"

There was only a slight hesitation. "I believe you."

"But the chief doesn't."

"But the chief doesn't."

Doug looked over at Billy and Tritia. "Why don't you go over to the car? I'll meet you there in a sec."

"Keys," Tritia said, holding out her hand.

He dug the keys out of his pocket and tossed them to her. She caught them in midair and, her arm around Billy's shoulder, headed toward the Bronco. Doug turned back toward the policeman. "He's not human, Mike."

There was silence between them.

"I got another letter from my fiancée yesterday. She said she wants to break up again."

"It's fake. You know that."

"I called her, but she hung up on me. Wouldn't even let me talk."

"Do you think—"

"I think he's sending her letters." The policeman took a deep breath. Around them, people were walking to their cars, heading for home. "I'm not sure whether I should try to stay out of his way, to stay as far away from you as possible, or whether I should come down hard on his ass and make him pay."

"You don't need me to tell you. You know the right thing to do."

"What right thing? You want to know the truth? I don't care about doing the right thing. I care about keeping Janine. That's what I care about. That's all I care about."

"I don't believe that," Doug said softly. "And neither do you. That's why you're talking to me right now."

"I don't know."

"You know, Mike."

"But there's nothing we can do. Not really. Nothing we can pin on him. Nothing we can prove. I'd like to be able to trip him up on something, to throw him in jail, but I can't."

"He's tampering with the mails. Get him for that."

"No proof."

"There will be when the post office calls you back."

"What if there isn't?"

"People are dying here, Mike. We have to do something."

"Yeah? What do you expect me to do? Hang up my badge? Go out and gun him down?"

"No. Of course not." But a small frightening voice within him was saying, *Yes yes*.

"I'm keeping my eyes open, like I promised. But I can't guarantee that I'll do any more than that. I'm a police officer, not a vigilante."

The young cop was looking for reassurance, Doug knew, but he had none to give. When it came to something like this, older did not necessarily mean wiser. He was just as afraid as the policeman and just as much in the dark about what to do. Still, he nodded. "That's all I ask."

"I have to get back to work. It's a rough crowd tonight."

"Yeah. I have to go too." Doug started to turn, but he looked back again. "Be careful, Mike. If he's sending letters to your fiancée, he knows about you."

The policeman said nothing, but moved away, between the cars, toward the grandstand. Silently, Doug walked back to the Bronco, where Trish and Billy were waiting.

He drove home slowly and carefully, though the anticipated drunks did not materialize. There were very few cars on the road, in fact, and most of the houses they passed as they drove through town were dark. He looked at the clock

THE MAILMAN 161

on the dash. Nine-thirty. That was strange. People were
usually up and about later than this on an ordinary Friday,
not to mention a holiday. It was like driving through a ghost
town, he thought. And even though Trish and Billy were
with him in the car, he felt a slight tingle of fear.

Willis was changing.

There was no mail on either Saturday or Sunday, and
when Doug went to the store on Monday and saw the
mailman unloading one of the mailboxes, he was gratified to
see that he looked paler than usual, and thinner, if that was
possible. Maybe he's sick, Doug thought. Maybe he's sick
and going to die.

But that was just wishful thinking. It wouldn't happen.

As always, the mailman smiled and waved at him as he
drove past.

26

Billy rode wildly through the brush, thick BMX tires rolling over weeds and rocks, plowing through thin bushes. He and Lane had both signed up weeks ago for the motocross competition, and while he had always planned on winning, it was now a necessity rather than a desire. He didn't really care at this point whether or not he came in first—he just wanted to beat Lane. To beat him bad.

He spun around a large boulder, taking the turn as sharp as he dared without slowing. He and Lane were about equal in skill and experience, and he knew it was going to take a lot of practice and dedication to beat his ex-friend.

But he *was* going to beat him.

He was going to make him eat dirt.

Billy had not been planning to ride anywhere in particular, but he found himself heading down the hill toward the archaeological site. He hadn't been down here since he and Lane had had their falling out, not because he hadn't wanted to, but because Lane had always done most of the talking for the two of them and he felt a little nervous going to the dig by himself.

Today, however, he found himself speeding down the hill toward the narrow valley. Ahead was a small natural ditch carved by runoff, and he yanked up on his handlebars, jumping it. The bike wobbled on the hard landing, but he maintained his pace and balance, pedaling furiously.

The ground leveled off, and he slowed as he approached the site, not wanting to startle anyone. When he reached the trees on the perimeter of the dig, he hopped off his bike and walked it the rest of the way.

But there was no one there.

The site was deserted.

He looked around. The university had not been scheduled to conclude their excavation until sometime in late August, but obviously they had decided to leave early. Billy's first thought was that they had all taken a day off, gone to town or to the lake or to one of the streams, but it was clear that they had packed everything up, finished their work, and gone home. Nothing was left save a few stakes embedded in the ground and a scattering of torn envelopes on the dirt.

Billy frowned. Something was wrong here. There had been no litter left behind on the dig last summer. None at all. The professor's motto had been "Pack it in, pack it out," and he'd made sure that his students left the area as close as possible to the way they'd found it.

He was suddenly scared, and he realized that he was all alone out here, that the closest person to him was up at the top of the hill. It came over him instantly, this feeling of being isolated, cut off from everything and everyone, and he quickly turned his bike around . . .

And he saw the mailman.

The mailman was striding toward him across the dirt, his hair a fiery red against the green background. There was no mail sack on his back, no letters in his hand, and the fact that he had come here to do something other than deliver mail scared Billy more than anything else. He jumped on his bike, swung it around, and began to pedal.

But he did not see one of the excavation trenches, and his front tire slid sideways, spilling him onto the ground. His head connected with the hard dirt. He was stunned but not hurt, and he jumped to his feet. The mailman was standing right next to him, smiling.

"Billy," the mailman said quietly, horrifyingly gently.

He wanted to run but was powerless to do so. All the will seemed to have been drained from his body. The forest around the archaeological site seemed heavy and impenetrably thick, like a tropical jungle.

The mailman put a hand on Billy's shoulder. His touch was soft and tender, like a woman's. "Come here," he said.

He led Billy with unused force across the empty dig to a large pit at the far end of the clearing. Billy could not remember seeing the pit before, and he tensed as the two of them drew closer to it. He knew he didn't want to see what the mailman wanted to show him.

"Look," the mailman said, smiling.

The pit was filled with bodies and parts of bodies, eyes staring upward, hands fallen limply over torsos. In the split second before he shut his eyes against the horror, Billy saw an alternating color scheme of pink flesh, red blood, and white bone, and he thought he saw, somewhere near the top of the pile near his feet, amid a tangle of arms and legs, fingers and toes, the bottom portion of the professor's face.

Billy awoke from the nightmare drenched with sweat, his mouth dry. For a second, the loft seemed strange, facing the wrong direction, the individual elements of its composition, the furniture and posters, slightly off. Then his brain kicked into its awake mode and everything fell neatly into place.

Well, not everything.

For the images of his dream stayed with him, not as something he had viewed secondhand, like a movie or a regular dream, but as a five-sensory recollection of an actual event, something he had actually experienced, and try as he might to repeat to himself, "It's only a dream It's only a dream It's only a dream," something inside him told him it was not.

27

"It's gotten to the point," Irene said, "where I'm afraid to open the mail."

Tritia, seated on the antique love seat, nodded. "I know what you mean. The first thing I do these days is check the return address. If it's unfamiliar, I toss it."

"I throw away all mail, even letters from people I've known for years. The last one I opened was from Bill Simms, accusing me of poisoning his dog. Can you believe that?" The old woman licked her lips nervously, and Tritia realized that her friend was frightened. Badly frightened. She frowned. Irene was not a woman who was easily scared, and Tritia was unnerved by the sight of her in such an uncharacteristic state. Something other than a few hate letters had made her so fearful.

Tritia put down her glass of iced tea. "What is it?" she asked. "What's the matter? This is more than just Bill Simms."

Irene shook her head. "Nothing."

"It's not nothing, dammit! Tell me."

Surprised by the vehemence of her reaction, Irene stared at her. Then she nodded. "Okay," she said. "You want to know what it is? Come here." Her voice was low, conspiratorial, tinged with more than a hint of fear.

Tritia followed her down the hallway into the closed room that had been her husband's den. It was now simply a storage room, filled with the physical forms of painful past memories, items either owned by or associated with her late husband. Tritia looked around. She had never been in this room before, had never even been brave enough to ask about it. Now she saw that it was dominated by floor-to-ceiling bookshelves that lined two opposing walls. Clothes and personal effects were piled high on an old oak dining

table that had been placed in the middle of the room next to
other unused pieces of furniture.

"There," Irene said. Her voice was shaking.

Tritia followed the old woman's pointing finger. On top
of the open rolltop desk, next to a dusty pile of old western
paperbacks, was a small box still half-wrapped in the brown
butcher paper in which it had been delivered. There was an
irregular trail of clearness, a skid mark through the dust on
top of the desk, which made it obvious that the box had
been thrown there in haste.

Irene stood in the doorway, tightly grasping the brass
doorknob. "It was sent to me yesterday," she said. She
swallowed with obvious difficulty. Her hands were shaking,
and Tritia could hear her uneven breathing in the silence of
the room. "There's a toe in there."

"What?"

"There's a toe in the box."

Tritia moved slowly forward. Her own heart was pounding loudly. She reached the desk, picked up the box, and
opened it.

She had known what to expect, but it was still a shock. A
toe, a human toe, lay in the bottom of the box, unnervingly
white against the brown cardboard. It was such a small thing
that she would have expected it to look fake, to look rub-
bery. But it was distressingly real. She could see the smooth
rounded tip, the curved lines around the joints, the individual hairs growing from the flat skin below the pinkish nail at
the top. It had been severed cleanly, cut somehow, but
there was no blood, not even a drop.

Tritia put the box down, feeling slightly nauseous. The
toe rolled over, and she could see red muscle, blue vein,
and a core circle of white bone. The room suddenly seemed
too closed, too cramped, and she backed up, away from the
desk.

"Jasper lost his big toe in a logging accident in 1954,"
Irene said quietly.

The severed joint seemed suddenly more sinister, invested
with a documented past that lent it a decidedly supernatural
aura. Tritia looked at her friend. Irene was pale, frightened,
and for the first time since Tritia had known her she looked
far older than her years.

Irene closed the door as soon as Tritia came out into the
hall, and led the way silently back to the living room. She

picked up her iced tea before sitting down on the sofa. Ice cubes rattled nervously against the glass. "He was working in the Tonto," she explained, "out by Payson, and was doing ax work when he swung and missed and chopped off his big toe. I don't know how he got that toe and missed the others, or how he didn't chop off a whole chunk of his foot, but he chopped off only the toe. He said he was screaming so loud that loggers miles away could hear the echoes through the trees. He said the spurting blood turned the green pine needles all around him red.

"They always had someone with them who knew first aid, because there were always logging accidents like these, and somehow they got the bleeding stopped and took him to the hospital in Payson. They didn't have surgical techniques like they do today, and the doctor said he wouldn't be able to sew the toe back on, even though they brought it with them. He said it would be better to close up the existing wound and let it heal." She was silent for a moment.

"What happened to the toe?" Tritia asked.

"Jasper called me, told me what happened, and I had someone drive me to Payson. I didn't drive in those days. The toe was in a jar in his hospital room, floating in this clear liquid, and he asked me if I wanted to save it, but I couldn't think of anything more repulsive. I hated just seeing it there, and I had a nurse cover the jar while I was in the room. I certainly didn't want a severed toe in my house, so I told him to have the hospital dispose of it." She shook her head at the recollection. "Instead, I found out later, he and his logging buddies got drunk, had a mock funeral in the woods, and buried it." She looked at Tritia, her eyes haunted. "That was a long time ago. There's not many left who even know that story. And I can't figure out how the mailman learned what happened, let alone how he found the toe again or how it could be in such good shape."

"Maybe it's not—" Tritia began.

"It is," Irene said firmly.

"Did you call the police?"

"What for?"

"This is against the law. Some—"

Irene put a hand on her arm. The old woman's fingers felt dry, cold. "Look," she said, "this is not a police matter. This is something private."

"No it's not." Tritia leaned forward. "You know what's

going on in this town. And you know there's no way we can
get the mailman. We have no proof to back up any of our
allegations." She gestured toward the hallway and the den
beyond. "Now we have proof."

"We have nothing. Do you know what will happen? He
will say that he only delivers the mail and is not responsible
for its contents, and he'll deny any knowledge of this. You
know that as well as I do."

Tritia stared into her friend's eyes. She was right. Much
as she hated to admit it, she was right. Irene knew exactly
what the mailman would do.

"At least let me call Doug, tell him. He'll get rid of it for
you. You don't want a—"

"No," Irene said. "I don't want anyone to touch it. And
no one but you will ever see it." She lowered her voice and
Tritia felt a chill creep down her spine. "It's evil."

Tritia nodded, feigning for her friend's sake an understanding she did not feel. Irene was slipping, she thought.
This had pushed her dangerously close to the edge, and if
something else occurred, it might push her all the way over.

Of course, that was exactly what the mailman wanted.

Tritia stood. "I have to go," she said.

"You can't go to the police," Irene said.

"I really think you should tell someone. This isn't right."

"No."

Tritia met her friend's gaze, then sighed. "Okay," she
said. "It's up to you." She walked to the door, turning
around before opening the screen. "Call me if you need
anything," she said. "Anything. Doug and I can be right
over, if there's an emergency."

"Thanks," Irene said. "But I'll be fine." She smiled.
"Maybe I just won't open my mailbox."

"That's probably not a bad idea."

The old woman laughed, and for a moment she sounded
almost normal. "Good-bye, hon," she said. "I'll see you."

Tritia walked slowly down the porch steps. " 'Bye."

She heard the sound of the door being locked behind her
as she walked out to the car, the deadbolt being thrown.

Tritia waved as she drove off, not checking to see if her
wave was returned. She turned onto the street, heading
toward home. She'd known that the mailman was responsible for the deteriorating state of affairs in town, for the
unpaid bills, the misdirected mail, the hate letters, and yes,

probably for the deaths. But the extent to which he was willing to go in order to get someone, the extent to which he was *able* to go in order to get someone, had never been brought home more forcefully than when she had looked in that box and seen the toe. Such random but well-thought-out malevolence was impossible for her to comprehend.

What frightened her even more was the realization that a mailman was the only person who had access to everyone in town, who dealt daily with each household, each individual. She had never been a religious woman, had not even been sure if she believed in such nebulous and culturally variable concepts as "good" and "evil." But she believed now. And she thought that evil had chosen a perfect form in which to do its work. If John Smith had been a preacher or a teacher or a politician, he would not have had access to nearly the number of people he did now and would not have been able to insinuate himself so subtly, so easily, so effortlessly into people's lives.

That bothered her, too. The passiveness of the town. The unwillingness of the people of Willis to face what was happening and do something about it. She and Doug themselves, for all their talk, had done very little to try to block the mailman, to put a stop to his plans. It was as if they were waiting for someone else to take on the responsibility, someone else to solve the problem.

But, then, what could they do? Even though they were aware of what was going on, had tried to effectively gird themselves against it, the mailman had made unwanted inroads into their lives. They had resisted the siren song of the mail, had turned deaf ears and blind eyes to the obvious psychological assaults on themselves, yet the ordeal had still subtly changed the dynamics of their family life. They had not drawn closer in the face of adversity but had, in a sense, retreated into themselves. There were no obvious walls or barriers, relationships were not tense or strained, but the comfortable spirit of joking camaraderie Doug and Billy had always shared was gone, replaced by a friendly but slightly more formal and less intimate set of roles. Her own relationships with Doug and Billy had gone through similar changes. She and Doug were more distant with each other; even their lovemaking seemed less a giving form of loving expression than the gratification of selfish needs, although the outward techniques had changed not at all. And lately she had taken to lecturing Billy in an authoritarian manner she had sworn she would never adopt.

She knew Doug had noticed these differences too, although neither of them had spoken of it to the other. She could see it in his eyes, read it in his attitude. It was expressed more by what he did not say than by what he did. They still talked of current events, household affairs, even, tentatively, of the mailman, but there was a superficiality to their conversations, a superficiality that extended even to subjects and thoughts that were not superficial, a failure to meet and communicate on the deep and important level so necessary to lasting relationships. More than once she'd felt as though they were talking at each other rather than to each other.

And it was the mailman's fault.

But she would not let him win. She refused to let him tear apart her family. It would be easy to succumb, to allow the breach between her and Doug to widen. But she vowed that she would not let things deteriorate any further. She was going to reach out to her husband and son, to put an end to this emotional lethargy, and she was going to force them to do likewise.

Part of her wanted to stop by the post office, to let the mailman know that she was no longer going to put up with his attempts to break her, that she was going to take a stand against him, but she remembered the last time she had tried to confront him, and the emotional clarity of the encounter remained horrifyingly undimmed. A field of goose bumps arose on her bare arms, the peach-fuzz hair at the back of her neck pricked. She was angry now, she was determined, but she was not stupid.

You're nice.

Never again would she go to the post office alone.

Tritia was nearly to the turnoff that led toward home when she realized she had forgotten to pick up food for dinner. She had come to town this afternoon not merely to see Irene, but also to pick up groceries. They hadn't been shopping in days and were in desperate need of milk and butter and other essentials as well as something for tonight's meal.

She made a U-turn, turning back toward the store. Usually, she planned out the family's meals a day in advance, but for the past week or so she'd been too tired and distraught to do anything but throw something together at the last minute, an attitude so entirely out of character for her that she wondered why she hadn't noticed it before. This craziness had affected not only the emotional life of her family but its culinary life as well.

She decided to stop by the delicatessen to see if they had any fresh fish. She was in the mood for trout, and if there'd been a good catch, she'd pick some up for dinner. Barbecued fish sounded wonderful right now.

She pulled into the parking lot of the shopping center. Although the spaces in front of Bayless were filled with cars, she was surprised to see that the area in front of the delicatessen was nearly empty. That was weird. Todd had the finest selection of cheeses and the best fresh fish in town, and usually when Bayless was busy, his store was even more crowded.

She parked in an empty space directly in front of the small store and walked inside.

She noticed the difference immediately. It was nothing she saw, more like something she felt. A tension. A strange uncomfortable feeling in the air that was entirely uncharacteristic of the store's usual atmosphere. She looked around. The deli was empty save for her and Todd behind the counter. She moved forward, examining the meats in the meat counter. She smiled at the shopkeeper, but he did not smile back, and she decided to quickly buy her food and get out of the store.

She pointed toward a selection of fileted trout on ice behind the counter. "Fresh catch?" she asked.

Todd nodded silently.

Her unease increased, and she said quickly, "I'll take three large fish."

The storekeeper opened the back of the counter, pulled out three trout, and placed them on the scale. "Tell your husband I don't appreciate what he's doing," he said.

Tritia frowned. "What are you talking about? What is he doing?"

"Tell him I don't appreciate it at all."

"Don't appreciate what?" Tritia stared at him. "Todd, tell me what's going on here. I don't know what you're talking about."

His reserve broke. He smiled at her as he wrapped the

fish, and there was sadness in the smile. "I know you don't."

"Todd?"

"I believe you. Otherwise you wouldn't be here." He gestured around the empty store. "You're my first customer today."

"What's wrong?" she asked. She leaned forward over the counter. "Is it the mail?"

His face grew stony, cold. "That'll be three-fifty," he said.

"Todd?"

"Three-fifty."

She paid for the fish and walked out of the store. As she backed up in the parking lot, she saw him standing in the doorway, staring after her. It looked as though he was crying.

28

Billy sat in the darkened living room watching TV. *Dick Van Dyke* segued into *Andy Griffith*, which segued into *The Flintstones*, which segued into *The Brady Bunch*. There was something comforting about the unchanging characters of the people on television, a reassuring element in the familiar plots and predicaments of the shows. Outside, things might be getting stranger, more chaotic. But on TV Mike and Carol Brady were still good-naturedly understanding parents trying to quell a war between the sexes that was brewing between their children.

A commercial came on and Billy got up to get something to eat. He had been glued in front of the TV set for most of the past three days, and though he enjoyed watching the shows, he was starting to feel a little restless and stir-crazy. He also felt a little guilty. His parents had never let him watch this much television before, and he could not help feeling that he was doing something wrong, that he should be doing something productive instead of wasting his time vegetating in front of the tube.

But his parents didn't seem to care. They were too preoccupied with other matters. His dad had not even commented when he'd walked through the house a few minutes ago, had not even seemed to notice that he was there.

Billy made himself a peanut-butter-and-jelly sandwich, then moved back into the living room and sat down in his chair before the TV. He had tried finding other things to do the past few days, but had been spectacularly unsuccessful. He had called everyone he'd known, asking if they wanted to go biking or go swimming or come over to The Fort, but his friends either weren't home or didn't want to talk to him. He had ridden by himself to the hill above the dig, but he knew without venturing down the slope that the archaeology students had gone, that the dig was over. He had pedaled as quickly as he could back toward home. The hill frightened him.

He wondered what Lane was doing.

He found himself thinking a lot about Lane lately, wondering how this estrangement could have happened to the two of them. He was aware that friendships often ended quickly and bitterly. He remembered how he and Frank Freeman, his best friend from fourth grade, had broken up after a relatively minor argument, and how alliances were quickly shifted, effectively redrawing the social map of the playground. He and Frank had ended up enemies, hanging out with rival factions of students, never missing an opportunity to hurt each other as deeply as possible.

And no one knew how to hurt more than an ex-friend.

But he and Lane had been buddies for a long time, had weathered fights both minor and major, and had still remained friends. It was hard to believe something like this could happen.

But Lane had changed.

A lot of people had changed.

The Brady Bunch ended and Billy switched the channel to the Flagstaff station to watch *Bewitched*.

He finished his sandwich, wiped his hands on his pants. He had never thought this was possible, had never thought this would happen, but for the first time in his life he was looking forward to the end of summer. He could not wait for the start of school.

Doug sat on the porch thinking about the mail. Brooding about the mail. This morning, he had received a slew of returned envelopes, some of them bills made out weeks ago, stamped with the notice "Not Deliverable as Addressed." There had also been an envelope addressed to Tritia, written in a flowery hand, smelling of perfume, which he had torn up and thrown away without opening.

The walk to the mailbox was really frightening him, he realized. Much as he tried to hide it, much as he tried to deny it, he felt nervous walking down the drive and was now almost hypersensitively aware of the bushes and trees on the way to the mailbox, knowing they could be used for possible hiding places.

He thought of moving the mailbox to a spot right next to the door, like mailboxes in the city, but he rejected that idea immediately. He did not want the mailman coming up to the house, coming that close to Tritia and Billy. He also thought of taking the mailbox down entirely. If they had no mailbox, they could get no mail, right? But that was not only cowardly, it was crazy. What the hell was he doing hiding from the mail? Did he think if he ignored the problem or tried to avoid it that it would go away?

Tritia pulled into the driveway. Doug looked away, toward the trees. He heard the muted clicking of the emergency brake being put on, the slam of the car door, followed by the sound of Trish's steps on the wooden porch. "I'm back," she announced.

When he did not respond, she walked over to him. "I said I'm back."

He looked up at her. "You want a medal?"

Her expression went from anger to hurt to a calm neutrality. He felt guilty and looked away. He didn't know why he was being so mean to her. She was only trying to be friendly. But there was something about her Pollyanna attitude, her pretending that everything was okay, that grated on him and made him mad. Made him want to hurt her.

He had been mad at her a lot lately, though he didn't really understand why.

"We're having fish tonight," she said. "Barbecued trout. I'll let you set up the barbecue."

"Did you buy any charcoal or lighter fluid? We're all out."

She shook her head. "Forget it. I'll broil it, then."

He stood up. "No. I'll go buy some. I want to get away from the house for a while anyway."

Tritia put a hand on his shoulder. "Are you all right?"

He stared at the hand, surprised. It had been days since they'd touched each other. He looked into her eyes and his voice softened. He felt some of his hostility, some of his tenseness, dissipate. He knew she was trying hard not to fight with him. "Yeah," he said. "I'm fine."

"Okay." She opened the screen door. "Better put some gas in the car too. We're almost out."

"Yeah."

As he walked down the porch steps and across the gravel to the Bronco, he heard the television shut off, heard Trish talking to Billy. The sound of her voice, used not in anger but in concern, was nice and familiarly comforting, like the voice of an old friend not heard in a while, and suddenly he felt much better.

The Bronco was nearly out of gas, the fuel gauge on empty, and the first thing he did was stop by the Circle K and put in five dollars' worth.

The second thing he did was drive to Howard's house.

He pulled to a stop in front of the low ranch-style home. It now looked definitely abandoned. The lawn was tan, even the weeds dried up and dead. Next door, a man was just getting out of his pickup and Doug quickly got out of the car and tried to wave him down. "Hey," he called.

The man took one look at him and hurried into his house.

Doug stopped walking. The whole damn town was acting squirrelly. He considered approaching Howard's neighbors on the other side, knocking on their door, asking if they'd seen the postmaster, but he had a feeling that he wouldn't get much cooperation from them. Or anyone else in the neighborhood.

He noticed that several other lawns were starting to look kind of ragged.

Knowing he would probably get no answer or response, he walked up Howard's driveway and knocked on the door. Pounded on the door. Yelled for Howard to come out. But his entreaties were met with no response. Again he checked the front door, the back door, the windows, but again everything was locked up tight. A darker, more solid drape seemed to have been put up behind the original curtains because now nothing could be seen inside the house, not even a shadow.

He wondered if he should call the police. Howard's house now showed definite signs of abandonment, and since no one except the mailman could claim to have seen him at all within the past few weeks, there seemed to him good cause to break into the postmaster's house and see if he was all right.

But he knew calling the police would do no good. He had told them the same story last time, and they'd done zippity shit. Besides, they'd never even try to get a search warrant or break into Howard's house unless they saw the mailman run inside the door with the postmaster's bloody head in his hands.

Doug shook his head. If there was one thing he hated about Arizona, it was the almost fanatic worship of land and property common to nearly everyone in the state. Here, people still had an Old West mentality, a perverse worldview that placed possessions above people in importance. He remembered one time when he and Billy had gone hiking out toward Deer Valley. They had been walking through a dry creekbed, following its course, when they happened upon a cabin in the woods. They turned immediately around, but not before they heard a young boy's voice call out, "Intruders, Pa!" A minute or so later, they heard the thunderous echoing sound of a shotgun blast. He'd felt like he was in some sort of damn movie. The noise was not repeated, but he and Billy had run the rest of the way back to the car, keeping low to the ground. When he told the police what had happened, the desk sergeant had merely smiled tolerantly and told him he shouldn't have been trespassing, as though death would have been fair punishment for a person who had inadvertently stepped on someone else's land.

It was this attitude that a man should be allowed to do whatever he wanted, with no restraints, that led to situations such as this.

Still, he got back in the Bronco and drove to the police station. It couldn't hurt to try. The chief, fortunately, was not there, but unfortunately, neither was Mike, and Doug ended up telling his story to a young female clerk who took down his statement and promised to give it personally to the lieutenant assigned to that sector of town. Doug was nice to her, cooperative, smiled at her, thanked her for her help, and left knowing nothing would be done.

Hell, maybe he should break in there himself, take this into his own hands.

But, no, the chief would just have him arrested and thrown in jail.

He drove to Bayless to pick up the charcoal and lighter fluid, aware that Trish was probably already starting to worry. He had gone to town to buy two items and had been gone for more than an hour.

He quickly went into the store, walked directly to the aisle containing nonfood items, and picked up a cheap bag of charcoal and a plastic container of store-brand lighter fluid. The express checkout lane was closed, and the three registers that were open had long lines of customers, so he picked the shortest one and got behind an elderly man carrying a handheld grocery basket piled with dairy products.

As he stood in line, Doug saw empty wire rack space formerly taken by the newspaper. The rack seemed sad and forlorn, if emotions could be ascribed to newsstands, and he found himself wondering what had happened to the risqué fortune cookies in Ben Stockley's desk drawer. He could still see in his mind the editor sitting behind his desk, but that image was beginning to fade, replaced by that of the bullet-riddled body he had seen on TV. What had happened to Stockley? A lump formed in Doug's throat and he forced himself to look away from the rack to the impulse items next to it.

It had been nearly half a month that the town had been without a paper. The *Weekly* had been, for all intents and purposes, a one-man operation, and when Stockley died, the paper abruptly ceased publication. Doug had no doubt that it would eventually get back on its feet once everything was sorted out—there were a few part-time reporters who could probably take over the editing duties, and the secretary pretty much knew how the business end of the operation worked—but for now the press in Willis was effectively shut down, and Doug couldn't help feeling that that was exactly the way the mailman wanted it. No independent means of disseminating information. No official way to learn what was going on.

Of course, news still traveled through unofficial channels. And traveled quite well. Through overhearing several unconnected conversations the past few minutes, for example, he knew that several more dogs had been murdered, not poisoned this time but decapitated, their severed heads stolen.

Gossip might be reviled in certain quarters for being unreliable—a children's party game of pass-the-message had been designed precisely to support that argument—but Doug knew from past experience that word-of-mouth was not nearly as faulty a means of learning news as it was made out to be.

He looked up to see Giselle Brennan walk into the store.

She saw him at the same time and waved. "Hi, Mr. Albin." She walked through the turnstile and around the cash register to meet him.

She was wearing no bra, he noticed immediately, and the hard points of her nipples were visible through the thin material of her tight T-shirt. Her large breasts jiggled as she walked toward him. She was grown now, he knew. An adult, a woman, but in his mind he still thought of her as a young teenager, and he felt strange seeing her in such an obviously sexual light. It disturbed him somehow, bothered him. He smiled warily as she approached. "Hi," he said. "How's it going?" He moved up in line.

"I got a job."

"Really?" he said. He placed his items on the moving black top of the register counter, automatically inserting a rubber divider behind it. "Where at?"

She grinned widely. "The post office. Can you believe it?"

The smile of congratulation froze on his face. Yes, he could believe it. "I didn't know they were hiring," he said carefully.

"Yeah, well, it's just temporary. I guess their sorting machine broke down and they were looking for someone to do it manually."

Doug moved forward. "Who hired you? Howard?"

"No, Mr. Crowell was sick. I guess that's one of the reasons they need an extra person. Mr. Smith hired me."

Doug forced himself to smile. "What do you think of Mr. Smith?"

Giselle's face clouded over for a second and he thought she was going to say something about the mailman, but instead she just shrugged. "I don't know."

The man in front of Doug paid for his groceries. Doug put a hand on Giselle's shoulder. She did not move away. "I don't know if you should work there," he said seriously.

She laughed. "My mom said the same thing. Don't worry. I'll be all right."

"Be careful," Doug warned her.

She smiled and pulled away. "Of course." She wiggled her fingers at him as she headed toward the frozen foods. "See you."

He watched her walk away, saw the outline of her tight ass beneath her jeans, the material pulled provocatively in at the crack.

"Two-eighty-five."

"What?" Doug turned around to face the cashier.

The young man smiled knowingly. "Two-eighty-five."

Doug took out his wallet.

In bed that night, Tritia snuggled next to him, laying an arm across his chest, holding him close in a way that she hadn't for quite some time. The dinner had been good and, more important, healthy. Trout and rice and asparagus stalks. She was back to her old nutrition-conscious self, and for some reason that made him feel more optimistic, less worried. Everything else might be going to hell, but at least they were going to be all right.

Her head shifted under the crook of his arm as she looked up at his face. "Do you still love me?" she asked.

"What kind of question is that?"

"Do you still love me?" Her voice was quiet and there was a seriousness in it he did not quite know how to take.

"Of course I love you."

"You never say it anymore."

"I didn't think I had to." He smiled. "God, we've been married for fifteen years. Why else would I put myself through this hell?"

"Be serious."

"Look, if I didn't love you, I wouldn't be with you."

"It's not that simple. Besides, I like to hear it sometimes."

"Michelle," he said. "That letter. That's what this is all about, isn't it?"

She said nothing but held him tighter. He kissed the top of her head.

"I'm afraid," she said finally.

"So am I."

"But I'm afraid for us. Our relationship. I mean, I get the feeling that you're keeping things from me, that you're afraid to talk to me. Or that you don't want to talk to me."

"That's not true," he protested.

"You know it is."

They were silent for a moment. "You're right," Doug said. "We have been drifting apart. I don't know why. I'd like to blame it all on the mailman, but I know that doesn't account for everything. It's my fault too."

"It's our fault," Tritia said.

And they held each other, and they snuggled closer, and Doug had the feeling that they had averted the disaster toward which they'd been heading, that they had bucked the trend that had been developing between them, and that they had successfully screwed up the mailman's plans.

29

Tritia awoke feeling jittery and out of sorts, the emotional residue of an unfortunately remembered nightmare that had, of course, been about mail. She'd been young, a child, but had been living here in this house, and she'd walked down the drive to the mailbox. It was a gorgeous day, the sky blue, the sun shining, and she was wearing her favorite pink dress with the little pinafores. She opened the mailbox and drew out a stack of brightly colored envelopes, the top one decorated with dancing teddy bears. Careful not to rip the beautiful paper, she pried open the sealed flap . . .

And a white hand shot out of the envelope and grabbed her neck.

She screamed, dropping the other envelopes, and they flopped open, hands shooting out from each of them. One hand shot immediately up her dress, grabbing her crotch. Two more stretched up to knead and fondle her fledgling breasts. Another shot up between the crack of her buttocks. Others grabbed her arms and legs. She screamed, but a final hand covered her mouth and she was pulled to the ground.

And then she woke up.

Not a good way to start the day.

It was her turn to fix breakfast, and she made bran muffins and squeezed the last of the oranges before going outside to check her garden. She felt tired and more than a little unpleasant, but she remembered her vow of yesterday, her promises to Doug, and she tried to push aside her negative feelings. She picked up the hose and turned on the faucet. Her plants had really gone to seed. She had continued to water them, but she had not weeded the garden for quite a while, had not taken the time to fight off bugs or prune leaves, and as a result, the vegetables this year were the worst she'd ever raised.

That too was going to change, she decided. She would

181

spend this morning taking care of her garden, putting it
back in shape. It was time for her to take control of her own
life and not let herself be manipulated by the mailman.

She thought of Irene. She would give her friend a call
today, make sure she was okay.

Doug awoke soon after, and when she heard the shower
water running through the pipes, she went back inside and
woke up Billy. They were all going to eat breakfast together
this morning. Like they were supposed to.

Following breakfast Doug washed the dishes, with Billy
drying, and when they were finished, she enlisted the aid of
both of them to help with the garden and the yard. Billy
tried to get out of it, tried to explain why it was more
important for him to watch television, but she and Doug
forced him to rake the drive, and for the first time in recent
memory he actually did the work without complaining. He
even seemed to be enjoying himself a little, and she
whisperedly pointed this out to Doug, who said there was
nothing like a short stint in hell to make a person long for
even the non-pleasures of everyday living.

They ate lunch on the porch together—bacon-lettuce-and-
tomato sandwiches—and afterward Doug and Billy decided
to go hiking out toward the old Sutpen ranch. She filled up
two canteens with water and ice, packed a sandwich apiece
just in case, and told them to be back by five or she was
calling the ranger station. They drove off in the Bronco,
waving.

When they were gone, Tritia called Irene.

She had thought about what she was going to say, had
planned out what she thought was a fairly compelling argument for her friend to tell the police what she had received
in the mail, or at least to allow her to tell Doug, but when
she heard Irene's frightened cracking voice, she knew that
no logical argument would be able to sway her.

"Hello?" Irene said.

"Hello. It's me, Tritia."

"I knew it was you. That's the only reason I answered the
phone."

Tritia took a deep breath. "Look," she said, "I'm your
friend—"

"No, I'm not telling anyone."

Tritia was taken aback by the old woman's determination.
"How do you know that was what I was going to say?"

"We both know why you called," Irene said. She coughed brittlely. "I have to work this out in my own way. Do you understand? This is something I have to do myself."

"Yes, but—"

"There are things you don't know," the old woman said, and there was something in her voice that sent a chill down Tritia's spine. "I shouldn't't've told you as much as I did."

"I just want to help."

Irene coughed again. "I know."

Tritia thought for a moment. "At least promise me you'll call if something happens, okay? Call if you need any help."

"You know I will."

"Okay." She was reluctant to hang up, but she could tell that Irene really didn't want to talk to her right now. "Are you sure you're all right?"

"I'm fine. I'll talk to you later, okay?"

"Okay."

The old woman hung up without saying good-bye.

Doug was wrong, Tritia thought, replacing the receiver. People weren't changing in ways entirely unconnected to the mail. Directly or indirectly, everything was connected to the mail. At the bottom of all that was occurring in Willis, at the root of all the hostility, all the craziness, was the mailman.

She walked outside to where she had left the mail she'd taken out of the box this morning before Doug and Billy awoke. There were two envelopes, both addressed to her, and all day she had debated with herself whether or not to open them.

Now she picked up a shovel and dug a deep hole on the forest side of the garden.

She threw the envelopes into the hole and buried them, unopened.

Tritia walked down the road toward the Nelsons' house. Hannah hadn't called for over two weeks. In fact, Tritia hadn't talked to her friend since Scooby had been poisoned. That was unusual. Ordinarily, she and Hannah went over to each other's houses or talked on the phone at least every other day.

She'd tried dialing the Nelsons' number more than once the past week or so, but she kept getting a busy signal, and when she'd called this morning, a decidedly robotic phone company voice had told her that the line had been disconnected and was no longer in service.

So she decided to walk over and see her friend.

There had been a light rain just after Doug and Billy had left, a short shower from a lone cloud that lasted less than ten minutes, and the dust on the road was packed down. For that she was grateful. Usually, dust flew with each footfall and she was filthy by the time she reached Hannah's house. But while the rain had settled the dirt, it had also upped the humidity, and that she could have done without. By the time she arrived, the sweat was dripping down the sides of her face.

The Nelsons' car was in the driveway, Tritia noticed immediately, so she knew they were home. She walked past the car up to the house, shoes noisily crunching the gravel beneath her feet. Her eyes wandered over to the metal stake where Scooby's chain had been tied. Next to the stake was an empty plastic water bowl. It was strange not hearing the dog's happy bark as she approached the house, and it made her feel uneasy, as though she had come to the wrong place.

She stepped up to the porch and knocked on the outer screen door. There was the sound of someone moving within the house, but the heavy front door did not open. She waited a few moments, then knocked again. "Hannah!" she called.

"Get out of here!" came her friend's angry voice from inside the house.

"It's me, Trish!"

"I said get the hell out of here!" Hannah Nelson opened the door, standing behind the screen. Her hair was tangled and unkempt, her housedress dirty. Tritia could not remember seeing her friend looking anything less than her best, ever, and the sight of her disheveled form was shocking.

"Hannah!"

"Get out of here, bitch."

Tritia stared, not knowing what to do, not knowing how to respond.

"Dog-killer!" Hannah screamed. She spat at her. The saliva, caught in the fine screen mesh, dripped down in thick sickening threads between them.

Tritia was confused. "What are you talking about?"

"We got the letter. We know all about it. Ron!" She

turned back toward the living room, leaving Tritia to stare at the glob of dripping saliva.

Ron emerged from the dim gloom of the living room, opened the screen door, and stepped onto the porch. He stood before Tritia, legs slightly spread in a stance of threatening belligerence. "I didn't think you'd ever have the guts to show your face around here again."

"I don't know what you—"

"Get out of here!" Hannah screamed.

Ron glared at Tritia. "You heard my wife. Get out of here. And don't you never come back."

Tritia backed off the porch, feeling for each step. "I really don't—"

"Go home, bitch." Ron spit on the ground in front of her. "And you tell your boy we don't want him around here neither. I know he's been coming here and stealing our lemons, and if he don't stop it, he's liable to catch a bullet in his butt. Get my drift?"

Tritia felt a rush of white-hot anger rush through her. "My son has never stolen anything in his life! He has been at home the past week. And if you weren't such an ignorant uneducated asshole, you might be able to figure that out!"

Ron advanced on her, fist outstretched, and she ran from him.

She turned back at the end of the driveway. "And if you thought about it some more, you'd know we wouldn't do anything to harm Scooby either!"

Ron picked up a rock and threw it at her. It went wide, missing her entirely, and she held up a defiant middle finger before running tearfully toward home.

She had regained her composure by the time Doug and Billy returned an hour later. She told Doug what had happened, and both of them marched down the road to the Nelsons' house, warning Billy to stay inside while they were gone.

But though the Nelsons' car was still in the driveway, though Doug knocked for five full minutes, no one came to answer the door.

30

The electricity went out on Tuesday morning during the second hour of the *Today* show. As before, the television simply winked off, the lights in the kitchen disappearing simultaneously. When Doug finally got through the wall of busy signals to the electric company, a very unsure man assured him that electrical service would be reestablished as soon as the problem could be identified and corrected.

"Approximately when will that be?" Doug asked.

The man cleared his throat nervously. "At this point I'm afraid I can't say, sir."

"Are we talking minutes or months here?"

"Possibly by the end of today. Maybe as late as tomorrow."

Doug hung up not knowing any more than he had before he called. It was stupid and ridiculous, but he had the strange feeling that the electric company's bill had gotten lost in the mail and that their machines couldn't work because they weren't paid up.

Or something along those lines.

Something to do with the mail.

By five o'clock that afternoon, the water, gas, and phones were out as well.

31

Strange, Doug thought, how they had not even considered leaving town, going to visit his parents for a few weeks or stopping off to see Trish's dad in California. There was nothing stopping them, no reason why they shouldn't get away from this madness for a while, but though they had not really talked about it, he knew that Tritia felt the same way he did: trapped in Willis, caged.

As far as he knew, no one had left town. They remained passively in place, like sheep, while a wolf prowled among them.

Why? he wondered. What was this malaise that had so gripped the community? What forced them to stay here, against common sense, against what must surely be natural instinct? The same thing that compelled people to remain in towns that were dying and rapidly heading toward ghost status, no doubt. Some illogical idiotic conception of "home."

The electricity was still off after three days, and he was getting mighty tired of cold baths and silent nights and sandwiches, but at least gas, water, and phone service had finally been restored. That was something he supposed he should be thankful for, but it seemed to him that the utility blackout period had served to sever ties among the people of the town more than anything else up to this point. He himself had talked to no one but Billy and Tritia for the past few days, and when he called Mike Trenton, the policeman had been cold to him and distant.

Hobie had not even answered his phone.

Which was why he was driving over to see him now.

He drove through the center of town toward Hobie's neighborhood. As much as anything else, he thought, it was the small things that were disturbing: the unmown grass at the park, the weeds protruding from the asphalt in the bank parking lot, the garbage cans lining the streets, filled with

187

uncollected trash—insignificant items on the surface, but telltale signs that something was seriously amiss. Just driving through Willis, Doug had the impression that many people were not at work, had not gone in today, that their jobs were not being performed. It was almost inconceivable that a single individual could have this much of an effect on an entire town, but the evidence was before his eyes and indisputable.

He pulled in front of Hobie's trailer. All of the cars seemed to be in place, so he was obviously home. Hobie never walked anywhere if he could drive.

Doug walked up the dirty path to the door, pushing the bell.

A moment later, Hobie answered the door, obviously shaken. He was wearing a black-and-gold Willis Warthogs T-shirt, and above the school colors his face looked pale, bleached, even his lips drained of pigment. "Hey," he said. "Long time no see."

Doug smiled, though he felt like doing nothing of the sort. "How're you doing?"

Hobie shrugged. "Not too good. But I'm glad you came." He opened the door wider and gestured for Doug to come inside.

The electricity was off here, as it was almost everywhere, but rather than open the drapes and windows, Hobie kept the curtains shut, relying solely on candles for illumination. The trailer was filled with the smell of burning wax and rotting food, and as Doug's eyes adjusted to the gloom, he saw that the refrigerator had been left open and that the food inside was spoiling. Trash and clothes were scattered everywhere, over both the living room and kitchen. He looked over at his friend. Hobie may have been loud and crude, but he had always been neat in his personal habits, and the shape of the trailer's interior frightened Doug more than he was willing to admit. Hobie's mental state had clearly deteriorated since the last time they'd spoken.

"I got another letter from Dan," Hobie said, sitting down on the dirty couch. "He wrote it last week."

Doug looked sharply up, but it was obvious that his friend was not joking. He was completely and totally serious. And he was terrified.

"Here. Read it." Hobie handed him a page of crude white paper on which was written a message in a thick bold

hand. Doug could not see to read, and he got up and pulled
open the drape, letting sunlight into the room.

In the light, the state of the trailer looked even worse and
more disgustingly filthy than it had in the dark.

"He says he's coming to visit," Hobie said quietly.

Doug read the letter:

Bro,
    Finally got some R&R. I'll be coming by to see you in a
week or so, soon as I can get a transport out of here. I'm
bringing some prime poon don't no one know about, so
we can have us some real fun. She's 12 and a virgin to
boot. At least that's what the guy who sold her to me
said.
    I'll be bringing my knives.
    See you soon.

It was signed "Dan," and it was dated last week.

Doug folded the paper and looked at Hobie. "You know
this isn't real," he said. "He's doing it. The mailman. He's
trying to—"

"It's Dan," Hobie insisted. "I know my brother."

Doug licked his lips, which had suddenly become very
dry. "What is this about a twelve-year-old? What does he
mean when he says he's bringing his knives?"

Hobie stood up and began pacing nervously around the
room. His face was tense, muscles strained. There was an
element of the caged animal in his walk. "I don't want to
see him," he said.

"What about the twelve-year-old girl and the knives?"

Hobie stopped pacing. "I can't tell you that." He looked
at Doug, eyes frightened. "I don't want him coming here.
He's my brother and I haven't seen him since I was sixteen,
but . . . but he's dead. He's dead, Doug." Hobie resumed
his pacing. "I don't want him coming here. I don't want to
see him." He took a deep audible breath. "I'm afraid of
him."

Doug heard the wildness in his friend's voice, the threat
of hysteria just below the surface. He stood up and grabbed
Hobie's shoulders, confronting him. "Look," he said, "I
know you recognize your brother's handwriting. I know he
says things in those letters that only he could know. But
listen to me carefully. It's a trick. The mailman's doing it.
You know as well as I do what's going on in town, and if

you think about it logically you'll realize that the same thing is happening to you. You said yourself that your brother is dead. I'm sorry to be so blunt, but do you honestly think that his rotted corpse is going to fly on a transport plane from Vietnam, land in Phoenix, and take a bus or cab or rent a car to come to Willis? Does that make any sense to you?"

Hobie shook his head.

"It's the mailman," Doug said.

Hobie looked straight into his eyes, and for the first time since he'd stepped into the trailer, his friend seemed rational, lucid. "I know that," he said. "I know the mailman's doing this. The letters come at night. I can't sleep anymore because I stay awake listening until I hear his car and hear him drop the letters in the slot. I'd like to go down to the post office and beat the living fuck out of the faggy son of a bitch, but I'm afraid of him, you know? Maybe . . . maybe he really can deliver letters from Dan. Maybe he can bring Dan back from the dead. Maybe he can bring Dan here."

"He's just trying to pressure you, to make you crack."

Hobie laughed a short nervous laugh. "He's doing a damn good job." He pulled away from Doug and walked into the demolished kitchen, picking up a bottle of Jack Daniels from the crowded counter and pouring himself a shot in a dirty glass. He quickly downed the liquor. "If he is faking those letters, writing them himself, then he knows a lot of things only Dan could know. He's even been able to copy Dan's handwriting perfectly. How do you explain that?"

"I can't."

Hobie poured himself another shot, drank it. "There's a lot of evil shit going down," he said. "A lot of evil shit."

Doug nodded. "You're right there."

Hobie looked at him. "He's not human, is he?"

"I don't think so," Doug admitted, and just saying that aloud made him feel cold. "But I don't know what he is."

"Whatever he is, he can bring back the dead. Dan's been writing to me. And now he's coming to visit."

"Maybe we should tell the police—"

"Fuck the police!" Hobie slammed down his shot glass, spilling whiskey. He shook his head, his voice softer. "No police."

"Why?"

"Because."

"Because why?"

"If you're going to act like this, then get the hell out of here and go home."

Doug held up his hands in acquiescence. "Okay, okay."

And he stood there silently as, shot by shot, Hobie finished off the bottle.

And he did not leave until after Hobie had passed out on the couch.

Five rings. Six. Seven. Eight.

On the tenth ring, Tritia finally hung up the phone. Something was wrong. Irene always answered her phone by the third ring. It was conceivable that she was out of the house, but it was hardly likely. She did not seem to be of a mind lately to leave the house for any reason.

Maybe she had to buy groceries.

No, Tritia thought. Something had happened.

As soon as Doug got back, the two of them would drive over there and see if Irene was all right.

She picked up the phone again and dialed Irene's number.

One ring. Two. Three. Four. Five. Six.

On an impulse, Doug pulled to a stop on the side of the road just after the crossing. It was midafternoon and the cicadas were out in force, their airplane humming the only counterpoint to the muted splash-babble of the stream. Near the road, the banks of the creek were narrow and rocky, with saplings creating a maze out of any attempted walkway. He was wearing his good tennis shoes and he knew he should stick to the bank no matter how awkward it was, but he stepped into the middle of the stream itself, waiting for a moment for his feet to acclimatize themselves to the coldness of the water before heading upstream.

He began wading purposefully upstream, toward the spot where Billy had discovered the mail. He had not been here since the day of the picnic, though he had thought of it often. Somehow, he had never heard whether the police had checked out the creek. They had taken his soggy samples, and Mike had confronted the mailman with them, but he did not recall hearing that the creek had been investigated.

Maybe he'd just forgotten.

Maybe not.

He was acutely aware of the loneliness of this place, of its relative inaccessibility. High cliffs rose up on both sides of the creek, and the sounds of man were nonexistent. Geographically, this area was not really remote; it was a mile or so from town, and fairly close to their settled section of the forest. But the lay of the land ensured that the creek remained as removed from civilization as the most out-of-the-way corner of the Tonto.

He moved forward. It was stupid of him to have come here by himself without telling anyone where he was going. He should have at least called Trish. If something happened to him . . .

He passed the spot near the path where they'd had their picnic and continued wading through the water. The bend was just ahead. How much mail would be there now? he wondered. Maybe it would not have been just dumped randomly. Maybe the mailman was now using the discarded mail for a purpose. He saw in his mind a mail city, small shacks constructed next to the creek from millions of dumped envelopes, letters meticulously arranged into foundations and floors, walls and roofs.

But that was crazy.

What wasn't crazy these days?

He stood just before the final turn, listening for any unnatural sounds, but could hear only the water and the cicadas. He moved slowly forward and peeked around the bend.

There was nothing there.

The mail was gone.

He was almost relieved. Almost. But his satisfaction in discovering that he had forced the mailman to dump the mail elsewhere, to find another spot in which to deposit the town's real correspondence, was offset by the knowledge that the mailman had been so frighteningly thorough that he had cleaned up the mail he had already dropped there, that, one by one, he had meticulously picked the thousands of envelopes from the water, from the ground, from the trees, from the bushes, and had taken them all away.

Billy was upstairs when Doug arrived home, watching his own TV because Tritia had on *Donahue* in the living room. The electricity, apparently, had finally been restored. Tritia was in the kitchen, chopping vegetables, but Doug made her

quit and dragged her into the living room, sitting her down
on the couch. He told her what had happened to Hobie, and
as she sat silently listening to his story, she grew increasingly
pale.

"He's doing the same thing to Irene," she said when he
was finished.

"What happened?"

She hesitated for only a second. Although she had promised Irene she would tell neither Doug nor the police what
had occurred, that promise was no longer valid. Her friend
might be in trouble, in danger, and it was more important to
help her out than to remain true to some ridiculous promise.

Tritia told him of the toe and of Irene's husband's accident, explaining also that she had tried calling four or five
times this afternoon but that no one had answered the
phone.

"Jesus! Why didn't you call the police?"

"I didn't think—"

"That's right. You didn't think." Doug strode across the
living room to the phone and picked up the receiver.

The phone was dead.

He slammed it down angrily. "Shit!" He looked over at
Tritia. "Come on, get ready. We're going to talk to the
police." He walked upstairs. Billy was lying in bed, watching *Bewitched*. "We're going into town," Doug told his son.
"Put your shoes on."

Billy did not even look at him. "I want to watch this
show."

"Now!"

"Why can't I stay here?"

"Because I said you can't. Now, get your shoes on or that
TV goes off permanently." He clomped back down the
stairs, checked the back door to make sure it was locked.
Tritia emerged from the bedroom, patting down her hair, a
purse slung over her shoulder. Billy's angry sullen footsteps
could be heard on the stairs.

"Let's go," Doug said.

They drove all the way to town in silence, Tritia worried
beside him, Billy, arms folded across his chest, angry in the
back seat. Doug drove into the parking lot of the police
station, pulling next to a beat-up Buick. He told Billy to
remain in the car, and he and Tritia walked into the building. The desk sergeant on duty came immediately to the

front counter when he saw the two of them standing there. "May I help you?" he asked.

Doug glanced around the office. "Where's Mike?"

"Which Mike?"

"Mike Trenton."

"I'm sorry, but information concerning the shifts and hours of department employees is confidential."

"Look, I know him, okay?"

"If you knew him well enough, you wouldn't have to ask. I'm sorry, but for security reasons we do not give out personal information concerning our officers. Now, is there anything else I can help you with?"

"I hope so." Doug told the sergeant about Hobie and Irene. At first, he left out the details, explaining merely that their friends were being harassed through the mail and had reason to believe that the mailman was behind it, wanting to let the police discover for themselves what had happened. But when the sergeant looked doubtful and started to give him a vague "we'll-look-into-it" answer, Doug decided to tell all.

"Hobie Beecham has been getting letters from his dead brother," he said. "Irene Hill was sent a severed toe through the mail. Hobie's dead drunk right now because of it, passed out on the couch where I left him. Irene's not answering her phone. Now, do you think, possibly, that you could spare a few minutes from your busy schedule to check this out?"

The sergeant's attitude had changed completely. He was suddenly eager to help, although there was a strange anxious nervousness to his manner. He took down Doug's and Tritia's names and address as well as the addresses of Hobie and Irene.

He knows, Doug thought. *He's been getting mail too.*

"I'll have an officer sent out to interview both Mr. Beecham and Ms. Hill," the sergeant said.

Doug glanced up at the clock on the wall. It was nearly four. The post office would be open for another hour. "What about John Smith? Are you going to send someone over to the post office to talk to him?"

"Of course."

"I'm going too," Doug said.

The sergeant shook his head. "I'm sorry, I'm afraid the civilians—"

"Fine." Doug smiled thinly. "Then I will just go to the

post office and happen to be there the same time as your man." He looked at Tritia. "Let's go."

The two of them walked out of the police station without looking back. Doug was sweating and his body was charged with adrenaline. Encounters with authority, even on such a minor level, still made him nervous, although he was getting increasingly used to them.

He had left the keys in the car for Billy, who had turned on the radio. His mood seemed to have improved during their absence, and he was no longer silently sullen when they got into the car.

"Why did we come here?" he asked.

"Because," Tritia told him.

"It's about the mailman, isn't it?"

Doug looked at his son in the rearview mirror as he started the engine. "Yes," he admitted.

"Are they going to get him?"

Doug nodded. "I hope so."

Billy sat back in his seat. "Probably not, though."

Doug did not respond. He waited for a moment until he saw Tim Hibbard and two other officers emerge from the building. Tim waved to him, motioned for him to follow, and Doug put the Bronco into reverse, pulling out of the parking space. He got behind the patrol car and followed it out of the lot, onto the street, and to the post office.

"Stay here," Doug said as he got out of the car. Tim was already waiting for him near the building's entrance.

Tritia unbuckled her seatbelt. "No way. I'm coming with you."

"Me too," Billy said.

"You definitely stay here," Doug told his son.

"Yes," Tritia agreed.

"Then why couldn't I just stay home and watch TV?"

Because I was afraid to leave you alone, Doug thought, but he only shook his head, saying nothing. He left the keys in the ignition, turned the radio to Billy's favorite station, and closed the car door. He and Tritia walked over to where Tim stood waiting.

The officer grinned as they approached. "The chief would croak if he knew you were here with me," he said. "He doesn't like you at all, you know."

Doug pretended to be surprised. *"Moi?"*

Tim laughed.

Doug looked toward the door to the post office. The afternoon sun reflected off the glass so he could not see clearly inside, but there appeared to be no patrons in the office. He turned toward Tim. "Where's Mike?" he asked.

"The truth? He was taken off this case because the chief thought he was getting too close to it."

"Too close to me, you mean."

"Well, yeah."

Doug frowned. " 'This case?' You mean the mailman?"

Tim smiled again. "Unofficially."

"Well at least something's being done. I was getting really worried about you guys."

"Don't stop worrying yet. The chief still thinks it's a load of crap, and we still haven't been able to substantiate anything."

"Until now," Tritia said.

"We'll see." Tim looked from Tritia to Doug. "You two ready to go in?"

Doug nodded. "Let's do it."

The day was waning, the air cooling, but the inside of the post office was extraordinarily hot and muggy. It had changed again, Doug noticed immediately. The walls, formerly a drab public-building grayish-green, had been painted a deep black. He had never before noticed the color of the floor, but the cement was now an unmistakable blood red. The philatelic posters on the wall were all of stamps that could not possibly exist. Bloody tortures. Unnatural sex.

Behind the counter, Doug saw Giselle. She was sorting through a pile of letters. She looked almost Nazi-like in her new blue uniform, Teutonic hair swept under her cap, and the sight of her in this place, in this position, made her seem like an entirely different person. She seemed tainted, corrupt, merely by her association with him, as though she had somehow turned her back on everyone else in town, on her parents and her old friends, and had betrayed them.

The thought crossed his mind that the mailman's goal all along had been to establish some sort of paramilitary organization using the local kids, a youth group that would usurp the power in the community. But, no, if that had been his plan, there would have been earlier signs and indications; he would have recruited other people already. Besides, that answer was too easy, too clean, too literal. The mailman's real goal, he felt sure, was not so simple, not so clearly defined.

If he had a goal at all . . .

Real life, Doug reminded himself, was not like literature. As an English teacher, he dealt constantly with the themes and motives of fiction, and he had a tendency to ascribe a similar structure to reality. But this was not a novel where acts were performed for a reason: to illuminate character, to reveal a truth, or to achieve an end. It was possible, more than possible, that the mailman was here in town not for a specific purpose, not as part of some evil grand design, but for his own entertainment or amusement. Or for no reason at all.

He found Tritia's hand and held it.

Tim cleared his throat, approaching the counter. He, too, must have been surprised by the state of the post office, but he let none of it register. "I need to speak with Mr. Crowell and Mr. Smith," he said.

Giselle looked up from her work and glanced from Tim to Doug and Tritia. She smiled at Doug, and he instantly regretted his superficial characterization of her. She had not changed, after all.

Then why was she working for the mailman?

"Is Howard here?" Doug asked.

Giselle shook her head. "He's still sick."

"Could you please tell Mr. Smith I'd like to talk to him," Tim said.

The mailman emerged from the back room. As always, he was dressed impeccably in his uniform. His hair, Doug noticed, was very nearly the same color as the floor. "Hello, gentlemen," he said. He smiled at Tritia, nodding his head. "Ladies."

Tritia tried to hide behind Doug. She did not like the mailman's eyes. She did not like the mailman's smile.

You're nice.

His eyes remained on her, holding her gaze though she wanted to look away. "How's your son?" he asked. The question was asked innocently, casually, but beneath the superficial interest was a deeper, obscene, frightening implication.

Billy's nice too.

"We didn't come here to chat," Doug said coldly.

"We've had reports that there has been some tampering

with the mails," Tim said. His voice was steady, even, but Doug could sense a hint of fear in it. He knew the mailman could too. "Two citizens have complained that they have been receiving"—he reached for a word—"rather bizarre items in the mail."

The mailman stared at the policeman calmly. "Such as?"

"Illegal items."

The mailman smiled patiently, understandingly. "The Postal Service is not responsible for the contents of the mail it delivers and under federal law cannot be held liable for damage caused as a result of its delivery. However, we are just as concerned as you are about abuses of the postal system and are willing to cooperate fully with any efforts designed to get to the root of this problem."

Tim did not know how to respond, and he looked to Doug for help.

"You're sending mail yourself," Doug said.

The mailman's gaze was unwavering and unreadable. "Of course I am," he said. "We all send mail. Are you implying that because I work for the post office I cannot send letters to people? Do you think that is some sort of conflict of interest?" He laughed, a false plastic laugh Doug knew he was supposed to see through. This conversation, Doug realized, was operating on two levels. The mailman was threatening him.

John Smith smiled. "I have to pay for postage just like everyone else. I don't even get a discount. But there is no limit to the amount of letters I can send. I can mail as many items as I want to."

"And have you mailed any threatening letters?" Tim asked. "Have you mailed any body parts?"

The mailman did not even pretend to be surprised. "I don't like your insinuation," he said.

"I'm afraid I'm going to have to ask you to let me search this post office."

"I'm afraid you're going to have to get a search warrant," the mailman said. "And I'm afraid you're going to find it fairly difficult to obtain a warrant to search an office of the federal government." He looked past Doug and Tritia out the window. "How's Billy today?" he asked.

"You leave him alone, damn you." Tritia glared at him.

The mailman chuckled.

Doug noticed Giselle backing away from the mailman behind the counter. She looked confused.

"I'm afraid you gentlemen"—the mailman smiled at Tritia— "and ladies will have to excuse me. I have work to do."

"I haven't finished talking to you," Tim said.

"I'm finished talking to you," the mailman replied, and there was something in his voice that made the rest of them fall silent. They watched him retreat back into the rear of the building.

Giselle tried to smile apologetically, but the smile did not quite work.

"Tell Howard to call me," Doug told her. "If you ever see him."

She glanced behind her to make sure she wasn't being watched, then shook her head slightly from side to side.

"To hell with the search warrant," Tim said angrily. "I'm going to get an arrest warrant. Let's get out of here."

They walked out of the hot dark building and into the fresh outside air. Behind them, from somewhere deep within the post office, they heard the mailman laugh.

32

The next day the telephones went out again, and Doug had
to drive into town to discover that the police had questioned
Hobie and Irene and that both of them had denied receiving
anything unusual in the mail.

He talked to the desk sergeant since neither Mike nor
Tim was in the office.

When he drove out to see Hobie afterward, his friend
refused to answer the door, pretending not to be home.

Irene did exactly the same thing.

33

Billy awoke early, his nose stuffed, his eyes itchy and watery, the nightmare from which he had awoken all but forgotten in the face of his overwhelming physical discomfort. He sneezed, then sneezed again, wiping his nose on the sheet, since there was no handkerchief handy. It was going to be one of those allergy days. He could feel it. He lay back on the pillow, eyes open. More than once, his parents had talked about taking him up to Flagstaff for tests, to find out exactly what he was allergic to, but when he'd learned that the tests involved needles, he promptly vetoed that idea. There was nothing he hated worse than needles. The allergy was horrible but bearable, usually not lasting more than a day or two at a time, and was infinitely preferable to being poked and scratched and jabbed.

He sneezed again. He had been planning to take Brad and Michael out to The Fort today to check out the *Playboy*s. The twins had never really believed that he and Lane had as many magazines as they said they did, and had often begged, had even offered to buy, their way into The Fort. Lane had always turned them down, insisting that only the original builders were allowed to see The Fort's interior, but now Lane was gone, and Billy had decided to invite the twins to come over and check it out for themselves.

Brad had sounded a little strange when he'd talked to him over the phone, hostile almost, as though he was mad for some reason, but since Billy had no one else to hang out with . . . Well, beggars couldn't be choosers.

Besides, it would be nice to see someone besides his family again. And he knew the twins would be impressed with the *Playboy* collection.

He forced himself to sit up. Behind his eyes, his head felt thick and heavy. He wasn't sure he should be walking through the forest with his allergy this bad; all the plants would probably only make it worse. But he didn't want to spend the whole day in bed. That was fine during the school year, when he could cajole his mom into bringing him toast and tea and could lie in his pajamas and watch cartoons and TV shows from morning to afternoon, but when it was summer and he had plans for the day . . .

He got out of bed and padded across the floor to the closet, taking out his bathrobe and putting it on. An old handkerchief was wadded up in the robe's pocket and he used it to blow his nose.

"Allergies?" his mom called from downstairs.

He didn't answer, hoping that if he ignored her she would go back to whatever she was doing and leave him alone. He moved over to the window, looking out. The sky was overcast, a cumulus ceiling painted with gradations of gray, and the morning sun was a hidden light dimly brightening a small section of cloud cover in the east. Above the pointed silhouettes of the pines he could see a lone hawk circling upward toward the top of the hill. Though it was not raining now, the ground was wet, the window misty.

Maybe he wouldn't be taking the twins to The Fort, after all.

He walked downstairs. The electricity was on again, and his dad was watching the morning news. His mom was standing in the kitchen at the sink, looking out the window at the forest, her back to him. On the counter were several boxes of high-fiber cereal along with freshly squeezed orange juice. Next to the toaster was a cut loaf of whole grain bread.

Things were back to normal.

Billy sneezed, wiping his nose on the sleeve of his bathrobe. He could barely breathe and his head was throbbing to the rhythm of his pulse, but when his mom turned around, a questioning look on her face, he said, "I'm fine," before she could even ask how he felt.

"You don't look fine," she said, walking over to the cupboard. She took out a glass and poured some orange juice, giving it to him. "You look sick."

"Allergy."

She nodded. "It's the rain. It gets those mold spores in the air. I want you to drink your juice and take some vitamin C."

He sat down at the counter and sipped from the glass. He

chose the least objectionable cereal, poured about half a bowlful, and sprinkled several spoons of sugar on top of it.

"What do you think you're doing?" his mom said.

"I can't eat this stuff without sugar."

"One spoon. That's all."

Billy smiled at her. "Too late now." He poured the milk in his bowl.

"Hurry up and eat and get ready," his dad said from behind him. "We're going to the store this morning, and I want to get it over with as soon as possible."

Billy swallowed his cereal. "I don't want to go."

"You have to go."

"My allergies are bothering me. I feel kind of sick. I think I'd better stay home."

"I thought you said you were fine. What a liar." His mom tried to make her voice light and playful, but he could hear an undercurrent of tension in it. He saw worried concern in the glance she shot over his head at his dad. "Why do you really want to stay?"

"Brad and Michael might be coming over. We were going to go play in The Fort."

"You're coming with us," his dad said.

"You guys always treat me like I'm a baby. I'm old enough to stay by myself. God, Lane's parents left him by himself for two days before."

"When?" his mother asked. "When you were staying overnight?"

"No," he lied.

"Where is Lane, by the way? I haven't seen him around lately. Did you two get into a fight or something?"

Billy looked at his mom, feeling his stomach knot up.

Naked.

"Yeah," he said. He dug into his cereal, focusing his attention on the bowl, not wanting to look at his mom, not wanting to think about Lane.

His dad came into the kitchen, dumped the last little bit of his coffee down the sink, and rinsed out his cup. "I think you'd better come with us today," he said.

Billy looked up at his father. "I think I'd be safer here," he said.

A look passed between them. Though none of them had said anything, the subtext of their conversation was clear to all of them, and Billy had obviously struck a responsive chord in his father with the word "safer." He was not sure if it was true, not sure if he really would be safer here, but he did want to stay, and he did not want to go to town. His dad continued to stare at him, but Billy did not avert his gaze, and he saw a host of conflicting emotions pass over his father's face.

His dad finally looked away and put his coffeecup on the drying rack. "Are you sure you'll be okay here by yourself?" he asked.

Billy nodded.

"You cannot leave the house," he warned. "I don't want you stepping outside that door until we come back. You understand?"

"Yes."

"If Brad and Michael come by," he added, "you just stay in here with them and watch TV or something, okay? Watch a videotape."

He nodded. "Don't worry."

His mom put a hand on his dad's shoulder. "I'm sure he'll be fine."

They finished breakfast in silence, his dad going back to the TV, his mom going into the bathroom to get ready. Something had happened here between them, something that he could almost but not quite understand, that barely eluded his grasp, and he wasn't sure if he was glad it had happened or not. He almost wished he had agreed to go to the store with them.

He sneezed, wiping his nose on his sleeve.

A half-hour later, his parents were ready to go. They said good-bye to him and gave him preparatory instructions that made it seem as though they were going to be embarking on a week-long journey instead of just going on a ten-minute trip to the store.

Billy watched them drive away, then he looked back into the kitchen. They had taken care of most of the breakfast dishes, but had left some for him to do. The sugar and orange juice and cereal boxes all still stood on the top of the counter, waiting for him to put them away. The TV was already off and he turned out the lights. The house grew dark, sliding into an artificial state halfway between night and day. He sat down for a moment on the couch to enjoy it. There was something special about being inside on a cloud-darkened day. Particularly when he was alone. It somehow made everything seem more valuable, more tentative and transitory and therefore precious. It was a strange feeling, as distinct from the feeling of safety and security he got from being warm inside the dry house on a snowy winter's night as it was from the claustrophobic feeling of being trapped inside on a warm sunny day, and it made him feel grown-up, as though he were already an adult and this was his house.

Outside, it began to rain. In the silence of the house, he could clearly hear the faint clattering sound of raindrops on the roof. He sat there for a moment, taking in the staccato rhythm of the rain, the modulating shift of daylight through the windows as the clouds above drifted, moved, overlapped.

He glanced at the clock. It was nearly nine-thirty. The twins were supposed to be here between nine-thirty and ten. Obviously, they wouldn't be able to go to The Fort if the rain kept up this way, but they could play a game inside or something until it abated.

First of all, though, he had to clean up the breakfast stuff. He sat up and walked into the kitchen. He put the orange juice in the refrigerator, put the cereal boxes in the cupboard. Moving over to the toaster, he glanced down at the counter.

Next to the loaf of wheat bread was a long white envelope.

An envelope addressed to him.

An icy finger of fear tickled Billy's spine. He stared down at the white paper rectangle. Had the envelope been there before? It couldn't have. If it had, he would have seen it.

He wanted to walk away, to go outside, to go back upstairs and wait for his parents to come home, to get away from the kitchen entirely, but the envelope beckoned him. He stared at it, unable to look away. He reached for the envelope as though it was booby-trapped, picking it up slowly, holding it at arm's length. He did not want to open it, was afraid to open it, but he had to see what was inside. Carefully, he pressed his fingers against the envelope, making sure it did not contain photographs.

His mother, naked.

His hand trembled. There were no pictures inside, the envelope was pliable, not stiff, and with one quick movement, he tore it open.

There were only four words typed on the plain white paper:

Come out and play

Come out and play. The words on their own were innocuous enough, innocent even, but the meaning behind them was anything but. He knew exactly who had sent the note, though there was no signature, and he knew exactly what the message meant.

Come out and play.

He dropped the paper on the floor, stepping away from it. He should have gone with his parents. He should never have stayed here alone. What the hell was wrong with him? The darkened house, which only a few moments before had seemed so wonderfully special, now seemed sinister and filled with shadows. He reached over and flipped on the light switch next to the sink.

Nothing happened.

The electricity was out.

He was scared now. He quickly rushed to the phone, picking it up.

It was dead.

Outside, beneath the low clatter of the rain, he heard the unmistakable sound of a purring car engine. He ran to the back door, checking to make sure it was closed and locked, then locked the front door. He moved next to the window, peeking out. Through the blurred drizzle outside the glass, he could see an indistinct form standing near the end of the drive by the road. A figure with a blue uniform, white face, and red hair.

Come out and play.

He backed quickly away from the window, closing the drapes. The second the curtains closed, he knew that it had been a stupid thing to do. Now he was trapped in here, helpless, blinded, unable to see what was going on outside. He almost opened the drapes again, but immediately dropped the cord. What if the mailman had sneaked up onto the porch and was standing right in front of the window waiting for him, grinning at him? What would he do? What could he do? He had seen the mailman move in the direction of the house the second before the curtains closed. Or had he? He couldn't remember.

His eyes darted toward the back of the house, toward his parents' bedroom. The drapes there were open, but the windows faced the forest. He would not be able to see anything other than trees.

And the mailman, if he sneaked around from that direction.

Billy ran upstairs. There was no door on the loft stairs, they simply came up through the floor, but his baseball bat was there and he could use that to protect himself if he had to. He picked up the bat and searched for something he could drop on the mailman's head if it came to that. He found several heavy old toys that he hadn't touched in years, and brought them with him to the bed. He gripped the bat tightly, waiting, ready to swing, listening for the sound of anything unfamiliar within the house.

But the only sound was the constant rain and he heard nothing else until his parents pulled into the drive an hour later.

34

Doug walked out to the mailbox. It had been quite a while since he'd actually looked at the mail, and he was more than a little curious to see what sort of letter the mailman was sending these days. For the past week or so, he had gotten up before Trish or Billy awoke and had dumped the mail directly into the outside garbage cans, making sure he buried them deep under the kitchen sacks and bathroom trash so they wouldn't be accidentally taken out of the can by a hungry dog or rambunctious skunk or raccoon.

Still, he was curious. It felt good to know that he was resisting the mailman's constant temptation, that whatever Postal Service pranks had been planned for he and his family had been successfully thwarted, but he could not deny that there was something inside him, that same stubborn something that had always made him do exactly what authority told him not to do, which made him now want to open up the mail and see what was inside, though he knew it was the dumbest move he could make under the circumstances.

He thought of Hobie and Irene, who had both stopped answering their doors or their phones.

His feet crunched in the gravel. He reached the foot of the drive and opened the mailbox. Inside was a single envelope addressed by computerized mailing label to "Occupant." Doug removed the envelope and slammed shut the box. He was still debating with himself whether to throw it away or look at it when his hands ripped open the sealed paper. He withdrew the contents of the envelope—a professionally typeset brochure and two photographs.

Nude photographs.

Of Tritia.

His mouth felt suddenly dry, his legs weak. He turned over the brochure and began to read. "Hi," it said. "My name's Tritia, and I want to be your very special friend. As an introduction to the Ranch Club, I am sending you two photos of myself, to show you what you get by taking advantage of our introductory offer. By night I am a wife and mother, but by day I am anything you want me to be. Your hot slut. Your love slave . . ."

He couldn't read any more. Breathing heavily with anger, revulsion, and trembling fear, he looked at the two photos. In one, a rear view, Tritia was bent over the back of a couch, offering to the camera a perfect shot of her white untanned ass.

Only . . .

Only it wasn't Tritia. The cheeks were too firm, and too round, the buttocks of a young woman in her late teens or early twenties. He looked closer. The small birthmark she had on her lower back was missing as well, and the fingers were too short and stubby. He looked at the other photograph, this one of Trish seated in a wicker chair, legs spread, eyes closed as she fingered herself. The breasts were wrong, he noticed. The size was about right, but Trish's nipples were much darker, much more prominent.

He tore up the photographs, tore up the brochure, tore up the envelope. The mailman had obviously pasted photographs of Trish's head onto someone else's body, although he did not know how or where the mailman could have gotten a hold of pictures of Trish. The photos were done well, flawlessly executed, with no visible seams, and would probably fool anyone else but him. But what was the point? Why go to so much trouble?

Maybe it wasn't just for him. Maybe the mailman had sent the same brochure, the same photos, to other people in town. Maybe other men were right now staring at the false body of his wife, reading the mailman's fake words, fantasizing, planning.

He pushed the thought from his mind as he walked back toward the house.

He threw the torn scraps of paper into the garbage before going inside.

The town had seemed nearly abandoned the other day when they'd gone to the store, with very few cars on the street, very few people visible anywhere, so Doug was more than a little surprised to see a crowd gathered in the parking

lot in front of the deli. He had been planning to go to the
hardware store, to pick up some more flashlight and radio
batteries before they were all sold out, but he pulled into
the Bayless parking lot when he saw the crowd. He parked
next to a gray Jeep Cherokee and got out. The group of
people standing in front of the deli was fairly quiet and fairly
still, but there was something threatening about them as
they stood in a rough semicircle around Todd Gold's station
wagon. Doug moved forward. He recognized the faces of
several students and several adults. They appeared to be
waiting for something, and although there was nothing unusual in either their individual expressions or stances, merely
being part of the crowd made them seem menacing.

Todd came out of his store, carrying a large white box.
He put the box into the open rear of the station wagon, next
to a score of others that had already been packed. He
slammed shut the hatch. Doug pressed through the group of
people to the front as the deli owner angrily waved the
onlookers away. "Get the hell out of here. Haven't you
done enough already?"

The crowd stood dumbly, silently watching as he went
into the store, emerged carrying several sacks, then closed
and locked the now empty deli. "Get out of here," he yelled
again. He dropped one of the sacks on the ground as he
took out his car keys.

Doug reached him just before he opened the front door.
"What is it, Todd? What happened? What are you doing?"

The storekeeper glared angrily at Doug. "I at least expected better from you. Some of these rednecks"—he waved
a dismissive hand toward the crowd—"I can understand.
They've never seen a Jew before, don't know what to do or
how to handle it, but you . . ."

Doug stared at him, confused. The man seemed to be
talking gibberish. "What are you talking about?"

"What am I talking about? What am I talking about?
What the hell do you think I'm talking about?" The storekeeper dropped a sack of mail onto his seat and began
sorting through it furiously, picking up envelopes, tossing
them aside, until he found what he wanted. He held it up.
"Look familiar?"

Doug shook his head dumbly. "No."

"No?" Todd read the letter aloud. " 'You Christ-killing
kike, we're tired of your greasy fingers touching our fish and

meat and food. How would your sheeny wife like a nice white cock up her ass?' "

Doug stared, stunned. "You don't think I—"

"Oh, you're telling me you didn't do it?"

"Of course I didn't!"

Todd looked down at the paper, reading. " 'Why don't I feed your wife some real knockwurst?' "

"Todd . . ." Doug said.

The storekeeper spat on the ground at Doug's feet. The expression on his face was one of intense hatred, a hatred borne of betrayal, and Doug knew that there was nothing he could say or do that could repair the damage that had been done, that could convince the storekeeper he had had nothing to do with this.

"Baby!" someone in the crowd yelled. "Crybaby!"

Doug looked up to see who had made the comment, but the faces all seemed to blur together. He noticed now that although the people were silent, they were by no means passive observers. There was anger on several faces, along with the ugly ignorant shadow of bigotry.

"Jewpussy," a man yelled.

"Go back to where you came from," a woman called.

Todd dropped the letter in the back seat and got into the car. He started the engine, put on his seat belt, and looked up at Doug. "I expected better from you," he said. "I hope you're happy."

"I'm on your side," Doug said, but the car was already backing up, turning around. Someone in the crowd threw a rock, and the rock hit the back fender of the departing station wagon, bouncing off. The car pulled onto the street, rounded the corner, and was gone.

Doug looked into the empty store and saw only the reflection of the crowd in the mirror. He saw faces he didn't know on people he knew. He saw people he didn't want to know at all.

He turned around.

"You're on his side?" a man said, demanded.

Doug held up his middle finger. "Fuck off," he said. He walked slowly back toward the car.

35

Tritia lay staring up into the darkness, needing to go to the bathroom but afraid to get out of bed. He was out there, she knew. Somewhere close. She had heard earlier the low quiet sound of his engine approaching and then cutting off, but she had not heard it start up again. She knew she should wake Doug, but he'd been so tense lately, under so much stress, and had had such a difficult time falling asleep that she didn't want to disturb him.

Upstairs, Billy's bed creaked as he shifted restlessly in his sleep. He had been nervous and anxious the past two days, ever since they'd left him home when they went to the store, and she was worried about him. He was becoming ever more secretive. Once again, something was bothering him that he refused to discuss with them, and though she was trying to be patient and understanding, it was hard not to feel frustrated with his lack of cooperation.

The pressure between her legs increased. She would have to go to the bathroom soon. There were no two ways around that. And she would have to decide whether or not to wake Doug. He snored softly next to her, his breathing rough and irregular, and she found herself thinking for some reason of sleep apnia, a disease in which the sleeping brain forgot to work the involuntary functions of the body, and a person stopped breathing and his heart stopped beating and he never woke up.

Stop it, she told herself. You're just being crazy.

The pressure increased yet again. She recalled with terrifying clarity the dream she'd had the night before. A dream in which she'd gone into the bathroom to take a bath and had lain in the warm sudsy relaxing water only to find that the mailman's body was beneath her. A hand had reached up from the bubbles to silence her scream as his burning organ entered her from behind.

She reached over and cautiously nudged her husband. "Doug?" she said softly.

"What?" He jerked awake, instantly alert, instantly on the defensive.

"I'm afraid to go to the bathroom alone," she said apologetically. "Would you come with me?"

He nodded, and even in the dark she could see the circles under his eyes. He stumbled out of bed, pulled on his robe, and they walked to the bathroom together. From the kitchen came the low sound of the refrigerator humming. Tritia reached around the corner, found the switch, and flipped on the bathroom light.

Sitting on the covered seat of the toilet was a white envelope.

"Oh, I left that there," Doug said quickly, picking it up, hiding it. But Tritia knew instantly with a feeling of terror that he had never seen the envelope before. She had been the last person to use the bathroom, just before going to bed, and there had been no mail in the bathroom at all.

He'd been inside the house.

"Check Billy," she ordered, running down the hall, through the kitchen. She was panicked, gasping for breath. She saw in her mind her son's empty bed, covers thrown aside, an envelope on his pillow containing a ransom note . . . or something worse.

Billy's nice too Billy's nice too. . . .

They ran crazily, Doug following her lead, up the steps to the loft.

Where Billy, alone, was fast asleep.

She had never really understood what a sigh of relief was, though she had read the phrase often enough in novels, but she breathed a sigh of relief now, an exhalation of the air she had been holding in her lungs as she prepared herself for the worst. Her eyes met Doug's, and both of them began silently searching through the loft to make sure the mailman wasn't hiding anywhere.

The loft was empty.

They combed the rest of the house, carefully searching the closets, the cupboards, under the beds. Doug checked the windows and the locks on the door, but everything was as it should be. Finally, satisfied that the house was clean, that there was no one there, they returned to the bathroom.

Doug put a reassuring hand on Tritia's shoulder.

"What the hell's the matter with you?" she demanded, pushing his hand away, turning on him.

He stepped back, surprised by her sudden fury. "What?"

"I said what the hell's wrong with you? You're all gung ho about going to the police and trying to get them to do something about the mailman, but when he comes in our own house when we're asleep and leaves a letter on the goddamned toilet, you pretend like you left it there and nothing's wrong."

"I didn't pretend like nothing's wrong."

"What did you do, then, huh?"

"I just didn't want to scare you."

"Didn't want to scare me? Didn't you think about our son at all? What if the mailman was still in the house? We all could've been killed."

"I wasn't thinking right, okay?"

"No, it's not okay. You endangered all of us. You didn't want to scare me? I'm already scared. I've been scared all summer! But I'm not some helpless little nitwit who has to be protected from what's going on. Goddammit, I at least expect you to treat me like an adult."

"You'll wake up Billy," Doug said.

"The mailman was in our house!" she screamed. "What do you expect me to do? Whisper?"

"We don't know that he was here. The door's locked, the windows are all closed—"

Tritia slammed the door to the bathroom, almost hitting his nose. He stood in the hall, furious with her, wanting more than anything to go back into the bedroom and crawl into bed and leave her alone in the damn bathroom. That would scare her enough to teach her a lesson. But as angry as he was, he was more afraid. She was right. They were in danger. The mailman had been inside their house, had invaded the one sacred spot where they had always felt themselves to be safe, had entered their fortress against the outside world. He stood there with his ear to the bathroom door, hoping he wouldn't hear the sound of anyone but Tritia.

The toilet flushed and she came out a few seconds later. "Let me see the letter," she said.

He took the envelope from the pocket of his bathrobe. "Maybe we shouldn't touch it," he suggested. "It might be evidence—"

Tritia ripped it open. The envelope was addressed to her, and inside was a sheet of white paper on which was written, in a flowery feminine hand, a single word:

Hi

Tritia began to tear the paper into little shreds.

"Hey," Doug said. "Don't do that! We need—"

"We need what?" she screamed at him. "This?" She continued to rip the letter. "Don't you know how he works? Don't you understand yet? Are you that stupid? He can't be caught. He can't be touched. The police will come and there'll be no fingerprints, no sign of forced entry, no proof of anything. Nothing for them to go on!"

Doug stared at her, saying nothing.

"He knows what he's doing, and he doesn't do things that will allow him to get caught. Even this letter doesn't mean a damn thing unless it has his fingerprints on it or we can prove that it's his writing."

She was right and he knew it, and the knowledge made him feel both angry and helpless. Tritia continued to tear the letter into increasingly tinier pieces, her hands working faster, more nervously, as tears escaped from beneath her eyelids and rolled down her cheeks. He reached out to grab her hands, to stop them, but she pulled away. "Don't touch me."

He moved closer still, putting his arms around her, pulling her close. She struggled. "Don't touch me," she repeated. But her struggles became progressively weaker, her protestations less adamant, and soon she was sobbing in his arms.

It was not yet eight, but Doug knew the post office would be open. He knew the mailman would be there—if he had returned from his nighttime rounds.

The Bronco sped over the asphalt past the Circle K, past the bank, past the nursery. They had not slept last night after they'd gone back to bed, but they had talked, discussing in whispered voices their fears and feelings, their thoughts and theories. Nothing had been resolved, nothing had been solved, but both of them felt better, safer, more secure.

Doug's anger, however, had not abated one whit, and with the coming of the dawn he had taken a shower, eaten a quick breakfast, and told Trish to stay home and guard

Billy. He was going to confront the mailman, and he wanted to do it while he was still mad enough not to be afraid. She had sensed this, understood this, and had not argued with him. She'd simply nodded and urged him to be careful.

He pulled into the parking lot of the post office. The only other vehicle in sight was the mailman's red car, and he parked right next to it. He got out of the Bronco and walked toward the glass double doors. They were being targeted, he and Trish and Billy, though he did not know why. Everything else at least fit together, made a kind of perverse sense. Ronda and Bernie had been killed because they were rivals; Stockley had been done away with to shut him up; the dogs had been murdered because, as everyone knew, mailmen hated dogs. But no such reasons or rationalizations could be found for the mailman's unceasing harassment of Doug's family and friends. Of course, other people in town were being harassed too, but not as subtly, not as purposefully. Doug knew what was going on, and the mailman knew that he knew and was playing games with him. The horrors were gradually increasing in intensity and proximity, moving in concentric circles toward he and Billy and Trish at the center.

The doors were open and Doug stepped into the post office. The morning chill had not penetrated the inside of the building. The temperature of the stale humid air felt as though it was in the high nineties. He walked up to the front counter, refusing to look at the twisted and repugnant wall posters. The floor felt wet and sticky beneath his feet.

The mailman emerged from the back, smiling. As always, he was wearing his full uniform. As always, his voice was smoothly plastic. "How may I help you, Mr. Albin?"

"Knock off the shit," Doug said. "We both know why I'm here."

"Why are you here?" The mailman's smile widened.

Doug leaned forward. "Because you're threatening my family. Because you came into my house last night and left us a note."

"What kind of note?"

"You know damn well what kind of note. It said, 'Hi.' "

The mailman chuckled. "That is pretty threatening."

Doug clenched his fist and held it up above the counter. "You can stop the innocent act. There's no one here but me and you, and we both know you broke into my house last night."

"I did no such thing. I was at home all evening with Mr. Crowell." The look on the mailman's face was an obvious parody of bruised innocence.

"And where is Mr. Crowell?"

The mailman grinned. "Unfortunately, he's sick today."

"I want you to stop it," Doug said.

"Stop what?"

"This. Everything. Just get the hell out of Willis, or I swear to God I'll make you get out."

The mailman laughed, and this time there was a harshness under the false nicety. His eyes, hard and blue and dead, bored into Doug's, and his voice, when it came out, had none of its usual calculated blandness. "You can't make me do anything," he said, and his tone made Doug's blood run cold.

Doug backed up a step. He realized that for the first time he was seeing the true face of the mailman, and he had to resist the instinctive impulse to flee. The fact that he had been able to goad the mailman into dropping his cover scared him much more than he ever would have thought. He shouldn't have come here alone. He should have brought Mike or Tim or another cop. But he refused to let the mailman sense his fear. He held his ground. "Why are you harassing my family?" he asked, and his voice came out strong, assured. "Why are you picking on me?"

"Because you know," the mailman said.

"I don't know anything."

"Because you complained."

"A lot of people have complained."

"Because I feel like it," the mailman said, and the random callousness of that admission, the utter lack of reason, struck Doug as the truth. He stared into those cold eyes and saw nothing. No passion, no feeling, nothing. Evil was not hatred, he thought. Evil was this.

The mailman smiled, and his voice was filled with an ugly undercurrent of threatening sexuality. "How's the little woman, little man?"

"You bastard!" Doug struck out at the mailman, but the mailman stepped easily back, avoiding the blow. Doug, thrown off-balance, fell against the counter.

The mailman chuckled, then his usual benign mask fell

into place. "I'm sorry, Mr. Albin. The post office is not open yet, but if you'd like to buy a book of stamps—"

"Just leave us alone," Doug said, standing straight.

"It's my job to deliver the mail, and I will continue to perform my duties to the best of my ability."

"Why? No one reads it anyway."

"Everyone reads their mail."

"I don't. I stopped reading it weeks ago."

The mailman stared at him, blinked. "You have to read your mail."

"I don't have to do anything. I take my mail directly from the mailbox to the garbage can, no stops in between."

For the first time, the mailman seemed to Doug at a loss for words. He shook his head as if he didn't understand what Doug was saying. "But you have to read your mail," he repeated.

Doug smiled, realizing he had hit a nerve. "I don't read my mail. My wife doesn't read her mail. We don't look at it at all. We don't even look to see who it's from or who it's addressed to. We just throw it away. So just stop wasting your time and leave us alone."

"But you have to read your mail."

Giselle walked into the office from the back.

"Just leave us alone," Doug said to the mailman. He turned and strode out of the building. He was trembling, shaking, as he walked out to the car.

He thought he heard the mailman say something to him as he left, but he didn't hear what it was and wasn't sure he wanted to know.

36

Doug drove through the night shirtless, his hair still uncombed, wearing only his Levi's and a pair of tennis shoes. He had driven this route a thousand times, but now he seemed to be moving in slow motion, the Bronco putting along at a pitifully inadequate speed. He hit the steering wheel as hard as he could, angry at the car and at himself. The horn bleated, and he almost drove into a tree as he turned a corner too sharply. He slowed down as much as he dared, but he had to get moving. He'd already taken far too long. The Bronco bumped onto the pavement as the dirt road ended, and he pressed down on the gas pedal.

He'd been scared a lot lately and he'd thought he'd reached the limit of terror, that he'd been as frightened as he could be, but when he'd picked up the phone from a sound sleep and heard Hobie's panicked high-pitched voice screaming of blood and virgins while in the background the static of a police radio crackled, he knew that fear had no limit. It was bottomless, and he just kept sinking deeper and deeper into it.

He saw the police lights from far down the street, a twin red-and-blue pulsing against the trees and houses of the neighborhood. The cars and the ambulance were directly in front of Hobie's house, so he had to park several houses away. He slammed the car door shut and ran down the cracked and dirty sidewalk. A gang of bathrobed men and women, neighbors, mingled about behind the yellow ribbon used to cordon off Hobie's trailer, and he pushed his way through them to reach the driveway.

"Hey!" a policeman yelled at him. "What do you think you're doing?"

"I'm here to see Hobie," Doug said.

"I'm sorry," the policeman said, blocking his way. "But you cannot move beyond the barrier."

"I called him," Hobie yelled from the doorway. "Goddammit! Let him in."

Doug looked over at his friend. Hobie's eyes were wide and wild, his short hair sticking out crazily in irregular clumps. He was wearing only Jockey shorts and a T-shirt, and Doug saw with horror that both were streaked with blood.

"Let him through," Tim Hibbard ordered from behind Hobie, and the first policeman motioned Doug under the barrier. Doug ducked under the ribbon and crossed the yard. Sealed plastic containers and boxes marked "Willis Police Department" had been placed next to the walk, and from inside the house came the hissing of radio static, the beeping of electronic instruments, and rough voices ragged with frightened disgust.

"I didn't do it, Doug." Hobie's voice was high and frightened. "I—"

Doug walked up to the door. "Don't say anything until you get a lawyer," he said.

"I didn't—"

"Don't say anything." Doug put a reassuring hand on his friend's shoulder, hoping he appeared calmer than he felt. Something worse than horrible had happened here, something that had turned Hobie into this frightened gibbering creature before him, and he wished for one cruel selfish instant that he had never met Hobie and that he could be one of the hundreds of other people in Willis sleeping right now, totally unaware and unaffected by what was going on. But then he saw the simple look of blind need on his friend's face and was sorry such a thought had even crossed his mind. He turned toward the closest policeman, a middle-aged man with a mustache he had seen around but did not know. "What happened here?"

The policeman looked at him with barely concealed disdain. "You want to know what happened here? You want to see what your buddy did? Come into the bedroom."

"I didn't do it," Hobie insisted. "I swear—"

"Shut up," Doug told him. "Don't say anything." He followed the uniformed officer into the bedroom, where another group of policemen were looking through the closet.

The smell hit him immediately. A thick sour-sweet stench that sickened his stomach and made him want to gag.

Blood.

"Oh, God," Doug breathed. "Oh, Jesus."

The girl's body was lying on the bed. Next to the knives. She was nude and on her stomach, facing away from him. The back of her skull was visible through the bloody hole that had been carved through her scalp. The bone had been chipped off in several places, revealing the pale red-tinged worm twists of her brain. Across her back were scores of stabs and slices, and the skin on her buttocks had been completely peeled off, exposing the wet muscle beneath. A stain of blood that took up half of the sheet spread outward from between her legs.

Doug looked up, unable to bear the sight. On the wall above the bed, snapshots of nude girls had been taped to the paneling. Dozens of them. All of the girls had been tortured and mutilated, sexually violated with knives identical to the ones lying on the bed.

"I didn't do it," Hobie insisted. "I swear to God I didn't do it. I just got here and found—"

The men by the closet turned around. Chief Catfield's eyes widened when he saw Doug. "Get him out of here!" the chief roared.

"I just wanted him to see what his friend did," the mustached policeman stammered.

"I don't give a flying fuck what you wanted!"

Doug staggered backward out of the room, gulping air, not needing to be told to leave. He could still smell the sickening heavy odor of fresh blood, could taste its disgustingly salty muskiness in his mouth. He stood for a moment with his hands on his knees, trying to keep down the gorge threatening to rise in his throat.

"I didn't do it," Hobie said. "He did it!" He grabbed Doug's shoulders, and Doug could see small flecks of blood splattered on his cheeks. "He set me up!"

"Who?" Tim asked from the other side of the room.

"The mailman."

"Don't say anything until you get a lawyer," Doug ordered. He glared at his friend, and Hobie looked subserviently away.

"We have his ass dead to rights," the mustached policeman said. "Ain't no way he's gonna get out of this."

"It wasn't me—"

"Shut up!" Doug roared.

"We'll do the shutting up around here." The chief emerged from the bedroom. "What are you doing here anyway?"

Doug was still trying to get the taste out of his mouth, the smell out of his nostrils. "Hobie called me."

"Are you his lawyer?"

"No. I'm his friend."

"Well, who let you through? Friends are not usually allowed on crime scenes."

Doug held up his hands. "You want me to leave, I'll leave."

"No!" Hobie cried.

"I'll find you a lawyer," Doug promised. "I'll get you whatever you need. Don't worry. There's nothing I can do here anyway."

"I didn't do it," Hobie said. Tears trickled down his cheeks, turning pink as they mingled with the flecks of blood on his skin.

"I know you didn't. And we'll get you out—"

"No you won't," the chief said.

"But you'll have to stay in jail for a few days until everything gets straightened out. Do you want me to call anyone? Your parents?"

"No!"

"Fine. But I'll do what I can, and I'll see you in the morning. Don't worry."

"Jeff!" Catfield motioned for the mustached policeman. "Escort Mr. Albin to the street."

The policeman nodded. "Yes sir."

"We'll get you out," Doug promised.

On the street, the neighbors were talking loudly and animatedly about what they thought had happened inside Hobie's trailer. One squat ugly woman with huge curlers in her hair insisted that she'd known for years the auto teacher was a practicing satanist.

Doug walked slowly back to his car. He wanted to run, he was so pumped up with adrenaline, but he forced himself to move deliberately, trying to keep under control the conflicting emotions raging through him. There was a lot to do. He had to find a lawyer, a good lawyer, get Hobie's stuff together, find out what Hobie's rights were, what could be done for him, whether he was going to be kept in Willis, taken to the county jail, or put in the state prison in Florence. But nothing could be done until morning.

He started the Bronco and backed up. He had not accomplished anything by coming over, he realized, had not helped his friend in any way, although perhaps he had succeeded in getting Hobie to keep quiet until he had legal counsel. What he really needed to do was to nail the mailman, to prove that the mailman had really committed the murder. But that was going to be impossible. There had been no witnesses, and Hobie himself was too far gone to be believable to anyone.

He turned the corner and saw the mailman's car on the next street over. He watched as the mailman's pale hand opened the mailbox in front of a house and inserted a stack of letters.

The hand rose up above the roof of the car and waved once, lazily.

Doug turned in the opposite direction, toward home.

37

Yard Stevens, the lawyer Doug retained for Hobie, was a southern gentleman of the old school who had emigrated to Arizona late in life and still retained many of the mannerisms of the Deep South. He lived and practiced in Phoenix but had a vacation home in Willis, where he spent the summers to escape the heat. He was well-known for both accepting and winning garish tabloid murder cases, and when Doug described to him Hobie's situation, he agreed to take it, even though it meant cutting his vacation short. Stevens' fees were so astronomical as to be unbelievable, but Doug was assured by a school-district representative that Hobie's insurance would cover the cost.

"You know," the lawyer drawled as they drove over to the police station in a huge white Lincoln, "I've been having trouble with the mail myself this summer. I have tried several times to speak to the postmaster about this, but he never seems to be in when I call."

Doug had debated whether or not to tell Stevens all, and he had decided it would be better for Hobie if he did not. At least not yet. He didn't want the lawyer to think both of them were nuts, and if Stevens discovered during his research what was really going on here, well, then they'd have another ally on their side. If he discovered nothing, Doug could always fill him in on the details later. "I've had trouble too," Doug admitted.

"If, as I believe, this is a townwide problem, we may be able to work this to our advantage."

Doug smiled. "Let's hope so."

The lawyer looked at him. "Do you think your friend's guilty? Tell me the truth. We're covered here by lawyer-client privilege, and it will never go further than this."

Doug was surprised by the forthrightness of the question. "He's innocent," he said.

"That's what I like to hear."

"What do you think?"

Stevens chuckled, a low mellifluous comforting sound. "I'll make my decision once I talk to my client."

At the police station, they were searched, then led into a small room empty save for three chairs and a table, all bolted to the floor. Hobie was brought in, handcuffed, and remained silent until his guard left the room. He looked even worse, even crazier, than he had last night, and Doug had a sinking feeling in the pit of his stomach. He'd been hoping Hobie would make a good impression on the lawyer.

"Okay," Doug said. "Now we can talk."

Hobie glanced furtively around. He looked under the table, felt under the chair, as if searching for electronic listening devices. Under other circumstances, the paranoia of Hobie's reaction would have been funny. But nothing seemed funny anymore.

"There're no bugs," Doug said. "Our police department can't afford any."

"And even if there were," Stevens said, "evidence gathered through their use would not be admissible in court."

"This is your lawyer," Doug said. "Yard Stevens."

The lawyer held out a thick pink hand. "How do you do?"

"How do you think? I'm in jail for murder."

"Did you do it?"

"Hell, no."

Doug felt a little better. Hobie still looked awful, but the shocked incoherence of last night and the dissolution of the past few weeks seemed to have disappeared. He seemed more confident now, closer to his normally abrasive self.

"Doug?" Stevens turned toward him. "I would like to speak to my client alone from here on. I may need your testimony in court, and I don't want to jeopardize its validity by allowing you access to privileged information."

Doug nodded. "Okay. I'll be waiting right outside."

"Fine."

"Thanks," Hobie said.

"I'll be by to see you later." Doug knocked on the closed door and it was opened from the outside. He was walking down the hall toward the front office when he heard a familiar voice behind him. "Mr. Albin? Can I talk to you for a moment?"

He turned to see Mike Trenton beckoning him from the doorway of an office.

"Doug. I thought I told you to call me Doug."

"Doug?"

He followed Mike into a small room dominated by a huge desk. Two walls were lined, floor to ceiling, with textbooks and bound case studies. "This used to be the police library," Mike explained, noticing his glance. "Well, it still is, but now it doubles as my office."

"What did you want to talk to me about?"

"Mr. Beecham."

"I thought you were off all mailman cases."

Mike shrugged. "It's a small department. A lot's been happening. We're shorthanded. Besides, this is not a 'mailman case.' "

"It is too, and you know it."

"I just wanted to ask you a few questions about Mr. Beecham."

Doug began pacing up and down the length of the tiny crowded room. "Come on, Mike. You know damn well that Hobie didn't kill that girl."

"I know no such thing. I'd like to help you, I really would, but Mr. Beecham's fingerprints—bloody fingerprints, I might add—were found all over the murder weapon and all over the room. And those photos on the wall . . ." He shook his head. "They're not proof of anything, but they're certainly a sign of a sick mind—"

"Those photos were sent to him by his brother."

"His dead brother?"

"What's the matter with you, Mike? What's happened? A week ago you had an open mind about this, now you're just . . ." He groped for the right word.

"Facing the facts," the policeman finished for him.

"Hiding," Doug said. "Grasping at any answer that fits into your police logic, that can be easily catagorized and catalogued and filed away and forgotten. I know you're scared. Hell, we're all scared. But you're looking for reassurance, and you're not going to find it. You want to believe that we're crazy, that none of this is happening, that life is going to go on as normal. But it's not going to go on as normal. People are dying here, Mike. You might not want to admit it, but everyone knows it. I know it, you know it, everyone in town knows it. People are dying because of the fucking mailman. Call it supernatural, call it whatever you want, but it's real, it's happening."

"His prints were on the weapon," Mike repeated tiredly.

"Be serious with me, Mike. Level with me. Don't hand me that official line crap. Be straight with me."

"It's an open-and-shut case—"

"Come on. I'm not your enemy here, Mike. Jesus, if we all just spent a little more time working together and a little less time trying to keep all of our goddamn roles so virginal and separate, we'd get a hell of a lot more done."

The policeman smiled slightly. "You were always a good talker. That's why you were one of my favorite teachers."

"I'm not just talking here."

"As far as I'm concerned, you are. We have proof, Mr. Albin. His prints are on the weapon. Blood was found under his fingernails, on his clothing, in his hair."

Doug opened the door. "Fine," he said, pointing an accusing finger at the young policeman. "Toe the party line, hide your head in the goddamn sand. But the next one's on your head. You could've done something about it. You want to talk to me about Hobie? Get yourself a subpoena." He slammed the door behind him, strode through and out of the police office, and stood in the open air, breathing deeply, trying to calm down. The warm morning air filled his lungs, tasting clean and fresh and good, reminding him of happier, far more different summers. His eyes scanned the small parking lot and found the shiny metal mailbox standing on a post at the juncture of the parking lot and the road, next to the low ranch fence. Sunlight glinted off the box's curved top.

He hated those aluminum pieces of shit.

He waited for Stevens by the car.

38

"Let me in! Let me in, goddammit!" Tritia stood on Irene's front porch alternately ringing the doorbell and banging on the door itself. She knew the old woman was home. The car was in the driveway and she had seen movement behind the lace curtains. Irene just didn't want to talk to her.

The cooler weather of the past few days was gone, and the hot afternoon sun beat at her back. She was already sweating, dying of thirst, and that gave her another idea. She decided to try a different tack. "Just let me in for a minute!" she called through the closed door. "All I want is a glass of iced tea! Then I'll be out of your hair for good!"

She waited a moment and was getting set to launch another pounding barrage when she heard the metal jingle of the chain being unhooked from inside, the sound of the deadbolt drawing out. A few seconds later the knob rattled as the lock was undone. The door was slowly pulled open.

Tritia barely recognized her friend. Irene appeared to have shrunk three or four inches and to have lost at least ten or fifteen pounds since the last time she'd seen her. She had never been a big woman, but now she appeared definitely small, shriveled. Her thin wiry hair was uncombed and spread out from her head in tangled wisps. Her face looked frighteningly gaunt, and she was wearing what looked like her pajamas. She glared at Tritia accusingly. "I told you not to tell anyone," she said.

"I'm sorry," Tritia apologized. "But I was worried about you. I knew what was happening, and I wanted to help—"

"You made it worse," the old woman said. She jumped suddenly with a cry of fright, whirling around, looking behind her as though searching for someone, but there was no one there. She turned nervously back toward Tritia, her eyes haunted. "Leave me alone," she said. "Please."

"I'm your friend," Tritia said. "I care."

Irene closed her eyes and sighed. She stepped aside, pulling the door open, and Tritia walked into the house. It was a shambles. Closet doors were open, their contents tossed into the center of the living room, cardboard boxes overturned on the Oriental carpet. Broken glassware could be seen through the doorway of the kitchen. Irene, cheeks sunken, staring eyes hollow, backed quickly away from the door, her hands nervously folding and unfolding.

Tritia swallowed heavily, feeling an ache of sadness in her breast as she looked at the frightened pitiful woman before her. A month ago, she would not have thought this possible. She would have said death, and only death, would be able to break Irene, and even then the old woman would go out kicking and fighting. But obviously the mailman had been able to do it just as well. She spoke softly to her friend. "Irene, what's happened?"

The old woman blanched visibly when Tritia spoke, cringing as though she were being yelled at, as though afraid of being hit. She suddenly cocked her head, listening to a noise that wasn't there, then dropped to her knees and righted one of the boxes on the floor, throwing in some of the small knickknacks that were lying on the carpet.

Tritia knelt down next to her. "Irene?" she said softly.

The old woman stopped picking up items off the ground and began to cry. Her voice was thin and reedy, the powerful assured voice Tritia remembered long gone.

Tritia reached out and hugged her friend. Irene stiffened noticeably at first, tensing as if preparing to be attacked, but she did not pull away, and gradually her muscles relaxed, giving in. She continued to sob, a seemingly endless flood of tears, and Tritia patiently held her, murmuring soothing noises in her ear.

When her crying finally stopped, she pulled away, wiped her eyes, and looked up at Tritia. "Come here," she said, standing up.

"What is it?"

"Come here."

Tritia followed Irene down the hall to her husband's den. She tried not to think of the toe, the severed toe, lying in the box, as Irene opened the door. Tritia peeked over her friend's shoulder. The room was filled with boxes of all shapes and sizes. They had been thrown into the room and left where they'd landed, right side up, upside down, on their sides. All were wrapped in brown butcher paper.

Tritia stepped around Irene into the room.

"Don't touch them," Irene screamed.

Tritia jumped. She turned around. She hadn't been planning to touch anything. "What's in them?" she asked, though she already knew the answer.

"Jasper."

"Your husband?"

"The parts of his body."

Tritia felt suddenly cold, chilled to the bone. She backed away from the open door. "None of the boxes are open," she said. "Maybe you're wrong."

"I don't have to open them." Irene pointed toward a square box big enough to contain a stack of hardback books. "I think that's his head."

Tritia closed the den door, pulling her friend away. "You have to get out of here," she said. "Why don't you come home with me?"

"No!" The old woman's voice was still capable of surprising sharpness.

"At least tell the police. Have them get these boxes out of here. You can't live like this."

Irene's face clouded over. "I'm sorry, I have no tea. You'll have to leave now." She jumped, crying out, and instantly looked at the floor behind her, but there was nothing there.

"Please," Tritia begged.

"It's my house. I want you out of here."

"I'm your friend."

"You *were* my friend."

"I'll call the police and tell them what I've seen and they'll come in here anyway."

"You do what you have to do."

Tritia felt like crying with frustration. She yelled at her friend. "Can't you see what's happening here? Can't you see what the mailman's doing?"

"I see better than you. Please leave now."

Tritia allowed herself to be pushed out the doorway. She remained on the porch for several minutes after the door was slammed shut, after she heard the sounds of locks and latches being drawn. She thought about the boxes in the den. The mailman might just be trying to scare her. They might not really contain body parts.

But they might.

What were they going to do? They couldn't just sit around until they were all knocked off or driven crazy. Something had to be done. But what? The police were no help. Apparently the higher-ups in the Postal Service weren't either.

Maybe someone should kill him.

The thought came, unbidden, but though she tried to push it away, tried to tell herself it was wrong and immoral and illegal, the idea stayed with her.

And by the time she had driven home it was starting to sound pretty damn good.

39

The phone rang, and Doug was awake instantly. He reached over Tritia's sleeping body and picked it up in the middle of the second ring. A feeling of heavy foreboding had awakened with him, and he glanced at the clock on the dresser as he brought the receiver to his ear, thinking with the fading vestiges of dream logic that he needed to remember the time of this call.

Two-fifteen.

"Hello?" Doug said. His voice was tired, tinged with annoyance at being disturbed, but there was an edge in it as well as he prepared himself for bad news. No one called at two-fifteen in the morning if it wasn't bad news.

"Mr. Albin?" It was Mike Trenton. Doug's throat felt constricted, his chest tight, and he had to force himself to swallow. The policeman sounded strange. Not exactly frightened, but something very close to it.

"What happened?" he asked.

"It's Mr. Beecham. He's, uh, he's dead."

Doug closed his eyes, letting his head fall onto the pillow, unwilling to make the effort anymore to keep it up.

"We found him on the floor of his cell," Mike continued. "His forehead is completely caved in, and there's blood all over the wall and floor. It's hard to tell, but it appears as though he butted his head against the wall until he smashed open his skull.

"We took away his clothes and shoelaces when we admitted him, but he didn't seem dangerous or self-destructive and we didn't think there was any need to restrain him or—"

Doug reached over Tritia's body and hung up the phone. After a second's thought, he took it off the hook.

"What is it?" Tritia asked groggily.

Doug said nothing but simply stared into space, and a moment later she had again fallen asleep.

He did not sleep until morning.

40

The funeral was short and sparsely attended. Hobie Bee-cham had not been the most popular man in Willis during the best of times, and the mailman's successfully slanderous framing of the auto-shop teacher had obviously taken its toll on Hobie's already low popularity rating. As Doug stood next to the open grave, he found himself wondering if anyone would have shown up even if the murder hadn't occurred. The mailman's continued psychic assault on the town seemed to have drained a lot of the energy from people, had made them less social, angrier, less trustworthy. He wondered if even Bob Ronda could draw the crowd today he'd been able to draw a month ago.

That was a strange way of looking at it, to see a funeral as a popularity contest in which final judgment was passed on a man's life by the number of people who attended, by the size of the crowd. But it was also strangely appropriate since many people did judge the worth of others by the quantity of their social relationships. Particularly in a small town like Willis. A man could be rich, famous, successful, but if he lived in Willis and he wasn't married, if he stayed home alone on Friday nights instead of going out with friends or family, there was definitely something wrong with him.

And there had always been something wrong with Hobie. He'd admitted it himself, many times. Making friends, as he was fond of saying, was not his major goal in life. Doug found himself smiling, though his eyes were moist. Hobie had been loud, obnoxious, iconoclastic, and fiercely inde-pendent. He was who he was, and if someone didn't like it, that was their problem.

He had also been a good friend and a damn fine teacher, and Doug thought that if all of the students whom Hobie had taught and befriended, had helped and counseled over the years, were still in town the cemetery would have been full.

He looked over at Tritia. No love had ever been lost between her and Hobie, but she was crying now, and more than the coffin in the ground, more than the gathered mourners, more than the carved tombstone, her tears made him realize that his friend was really and truly gone.

Doug looked into the sky as the tears rolled down his own cheeks, trying to think of something neutral, something unconnected with death, so he would not start sobbing.

Billy was taking it really hard. This time, they had sat him down and discussed it with him and left it up to him whether or not he wanted to attend the funeral. He had almost said yes because he felt obligated, felt he might not be showing how much he cared if he did not attend, but Trish had assured him that they did not expect him to go, that it was not required, that Hobie, wherever he was, would understand, and Billy had elected to stay home. There was no sitter for him this time and both of them worried about leaving him alone, but he promised to keep all the doors locked, the windows shut, and to remain upstairs until they returned. Doug told him that it was all right if he watched TV downstairs or made himself food in the kitchen, but Billy declared with an adamance that surprised them both that he would not go downstairs until they returned.

The morning, appropriately enough, was overcast, funereal. The storm season was upon them, and the weather from now until fall would be characterized by the dichotomous extremes of dry heat and cold rain. Doug said a few words over the casket, as did several other teachers, and then the nondenominational minister began his eulogy and consecration. Before the minister had finished, light drops of rain were falling, and by the time the graveside service was over it had turned into a real downpour. No one had brought umbrellas, and everyone ran through the cemetery to their cars or trucks.

Doug thought of the cars and car parts sitting in Hobie's yard and wondered what would happen to them.

He and Trish were the last to leave the gravesite, and they walked slowly between the stones, even though the rain was coming down hard. They watched Yard Stevens' Lincoln pull out of the parking lot, following the small line of vehicles heading down the road.

Hobie's parents had not come, although Mike said they had been notified and were the ones who had made all the arrangements, and Doug found himself wondering if perhaps they had missed their son's funeral due to a mixup in the mail. It was entirely possible that they had received a letter from the funeral director telling them that, due to scheduling conflicts, Hobie's funeral had to be put back a day, and that they would arrive in Willis tomorrow to find that everything was over, their son buried, services finished.

"He killed him," Doug said aloud. "He killed him as surely as if he put a bullet to his head."

"I know," Tritia said, squeezing his hand.

Doug was silent for a moment as they walked. His shoes sunk in the mud. "Let's leave, he said. "Let's get the hell out of this town." He looked at her. "Let's go."

"Permanently or for a vacation?"

"Either."

"I don't know," she said slowly. "It doesn't seem right to just abandon everyone here."

"Abandon who?"

"Everyone. Our friends."

"The ones that are dead, the ones that are crazy, or the ones who've disappeared?"

She turned on him. "What's the matter with you?"

"Nothing's the matter with me. I just want to get out of here so we can get our lives back together while we still have lives."

"And who's going to stop him?"

"Who's going to stop him if we are here?" Doug ran a hand through his wet hair. "In case you haven't noticed, we haven't exactly sent him packing. Hell, we're batting 0 for 0 here. We haven't done a damn thing. Maybe if we leave things'll calm down."

"And who'll be here to fight him?"

They stared at each other through the thin wall of rain between them. Doug glanced down the hill toward the post office and saw that the flag was flying mockingly at half-mast.

"We can't leave," Tritia said gently. "We have a responsibility here."

"I'm tired of responsibility."

The rain died, cut abruptly off as though a spigot in the sky had been turned, but wetness continued to run down Doug's face, and he discovered that he was crying. Tritia reached out to him, tentatively, touching his cheek, his forehead, his chin. She moved forward and put her arms around his back, drawing him close, holding him, and they stood like that for a long long time.

For dinner they had chicken tortilla crepes. The meal was one they all enjoyed, and Tritia had spent much of the afternoon preparing it, but none of them seemed to have much of an appetite and they picked silently at their food, lost in separate parallel thoughts.

The electricity went out again in the middle of the meal, and Tritia picked up the matches and lit the candles she had placed on the table. The power had been going on and off so often lately that she now kept candles and flashlights in each room of the house for backup sources of light. It was getting to be almost second nature. If this ordeal was teaching them anything, it was teaching them to be self-sufficient, teaching them that they did not really need all the amenities they'd always thought they'd needed in order to survive. She wondered how some of the other, older people in town were getting along. Her family, at least, had had a head start—she had always made food from scratch and over the years had implemented many of the independent natural living suggestions she'd learned from *Mother Earth News*— but adjusting might be a little more difficult for some of the other residents of Willis.

The reason for these constant outages was obvious: the mailman wanted to break down their resistance, to make sure they knew that nothing could be relied upon, nothing was safe. The security blanket of civilization was one that he could rip off at will, exposing their helpless nakedness, and doing so was something he clearly enjoyed. Exactly how he accomplished the blackouts, how he brought about the cessation of water and gas and phone service, was still not known. She and Doug had talked to people at the offices of each of the respective utilities until they were blue in the face, but the answers they received were vague and inconclusive, having something to do with fines and penalties, work orders and correspondence.

Paperwork that had gotten fouled up through the mail.

According to a representative for the town's department of water and power, it could not provide services because *its* water and electricity had been cut off at the source—the Salt

River Project in Phoenix. The project had said, alternately, that the department had not paid its bills and that its quota of services had already been provided. Cited as proof were invoices received through the mail.

But the representative assured Doug and Tritia that the problems would soon be solved, and water and electricity restored.

The man at the phone company, the same manager Doug had talked to before, was even less specific and promised nothing.

It was ironic that the people who were probably having the least difficulty adapting to these circumstances were the ones living on the outskirts of the town, those who normally lived in the most primitive conditions. Now, with their wells and septic tanks and butane generators, their lives were going on as normal, while the rest of them ate cold food and took cold showers and lit candles for light.

"I hope this doesn't last all night," Tritia said.

Doug took a bite of his tortilla crepe. "It probably will."

Billy dropped his fork, and it fell loudly onto his plate. He had hardly eaten anything, had merely cut up and smeared and played with his food.

Tritia fixed him with a no-nonsense stare. "Finish eating your dinner," she said.

Billy groaned. "I don't—"

A rock crashed through one of the front windows, glass shattering explosively, muffled not at all by the closed curtains. There was the sound of another rock hitting hard against the outside wall.

"Fucker!" someone yelled angrily. The voice was that of an adult male, not a child, not a teenager.

Doug quickly pushed back his chair, knocking it over as he scrambled around the table toward the front door.

"Don't!" Tritia yelled. Her face was white with fear.

Billy, too, looked scared, and Doug could feel his own heart pounding within his chest, but he rushed to the door anyway.

Another rock hit.

"Fucker!"

And then there was the sound of flying gravel, a pickup peeling out and speeding away.

Doug pulled open the door and ran onto the porch in time to see the taillights of a truck disappearing between the trees. There was still a cloud of dust in the drive. He looked down. At his feet on the porch were several rocks approximately the size of softballs. Although only one had hit the window, two of the others had hit the wall and had been thrown with enough strength to make small splintered indentations in the wooden front of the A-frame. How the hell had someone been able to drive close enough to the house to throw rocks this size and not be heard?

From down the road in the silent forest, he heard the sound of triumphant whooping and hollering, growing fainter as the truck sped farther away.

"What was it?" Tritia stood in the doorway, trembling, holding Billy's shoulders.

"I don't know."

"Why?"

"Why do the Nelsons think we killed their dog? Why did Todd think I was persecuting him?" Doug looked at his son. "You don't know who did this, do you?"

Billy shook his head, still frightened.

"I didn't think so. Come on. Let's go inside." He herded Tritia and Billy through the door, then closed and locked it behind him. Tomorrow, he'd have to find someone to replace the window. He glanced around the front of the living room. In the candlelight broken shards and bits of glass glittered on the chair and part of the couch. They would have to rearrange the furniture in case something like this happened again. He didn't want Tritia or Billy hit by a rock or cut by a stray piece of glass.

His muscles were still tight, knotted. Although he wanted to know who had thrown the rocks, who had been in the truck, he found himself strangely unangry with the men involved. He was beginning to see the people of Willis as either victims or puppets, manipulated by the controlling will of the mailman. It was the mailman he blamed for everything, from the deaths of dogs and people to racial attacks to utility failures, and that worried him a little. His attitude seemed too close to that of classic paranoia for him to feel entirely comfortable with it. But, farfetched as it sounded, he knew it was the truth. He was not ascribing an omnipotence to the mailman he did not possess; he was merely recognizing an existing situation. He would not be at all surprised to learn that the mailman had orchestrated everything to occur in such a manner that it would engender within him exactly the sort of doubts he was harboring now.

He shook his head. He really was getting paranoid.

Tritia was already clearing the dinner dishes. They had not finished, but no one felt like eating right now. Doug walked over to help her. Even Billy took his plate to the kitchen, though he normally would not be caught dead voluntarily doing any sort of labor connected with the family.

A car drove by on the road, stereo blasting, and all three of them tensed as they waited to hear whether it would turn into their drive. The car continued down the road, the sounds of the engine and stereo fading. They looked at one another silently, then continued to clear the dishes.

The curtain covering the broken window blew inward with the light night breeze.

41

After breakfast, Doug called around trying to find someone who would replace the window. Harmon's carried the glass, but there was no one available to do the installation. If Hobie were here, he would have known how to install the window, but Doug was not even willing to attempt it. Aside from the simplest and most necessary household chores, he was incompetent at manual labor. The shed was one thing—it was designed for construction by people like himself and came with simple step-by-step instructions—but the window was something else. He called several handymen listed in the phone book, but two did not answer and one refused to perform the work. The only man who would even consider doing the job said the labor would cost $150, and he would not be able to get to it for another two weeks.

Doug was tempted to just board the damn thing up and hang a picture of a window in front of it.

He made some more calls, then went back to the original handyman, whose price had now gone up to $175, apparently as punishment for daring to shop around and try to find someone else.

He hung up the phone and felt Tritia's hand on his shoulder. He turned around. She was dressed in jeans and a nice blouse, and her purse was over her shoulder. "Do you have the keys?" she asked.

"Where're you going?"

"Irene's. I'm worried about her. I try to call and there's never any answer, and after what happened to Hobie . . ." Her voice trailed off, not needing to finish the sentence.

Doug pulled the keys from his pocket. "I'll go with you."

"I think it's better if I go alone. She's not really up to seeing people right now. I don't even know if she'll see me. You just stay here with Billy."

Doug's eyes met hers, and she saw worry in them, concern. "It's dangerous out there."

"I know. I'll be careful."

"Why don't I drop you off and park down the road? You can—"

"No," she said firmly. She took the keys from his hand. "Don't worry. I can take care of myself. I'm just going to check on her and be right back. You won't even notice I'm gone."

"Why don't you have the police check on her? She's an old frail woman, tell them you think she might have slipped and fallen in the bathtub. They'll do it."

"No," Tritia said. She gave him a quick kiss. "I'll be back in twenty minutes."

"The car's almost out of gas, but there's enough for you to get there and back. Don't buy any. I'll get it later."

"Okay," she said.

Troubled, he watched her get in the car, back up the drive, and head through the trees toward town.

Something was wrong. Tritia felt it the instant she stepped out of the car. The atmosphere was changed, strangely and indefinably altered. The air was still, even the birds and insects quiet, as though some vast invisible soundproof barrier had been placed over the property. The house itself seemed empty, abandoned, though nothing physical appeared to have changed. She shivered. Death hung over Irene's house. She knew it as surely as she knew today was Tuesday. She pushed the thought from her mind. She was just being foolish. Superstitious. She forced herself to walk across the dirt to the front door. Peering through the lace curtain, she saw no sign of movement.

She knocked on the door. "Irene!"

Her voice died flatly, without even the faintest hint of an echo.

Still no movement inside. Something was definitely wrong. She knocked harder, rang the bell. "Irene!"

What if the old woman really had fallen down and had broken something and couldn't move? What if she had had a heart attack or a stroke?

What if the mailman had gotten her?

"Irene!" Tritia rattled the doorknob, but it was locked as usual. Worried now, she moved around the side of the house to the back door, weeds scratching her bare ankles. The back door was unlocked and she pushed it open carefully. A bad sign. Irene always locked both doors.

Maybe he was in the house.

"Irene!"

The house was silent.

Tritia's heart was pumping crazily, pounding with an amplified fear rhythm she could feel in her stomach and throat and could hear in her head. She should get out of here now, fast, and drive straight to the police station and bring someone back. The last thing she should do was explore on her own. But her feet carried her forward into the kitchen. The floor was littered with pots and pans and broken china, and she stepped gingerly over the smashed pieces of shattered glass. On the counter, she could see a loaf of homemade bread covered with splotches of green mold. In the window, Irene's plants had grown wildly before succumbing to the brown dryness of a waterless death. The room was filled with the mingled odors of spices, herbs, and decay.

"Irene!" she called.

No answer.

She continued through the doorway into the living room, took in at a glance the ripped upholstery of the antique furniture, the overturned television, the debris on the Oriental carpet, and realized that Irene was not here.

She recalled the parcels in the den, and she thought she knew in which room she would find her friend. She felt a sinking feeling in the pit of her stomach. "Irene!" she called.

No answer.

Now was the time for her to leave, or at least to pick up the phone and call the police, but she continued to move deeper into the house. She would check the other rooms first. If Irene was not in any of them, if it was clear that she was in the den, then she would call the police.

Tritia walked down the hallway. She glanced into the bedroom. The pillows had been ripped open, feathers were everywhere, but there was no sign of her friend. She saw her own reflection in the cracked mirrored door of the busted armoire. She had not realized how truly frightened she was until she saw the anxious expression on her pale face.

She moved down the hall to the bathroom.

Where the tiled floor was covered with ripped brown packaging paper, untied string, opened boxes.

Where Irene was lying in the tub, wrists slit.

Tritia stared at her friend. She had obviously been here for some time. The skin on her body was white and water-logged, her sightlessly staring eyes glazed over with dried cataracts. The blood had settled, separating from the lighter water, and the bottom portion of her body was hidden beneath a heavy red liquid blanket. Around her floated the individual pieces of her husband's body. Arms. Legs. Hands. Head. The pieces were white and bloodless, pruned with water, and they bobbed in the bath, crowding for space.

Floating between Irene's outstretched legs was a small severed, castrated penis.

Tritia wanted to look away but could not. Her gaze was fixed on the bloody bathtub.

She did not realize she was screaming until her throat began to hurt.

42

Doug made lunch, hot dogs, and as he spread mustard over the buns, he glanced worriedly out the window at Tritia. She was working in her garden, trying once again to get it into some semblance of order. He was concerned about her. After her initial shock at finding Irene's body, she had quickly returned to normal. Two days later, she was her usual self. She was not disturbed, not frightened, not withdrawn, not anything. That wasn't right, he knew. That wasn't natural. He himself was still coming to grips with Hobie's death, and he had not even seen his friend's body. Tritia had discovered Irene in the tub, wrists slashed, surrounded by body parts, and she was acting as though nothing unusual had happened, as though nothing was wrong. He had not talked about it with her, had not brought up the subject of Irene at all for fear of disturbing her unnecessarily. He had assumed that when she was ready to discuss it, she would do so. But so far she had not been inclined to bring it up, which was definitely out of character for her.

He watched her through the window, pulling weeds, wondering if this was some sort of elaborate denial, if one day, unexpectedly, she was just going to snap and all of her pent-up emotions would explode.

Maybe he would broach the subject with her, bring it up gently.

As usual, the mailman had gotten off scot-free. The police had questioned him, but he had pulled the old the-Postal-Service-is-not-responsible-for-the-content-of-the-mail-it-delivers crap, and as usual, there was not a damn thing anyone could do about it. There was nothing linking him specifically to the mail sent to Irene, nothing anyone could prove.

The mailman promised that he would institute a thorough

Postal Service inquiry to discover the source of the body-part packages.

A thorough Postal Service inquiry . . .

Shit.

The hot dogs were boiling, and Doug told Billy to run outside and get his mother, it was time for lunch.

"Wait," Billy said. "It's almost time for a commercial."

"You've seen that show a thousand times. Go get her now."

"Wait a sec."

Doug sighed, shaking his head. He opened the window, letting in a breath of warm summer air. "Time to eat," he called.

She looked up at him, squinting, and waved. "Be right there."

He watched her put down the trowel, brush off her hands and knees, and jog toward the porch. They should have gotten out of here. They should have left Willis a long time ago, when everything first started, before it all got too deep. Now it was too late. They were stuck. The gas stations in town had run out of gas, and no new fuel was scheduled to be delivered because none of the stations, not even the name franchises, had paid their bills.

The checks had gotten lost in the mail.

Doug turned off the stove, took out the hot dogs, and used a fork to pick them up, putting them in the buns. The gas shortage was only temporary, he knew. Phone calls were being made, problems explained, deals negotiated, but for at least the next three or four days no one could leave Willis unless they already had a full tank of gas. The Bronco was only half full.

He couldn't help feeling that everything was coming to a head, that three or four days was all the mailman needed to accomplish whatever it was he had set out to do.

Tritia came in sweating, wiping her forehead. "Whew! It's hot out there today. I hope we get some rain this afternoon to cool it off. Anybody hear the weather?"

Doug shook his head. Billy, watching *Dick Van Dyke*, did not even hear the question.

Tritia washed her hands and face in the bathroom. She gratefully accepted the plate of hot dogs, though her face clouded over for a second when he handed her a glass of iced tea. She took her food onto the porch and Doug followed her outside, bringing his own lunch. They sat next to each other at the table.

Tritia took a bite of her hot dog. "What are your plans for this afternoon?" she asked.

He frowned. "Plans? I don't—"

"Good. I want you to dig up that manzanita by the side of the house. I want to expand my garden."

"Look—" he began.

"You have something more important to do, Mr. Teacher?"

He looked at her, and the worry must have shown in his eyes because she looked away, refusing to meet his gaze. "No," he said softly. "I don't have anything else to do. I'll help you with your garden."

"Thank you." She took another bite of her hot dog.

Inside, the phone rang, its tones clear and pure in the still noon air. Doug stood up, pushing back his chair. "I'll get it," he called. He hurried inside and picked up the receiver. "Hello?"

A woman's voice jumped out at him. "Help me! Dear Jesus God, help! Oh, God! I'm here by myself!"

Goose bumps arose on Doug's arms. "Who is this?" he asked.

"Tritia? Help me!"

"This isn't Tritia, this is—"

"Oh God oh Jesus I hear him now!"

"What is it?"

"Tritia!" the woman screamed.

"Trish!" Doug yelled. "Get in here fast!"

Tritia ran inside and took the receiver from his grasp. "Hello?"

"He's here again!"

Tritia recognized the voice. Ellen Ronda. She had not called since the time Tritia had been alone at the house, and she sounded much worse now. Hysteria had not merely crept into her voice, it had transformed it completely, until she no longer sounded even remotely like herself. The woman on the other end of the line was not someone who could have ever been referred to as The Rock. This was a woman firmly in the grip of madness, a gibbering fool, a babbling idiot.

"What is it?" Tritia demanded.

"He's coming after me," Ellen screamed. "With a baseball bat!"

"Calm down," Tritia told her. "Just—"

And then she heard the sound of glass breaking.

The sound of a baseball bat hitting a wall.

"Get over here!" Ellen screamed. "Bring the police! He's—"

There was a loud crack as the line went dead.

Tritia dropped the phone and grabbed Doug's hand. "Let's go," she said.

"What's happening?"

"Ellen's being attacked! Right now!"

"Let's call the—"

"There's no time!" Tritia pushed open the door. "You stay here," she yelled at Billy. "Lock the doors! Stay inside!" She pulled Doug across the porch toward the car. "Let's go. Now!"

Doug drove as quickly as he could, but the Rondas' house was on the other side of town and there was no shortcut. The Bronco bumped along, splashing through the creek crossing, bottoming out in the ruts. As they sped through town twenty miles over the speed limit, Doug hoped that a cop would see them and chase them, but the street seemed to be deserted. He glanced quickly over at the post office as they sped past it. The parking lot was empty. Even the mailman's car was gone.

The front door of the Rondas' house was wide open. Doug pulled to a quick stop in the driveway, then ran inside the house without waiting for Tritia. He had nothing in his hand and cursed himself for not taking out a tire iron or something that could be used as a weapon.

He ran through the wrecked living room, through the trashed family room.

Ellen was lying on the floor of the kitchen, naked. Dead. A knife was clutched in one hand; her other hand was clawed into the linoleum. She had died with her mouth open, screaming or trying to scream, and her face was frozen in a rictus of terror.

But it was not the upper half of her body that commanded Doug's attention.

He stared down at Ellen's body as Tritia came up behind him. The old woman's legs were broken and spread wide apart, the ankles jutting out at impossible angles. Whatever had been used to assault her vagina had left behind a huge gaping hole from which hung small clinging pieces of flesh. The skin up to her navel had been split, and blood was everywhere, covering her legs, the floor, the kitchen table, thickly, darkly red.

"Oh, God," Tritia said. "Oh, my God." She rushed outside and promptly threw up.

Trying to keep his own lunch down, Doug called the police.

They were seated in the Rondas' living room, listening to the sounds of the police and the coroner working in the kitchen. Doug found his eyes fixating on a photograph of Ronda, his wife, and both boys displayed on the mantel above the rock fireplace. Next to him Tritia sat silently. He held her hand, periodically giving it a small squeeze, but she said nothing and her hand did not react back. He heard a noise behind him as someone emerged from the kitchen.

"We'll get him," Mike said. "We'll get him now."

"Kind of late, don't you think?" Doug stood up, turning to face the policeman, but the anger within him dissipated as he saw the look of devastation on the young officer's face.

Mike closed his eyes, trying to catch his breath. "Yes it is," he said. "Way too late."

The coroner emerged from the doorway behind him. A sharp hawk-nosed man with the lean look of a meaner Harry Dean Stanton, he alone seemed unfazed by what he had seen. He handed Mike a clipboard and several forms.

"What caused it?" Doug asked.

The coroner looked at him. "Her death? The official story will be that she was raped and murdered."

"What is the unofficial story? The real story?"

"The real story? You saw for yourself. She was raped to death. She was raped and sodomized with a large blunt object, approximately the size of a baseball bat. Her intestines are ruptured, her liver and kidneys smashed, and her gall bladder has been completely torn apart. I'll have to conduct an autopsy and examine her more thoroughly before I can determine the exact extent of the damage and the precise organ stoppage that caused her death."

Mike looked over the forms, signed the top one, then handed the clipboard back to the coroner, who went back into the kitchen. Mike followed. Through the doorway, Doug saw two white-suited men unrolling a plastic body bag.

Doug sat back down on the couch, grasping Tritia's limp hand. A moment later, Mike emerged from the kitchen with Chief Catfield.

"Mr. Albin," the chief said, nodding in acknowledgment.

Doug glared at him, pointing toward the kitchen. "So, tell me, Chief, did she kill herself too?"

"That's not funny, Mr. Albin."

"You're damn right it's not funny. I told you assholes about the mailman weeks ago. I told you something like this would happen. I warned you. Are you happy now? Now do you believe me?" He slammed his palm angrily against the table in front of him. "Shit!"

"For what it's worth, I believe you, Mr. Albin. But it's not as simple as you seem to think it is. Of course, we're going to question Mr. Smith. But unless we find some prints or threads of clothing or other physical evidence, or unless we can find a witness who can place him at the scene of the crime, there's no way in hell we'll be able to detain him for more than an afternoon."

"Ellen told my wife this was going to happen! She said the mailman was going to kill her! Isn't that proof enough? Doesn't that count for something?"

The chief turned toward Tritia. "What exactly did she say, Mrs. Albin?"

Tritia stared at him dazedly for a moment, then shook her head as if to clear it. Her voice, when it came out, was rational, lucid, and completely normal. She looked from Doug to Mike to the chief. "Actually, she did not say the name of the man who was after her. She just said 'he,' although I knew immediately who she was talking about."

Doug ran an exasperated hand through his hair. "Can't you get the federal authorities involved here?"

"How?" Mike said. "This doesn't involve interstate commerce, international terrorism, or anything else the feds would ordinarily investigate."

"It involves the mail."

"Easier said than proven," the chief said.

"What about the state police?"

"We'd prefer to tackle this on our own," Catfield explained. "This is a local matter, and I think we can handle it better without any outside interference."

"Yeah, I can tell. You're doing a hell of a job."

"For your information, Mr. Albin, even if we did want to

get the help of an outside agency, the state authorities require more than just a phone call before they get involved in a matter that clearly should be under local jurisdiction. Documentation must be provided, forms must be completed—"

"All of which are sent through the mail," Mike said.

"Shit!" Doug stood up. "There has to be something we can do."

The chief turned back toward the kitchen. "We'll do what we can."

The electricity was on, and Billy was upstairs watching his usual Thursday-night shows. The television was off downstairs, and both Doug and Tritia were reading—he an old John Fowles novel, she a new Joseph Wambaugh book. They'd told Billy what had happened, in simple nongruesome terms, but they had not spoken of the afternoon since then, and dinner had been marked by long silences and irrelevant conversation.

The phone rang and Tritia got up to answer it. "Hello?" She turned around and offered the receiver to Doug. "It's for you."

He put down his book, stood up, and took the phone from her hand. "Who is it?"

"Mike Trenton."

He held the receiver to his ear. "Hello?"

"Doug? Mike. We found the bat. It was in a ditch down the street." There was a pause, a beat. "It was covered with bloody fingerprints."

Doug frowned. The news was good, exactly what they'd wanted, what they'd been looking for, hoping for, but the policeman's voice was neither excited nor happy. It was flat, unemotional, devoid of any feeling. Something was wrong. Things hadn't worked out the way they were supposed to. "What's the matter, Mike?"

"The fingerprints are Giselle Brennan's."

Doug was silent.

"You still there?"

"Yeah, I'm here."

"We took him in and held him, but there's nothing we can do. We had to let him go."

"He did it, Mike."

"I know," the policeman said. He was silent for a moment, and when he spoke again, his voice was low, conspiratorial. "Is it all right if I come over? There's something I'd like to show you."

"Of course. When do you want to come by?"

"Would right now be okay?"

"Fine."

"I'll see you in a few minutes."

Doug hung up the phone and turned toward Tritia. "They found the bat used to rape Ellen, but the fingerprints on it were Giselle Brennan's."

"Oh, my God."

He nodded. "They're going to throw her in jail. Mike's coming over right now. He said he has something to show us."

She closed her book, dropping it on the floor next to her. "When is this all going to end?"

"Soon I hope."

Tritia was silent for a moment. "What if someone kills him?"

Doug was shocked. "What?"

"I've been thinking about this for a while." She stood up excitedly. "What if someone cuts his brake lines or shoots him or—"

"Trish!"

"Why not? Can you think of any reason why not?"

"Because . . . because it's wrong."

"That's not much of an argument."

"Killing is not an option," he said. "I don't want to discuss it anymore."

"Fine." She picked up her book from the floor, turned to the page she had marked, and began reading. He stared at her as she read, but there was no anger in her face, no defiance, no resignation, nothing but a relaxed ease. He realized that he was worried about her, about what she might try. He didn't entirely trust her. He was going to have to watch her very carefully from now on.

True to his word, Mike pulled up in the drive fifteen minutes later. He was wearing not his uniform but his street clothes, and under his arm he carried a large photo album.

Doug met him on the porch. "Hi."

Mike looked around. "So this is where you live. I always wondered what a teacher's house looks like."

"The same as everyone else's." Doug pointed toward the boarded-up window and the splintered holes in the wall.

"Compliments of some of our mailman's rock-throwing friends."

"Did you report that?"

Doug shook his head. "What's the point?"

"Well, if we can ever find a way to tie all these together, we can nail his ass once and for all, put him away for good."

Doug smiled wryly. "Yeah. Right." He opened the door. "Come on in." Mike followed him inside. "So you have the weapon."

"That's right."

"What does Giselle say about it?"

Mike shook his head. "We don't know."

"What do you mean you don't know? Don't you have her in custody?"

"We can't find her," the policeman admitted. "Her mother says she hasn't been home for three days. Smith claims he hasn't seen her since the afternoon of the murder."

"You think he killed her?"

"Who knows?" Mike shrugged. "Anything's possible."

"Why don't you hold him on suspicion of murder?"

"Without a body?"

"Kidnapping, then."

Mike sighed. "We're doing what we can."

"I've heard that before."

Tritia stood up and Mike nodded to her. "Hello, Mrs. Albin."

She smiled back. "Hello." She glanced at Doug. "I'm going to bed. You don't need me for anything out here, do you?"

He looked over at the clock. "It's only eight-thirty."

"I've had a busy day."

"Yeah," Doug said. "We all have."

"I'll see you later." She waved to Mike. "Good night, Mr. Trenton."

"Good night."

Doug pulled a chair next to the coffee table and motioned for Mike to sit down on the couch. The young policeman sat down tiredly, placing the photo album on the table before him. "Did you know Mrs. Ronda painted?"

"What?"

"She painted. You know, art. She was like an amateur artist."

Doug shook his head, puzzled. "No, I didn't. But what does that have to do with anything?"

The young policeman reached for the photo album. "We found some paintings in her closet. She kept them secret." He opened the book and Doug suddenly knew what was coming next. "I'm not supposed to show you this. This is police evidence. The chief said these paintings mean nothing, that if anything they're merely signs of a disturbed personality, but . . ." He looked up at Doug and pushed the open album across the table.

The paintings were indeed disturbing, done in bright garish colors, executed in an angular expressionistic style. Doug stared at the picture of the first canvas. A blue-uniformed man, carrying a jagged baseball bat, was treading on a field of anguished screaming faces. The sky was an apocalyptic red, the same color as the man's fiery hair. The man's face was a grinning white skull.

The next picture was of a monster, a hideous creature with a sharply fanged mouth that took up a full half of its malformed face. The monster held in its obscenely twisted claw a white letter. The street down which the creature was walking was an off-center path dividing identical rows of mailbox houses.

The pictures were all variations on a theme, personal and highly idiosyncratic depictions of a horrific mailman.

In the last, unfinished painting, the mailman was dressed as the Grim Reaper, and the blade of his scythe had shish kebabbed several women between their legs.

"She knew," Mike said.

Doug closed the album. "So what? Who doesn't know?"

"But she knew what was going to happen to her. Did you see those women? Did you see that baseball bat?"

"Yes."

"Well, my idea is that if she knew, others do too. We just have to find them. It'll be tough. People aren't being real cooperative right now. But if we can find his next victim, we can stake him or her out and catch Smith with a sting operation."

It sounded good, but Doug did not think that the mailman was a killer who was methodically murdering people in town. He was something far worse than that. Murder was merely one tool he used to get what he wanted. For all they knew, he had killed all the people he needed to kill and now he was moving on to something else.

Or perhaps he was going to kill them next.

"I think it's a good idea," Doug said. "I hope it works."

Mike frowned. "But I need your help. I was hoping you'd—"

"Sorry. I don't think I have any help to give."

"Sure you do—"

"You want my opinion?"

The policeman nodded. "Of course."

"Don't wait for him to do something else. Get him now. Charge him with anything, charge him with everything. If nothing sticks, fine. But at least you'll have kept him off the streets for a while. And maybe by that time, with the hearings and jailing, the Postal Service will have appointed someone else to the job and we can get rid of him for good."

"That's your plan?"

Doug leaned forward. "He's a fake. I called the main post office in Phoenix, and they have no record of him. When you guys called, their computer was mysteriously down and my story couldn't be corroborated. But he's not a real mailman. If you can get a postal inspector up here, if you can get the federal authorities to charge him, I think we'll be safe. The problem is, you're not going to be able to get through by mail or phone. You're going to have to go to Phoenix in person."

"No gas," Mike reminded him.

"That's why you throw his ass in jail until you can get someone up here, put him out of commission for a while."

"I don't know," Mike said.

"Well, then, don't throw him in jail. But at least try to get a representative from the post office up here. He's not a real mailman, but he recognizes the authority of the Postal Service. Hell, it's the only authority he does recognize."

"What makes you think so?"

Gooseflesh cascaded down Doug's arms as he remembered the mailman dancing on the ridge. "I just know."

"I still want to stake him out."

"Then stake him out. Tail him. Follow him wherever he goes. Maybe you'll be able to catch him that way."

"But you don't think so?"

"I don't think so."

Mike stood up, picking up the photo album. "I'm on my own on this, you know. The department's not behind me. The chief would shit if he knew I was even talking to you."

"Why?"

"I don't know. But I do have a few others with me. Tim, of course. And Jack and Jeff. We all know what's going on."

"I think you should nab him now."

Mike walked to the door. "I'll think about it." He turned on the porch. "It would mean my job, though."

"It may mean your life if you don't. Or mine."

"Maybe he'll just go away."

Doug smiled grimly. "No. That's what I was hoping, too. But that's the one thing he won't do: he won't go away."

Mike walked out to his car, got in, and backed up the drive, and Doug stood on the porch until the policeman's taillights were gone and the noise of his engine had faded into the sounds of the night.

43

But Doug was wrong. The mailman did disappear. He was gone the next day, and when Doug drove by the post office in the afternoon, it was closed. At the police station, Mike said that Smith Tegarden, the officer assigned to man the speed trap at the edge of town, had seen John Smith's car heading toward Phoenix.

The next day passed, and the next, and there was still no sign of him.

When the weekend rolled by and Monday arrived with the post office remaining closed, Doug began to relax.

It looked like it was over.

The mailman was gone.

44

The morning dawned clear and cool and sunny, the first August merging of the disparate weather trends that would eventually crystallize into fall. Doug awoke early, showered, shaved, and went out to check the mailbox. He was gratified to find that it was empty.

By the time he'd walked back to the house, Tritia was up and making coffee. There was annoyance on her face as he said "Good morning" to her, and when he repeated the greeting, she refused to respond, unintelligibly grunting some sort of reply.

Doug turned on the television, and the familiar set of the NBC *News at Sunrise* blinked into existence. There had been no problems with the electricity since the mailman left, and gas, water, and phone services had continued uninterrupted. Life, it seemed, was settling back into normalcy.

Billy was still asleep, but Tritia ordered Doug to wake him and make him come down for breakfast. She was making Spanish omelettes for each of them, using vegetables she had grown in the garden, and she refused to suspend her culinary efforts until Billy graciously decided that it was time for him to awaken. "Get him up now," she said.

They ate breakfast together, and Tritia announced that this morning they were going to go to the store and do some serious shopping. The cupboards were nearly bare, as were the refrigerator shelves, and she had a stack of coupons whose expiration dates had nearly arrived. She began making out a list of items they needed while Doug washed the dishes and Billy dried.

"Okay," she said finally. "Ready."

"I don't want to go," Billy said.

"You have to go."

"Why?"

Tritia looked at her son. He was mature for his age,

intelligent, strong, but he had been forced to absorb far too much the past two months, had been expected to deal with things that most adults never had to deal with. She felt a strange sadness settle over her as she looked at his weary face. She had always wanted Billy to remain a child as long as possible and not grow up too fast. Childhood was a magical special time and could only be experienced once. Yet at the same time, she did not believe in sheltering children from reality. Like it or not, they eventually had to live in the real world, and they could adjust to that world better if they were adequately prepared to deal with it.

This summer, however, had not been the real world. The horrific events of the past two months would not prepare Billy for things to come. Nothing like this would ever come again.

She stared at him, saw the pleading in his tired eyes. Her tone of voice softened. "Okay," she said. "You don't have to go."

Billy smiled, relieved, although there seemed to be something else in his eyes, something lurking just beyond the obvious emotions mirrored in his face. This had probably scarred him more than she would ever know. "Thanks," he said.

"But," she warned, "you have to stay in the house. Keep all the doors locked and don't let anyone inside until we get back. Understand?"

He nodded.

"Okay." She looked over at Doug and saw his slight smile of approval. It never hurt to be careful.

Billy got dressed and stood on the porch as his parents got in the car and backed up the drive. "Lock the door," his dad called.

"I will."

He went back into the house and locked the door. His eyes were drawn to the piece of plyboard still covering the broken window. He hoped the guy was going to come and fix the window soon. The board helped television viewing in the afternoon, virtually eliminating the glare from the sun, but it also made the house seem far too dark.

He didn't like darkness.

He wasn't sure what he was going to do today after his parents got back. He thought of calling the twins, but then decided he really didn't want to see them. What he really wanted was to do something with Lane, but he was afraid to call his old friend. With the mailman gone and everything over, Lane might be back to normal. But then again, he might not, and Billy wasn't brave enough to find out.

Right now, he had to go to the bathroom, and he walked through the kitchen to the hall. He went into the bathroom, already unbuckling his belt. He froze.

An envelope was perched on the edge of the sink.

Another lay atop the closed lid of the toilet.

He wanted to scream, but he knew no one would hear him. His cries would only alert whoever—

the mailman?—was out there.

Or in here.

He backed into his parents' bedroom. He saw one sealed letter on the dresser, another on the bed.

The house seemed suddenly much scarier, much more frightening. He walked slowly, silently toward the front room. The board over the window cut off an awful lot of light, he noticed, throwing nearly half of the room into darkness, creating pools and boxes of shadow within which a figure could hide. He saw a trail of envelopes leading upstairs to the loft, to his bedroom.

He carefully picked up the phone next to the TV. It was dead.

He heard a rustling noise upstairs.

He had to get out of here. But where could he go? There were not many homes nearby. He certainly couldn't stay at the Nelsons'. He couldn't go to Lane's house.

The Fort.

Yes, The Fort. He could go to The Fort and wait there until his parents came home. He and Lane had purposely built the structure sturdily in order to withstand outside attack, and he would be able to hide safely in there.

As quietly as possible, he opened the front door and stepped out onto the porch. The boards creaked beneath his feet and he stood still, unmoving, listening for any reaction upstairs, ready to run at the slightest sound, but he heard nothing.

He had never realized before how noisy the porch really was, and it seemed like a squeaking creaking eternity before he reached the steps and hurried down. Beneath his feet, the gravel crunched with thunderous volume, but he ignored it and ran as fast as he could down the path toward The

Fort. He leapt over familiar rocks and logs, skirted known sticker bushes. With one leap and expert footwork, he was on top of the camouflaged structure's roof, and then he was dropping inside, closing and locking the trapdoor.

He lay panting on the floor for a moment, trying to catch his breath, listening for any sounds that he had been followed, but the only noise he heard was the obnoxious cawing of a blue jay in a far-off tree.

He was safe.

He stood up, praying that his parents would come home soon. Praying that when they did come, he would be able to hear the noise of their car. He listened again for foreign sounds, alien noises, but the woods were clean.

He looked around the Big Room. The Fort seemed different with Lane gone, abandoned. The other time he had come in here without Lane, it had felt strange, but it had still been *their* Fort. Now he wasn't sure whose it was. The structure was in the green belt by his house, but the materials had come from Lane's father and they had done all the work in tandem. He walked slowly through the room like a stranger, touching objects which had once been familiar to him but from which he now felt impossibly distanced. Everything seemed weird, as though it had once been his but was his no longer.

He supposed this was what a house must feel like to people who got a divorce.

Every so often, he stopped in his tracks, unmoving, listening to hear if there were any sounds outside, but always there was nothing.

He walked into the HQ, looking down at the pile of magazines on the floor. Even the *Playboy*s no longer seemed as though they belonged to him, although they did not seem as though they belonged to Lane either. They were caught in some timeless netherworld in-between, ownerless. He picked one up. The page opened to the spread of "Women in Uniform," and he saw the naked body of the female postal carrier.

"Billy Albin."

He stopped moving, holding his breath, trying not to make any sound. His heart was trip-hammering wildly.

"Billy Albin."

The mailman was just outside The Fort. He had tracked him somehow and had found him. Billy was too terrified to

THE MAILMAN

move. He tried to exhale silently, unable to hold his breath any longer, but the noise sounded like a hurricane in the silence. Outside, the feet stopped moving.

"Billy."

He did not move.

"Billy."

Now the voice came from the other side, although he had heard no scuffling feet, no rustling leaves, no sound of any kind.

"Billy."

The voice came again, a low insistent whispering. He wanted to scream, to cry out, but he dared not. The mailman obviously knew he was here, but Billy did not want to confirm his presence. Maybe if he pretended that he wasn't here, if he just laid low and waited it out, the mailman would go away.

"Billy."

No. He wasn't going to go away.

Billy stood stock-still, only his mind moving, his brain trying desperately to think of something he could do. There was only one entrance to The Fort, no way to get out without the mailman seeing him. He and Lane had often talked about making an escape hatch, an emergency exit, building an escape tunnel under the dirt, but they never had. Now, he considered his choices. Or his choice. He had only one, really. If he could make it up to the roof, through the trapdoor, without the mailman seeing or hearing him—

"Billy."

—he could jump and haul ass to safety.

Tiptoeing carefully, lightly, quietly, he stepped into the Big Room.

"Billy."

The voice was closer this time. Extremely close. Billy looked up.

The mailman stared down at him through the open trapdoor, grinning. There was corruption in that smile, a twisted cruelty in the hard blue eyes.

"Want to have a good time?" the mailman asked.

Billy backed into the HQ. He glanced down at the stack of *Playboy*s as he retreated, but they were not *Playboy*s. They were *Playgirl*s.

"Billy," the mailman said again.

Panicked now, he began kicking at the back wall of the

HQ, trying to knock off one of the boards so he could crawl through and out. He kicked with all of his might, putting the strength of desperation behind each kick, but they had built The Fort well—too well—and the boards would not budge.

He heard the mailman drop through the trapdoor to the floor of the Big Room behind him.

"I brought you a present, Billy," the mailman said.

"Help!" Billy screamed at the top of his lungs. He kicked furiously at the wall. "Mom! Dad!"

"Want to have a good time?" the mailman asked.

Billy turned around and saw over his shoulder the mailman smiling, holding forth his present.

When Billy was not home when they came back from the store and had still not returned an hour later, Tritia began to panic. She had Doug call Mike at the police station, who promised to comb the town, starting with the post office, and she began calling all of Billy's friends. She dialed the Chapmans' number and Lane answered the phone.

"Hello," Tritia said. "This is Mrs. Albin. Is Billy there?"

"No." Lane's voice sounded at once cold and suggestive, not unlike that of the mailman, and the fear grew within her.

"Have you seen him at all today?"

"No." Lane paused. "But I've seen you."

There was a click as the connection was broken.

Tritia hung up the phone. What the hell did that mean? She didn't know, and she didn't think she wanted to know. She started to dial the twins, when she heard Doug come in through the back door.

"He's not under the house or by the clothesline," he said. He was trying to keep the worry out of his voice, but he was not having much luck. "His bike's still here. I'm going to start looking in the back, around the green belt."

"Okay," she agreed. "I'll keep calling."

Doug walked out the front door.

God, she prayed silently, let him be all right.

Doug walked across the length of their property, venturing into the green belts on both sides, searching under every bush, looking up in every tree, calling his son's name. "Billy! Billy!"

Lizards scuttled out of his way, frightened by the noise. Quail flew frantically up from their herbaceous hideaways.

"Billy!"

He continued pressing toward the hill in back of their house until he saw the camouflaged exterior of The Fort before him. "Billy!" he called.

There was no answer.

He stared at The Fort, and there seemed to him something ominous about it. He had never before thought of the wooden structure as anything more threatening than a children's playhouse, but as he looked at it now, it seemed low and dark and claustrophobically closed, and he realized that the feeling he got from it was uncomfortably close to the feeling he had had when he'd looked at the house in which Ellen Ronda had been killed.

He took a tentative step forward. "Billy?"

He pressed his ear to the wooden wall. From inside The Fort, he could hear a low steady whimpering. "Billy!" he cried. He looked frantically for a weak point in the structure where he could pull off a board and get inside, but the makeshift building was remarkably well-constructed, with no protruding panels or obvious weak points. Desperate, he grabbed hold of the roof and tried to pull himself up. He was horrendously out of shape, and even a partial pull-up caused him to grunt and strain with the effort. A sliver slid into his palm, and his right ring finger pressed painfully against the bent head of a crooked nail, but with the aid of his feet kicking against the side wall for support, he managed to reach the roof and roll on top of the clubhouse.

Nearby, he saw the square open trapdoor that led down into The Fort. He peered in but could see nothing; he quickly dropped through the opening, landing hard. The whimpering was louder now, and he whirled around. "Billy?"

His son was crouched in a dark corner of the room in a modified fetal position, knees drawn up to his chin. His shirt was ripped and tattered, covered with grease and dirt. His face was blank.

He was wearing no pants.

"Billy," Doug cried, rushing forward. He was screaming and crying all at once and he fell to the ground, hugging his son. Within him the rage and fear and pain had coalesced into one horrible all-consuming feeling of hatred, and tears flowed down his cheeks as he gripped Billy tightly.

"No," Billy was saying softly. "No. No. No. No . . ."

Doug moved back, still holding his son. Through his tears, he looked into Billy's face. The boy's eyes were wide and scared and staring.

"No. No. No. No . . ."

On the dirt next to him was a soiled wedding dress.

And a pair of bloody underwear.

And several postmarked packages and envelopes.

A bolt of emotional pain wrenched Doug's midsection, so sharp it was physical.

Billy's faraway gaze focused on him for a moment. "I won't wear it!" he screamed. "You can't make me." His entire body shook.

Doug pulled him close. He realized for the first time that his son's skin was warm, feverish. He pulled himself together, forcing himself to act logically, though the bitter hatred that flowed through his veins rebelled against all rationality. He stood and was about to pick up Billy when he noticed the corner of an envelope protruding from underneath one of the folds of the soiled dress. He reached down and grabbed it, saw his name on the front, tore it open. There were only five words and an exclamation point on the otherwise blank page:

I like your wife too!

"No!" Doug screamed, a loud primal denial directed to no one who could hear.

"No," Billy repeated. "No. No. No. No. No . . ."

Doug picked up his son without thinking and with adrenaline strength pushed him up through the opening. He guided the limp body away from the hole, then lifted himself up. His muscles were aching, his tortured insides on fire, but he forced himself to move across the roof. He had to get home to Tritia.

Tritia hung up the phone, palms sweaty, the fear feverishly alive within her. She walked into the kitchen to get herself a glass of water, and it was then that she saw the envelope on the counter next to the microwave. Frowning, she picked it up. She could not remember seeing it on the counter before. She certainly hadn't checked the mailbox today, and she was pretty sure neither Doug nor Billy had either. She looked at the front of the envelope. It was addressed to her, but there was no return address.

It's starting again, she thought. And Billy's missing. But she refused to let herself think that way. She tore open the envelope and pulled out the piece of paper inside.

I'm in the bedroom.

The words jumped out at her, hitting her with the impact of a blunt cudgel. He was back. It hadn't ended.

He was back and he was after her.

Fumblingly, she opened the top drawer nearest the sink. She drew out a carving knife and gripped it tightly, holding it before her as she walked slowly down the hall toward the bedroom, prepared to lash out at any sign of movement. She knew that it was stupid and foolhardy to try to take on the mailman by herself—she should run to a neighbor's house, call the police—but he had pushed too far. She had reached her limit and she was damned if she was going to let him terrorize her anymore.

If he was here, she would kill him.

She would slit his fucking throat.

He was not in the bedroom. Knife in front of her, poised to stab, she checked the closet, looked under the bed. Nothing. She poked her head in the bathroom. All clear. She knew he was neither in the kitchen nor in the living room because she had been in both.

That left the loft.

She thought she heard a footstep creak upstairs.

Run, a part of her brain—the intelligent part of her brain—was telling her. Get out of here now. But she gripped the knife tighter and headed through the kitchen, through the living room, to the stairway. It was day, but the loft's small lone window was not able to illuminate the entire room, and the top of the stairs was in shadow.

She crept upward as quietly as possible, fingers white on the knife handle. She was almost to the top of the stairs and was bending over to keep her head below the level of the floor so he would not be able to see her approach, when her foot landed on a loose board. The stair groaned. She froze, not daring to breathe, but there was no sound from the loft. Holding the knife before her, she dashed up the last five steps, ready to lash out.

The loft was deserted. There was no one there.

Still holding the knife, she made a quick check of the closet, of the area behind Billy's bed, but the loft was empty.

He had gone.

The house was clean.

She made her way downstairs. In the living room, she peered out the window, trying to spot any unnatural objects in the drive or in the surrounding trees and bushes, but the property was disturbed only by a pair of battling blue jays. She double-checked first the front door, then the back, and when she found that both were locked, she allowed herself to relax a little.

Her bladder had been considerably weakened by the tension, and she walked into the bathroom, still clutching the knife. She no longer had a death grip on the handle, but she was taking no chances—she might have missed him in her cursory examination of the forest in back. He could have been hiding behind a tree, knowing she would not go out of the house to search for him, and he might be waiting outside right now, listening in at the door, waiting for precisely a moment like this, a moment when she was vulnerable, to come inside and attack.

She left the bathroom door open and quickly pulled down her pants, sitting on the toilet.

The mailman stepped out of the shower.

She screamed in terror, dropping the knife, then immediately reached down with scrambling fingers to pick it up off the floor. He stepped on top of it, his shiny black shoes completely covering the blade. He was fully dressed, wearing his pressed postal uniform, but she could see the huge bulge in his trousers as he stood in front of her. She covered her exposed lap with one hand and held the other tremblingly in front of her to push him away.

She had not stopped screaming, but he did not seem to mind. He smiled at her. "Nice bush," he said, and the crudity of his words, juxtaposed against the smoothness of his voice, was somehow more terrifying than if he had simply come out and attacked her.

Why the hell hadn't she checked the shower?

He bent down to pick up the knife and she leapt off the toilet and out of the bathroom in a frantic, instinctive escape attempt. Her body slammed against his in the constricted space before the doorway, and for a sickening second as she

flew past him, she felt his clothed hardness against her
naked skin. And then she was across the hall and in the
bedroom, slamming the door shut. She fumbled with the
knob for a second before turning the lock. Her eyes darted
around the room as she searched for something, anything,
that could be used as a weapon.

Outside, in the hall, she heard a clattering sound as the
mailman threw the knife across the floor into the kitchen.
Obviously, he didn't want to kill her.

Then what did he want?

She pressed her shoulder against the bedroom door and
let out an involuntary sound of raw animal fear. She was too
afraid to cross the room to reach the telephone. The door
lock was cheap and flimsy, and if she let up on her support
for even a second, he would be inside.

Inside.

She closed her eyes, willing herself not to be overwhelmed
by the fear. "Get out of my house," she ordered. Her voice
was wavering, unforceful. "Get out of here now!"

"You want it," he said, his voice coolly unperturbed.
"You know you want it."

"Get the fuck out of here!" she screamed. "I'm calling
the police."

His voice dropped an octave to a tone of low insinuating
intimacy. "Do you like your mail delivered at the back
door?" he asked.

"Help!" she screamed at the top of her lungs. She meant
for the scream to be loud and piercing, a cry of terror and
rage, but the shout was almost a sob, desperation eating
away at its edges, and she abruptly fell silent, unwilling to
let the mailman sense her weakness, the stubbornness within
her unwilling to concede anything to the monster outside
the door.

"Do you like blood?" the mailman asked in that same low
intimate tone. He was right next to the crack of the door;
she could hear the sound of his dry lips pressing together as
he spoke. "Do you like warm, thick, salty blood?"

"Help me!" she cried, and this time it really was a sob.
She heard the mailman's low answering chuckle.

And the sound of a zipper being pulled down.

"You know you want it," he repeated.

She held her breath.

There was the quiet slapping sound of skin against skin.

He was playing with himself.

"Billy likes his mail delivered upstairs and at the back door."

That gave her the strength that had been eluding her. White-hot anger coursed through her veins. "You son of a bitch!" she screamed. "Don't you dare touch him!"

From outside the house, from the rear, she heard Doug's voice. "Trish!" Again: "Trish!" He was running; the amplification of his words came at a pace much faster than it would have had he been moving more slowly. Something had happened. She could hear the fear in his voice, and the burning anger. Something had happened.

But she was just thankful to hear his voice at all. She was saved. Whatever else had happened, he was here to save her. "In here!" she yelled as loud as she could. "I'm in the bedroom!"

She had not heard the mailman leave, but from the silence on the other side of the door she knew he was gone.

There were heavy running steps on the porch. "Trish!" Doug called frantically. The screen door slammed shut.

"I'm in here!" She fumblingly opened the bedroom door and flew out of the room, sobbing. "I—"

Her sobs stopped when she saw that Doug was carrying Billy into the living room. She stopped breathing. Time stood still. The boy's unmoving body was draped limply over his father's outstretched arms, and for one sick second she was reminded of a scene from *Frankenstein*. She had to will herself into action. She snapped out of her trance and ran forward, putting an ear to her son's chest. "What happened?" she demanded.

"I found him in The Fort." Doug's voice was a shocked emotionless monotone. "The mailman found him first."

Tritia noticed for the first time that Billy was wearing no pants.

Doug placed his son carefully on the couch. Billy's skin was grayish, pale. His lips moved silently in unbroken fever sentences. Tritia could not make out what he was saying.

"When we get to the hospital, I'm calling the police," Doug said in the same flat tone. "And if they won't go after him, I'll kill him myself."

Tritia felt Billy's forehead with a trembling hand. "What happened?"

"I don't know. He was lying in The Fort like this. His

pants were off and his underwear was bloody and there was a . . . a wedding dress next to him."

Tritia put a hand to her mouth. "Oh, my God."

Doug felt the hot tears spilling onto his cheeks. His voice cracked. "I think he was raped."

"We have to get him to the hospital. I'll call the ambulance."

"Fuck the ambulance. There's not enough time."

Tritia cradled her son's head in her arms.

"No," he murmured. "No I won't. No. No. No. No . . ."

"Let's go," she said.

The thoughts that ran through Doug's mind as the Bronco sped over the rough dirt road were fragmented, disjointed: what he should have done, what he could have done, what he did wrong, what he would do over again if given the chance. Billy moaned in the back seat, a muffled delirious sound followed instantly by Tritia's soft soothing. Doug cursed himself for not living closer to the hospital.

They sped past the trailer park and bumped onto paved road. The shock had left him, had disappeared as quickly as it had come, and had been replaced by a seething bottomless anger that could be assuaged only by revenge. Once Billy was okay, he would go to the police. And if the police refused to do anything, he would go after the mailman himself. There was no way in hell he was going to get away with this.

Willis Community Hospital was a low white brick building located off the main road in the center of town. It was situated between the Presbyterian church and a short row of tract houses, the model homes from one of the town's aborted real-estate developments. Although the hospital was the newest and best-equipped medical facility in the county—it even had its own heliport for the transporting of serious cases to Phoenix or Flagstaff—it now seemed to Doug small and seedy and hopelessly out of date. He wished they lived in a metropolitan area with access to state-of-the-art medical technology.

They pulled into the emergency loading area, and Doug ran around the back of the Bronco to open the passenger door. He let Tritia out, and she ran into the hospital to explain the situation while he carefully lifted Billy from the back seat and carried him into the building.

A doctor, an orderly, and two nurses were already wheeling out a gurney, and Doug placed his son gently down on the crinkling sanitary paper that covered the gurney's thin mattress. The doctor introduced himself as Ken Maxwell, and he fired off questions one after another as they headed through the double doors and down the hall, asking a follow-up before Doug or Tritia had time to adequately respond to its predecessor. The pinched-faced woman at the admissions desk tried to insist that someone had to stay and fill out forms, but the doctor snapped at her, telling her to shut up and leave it for later as he followed the orderly pushing the wheeled stretcher through the corridor. The two nurses had already hurried ahead to prepare the examination room.

The gurney was pushed next to a stationary operating table in the center of the room, and the doctor helped the orderly shift Billy onto the raised platform. He listened with a stethoscope to Billy's chest, checked his eyes with a penlight. His hands expertly prodded and probed the boy's prone form, but Billy noticed nothing. He neither moved nor flinched, and he kept up the low insistent words he had been repeating since Doug found him.

Doug licked his dry lips. The doctor was busy. This would be a good time to call the police. He caught the eye of the orderly. "Is there a phone around here?" he asked. "I have to call the cops and tell them what happened."

"There's one out in the waiting room."

The doctor finished his external examination of Billy's body and said something to the nurse nearest him. He looked up at Doug and Tritia. "I will have to give him a thorough examination," he said. "And I'll have to take some X rays, perform a few standard tests." The nurse handed him a pair of clear rubber gloves taken from an unopened package. "As you're his parents, you may remain here if you wish, but it may be a little rough to watch." He pulled on the gloves and picked up his penlight. Both nurses carefully rolled Billy over onto his stomach. Doug could see the smeared dirt on his son's buttocks, and he turned away.

"I'll stay," Tritia said, giving his hand a small squeeze. "You go make your phone call."

Doug nodded slowly. He really did have to call the police, but he was glad that he did, grateful to have that excuse to fall back on, and for that he felt guilty. He knew he should be there for Billy, but he could not watch the doctor examine his son. Tritia knew that, and this was her way of telling him it was okay. But he still felt awful about it. He had always been like this. He had not wanted to watch his son's birth and had thrown up himself when Billy was an infant and had vomited on his shoulder. Sickness involving members of his family made him squeamish, particularly if it involved blood and bodily functions. He wished he didn't feel this way, wished he could let it not affect him, the way Tritia did, but he had no control over his reactions. He had often wondered if this was a trait common to all fathers, and he thought that perhaps this was one reason why young children inevitably felt closer to their mothers and turned to their maternal parents when they needed comfort. After sharing bodies for nine months, mothers did not seem to mind a little blood or pain. It wasn't as alien to them as it was to fathers.

He looked over at his son, saw the smeared dirt, saw red lines that looked like scratches.

"No," Billy was murmuring. "No. No. No. No . . ."

"You go," Tritia prodded him.

The doctor bent over Billy's body.

Doug squeezed Tritia's hand and walked quickly out of the room. He was angry at himself and he flinched as Billy's murmurs cut off with a sharp gasp. The door swung shut behind him, and he was in the corridor. He hurried back the way they had come in. At least the doctor seemed to know what he was doing. He had wasted no time, had reacted instantly to the situation, had cut the red tape off at its source, and had exhibited a no-nonsense attitude in his quick appraisal of what was to be done. For that Doug was grateful, and despite his initial paranoid misgivings, he was now confident that his son would receive the best medical attention possible.

There was going to be hell to pay in the psychological department, though. The damage here was not entirely, or even predominantly, physical. What had happened to Billy would probably scar him emotionally for the rest of his life. The anger burned through Doug, unwavering, undiminishing. They were going to have to really search around and make sure they found someone who could help Billy.

But now it was time for the mailman to pay.

The pinched-faced woman glared at him from behind her glass-walled room as he walked up to the pay phone in the waiting area. He ignored her and dialed the number of the police department. He closed his eyes. The phone rang once, twice, thrice.

An unfamiliar voice answered. "Willis Police Department."

Doug cleared his throat. "I'd like to speak to Mike Trenton, please." He sounded like a stranger to himself.

The voice on the other end of the line was cautious. "Who shall I say is calling?"

"Doug Albin." There was a pause, then Mike came on the line. Doug gripped the receiver tightly, not bothering with pleasantries. "The mailman's back."

"I know."

"He attacked my boy, Mike, and he threatened my wife. I'm going after him."

"We're going after him too. He killed the chief."

It took a moment for the information to sink in. Doug felt cold, frightened. The mailman was no longer playing around. He was not hiding behind rules and regulations, not working through letters. He was coming in for the kill. But though the fear was strong within him, it paled next to the towering strength of his anger.

"We just found the chief's body a few minutes ago," Mike said. "How's your son? Is he going to be okay?"

"We don't know."

"We're gathering everyone together. We'll be leaving in ten minutes."

"Wait a sec, Mike." Doug felt weak. He saw Tritia running down the hall toward him, nearly tripping on the slippery tile. She was crying, sobbing, and with a sinking feeling in his stomach he knew that Billy was dead. Then she drew closer, and he saw that she was crying and laughing, sobbing and smiling.

"He's okay," she cried. "He's all right."

"Hold on, Mike," Doug said into the receiver. He left the phone dangling as he took Tritia's hand and ran down the corridor to the examination room. The doctor was just maneuvering the large cranelike X-ray machine over Billy's back.

"Is he okay?" Doug asked.

"There's been no real physical damage," the doctor told him. "Billy is clearly suffering from traumatic shock, but he seems to have sustained no actual injuries. There're a few scratches and bruises, and I'll continue the tests, but I think you're safe."

"He wasn't . . . ?" Doug left the question unfinished.

"There does not appear to have been any penetration," the doctor said quietly, "although I have no doubt that he was assaulted."

"But the blood on his underwear . . . ?"

"It's not Billy's blood."

A flood of relief washed over Doug, and he held Tritia, who continued to sob. The doctor gave him a quick reassuring smile, then moved the X-ray camera into place.

Five minutes later, Doug was back in the waiting room. He picked up the receiver. "Mike? You still there?"

The other end of the line was silent. "Mike!" He heard a low knock as someone obviously picked up the phone from where it had been lying. "Mike?"

"Yeah?"

"He's okay."

"Thank God."

"I want to be in on this," Doug said.

"I can't—"

"Mike?"

Silence.

"Mike?"

"All right," the policeman conceded. "How fast can you get over here to the station?"

"I'll be there as soon as I can. Wait for me."

"Make it fast. We want to get him before he leaves town. You have five minutes."

"Goddammit!"

"All right," the policeman said. "Sorry. We'll wait."

"Thank you. I'll be there in ten."

"Meet you here." Mike hung up and Doug did the same. He returned to the examination room, where the doctor was putting away a hypodermic syringe. One of the nurses covered Billy with a sheet. "Get him a room," the doctor ordered. He looked from Doug to Tritia. "He'll be sleeping for a while now. I suggest you try to get some rest. He'll be coming out of it before morning, and he's going to want you nearby."

"I'm staying," Tritia said.

The doctor nodded. "We can set up a chair in his room. Or even a cot, if you'd like."

Tritia looked up at Doug, who put his arms around her. "Have they caught him?"

He shook his head. "We're going after him now."

" 'We?' "

"We."

The doctor, orderly, and nurses worked busily next to Billy.

Doug squeezed Tritia tightly. "Watch him," he said. "Take care of him."

She shivered as he pulled away, rubbing her arms. "Where are you going? What are you going to do?"

"I'll meet them at the police station. Then we'll go to the post office."

They both followed the hospital team as they wheeled the now sleeping and silent Billy into his room, a large private room with a raised color television and two adjoining beds. Doug gave Tritia the pertinent insurance information from his wallet, and she promised to take care of everything.

She followed him out to the waiting room. "Be careful!" she called after him as he walked between the sliding glass doors.

45

Doug ran into the police station. He noticed the difference immediately. No one was working or talking. The room was still and silent. The policemen were standing around the front office, visibly nervous, unsure of what to do. Mike seemed to have taken charge, though there were one or two officers above him in rank, and he alone appeared to be thinking clearly and rationally. He was on the phone, apparently talking to someone important in Phoenix.

There were piles of unopened letters on each of the desks, Doug noticed. The letters were untouched, as if everyone was afraid to go near them.

Mike got off the phone, saw Doug, and hurried over. "Finally," he said. "How's your boy?"

Doug nodded. "He'll be okay."

"Your wife?"

"All right."

"Good." He was holding a letter in his hand, and he handed it to Doug. "Read this."

Doug looked down at the paper. Scrawled in smeared pencil was a simple sentence:

> Your services are no longer needed.

It was not dated, it was not signed.

"We found this in the chief's hand."

"Where—?" Doug began.

"Come on." Mike led him quickly into the hall and down to the closed office at the far end. "Brace yourself." He opened the door.

Catfield was in his desk chair, facing the door. He had been thrown back against the wall behind the desk and was staring at them. Or would have been staring at them had he had a face. For the shotgun propped on the desk before him had taken off half of his head, including his nose and eyes,

275

leaving only a twisted bloody mess of bone and tissue. Five or six remaining teeth grinned out of the grotesquely misshapen hole that had been a mouth. The diplomas and certificates on the wall were splattered with a Rorschach of blood and brains.

"Jesus," Doug breathed. He looked at Mike. "You waited to call me?"

"No," the policeman admitted. "But I didn't want to argue. We went over to the post office, found nothing. I have five men and six volunteers combing the town right now."

"Have you tried Howard's house? That's where he lives."

"That's where the rest of us are going."

"Let's go," Doug said. He closed the door to the chief's office.

The mailman's car was not in front of Howard's house, but the convoy of two police cars and two pickups parked catty-corner in the center of the street just in case, effectively blocking off any attempt to escape. The house looked even worse than it had the last time Doug had been by. The paint wasn't peeling, the shingles not falling off, but the house's overall appearance was so dilapidated that it gave the illusion that they were. The lawn was a brown weed jungle.

They got out of their cars and moved forward, two policemen in the lead, guns drawn. No one came out of any of the other houses on the street, and Doug found himself wondering if their owners had left, were dead, or were merely too frightened to come out.

A policeman knocked on the door, rang the bell, called out for someone to answer, then used a device to jim open the door. They walked inside.

The interior of the house was completely dark, the only illumination entering through the open door behind them. The heavy unmoving air stank of festering decay. Doug put his hand over his nose to block out the smell. He looked around, frowning. The entryway seemed narrower than he remembered, the walls rougher and more irregular. He reached out to touch the wall next to him, and his fingers touched packed paper. "Jesus," he whispered.

Stacks of envelopes stretched from floor to ceiling, covering every available inch of wall space, completely blocking the windows. The envelopes were fitted so neatly and precisely together that there was no space between them; they effectively formed an inner wall to the house.

The rest of them waited in place while two policemen went out to their cars for flashlights. Doug's eyes gradually adjusted. He could see into the living room beyond, and he noticed that the furniture had remained untouched. The couches and tables were not covered by mail, but the walls were concealed with an inner layer of piled envelopes, and in the center of the room additional stacks of mail had been used to form low shapes, sculptures, vaguely geometric, vaguely pyramidic forms.

The lights came, strong halogen beams that penetrated the dimness and brought to their eyes the enormity of what they were up against, the sheer single-minded craziness of the mailman. Doug stared at the letter walls, at the patterns formed by precise placement of colored envelopes and overlapping stamps. He was reminded of the Aztecs or Mayas or Incas, one of those ancient civilizations that had been able to fit stones together so perfectly that their structures were still standing today without the aid of mortar or cement.

They moved forward, slowly.

"Mr. Smith," Mike called out. "Mr. Smith, are you here?"

The house was silent save for their own breathing and footsteps. They walked through the living room, family room, dining room, kitchen, marveling at the completeness of the mailman's insane renovation. The horrible, putrid smell grew stronger as they moved into the hallway. Mike, in the lead now, pushed open a bedroom door.

And there was Howard.

It was clear from the strength of the stench, a sickening acrid odor of gas and bile and feces, that Howard had long since started to rot, but the signs were not readily visible on his face. The mailman had crudely painted Howard's lips with a dark-red lipstick, and ineptly applied eye shadow ringed the postmaster's widely staring eyes. There were twin rose circles of rouge on his pale sunken cheeks. Howard's hair had continued to grow after death, and it was piled on top of his head in a feminine swirl, held in place by greasy perfumed mousse. His toenails and fingernails had continued to grow as well and were obscenely long. The mailman had painted them a bright red.

He sat in a chair in the center of the room, staring at a

dead television set, the only other piece of furniture in the room. On the floor surrounding him were crusts of moldy bread, old Twinkie wrappers, and the bones of rats.

Mike took a walkie-talkie from one of the other policemen and told the patrolling officers what they had found, requesting that the coroner come to Howard's after he had finished with the chief.

Doug stepped out of the room and walked down the hall, through the living room, and outside to catch his breath. Even with his nose plugged he had been able to smell the rot, and his stomach had churned as he saw what had been done to the postmaster. Part of him had wanted to grab Mike and shake him and say, "I told you so," but he knew that that was stupid and petty and that this was not the time or place for it.

He stood on the dead lawn, staring up at the sky, breathing. It was getting late. The sun was beginning to sink, the shadows to lengthen. In other towns throughout the state, throughout the country, people were settling down to dinner, talking, watching the news. But here such normalcy was merely a memory.

He felt a hand on his shoulder. Mike. "The patrols report no sign of him. Do you have any idea where he might be?"

The creek, Doug started to say, but then he saw the thin sliver of moon hovering over the dimming horizon in the east. He remembered the mailman's dance of triumphant celebration. "I know where he is," he said, looking confidently into the policeman's eyes. "Get everyone together. Everyone. We can't let him get away this time."

"He won't get away," Mike said softly. He patted Doug's shoulder and went back into the house. Doug could hear his voice, though he could not tell what he was saying, and a few moments later he heard the sound of footsteps behind him as the policemen hurried outside.

The rocks of the ridge were orange in the light of the setting sun, the trees black triangular outlines. Venus had already appeared low in the west, and in the east the moon had risen, brightened. They drove up the narrow road slowly, in single file. Below them, the lights of the town seemed deceptively tranquil, benign, as though nothing out of the ordinary could ever happen in such a sleepy little community.

Doug drove with Tim in his pickup, and neither of them

spoke on the ride up the ridge. The radio was off as well, and the only noise was the rattle and clatter of the truck as it bounced over the ruts and washboards of the rough road. Doug looked in the side mirror and saw Mike and the other policemen following close behind in their patrol cars, the other pickup bringing up the rear. When they reached the top of the ridge, Doug told Tim to pull over and motioned out the window for Mike to follow suit.

They all got out of their vehicles. The night was cool, an advance scout for the coming fall. There were no clouds, and the new moon was surrounded by a faint hazy white halo.

"Why are we stopping here?" Mike asked.

Doug put a finger on his lips to tell the policeman to be quiet. "We have to walk the rest of the way. It's the only way we'll catch him. If he hears all those cars and trucks driving up the road, he'll be gone before we even get there."

Mike nodded. "All right, then. Lead the way."

They walked slowly across the bumpy ground, the policemen with their guns drawn, everyone nervously alert, on edge, listening for the smallest sound, looking for the smallest movement. They passed through a patch of sticker bushes, maneuvered through the giant manzanita.

And then they heard it. The familiar rhythmic chanting that brought a chill to Doug's blood, raised goose bumps on his arms.

He looked back at Mike, who nodded for him to keep moving. They crept forward slowly, quietly, until they were at the edge of the field. Doug stopped.

The mailman was dancing, as Doug had known he would be, arms flailing with wild abandonment, legs kicking up in spontaneous counterrhythm.

And the chant.

". . . rain nor snow nor sleet nor hail . . ."

The chill that had enveloped Doug increased as they approached. There were ten of them all together, he was not alone, but he felt as afraid as if he had been facing the mailman by himself.

The mailman continued to dance. He looked extraordinarily thin, and he seemed ghostly in the moonlight, his red hair fake.

"Okay," Mike whispered, gathering them around. "We'll spread out in a net, a half-circle. He can't go down the cliff, so he'll be trapped." The policeman looked at Doug, then back at his colleagues. "He's not armed, but he's dangerous. If he tries anything, shoot him."

The other policemen nodded.

"Let's go."

The grass and bushes rustled as the men spread out, but the noise was more than covered by the mailman's chanting. Doug, weaponless, stayed close to Mike. When the policemen saw that they were all in place, he stepped forward. The others followed suit.

The mailman saw them but did not falter in his ritual, continuing to dance without pause, raising his arms toward the sliver of the moon.

"I am placing you under arrest," Mike announced.

The mailman laughed, changing the words to his chant: "Neither men nor women nor hail of bullets shall keep this mailman from his appointed rounds."

Mike stepped forward, Doug next to him. The half-circle began to close in.

The mailman danced away from them, across the rocky field toward the edge of the ridge.

"Stop right there," Mike ordered.

The mailman laughed, leapt, danced, chanted. "Nor dark of night . . ."

They followed as he led them toward the ridge's edge, closing in, tightening their trap until they were almost upon him.

The mailman stopped dancing. He was not sweating, not even breathing hard. He grinned at Doug. "Billy is such a nice boy," he said. "Such a *nice* boy."

"Put your hands above your head," Mike ordered.

"What for, Officer?"

"Put them up!"

"You have no proof."

"We have all the proof we need."

The mailman smiled as he looked around the semicircle. "Fuckers," he said quietly.

"Put your hands above your head," Mike repeated.

"Fuckers," the mailman said softly. He moved backward to the very edge of the cliff, darting agilely from rock to rock, moving surefootedly across treacherous stretches of loosely packed dirt away from them.

Mike fired a warning shot in the air, and the mailman

stopped. Mike aimed the pistol at him. "If you make one more move, I'll kill you. Do you understand?"

Doug was not sure whether Mike was serious or not, but the mailman thought he was, and he remained in place.

"Tim," Mike said, "cuff him."

Tim nodded, moved forward, open cuffs in hand. "Mr. Smith, you are under arrest for—"

He never finished the sentence. The mailman quickly reached out and, before Hibbard had a chance to react, grabbed the handcuffs and yanked them from the policeman's grip. Tim lunged for the cuffs, but the mailman stepped neatly aside and with a quick well-placed push sent the young policeman over the edge of the ridge. There was a raw scream of terror that was cut off almost immediately. Doug heard the sickening thump-crack of the body hitting rock and, for a second, a faint echo of the scream before the echo, too, was cut off.

The mailman grinned. "Next?"

It had happened in a matter of seconds, almost before Doug knew what was going on, but Lt. Jack Shipley was already in action, moving forward, pistol pointed directly at the mailman's midsection. The mailman's white hand darted out, reaching for the gun.

Jack shot.

The bullet hit the mailman full in the chest, blood spurting from the ragged hole. The mailman toppled backward from the force of the blast, but he managed to grab the gun anyway. With a quick yank, he pulled the policeman with him over the edge. Jack was too startled to scream or react in any way. The mailman fell over the cliff, clutching tightly to the policeman, and the two of them tumbled to the rocks below. In the second before he fell, Doug thought he saw a smile on the mailman's bloody lips.

The rest of them ran to the edge, looking down, but the ground below was dark. Several policemen switched on their flashlights.

The intersecting beams quickly found and illuminated Jack's broken unmoving form.

The beams crossed and crisscrossed, searching the rocky floor below, spotlighting inch by inch the ground surrounding the spot where Jack had fallen. Tim lay nearby, arms twisted to the sides in impossible angles, head cracked open on a boulder. The lights lingered, then moved on, hitting trees, hitting bushes. Doug said nothing, and neither did any of the other men, but they were all thinking the same thing, and they were all scared shitless.

The beams continued to explore the terrain below the ridge, covering and recovering the same area.

But there were only two bodies on the ground.

The mailman was gone.

46

Doug sat on the porch and looked at his watch. It was after midnight already. He had been here for four hours, since leaving Trish at the hospital. He had wanted to stay too, but the doctor on duty, not Dr. Maxwell, had said that only one parent would be allowed to spend the night.

Doug had driven home alone.

On the ridge, he had hitched a ride back with Jeff Brickman, the officer who had volunteered to return to the station and coordinate communication while the other men figured out how to bring up the bodies. Jeff was going to try to get through to the county sheriff's office or the state police, and Doug seriously hoped he succeeded. For now, the policemen were following Mike, but he could already see them falling into disarray with the regular chain of command broken. When he had left, they were almost to the drawing-straws level of assigning responsibilities. It frightened Doug to see how easily such a trained group of individuals, such a structured organization, could fall apart, and he was glad when he was once again in the Bronco and driving.

He wondered now what the police were doing.

He thought of calling, but decided against it.

He finished off the last swallow of his fifth beer and stared up at the stars. Far above, one of the lighter heavenly bodies was traveling west to east in a steady line. A satellite. Lower, he saw the blinking lights of an airplane pass by, though the airplane made no sound.

Outside Willis, the world continued on.

He had called Tritia every half-hour, but she kept telling him there was no change, Billy was still sleeping. The last call had obviously woken her up, and she had irritably told him to stop calling, she would tell him when something happened.

Stop calling.

He wondered if she blamed him for what had happened.

He lay back in the soft seat, unmoving, unthinking, ready himself to drift drowsily into sleep, when he realized suddenly that the atmosphere had changed. Something was not quite right. He sat up, alert and awake. The crickets were silent, he noticed. There was no sound, no noise at all.

Yes, there was a noise.

From up the road, from the direction of the Nelsons', he heard the low purr of an engine drawing closer.

He froze, unable to react, unable to do anything.

The sound approached, growing louder in the stillness. He wanted to run and hide, to get into the house and lock the door and shut the curtains, but he remained in place.

And there it was, at the far end of the drive, the red car of the mailman, pulling in front of the mailbox.

He was dead. Doug had seen him shot, had seen him fall over the edge of the ridge. He was dead.

Doug stared at the red car. The driver's window rolled partially down and a white hand emerged from the dark interior, placed a letter in the box, then waved tauntingly good-bye as the car pulled away.

It was several moments later before the crickets started up again.

Doug's heart slowed, but he remained on the porch, unmoving. The mailman could not be killed. He could not die. There was nothing they could do. Doug prayed to a God he had not talked to in decades, but there was silence on the other end of the line. He sat there, unmoving.

He was still awake five hours later when dawn arose in the east.

47

He called the hospital before he went over, but Billy was still asleep. Good. That would give him time to get there. He wanted to be at his son's side when he awoke.

Tritia was seated, bleary-eyed, on her bed next to Billy's. She was dressed, her clothes wrinkled from having been slept in, her hair mussed and tangled. He hugged her tightly.

"You look like hell," she said.

"You don't look much better."

They both looked at Billy. Asleep, his features seemed restful, normal, as though nothing had happened to him and he was going to awaken the same as always. But he would not be the same. He would never be the same again.

"He's back," Doug said. "The mailman. I saw him last night. He delivered our mail." He had told her the mailman had been shot and killed, leaving out the part about his disappearing body, hoping against hope that they had merely not seen him in the night, that the flashlights had not illuminated the contents of an overlooked shadow or that he had crawled off somewhere to die.

Tritia paled. "He died and came back?"

"Or he didn't die at all."

Her expression collapsed, bravery fleeing in the face of overwhelming despair. "That's it, then."

Billy stretched, yawned, groaned in his sleep. Doug sat down on the edge of the bed and put a hand on his son's forehead. He found himself wondering why the mailman had not actually harmed Billy or Tritia. The mailman had been after him and his family from the beginning, but when he had finally caught Billy and Tritia, when he had had them in his power, he had done virtually nothing to them.

Maybe he couldn't do anything to them.

Billy sat upright in bed. "No!" he screamed. "No!"

Doug grabbed Billy's shoulders, guiding him down. "It's

okay, Billy," he said gently. "You're safe now. You're in the hospital. It's over now. You're safe."

The boy looked around with wild-rabbit eyes.

"We're here. It's okay."

Tritia moved over to the bed and hugged Billy. She was crying. "We're here," she said. "We're with you. Everything's going to be all right."

Doug felt the tears in his own eyes as he held his son's hand.

"Mom?" Billy said tentatively. "Dad?"

"Is everything okay?" The doctor hurried into the room. He saw that Billy was awake and moved over to the bed. "How are you feeling?"

The boy looked at him dully. "Tired."

"Effects of the tranquilizer," the doctor explained to Doug and Tritia. He turned toward Billy. "You're not in any pain, are you?"

Billy shook his head.

"Good. Probably just the shock, then." He smiled at Billy. "I'll be wanting to do a few tests later, when you feel up to it. Right now, I'll leave you alone with your mom and dad, okay?"

Billy nodded.

The doctor smiled at Doug and Tritia, gave a surreptitious thumbs-up sign, and left the room.

Left alone, the three of them were silent for a moment.

"Do you remember what happened?" Doug asked softly.

"Doug!" Tritia glared at him.

"Do you remember?"

"Leave him alone."

Billy nodded silently, not able to look at his parents' faces.

"Did he hurt you?" Doug asked.

Billy shook his head. "He couldn't touch me," he said. His voice was a cracked whispered croak. "He wanted to, but he couldn't."

Doug's blood was racing. "What do you mean he couldn't touch you?"

"He couldn't touch me."

"Why?"

Billy turned toward his father, then looked away, ashamed, embarrassed, unable to make eye contact. "I don't know."

"Think."

"Doug," Tritia said.

"He tried to give me mail," Billy whispered. "He wanted me to read it and he got really angry when I didn't. He said it was an . . . an invitation. I thought he was going to hit me, but it was like . . . like he couldn't touch me. Like something was stopping him. He started yelling at me and calling me names and threatening me, but I wouldn't take his invitation and he started going crazy, but he didn't touch me."

"You've been through a lot," Tritia said. "It's no wonder you think—"

"Let him talk." Doug nodded encouragingly at his son. "Go on."

"That's it."

"He couldn't touch you?"

Billy shook his head.

"What about the dress?"

Billy buried his face in the pillow. His voice was muffled. "I'm tired now," he said. "Stop asking me questions."

"What about the dress?"

"He wanted me to wear it, okay? He wanted me to put it on."

Doug patted his son's back. "Okay," he said. "All right." He stared at the headboard of the hospital bed and tried to recall whether or not he had ever seen the mailman touch anyone. He had not.

The reason the mailman could not be implicated in any of the murders, Doug realized, was because he had never performed any of them. Ronda and Bernie really had killed themselves, as had Irene. Stockley and Hobie had themselves been driven to murder. Unimaginable as it was, Giselle had actually raped and killed Ellen Ronda with the baseball bat.

John Smith's only power was the mail.

What was it Howard had said? The mailman spent all day Sunday hibernating in his room? And when he came out on Monday, he was tired, like he'd been sick? Doug remembered how pale and weak the mailman had seemed after the Fourth of July holiday.

He needed to deliver the mail to survive.

Tritia pushed Doug away and stroked Billy's hair. "What's the matter with you?" she asked angrily. "Hasn't he been through enough without his own father making him relive it?"

"I have an idea," Doug said. "I think I know how to get rid of the mailman."

Her eyes met his, and he saw in them a spark of hope.
"How?" she asked.

"It's crazy and it may not work."

"If it doesn't, we can go to Phoenix and never come
back." Her expression darkened. "If he doesn't follow us
and find us." She held his gaze. "What is your idea?"

"We cut off his power supply. We stop the mail."

"What?"

"That's the only way he can get to us. You heard Billy.
The mailman couldn't touch him. And what about you? He
didn't touch you either, did he?"

Tritia recalled with sickening clarity the feel of his hardness beneath his uniform as she'd shoved her way past him
in the bathroom. She slowly shook her head.

"You see? All he can do is manipulate people through the
mail. That's it. If we can just stop people from reading or
sending mail, we can get rid of him. But we have to get
everyone in town together. Every last damn one of them. If
this is going to work, it'll require the cooperation of every
person in Willis."

"I was talking to one of the nurses," Tritia offered. "I
don't think that will be a problem. They all know what's
going on. They're all scared. They'll do anything."

"We have to get the word out fast. I'm going to ask the
police to help me, call some of the other teachers. If we can,
I want to have a meeting of everyone in town tonight."

"Tonight's too soon. Word doesn't travel that fast." Dr.
Maxwell stood in the doorway. He walked into the room. "I
heard what you said, and I'm willing to try it."

Doug looked at him, smiled. "Thanks."

"I think you'll have to make it for tomorrow night. I can't
be there, and neither can most of my staff, but you can talk
to them beforehand. I think they'll go along with you on
this." He looked at Billy, who was still facedown in the
pillow. "We have to stop him."

"If he can be stopped," Tritia said.

"I think he can," Doug said.

Billy's voice was muffled by the pillow, but it was clear.
"I think he can too," he said.

Doug grabbed Tritia's hand and squeezed it tight.

48

They drove to the meeting together. Tritia had wanted to stay with Billy, but Doug said he needed her for this and she agreed to go along. They would return to the hospital afterward.

They had both stayed with Billy the night before, and although he was plagued with nightmares so powerful that twice Doug had to wake him up, he was unsedated, and in the morning he was lucid and cognizant of what was going on. He even made specific requests for breakfast, and by late afternoon he seemed almost like his normal self.

Dr. Maxwell got in touch with a friend of his in Phoenix, a psychiatrist specializing in childhood trauma, and he agreed to drive up and see Billy tomorrow.

Maybe things would be okay.

They drove past the post office on their way to the meeting. The character of the small building had changed completely from the days in which Howard Crowell and Bob Ronda had happily worked behind its doors, from the days in which the entire town had purchased stamps and dropped off mail between its walls. The staid nondescript structure now appeared decidedly malevolent. The windows had been smashed, their openings hastily covered up with irregular lengths of board nailed from the inside. Piles of ripped and dirty envelopes, as well as broken pieces of the mail-sorting machine, were scattered over the concrete steps. In a defensive line directly in front of the post office a row of rural mailboxes had been placed upside down, the metal boxes on the ground supporting their inverted posts.

On top of the posts were nailed the severed heads of town dogs, the animals' glassy eyes staring, unseeing, toward the street.

The dogs' headless bodies, ten or fifteen of them, littered the small parking lot.

Doug shivered as he and Trish sped by. The mailman was inside there, he knew. Probably peeking out at them. He felt suddenly nervous. Maybe he shouldn't have made Tritia come. Maybe he should have had her stay with Billy.

No, Billy would be all right. The hospital staff and Dr. Maxwell would look after him.

The street in front of the school was already jammed with cars. Someone had opened the gym and turned on the lights and people were filing in. Doug and Tritia parked on a side street and walked, rather than trying to find a closer parking space. They were greeted at the door by Mike, who told them that everyone who could would be there. The police had combed the town for two days, spreading the word.

Doug thanked him and stepped inside the gym. He and Tritia made their way through the crowd by the door and stood near the entrance to the boys' locker room. All four walls of bleachers had been brought down, and three of them were nearly full. There would not be enough space in here for everyone, he realized. Many people would just have to stand or sit on the floor.

He glanced around, trying to gauge the mood of the crowd. People seemed tentative, hesitant with one another. Awkward. Grudges had been formed and fanned through the mails, words of hate had been received and responded to, acquaintanceships had been reforged and realigned on the basis of faulty information, misdirected emotions, lies. Everyone knew that now. Everyone realized that the hate mail they'd been receiving, all of the gossiping innuendo, had not been sent by their neighboring townspeople but had been forced upon them by the mailman.

Still, feelings formed during that troubling period could not be instantly discarded, and there was tension among many members of the crowd. Arguments erupted. A small shoving match started in the stands, but was quickly stopped by a policeman.

And still people continued to arrive. People who had never before attended any civic function, people whose faces Doug did not even recognize, took seats on the bleachers. There were lone men in dusty hats and cowboy boots, impeccably dressed old couples, trendy young newlyweds, average families with children.

By eight o'clock, the appointed time, the gym was full, and Doug felt a little overwhelmed when he saw the size of

the crowd. It was not speaking before so many people that
daunted him—he was a teacher and was used to speaking in
front of groups—it was taking the responsibility of leading
so many individuals, of making the decisions for so many
people.

He saw in the packed bleachers the faces of school-board
members, city-council members, policemen, the fire chief:
people elected or appointed to positions of power. These
men and women, supposedly trained to deal with public
crises, did not know what to do in this situation and were
looking to him for answers. The thought was intimidating,
made even more so by the looks of worry and hope he saw
on the faces of people he didn't even know, by the frightened murmurs of adults and the crying whimpers of children.

The room felt hot, the walls claustrophobically close, the
air filled with the smell of old and new sweat. Tritia squeezed
his hand, a gesture of faith and support that more than
anything else gave him the strength to stride across the
polished wood floor to the center of the gym.

There was no need for him to be nervous or worried or
intimidated, he told himself. He was taking control in this
crisis because he had to, because he was the only one who
knew what had to be done. He had to think positively.
There was no room for doubt. Not now. There was too
much at stake. This was no time for indecision. They had to
fight the mailman with everything they had, with their com-
bined faith and belief. They had to do it or die.

The crowd was silenced immediately; he did not even
have to raise his hand. The talking died down, and parents
hushed the crying of their children. Only the wailing of a
few small babies disturbed the stillness.

"You all know why you're here," Doug began. "Why
we're here. We're here to free our town from the tyranny of
the mailman. He has held us captive all summer, has used
the mails to pit brother against brother, friend against friend.
He has stopped our utilities, disrupted our lives, ruined our
relationships. He has killed directly or indirectly, and he has
brought our town to this." He gestured before him, toward
the world outside the walls. The people were silent. He
had their attention. "Many of you may not know it, but we
found Howard Crowell yesterday in his home. Dead."

A wave of words passed through the crowd.

"He killed my Darla too!" David Adams called out. His

voice was frightened, close to hysteria. "He promised her things! He lied about me and he made her . . . he made her . . ." David's voice trailed off.

"My business is ruined because of that son of a bitch!" Hunt James announced. "And so is Dr. Elliott's! He spread rumors about us and these assholes believed it!" He motioned toward the people surrounding him.

And now a lot of voices were speaking at once, people standing, yelling, screaming, competing for attention.

"—knew my mother had a heart condition!"

"—We've always paid our bills on time! Always!"

"—never hurt an animal in my life!"

"—illegal to send those kinds of things through the mail! Those videotapes! And those rubber—"

Doug held up his hands for silence. It took a few moments, but when the crowd quieted down, he continued. "We have to get him out of our town," he said. "We have to exorcise him."

"Let him do the rope exercise!" someone called out.

Doug shook his head. "Lynching won't work."

In the front row of the bleachers right before him, Tril Allison, the owner of Allison's Lumber, stood up. He was not used to public speaking, and he shifted nervously from one foot to the other. Next to him on the bleachers sat his sons, Dennis and Tad, both of whom had been in Doug's English classes last semester. Tril cleared his throat. "What is the mailman?" he asked.

It was the question that had been on everyone's minds, if not everyone's lips, and Doug was about to respond when a shrill voice sounded off from somewhere in the upper portion of the bleachers.

"He's the devil!" An old woman stood up, a woman Doug did not recognize. "Our only hope is prayer! Our only hope is to ask Jesus Christ for forgiveness and beg Him to protect us!"

There were low murmurs of frightened assent.

"He's not the devil!" Doug announced, raising his hands for quiet.

"Then, what is he?" Tril asked. "He certainly ain't human."

"No," Doug said, "he's not human. To be honest, I don't know what he is."

"He killed my daughter!" someone yelled.

"I don't know what he is!" Doug repeated, louder. "But I do know this: he can be stopped. We can stop him."

Smith Tegarden, one of the police officers who had been on the ridge the other night, walked out of the crowd and onto the gym floor. There was confidence in his step, but Doug could see that that was merely habit, reflex. The veteran cop was frightened. He stood in front of Doug. "We shot that bastard point-blank, and he didn't die," he said. "He fell off the ridge and walked away. How do you propose to stop him?"

Doug took a deep breath. "We're going to starve him," he said. "We're going to cut off his mail."

"Cut off his male what?" someone yelled from the crowd, and there was a chorus of tension-relieving laughter.

Doug smiled. "We're going to stop sending or receiving any mail. Whatever he delivers, don't take it, don't pick it up. Let it sit in your mailboxes. The mail is his only real power. That's all he's ever really done to us." He thought of Billy, thought of Tritia, thought of Howard. "The mail is how he's gotten to us. It's how he's brought us to this point. It's his only weapon. If we can stop the mail, we can stop him."

Arguing broke out and Doug could tell immediately that his idea had not gone over well. He had been afraid of that. It sounded so stupid, so weak, so ineffectual, that it didn't seem as though it would do any good. He saw a couple of people heading for the door.

"Wait," Mike's voice cut authoritatively through the cacophony. He walked across the floor to stand next to Doug. "Hear him out."

The noise abated.

"I know it sounds idiotic," Doug continued. "But we have nothing to lose by trying. The police officer's right. Bullets won't stop him. I don't think he can be killed. But I've been watching him. There was a holiday on the Fourth of July. No mail was delivered. The next day he was thin and sick. This week, when he came back after disappearing, he was even thinner. He needs mail to survive. That's where he gets his energy or his power or whatever it is. If we cut him off, if no one sends any mail or receives any mail, he will have nothing to do. He will die."

"Maybe he won't die. Maybe he'll just leave," a woman said.

"Fine. At least we'll be rid of him."

"Then he'll come back."

"And we'll do it again. Or maybe by that time we will have found something else."

People were starting to talk again.

"We all have to do it. Every one of us. If even one person gives him mail, it may be enough to keep him alive." Doug swallowed. His voice cracked. "Look, he attacked my wife and my son. Or he tried to attack them. But he couldn't do anything. He couldn't touch them. He wanted to, he tried to, but in the end the only thing he could do was try to get them to read his mail. That's all he has. That's his only power."

The sound of the crowd was different this time, louder, less argumentative, hopeful. They wanted to believe. Next to him, Tritia held his hand. She looked up at him and smiled. "No mail!" she yelled. "No mail!" She began to chant in a cheerleader cadence. "No mail! No mail! No mail! No mail!"

It was picked up by Mike and by some of the people in the front rows. Two of the school's real cheerleaders took up the cause, lending their considerable vocal talents to the chant, and from elsewhere in the audience the other cheerleaders followed suit.

"No mail! No mail! No mail! No mail!"

The sound grew, spread, and soon the entire gym was filled with the echoing reassuring sounds of the impromtu cheer.

"No mail! No mail! No mail! No mail!"

Never before had Doug experienced such a sense of community, such a spirit of cooperative togetherness, such a willful optimism. For the first time, he really and truly believed that they might have a chance to put a stop to this nightmare. He grinned at Tritia, and she grinned back.

The lights in the gym flickered.

"Stay calm," Doug ordered. "Don't panic!" But his voice was lost in the cry of the crowd, in the thump of stamping feet.

A moment later the electricity went off for good.

But no one seemed to notice and the people of the town continued to chant.

"No mail! No mail! No mail! No mail!"

49

In the morning Doug awoke to see outside his window a winter wonderland. The sight was beautiful. It had snowed during the night, and ground and porch, trees and bushes were all completely covered with pure glorious white.

Only . . .

Only the air was warm and humid, the sky cloudless, and the ivory blanket that covered the world outside seemed smoothly even, strangely symmetrical.

He opened the back door and looked down.

The ground was not covered with snow.

The ground was covered with envelopes.

He stood there stunned. The envelopes had been placed, facedown, end-to-end over everything, their flat edges fitting perfectly against the side of the house in a straight line and continuing over the back porch, over the storage shed, over the manzanita bushes and the trees. The enormity of such an effort was overwhelming, and the fact that it had been completed in one night, directly outside his house while he had been sleeping undisturbed inside, was terrifying.

He was glad that Trish had spent the night at the hospital with Billy. He would not have wanted her to see this.

Gingerly, Doug bent down and picked up the envelope nearest the door, turning it over. It was addressed to him from his mother. He picked up the one next to it, addressed to him from his father. The one next to that was from his Aunt Lorraine.

He had the feeling that the mailman had grouped the envelopes in a specific order and that, if he made the effort to trace the pattern, he would find that the lineage of his life spread outward from that point in the return addresses of the letters.

Doug stood up. He'd thought at first that the whole town had been covered by mail, but he saw almost instantly that past the white blanket covering his own trees was the natural green of real nature. He slipped on his sandals and stepped onto the back porch. The paper crinkled beneath his feet, but he continued forward, determined to see how far the mailman had gone. When he came to the first bush, its leafy shape entirely hidden by the back-to-back envelopes that domed its true form, he extended a cautious hand, curious to see how the envelopes had been attached together.

The dome collapsed.

A house of cards. The mailman had used the envelopes to construct a house of cards, balancing them one on top of the other with no adhesive until they covered the bush.

He walked across the white ground to the first tree, touching it.

The tree covering, too, collapsed in a rain of letters.

In the house the phone rang, its jangling loud in the early-morning stillness. He knew it was probably Trish calling, but he still hurried forward through the bushes and trees, away from the house, starting off letter landslides as he ran. He had to see how far this extended.

He was not surprised to discover that the white blanket stopped at the exact edge of his property line, that the straight sides of the carefully placed envelopes marked a perfect border around the irregular shape of his land.

He dashed back to the house, experiencing a perverse sense of pleasure as the envelopes crunched beneath his feet. The phone was still ringing, and he ran into the bedroom, picking it up as he fell back onto the bed. "Hello?" he said.

"Letters," the mailman sang in a cruel parody of a Las Vegas lounge singer. "We've got letters!"

Doug hung up the phone, his hand suddenly sweaty. His heart was pounding, and not just with the exertion of running. He lay there for a moment, breathing, thinking, then picked up the phone again to dial Mike.

"Letters," the mailman sang through the receiver.

Doug hung up. The mailman was staying on the line, keeping it open, not letting him make or receive calls.

Fine, Doug thought, his mouth set in grim determination. If the mailman wanted to play hardball, hardball was what he was going to get.

He unplugged the receiver. First he would drive to the

hospital, see Billy and Trish. Then he would go to the police station. Then he would go to the hardware store and buy some extra garbage cans.

Then he would come back here and rake the yard and throw away all of that fucking mail.

Tritia said that she'd stay at home tonight if Doug wanted, keep him company. Billy was feeling better, she said, and wanted to be alone, didn't want his parents hovering over him every second of the day like he was some kind of baby. But Doug insisted that she remain with their son, telling her that it was important for the boy that she be with him. She said that in that case it was important for both of them to be there, but he told her that he and Mike had a strategy meeting to conduct. They had things to discuss and plan out. She should stay at the hospital.

It was a wise decision, for the next day the property was again covered with mail, although the pure white envelopes of the previous morning had been replaced by an odd assortment of strangely shaped packages, poorly wrapped parcels and filthy postmarked bundles. As before, every inch of ground was covered. The mailman had somehow managed to fit the pieces of this motley collection together like some giant jigsaw puzzle, finding complementary curves for the sides of bent boxes, finding corresponding accordion sides to match mishandled packages.

Doug opened the door and stepped outside. The smell hit him immediately, a rancid fetid odor of rot and decay. Through the ripped corner of one of the packages nearest him he saw a bunch of moldy grapes. The package was addressed to Tritia, obviously one of her Fruit-of-the-Month Club deliveries. Next to that was an irregularly shaped, awkwardly wrapped object covered with postage stamps that could only have been a cat. Blood had soaked through the brown butcher paper. It too was addressed to Tritia.

Doug surveyed his property, a feeling of dread settling over him. Obviously his plan wasn't working. The whole town was supposed to be ignoring their mail, sending and receiving nothing, and according to Mike, everyone was complying. Yet still the mailman had enough power to do this, to manufacture or gather together hundreds of packages of perversities and within the space of a single night arrange them over his entire property. How could they even hope to fight a being who could pull off something of this magnitude?

But maybe that was the point. Maybe that was why this whole scene had been staged. Maybe that's what the mailman wanted them to think. Maybe the mailman was scared and on the ropes, using everything he had, trotting out his big guns in an effort to demoralize them and bully them into submission.

Or maybe, Doug thought, his disposal of the envelopes yesterday had given the mailman an energy boost. It was possible that *any* action involving mail, even its disposal, empowered the mailman to a certain extent.

He immediately retreated into the house, threw on his clothes, grabbed his keys, and drove into town to talk to Mike. He asked the policeman to have his men tell everyone that, no matter what happened, they were to leave their mail untouched, not burn it, not throw it away, not do anything with it. Let it pile up if they had to, but don't touch it.

Doug practiced what he preached, leaving the packages in his own yard and spending the night at the hospital with Tritia and Billy. When he returned home the next afternoon, the yard had been cleared. All of the packages were gone and nothing had been left to take their place.

Doug smiled. That, he was certain, had been a tactical error on the mailman's part. The stench and the disease accompanying the rotting fruit, animals, and whatever else had been in the bundles would have eventually forced him to clean his yard, thereby granting the mailman more power. Instead, the mailman had been forced to expend power in order to remove the packages.

The signs were subtle, but they were there.

The mailman was getting scared. He was getting sloppy.

He was slipping.

They just had to wait him out.

50

The days were long. The nights were longer.

The utilities had been off since the day after the packages had disappeared, and both Doug and Trish smelled from not bathing. For meals they had sandwiches and barbecues, drank warm beer and Cokes. During the interminable days, they waited on the porch, trying to read but not reading, or went to the hospital to sit with Billy. The hospital had its own self-powered emergency generators, and while they were not allowed to use the rationed water or spend the night in semi-air-conditioned comfort due to the new over-crowded conditions, at least they had the satisfaction of knowing that Billy was being taken care of.

The psychiatrist who had come up from Phoenix told them after an afternoon-long meeting with Billy that he was a healthy and extremely well-adjusted young man and that with the proper counseling he should be able to recover nicely.

At night Doug's fitful sleep was disturbed by dreams. Dreams in which Willis was a ghost town and all of the buildings were made from mail. Dreams in which Tritia lay naked and beckoning on the bed, covered head to toe with canceled stamps. Dreams in which Billy wore a Postal Service uniform and grinningly accompanied the mailman on his hellishly appointed rounds.

The gas in the Bronco was getting low, but Doug couldn't help driving into town to check with the police. Each night the mailman came, delivering mail, depositing it now in the mailbox, and Doug kept thinking that with no visible progress someone was going to crack, was going to accept a letter or, worse, send one. But Mike and Tegarden said each time that as far as they could tell, the dam was holding.

The sixth day passed.

The air-conditioning was shut off in the hospital to save

the generator fuel, but the windows were open and a slight breeze cooled Billy's room. The two of them played Monopoly while Tritia watched, then Tritia and Billy played Parcheesi while he watched.

How thin was the veneer of civilization, Doug thought. How little it took to send them scurrying back to the caves. It was not laws that separated man from beast. It was not reason. It was not culture or government. It was communication. Communication made possible the niceties of modern life, ensured the continuation of society. A breakdown in communication, particularly in this global age when so much depended on the proper relay of correct information, left people feeling lost and helpless, resulting in an arrest of the normal rules of behavior, paving the road for chaos.

But he was waxing pretentious again. He found himself doing that often, even aloud, which annoyed the hell out of Tritia. He should have learned by now to save those sorts of ruminations for the classroom and not to inject them into real conversations.

The classroom.

How far away school seemed, how quaint and innocent. He tried to think of when school was going to be starting, but though he thought it was pretty soon, he wasn't sure. He realized he didn't know what date it was.

He left Tritia at the hospital while he went to the police station to see what was happening. On the way, he passed by the Circle K, and he slowed down as he saw the mailman opening the blue mailbox in front of the convenience store. The mailbox was completely empty and he slammed the metal door shut angrily. He looked bad, Doug thought. He had always been thin, but now he seemed gaunt, almost skeletal. His pale skin was bleached nearly bone-white, and there was no differentiation in color between his lips and the rest of his skin. Even his once fiery red hair seemed faded and lackluster.

Doug's heart leapt hopefully in his chest. It was working. He had been right. The mailman might be able to substitute mail, even to generate mail, but to do so he had to have other mail coming in. He smiled to himself. Mail, he thought, could be neither created nor destroyed.

Doug watched the mailman stand. He seemed weak, frail. All they had to do now was wait him out.

The mailman suddenly turned toward him and grinned,

eyes fastening sharply and instantly on his own, as though he had known exactly where Doug had been watching the whole time. The effect of those perfect teeth in that skeleton face was horrifying. A comic-book monster come to life. The mailman reached into his bag and pulled out a handful of envelopes, fanning them like cards, offering them to Doug. But Doug pressed down on the gas and sped past the Circle K not looking at the mailman, heart hammering in his chest.

His fear did not survive the trip to the police station. He ran inside. For the first time, he had something to tell them, good news, and when he described what he had seen, the policemen cheered.

"No mail," Mike said, grinning. "No mail! No mail!"

The others took up the chant.

"No mail! No mail! No mail!"

51

Tril Allison stood in front of the living-room window with his sons, watching as the mailman's red car pulled in front of their driveway. Annie stayed in the kitchen, refusing to look, afraid to look.

The car came to a full stop and the mailman got out. He looked extraordinarily thin, almost emaciated, and even from here, Tril could see the bony fingers emerging from the drooping uniform, could see the haggard gauntness in the pale face. Tril's hands tightened on the windowsill. He was scared, but he was also exhilarated, horrified and at the same time thrilled. It was working. The English teacher had been right. Without any mail to deliver, John Smith was losing his strength. He was dying.

Through the window, he met the mailman's gaze, and for the first time in a long while he did not look away.

The mailman moved over to the wooden mailbox and opened the hinged door. Out spilled envelopes, white and manila, thin and stuffed, large and small: the untouched mail that had been delivered over the past few days. The mailman looked up again at the house, and Tril could see in the white skeletal face a ferocious rage, an expression of pain and hate so raw and unfettered that both boys moved back from the window, too frightened to watch.

But Tril watched.

He watched as the mailman angrily picked the envelopes off the dirt and shoved them back into the box. Watched as he brought more mail from the car and shoved it in as well. Watched as he slammed shut the mailbox door.

The mailman moved around to the driver's side of the car. He glared at the house and mouthed something Tril could not make out before getting in and driving off in a cloud of dust.

Tril waited a few moments to make sure he was not going

to return, then looked back at Annie, at his sons, picked up
the hammer and nails, and went outside to nail the mailbox
shut.

Hunt James pulled into the six-space parking lot in front
of the building he shared with Dr. Elliott. He had come
here to tape up the mail slot in his office door, to make sure
that the mailman would not be able to deliver anything to
his business address. He strode across the faded and broken
asphalt and stepped onto the short sidewalk. In the window
of the dentist's office, next to the familiar "No UPS today"
sign, he saw a hastily lettered square of white cardboard
that said "NO MAIL EVER!"

Good idea, Hunt thought. He used his key to open the
door to his own office and flipped on the lights. He strode
purposefully across the carpeted floor. From his secretary's
desk, he took a thick black felt-tipped pen and a sheet of
typing paper as well as a roll of masking tape. Smiling to
himself, he began to write.

The mailman drove by the house three times before stopping. David Adams grinned to himself as he saw the red car
brake in front of the house. He had dug up the mailbox,
had filled in the post hole, and had dumped the whole thing into
the back yard. Later, after breakfast, he would cut up the
post for kindling and smash the mailbox itself.

The mailman got out of his car and, letters in hand,
walked straight up the driveway toward the front door.

David quickly locked the screen door, shut the real door
and pulled the curtains, still grinning. The mailman was
getting pretty damned desperate. He looked like hell, and
he was even delivering mail in the daytime. They had the
bastard on the ropes now.

There was a knock at the door. "Mr. Adams!"

David said nothing, did not move.

Another knock. "Mr. Adams!"

David did not respond.

"I know you're in there," the mailman said. He knocked
again, loudly, more forcefully. "Mr. Adams? I regret to
inform you that you are in violation of federal statute. Since
you do not have a post-office box or drawer, you are required by law to have either a mailbox or mail slot at your
place of residence so that mail can be properly delivered. If

you do not have a mailbox or mail slot, you are interfering with the daily operation of the federal government and, as such, can be prosecuted."

David smiled. There was a hard edge to the mailman's voice and more than a hint of desperation.

"I know you're in there," the mailman repeated. His voice took on a sly tempting quality. "I have things here that I know you'd like to see. Darla's last letter. A letter from her lover. This is good mail today, Mr. Adams. Good mail."

David said nothing, though he wanted to scream at the son of a bitch; remained unmoving, though he wanted to attack. He heard the mailman angrily throw the letters on the stoop and stalk off. A moment later, he heard the start of a car's engine and then a decreasing purr as the car pulled away. David opened the door, opened the curtains, breathed deeply, feeling good.

It was only a matter of time.

52

Doug and Mike and Tegarden sat silently on the lone bench in front of Bayless. From this vantage point, they could see most of the town's business section, and for the past hour they had watched as the mailman had driven up and down the street, desperately trying to find a place to deliver mail. All of the businesses had disposed of their mailboxes or blocked off their mail slots, and most of them had put up signs, some elaborately hand-painted on posterboard by wives and children, some banner-printed by home computer, some crudely scrawled on cardboard:

> NO MAIL ON BOARD
>
> ONE LETTER CAN RUIN YOUR WHOLE DAY
>
> I WON'T TOUCH A LETTER UNLESS YOU
> PRY IT INTO MY COLD DEAD FINGERS
>
> MAIL IS NOT HEALTHY FOR CHILDREN
> AND OTHER LIVING THINGS
>
> MAIL SUCKS

The mailman's behavior had become increasingly frantic as he darted from shop to shop, gas station to office, his driving increasingly crazy as he sped for the fourth, fifth, and sixth times over the same section of street. Observed from this vantage point, he seemed like a trapped and doomed bug trying to escape from the lethal confines of a killing jar.

Doug was nervous and excited, and he knew the other two men were too, but all three of them had for some reason assumed masks of laconic disinterest, as though they were three old-timers whiling away their hours on a park bench and casually commenting on the sights that passed before their eyes.

"Looks like he's going back to the donut hut," Tegarden drawled.

"Yep," Mike said.

A part of Doug felt sorry for the mailman. He did not like to see anything hurt or wounded. But he had only to think of Trish and Billy, of Hobie and Stockley and everyone else, for that sympathy to disappear and be replaced by a grim feeling of satisfaction.

The mailman was getting what he deserved.

"He's trying to shove mail under the door of the catalog store," Mike observed.

"Won't work," Tegarden said.

The mailman ran wildly back to his car and drove back up the street for the eighth time.

53

The water came on sometime during the ninth morning, the electricity that afternoon.

By the end of the next day, both gas and telephone service had also been restored.

54

The mailman had not been seen for over two days, and when Doug called the police station, Mike told him that the mailman's car had not moved from the front of the post office for fifty-two hours. "I think it's time for us to go in there and check," he said. "Let's see what's going on."

They drove together, in four cars, and Doug couldn't help thinking about Jack and Tim. When this was over, they would have to have a memorial service for them. For all the victims of the mail.

Flies were buzzing on the dried heads of the dead dogs. The air was thick with the putrid odor of the decapitated carcasses. The eight men strode across the parking lot. Directly in front of the door, behind an overturned bench, Doug saw something he hadn't before.

An infant's head.

Speared on a fallen mailbox post.

He looked at Mike, but neither of them said a word. The child's head, like those of the dogs, was dried and old and swarming with flies. The small eyes were clear deflated sacs.

Mike motioned to Tegarden, the biggest, strongest man on the force. "Kick it in," he said, gesturing toward the glass door.

Tegarden obliged happily and shattering shards exploded inward.

They stepped through the open door frame.

The interior of the post office was dark, windows completely boarded up, lights off. Brown packaging paper covered the walls and floor and ceiling. The men stepped hesitantly inside, Doug first. The sounds of their movement were loud in the stillness. "Where the hell are you?" Doug called.

There was no answer, and they moved carefully forward as one. The room was a shambles. The tall metal table that had stood against one wall was overturned, and the floor was littered with paper and boxes and pieces of broken furniture. The body of a rat lay on the front counter, its head gone, chewed off. Next to it, large bones, probably from a dog, had been arranged in precise geometric patterns. The entire countertop was covered with dried blood.

Doug stepped slowly around the counter. The post office seemed empty, felt dead, but he was nervous nonetheless. He tiptoed toward the open door that led to the back room.

From inside the room came a long low sigh.

And a frightened whimper.

Doug stopped in his tracks, heart pounding. Looking behind him, he saw fear on the faces of both the old and young policemen. All of them had heard the noise, and none of them knew what to make of it. Only Mike seemed unaffected. He pushed roughly past Doug, preparing to lead the assault into the rear of the post office, but Doug held him back. He was scared, but he was not about to let Mike do what he knew was his responsibility. "No," he said.

The policeman looked at him.

"I want to go alone."

Mike shook his head, pulling out his revolver, snapping off the safety. "It's too dangerous."

"It's not dangerous. Not anymore." He looked into the policeman's troubled eyes. "This is between me and him."

Mike was silent for a moment, his gaze searching, then he nodded, something like agreement or understanding entering his expression. "All right," he said. "But take this." He handed Doug the gun. "You know how to use it?"

Doug shook his head. "Not really. But it doesn't matter. It won't work on him anyway. You know that."

"Take it just in case."

The whimper came again. It sounded like someone in pain.

"That's it—" Mike began, moving forward.

"No," Doug said, grabbing his arm, pulling him back. "I'm going in alone." The policeman stopped, stared at him, but did not move away. Doug held his gaze, hefted the revolver in his hand. "I'll be okay."

Mike nodded slowly. "Okay," he said finally. "But we'll be right here if you need us." The policeman's words were reassuring, his tone anything but. "If I hear anything weird, I'm going in."

"Got it."

Doug stepped into the back room.

Into the lair of the mailman.

He glared at Doug from the rubble. Or, rather, *it* glared at him. For the mailman now appeared only vaguely human. His body had shrunk, become thin and twisted and malformed like that of some giant insect. The red hair on top of his head, now blondish pink, had grown out tremendously and hung down in thick irregular tufts. His teeth looked overlarge in his caved-in head and sharp, as though they had been filed. Around him the desks and shelves, machines and bins, canvas bags and postal paraphernalia, were littered in a jumbled chaotic mess.

Behind Doug the door slammed shut.

The mailman laughed, a rasping chuckle that sent a shiver of primal fear down Doug's spine. The air was filled with a strange heaviness, a crackling eddying current of power that felt like charged electricity.

In the shifting emphasis of light caused by the closed door, Doug saw for the first time that he and the mailman were not alone in the room. In the far corner, against the wall, almost hidden by the shadow of a vertically overturned table, was an unmoving figure with wildly uncombed hair. The figure whimpered pitiably. Doug stepped forward until he could see a face.

Giselle Brennan.

His breath caught within him. Giselle was wrapped, mummylike, in brown packaging paper. One arm had broken free from the covering and was twisted at an unnatural angle, affixed to her side with rubber bands and encased in layers of folded orange and blue Express Mail envelopes. Blood had seeped through the wrapping in innumerable spots and had blackened and dried in even, regular stripes. Giselle's face, her neck and chin and cheeks, were crisscrossed with paper cuts, straight intersecting lines that sliced through skin and formed a field of squares, rectangles, parallelograms. Paper cuts also scored her lips, making it appear as though they had been sewn shut. One ear was torn off.

"Giselle," Doug said, moving forward.

She moaned.

It was then that he saw on the white skin of her forehead

several wavy lines of black ink protruding from a circle filled with writing.

The mark of cancellation.

From under her hairline he saw an even row of pasted stamps.

He turned on the mailman. "What is this?" he demanded. "What happened? What the hell have you done to her?"

The mailman laughed again, the rasping sound as grating as that of fingernails scraping across a chalkboard. "Mail accident," he said. His voice was a low whisper, barely recognizable.

"You bastard," Doug breathed. He suddenly realized what the mailman had done. He had turned her into a package. A fucking package ready to be mailed.

The creature coughed. "The Postal Service cannot be held responsible for injuries occurring as a result of delivered mail. If she had been injured as a result of her work, she would have been covered under federal employment statutes. But she is a part-time worker injured in a nonjob related accident. I have helped her as much as I can. I have bandaged her wounds. I can do no more. Now it is up to you." There was hunger in his insectile eyes. "If you do not take her to the hospital immediately, she will die. It may already be too late."

This time the young woman's moan was a word. "Help."

Doug stood unmoving, not knowing what to do. The seconds seemed like hours, endlessly long. He could almost hear them ticking off, one after the other. The room was still, silent, and so, he noticed, was the room out front, the town outside. Not a sound disturbed the perfect quiet. It was as if the whole world awaited his decision.

"Help me," Giselle pleaded. Her voice was weaker than her moaning. Fresh blood spread over her chin from her serrated lips.

"She will die unless you save her," the mailman whispered.

This was not something that could be decided quickly. This was not the sort of answer that could be decided by eeny-meeny-miney-moe, in which the outcome didn't matter. The outcome *did* matter, and both the possibilities were wrong. He took a deep breath. If he had been a doctor, he might have been able to judge if recovery was possible or death inevitable, he might have been able to base his decision on knowledge and experience. But he knew nothing.

He needed time to figure this out. He needed time to ponder, analyze, study the situation.

But there was no time.

"Mr. Albin," the mailman whispered.

"Help," Giselle pleaded.

Doug closed his eyes. Everything within him, his heart, his soul, all of those elements that made him human were telling him to get moving and take her to the hospital. But a stubborn core of icy resolve kept him from acting. If he helped Giselle, all would be lost. The mailman, obviously, was near death. This was merely a last gasp, a final attempt on his part to turn the tide. If Doug accepted this "mail," it might energize him enough that he might be able to really fight back. If mail's power was proportionate with its weight or value, Giselle was the equivalent of hundreds of checks and letters.

"Help me."

He could not let her die. She might die anyway, but he could not be responsible for her death. It would mean sacrificing all of the work, all of the effort performed by himself and everyone else in town; it could even mean that the mailman would be restored to full power, free to kill other people. But Doug could not stand idly by and watch Giselle die. He had to take her to the hospital. By refusing to condemn her to death, he might be condemning others to death. But he had to take that chance.

He took a step forward. Out of the corner of his eye, he saw the mailman's skeletal arm trace a pattern in the air. He stopped, turning.

A tear rolled down Giselle's cheek, diverted by the paper cuts into increasingly smaller rivulets. "Mr. Albin," she cried softly.

The mailman's twisted lips moved silently. His eyes were closed.

"Don't let me die," Giselle pleaded.

Her voice sounded different than usual, Doug noticed, more rhythmic, less natural, and there was something about her words that seemed stiltedly formal, which did not ring true. He looked from Giselle to the mailman and back again.

The mailman's head moved to the right.

Giselle's head moved to the right.

He stood unmoving, unsure of what to do.

"You're the only one that can save me," Giselle pleaded, her voice fading.

Doug stiffened. "The only one *that* can save me."

That.

Giselle would have said "who."

She was already dead. She had been dead even before he had stepped through the door. He looked closely into the young woman's face, saw now the slightly glassy sheen of her eyes, the vaguely translucent thickness of the tear that had coursed down her serrated cheek. She had died sometime earlier, maybe today, maybe yesterday, maybe the day before, and the mailman had kept her here to use as bait, knowing Doug would come eventually and knowing that he would not be able to let her die. The mailman had played her like a puppet, manipulating her limited facial expressions, using her voice to say his words, animating her dead form with whatever was left of his power.

"Nice try," Doug said coldly.

The mailman opened his eyes, glared. Their glances locked, and this time Doug did not look away. His gaze remained hard, even, unblinking. The mailman's stare was equally unwavering, but the strength was tentative, a front maintained at great cost. There was defeat behind the iron, fear behind the aggression, recognition that he had miscalculated. He had lost, and he knew that he had lost, and he knew that Doug knew he had lost.

"You're finished," Doug said.

The mailman hissed. Behind them, Giselle's body slumped to the ground in a loud crinkle of paper as around the room letters, envelopes, bills, began swirling up from the floor as though caught in a dust devil. Doug half-expected the mail to attack him, to fly at his face, but all it did was circle impotently upward in the air.

The mailman did not even have enough power left to control a few small envelopes.

"It's over," Doug said.

The door flew open, Mike, Tegarden, and the others bursting in. "We couldn't—" Mike began. He saw the swirling letters, saw Giselle's body. "Jesus!"

Tegarden aimed his revolver instantly and fired at the mailman. The bullet passed harmlessly through him. The mailman laughed, a rasping chuckle that was supposed to be frightening but somehow was not.

Doug suddenly remembered that he was holding a weapon himself.

The mailman pulled an envelope from the air. He lurched forward on skeleton feet, the envelope in his outstretched claw. He smiled up at Tegarden. "For you," he croaked.

The policeman shook his head in disgust.

The mailman's smile faltered.

"Let's get out of here." Doug's voice was calm and self-assured. "We'll come back in two more days." He returned the revolver to Mike.

Mike looked from Doug to the mailman, then back again, taking everything in. He nodded silently and motioned the others to leave.

"No!" the mailman rasped, screamed.

They ignored him as they walked over the broken glass out of the office.

55

Doug awoke fully alert, the dream he'd been experiencing disappearing instantly without leaving even a vestigial memory. At first he thought he must have been awakened by a noise—the telephone, a knock on the door, something falling over—but the air was still and silent, only the ever-present sound of the crickets outside disturbing the peaceful night air. He glanced at the clock, its blue letters glowing in the darkness. Three. Three o'clock. The dark hour of the soul. He had read that somewhere, "the dark hour of the soul." Three in the morning was supposed to be the time when the human body is physically closest to death, when all functions are at their lowest ebb.

So why did he feel so up, so alert, so aware?

Outside, the crickets stopped chirping and in the resulting silence he heard a low bass oscillation, a slight auditory disturbance that he knew would resolve itself into something familiar but that he now could not quite place. The noise grew louder, approaching, and he realized that it was the sound of a car engine.

The sound of the mailman's car engine.

It wasn't possible. Yesterday the mailman had been too weak to move, almost too weak to stand, in nowhere-near-good-enough shape to drive a car. Even if he had successfully delivered a letter, or several letters, between then and now, it was impossible for him to have so suddenly improved.

But there was no mistaking the sound of the car. In the stillness of the night he heard its tires crunching gravel, heard the low purr as it idled at the foot of the drive.

The low purr.

The sound was not frightening to him, but it was compelling, and he sonically followed its approach.

The purr.

The alertness with which he'd awakened began to fade.

He wanted to sit up in bed, to walk to the living room and peek out the front window to see just what was happening, but either his mind was too tired to issue the command or his leg muscles were too tired to follow it, and he remained in bed, listening to the purr.

The purr.

He realized that the low drone was acting as a somnolent, that its unchanging rhythm was hypnotizing him back into sleep, but he was unable to fight against it. His eyes began to close. He faded back into dreamland still hearing the low sound of the quiet engine.

He knew when he awoke that the mailman was gone. He knew without hearing, without seeing, without checking. It was a feeling, a subtle difference in the air, in the atmosphere, that he could not have explained if he'd had to. An oppressiveness was missing; and the feeling of lurking dread to which he had grown accustomed, which had awakened with him each morning, which had seemed after all this time to have become an integral part of his makeup, had disappeared.

He picked up the phone and called Mike. The policeman was not at home, but he was at the police station, and he answered immediately. "Willis Police Department, Mike Trenton speaking."

"Mike? This is Doug."

"He's gone."

Doug was silent for a moment, closing his eyes, feeling the relief wash over him. Confirmation. He was gone. "I knew he would be," Doug said.

"I noticed this morning as I drove in that his car was not in the post-office parking lot, and I went in there with Tegarden and Jeff. Nothing. The place was empty. He may be coming back, though—"

"He's not," Doug said.

"We don't—"

"He's not."

"You may be right," Mike said slowly. "We got a report this morning over the radio, from the DPS, that there was a single-vehicle accident out on Black Canyon toward Camp Verde. There're no details, but it could be him; the car was headed in the right direction. The vehicle and driver were so badly burned that they were unrecognizable, but we'll know soon enough. Even if we can't find dental records, an examination of the car should show if it was his make and model, and we can go on from there. We should know in a few days."

"It doesn't matter," Doug said.

"It doesn't matter? You don't seem too concerned about this."

"He's gone. Can't you feel it? I don't know whether we drove him out or he accomplished what he wanted to accomplish or he died or whatever. But he's gone. He's not here. He's not coming back."

"I hope you're right."

"I am right."

"Wait a minute." There were muffled voices on the other end of the line as Mike put his hand over the receiver. "You still there?" Mike asked.

"Still here."

"I just got a note from Jeff that a postal inspector called. He's coming up later this week."

Doug smiled. "A little late, isn't he?"

The policeman chuckled. "A little."

They were silent for a moment, and Doug realized that for the first time in over a month the two of them had nothing to say to each other. "Well, I'll let you go," he said. "But I'll be by later. We'll talk."

"Okay."

"It is over, Mike."

"I believe you."

Doug laughed. "*Now* you believe me."

"Get out of here."

"Later," Doug said. He hung up the phone. What had the mailman been after, he wondered, and had he found it or done it or completed it? He had arrived in Willis two months ago and had left the town a shambles. Had that been what he wanted? Or had it been something else, something more? Perhaps they had thwarted him before he could finish what he had started. Or perhaps he had really had no motive.

Unbidden, Doug thought of the letter of resignation William Faulkner had tendered after working for a short time for the Postal Service: "I will be damned if I propose to be at the beck and call of every itinerant scoundrel who has two cents to invest in a postage stamp."

Perhaps it had been a motive as simple as that.

But they would never know, he realized. They would never know what the mailman had wanted, or whether he had failed or succeeded.

It didn't matter, though.

None of it mattered now.

It was over. It was finished.

He and Tritia brought Billy home from the hospital later in the morning, and Doug turned on the television while Trish made a bed for their son on the couch. For the first time in nearly two weeks the house did not seem to Doug like a violated fortress, like a temporary shelter in which he slept. It felt once more like a home.

Tritia poured Billy a glass of 7-Up and took it to him.

"Dad?" Billy asked from the couch.

Doug turned. "Yes?"

"It's over, isn't it?" he asked.

He nodded at his son. "Yes," he said. "Finally."

"Finally," Billy breathed gratefully, settling back on the pillow.

They made sure Billy was comfortable, then Tritia went into the kitchen to fix his favorite lunch—macaroni and cheese with chopped-up hot dogs. It was about as nutritious as lint, but this was a special occasion and he deserved a special lunch to go with it.

Doug turned the TV to Channel 5 so Billy could watch *Dick Van Dyke*, and he watched it with him for a few minutes. On an impulse, during a commercial break, he walked outside, onto the porch. He stood there for a moment, then began to walk down the drive to the mailbox. It was a beautiful late-summer day. The temperature was hot but not uncomfortably so, the harshness of June and July mellowed and gone. In the trees, bluebirds chattered happily and the sky above was cloudlessly blue. There was a slight breeze, not strong enough to disturb anything, but strong enough to act as a natural fan and keep his face cool as he walked.

He reached the mailbox and stopped. The box was open and Doug moved forward to peer inside.

Three coal-black envelopes lay neatly stacked next to the opening.

He remembered the sound of the car the night before,

and he felt the return of a familiar coldness. Reaching in, he pulled the envelopes out. The paper felt strange and thick to his touch, slightly slimy, as though it was made from something organic. The contents were heavy and oddly shaped. A wave of revulsion passed through him. He had the sudden urge to drop all three envelopes on the ground, to stomp on them, to bury them with dirt. Without looking at their contents, he knew that whatever was inside the envelopes was evil.

He examined each piece of mail. On the front, in red scripted Old English letters, were his, Tritia's, and Billy's names. No addresses.

He wondered if other people in town had received letters like these. If everyone in town had received letters like these.

He stared down at the mail.

Inside the envelope addressed to him, something squirmed.

He dropped all three envelopes on the ground and involuntarily jumped back. He was about to stomp on them, to kill and crush whatever was enclosed within the black paper, but he had a better idea and ran as quickly as he could back up the drive to the car. Pulling open the driver's door, he leaned across the seat and opened the glove compartment. He dug down under the flashlight, the repair receipts, the Handi-Wipes, and the AAA maps until he found what he was looking for.

A book of matches.

He ran back down the drive to where the three envelopes lay in the dirt. Gingerly, he picked up the two marked with Tritia's and Billy's names and placed them atop his own. He struck a match, but it blew immediately out. He tried again, cupping his hand around the timid flame, and was rewarded when the fire grew. He bent down, holding the match to the edge of the top envelope, hoping it would catch on fire.

It did, and he watched as the strange multicolored flames, now blue, now red, spread over the thick slimy paper. He had half-hoped to see what was inside once the fire had eaten away the envelope, but at the last second he looked away.

Something told him it was not knowledge he wanted to have.

The envelopes burned quickly, brightly, and when the fire had done its work, there was only a small pile of smoldering ashes left. Doug kicked the pile, and blackened flakes scattered in the road, the light breeze sending the burned dust skittering across the dirt, fanning out in all directions. He watched the ashes dance into the ditch, under the brush, over the groundcover, mingling with the elements of the forest until all trace of them had disappeared.

He stood there for a moment, staring at the spot where the letters had been. Looking over at the empty open mailbox, he realized that this was the first time since the beginning of the summer that he was not afraid of it.

He was free.

The town was free.

The mailman was gone.

He breathed deeply. Lunch was waiting for him. He smelled hot dogs on the breeze. And macaroni and cheese. From the house he heard the welcome sounds of Billy's voice and Tritia's voice and a television laugh track.

He had things to do. He had a storage shed to build. Smiling, feeling happy, feeling good, he closed the mailbox door and walked back up the drive toward home.

BEWARE OF STRANGERS . . .

The car pulled into the parking lot. The passenger window slowly lowered, and against the darkness of the interior, Billy saw the mailman's milk-white face and bright red hair.

The car stopped next to him. "Need a ride?" The smooth voice was suggestive.

"My dad's coming to pick me up," Billy said. His heart was pounding so crazily that he thought he might have a heart attack.

"Your dad's not coming," the mailman said. His voice was still silky, but there was an undercurrent of menace in it. The passenger door opened. "Get in."

"Your dad's not around anymore," the mailman said, and chuckled. Something about the way he stretched out the word "around" sent goosebumps down Billy's arms. "Get in."

"No," Billy said.

"You'll get in, and you'll like it." The mailman's arm stretched out through the open door.

And continued to stretch.

And continued to stretch.

Until his cold white fingers were clamped around Billy's throat.

THE MAILMAN